a clash
of spheres

Books by P.F. Chisholm

The Sir Robert Carey Mysteries
A Famine of Horses
A Season of Knives
A Surfeit of Guns
A Plague of Angels
A Murder of Crows
An Air of Treason
A Chorus of Innocents
A Clash of Spheres

Writing as Patricia Finney

The Lady Grace Mysteries
Assassin
Betrayal
Conspiracy
Feud

Children's Books
I, Jack
Jack and Rebel the Police Dog
Jack and the Ghosts

Other Novels
A Shadow of Gulls
The Crow Goddess
Gloriana's Torch
Unicorn's Blood
Firedrake's Eye

a clash of spheres

A Sir Robert Carey Mystery

P.F. Chisholm

Poisoned Pen Press

Copyright © 2017 by P.F. Chisholm

First Edition 2017

10 9 8 7 6 5 4 3 2 1

Library of Congress Catalog Card Number: 2016955447

ISBN: 9781464208287   Hardcover
      9781464208300   Trade Paperback

Poisoned Pen Press
6962 E. First Ave., Ste. 103
Scottsdale, AZ 85251
www.poisonedpenpress.com
info@poisonedpenpress.com

Printed in the United States of America

This book is dedicated to all the wonderful people who read my book in draft. I call them my beta-readers. They not only save me a huge amount of time and effort, but make my books so much better. Thank you!

Brenda James
Carol Matson
Chris Luke
Elizabeth Bozzell
Gail Hourigan
Gereg Muller
Hadas Kozlowski
Hilary Silvert Newell
Karen L Black
Kendall Britt
Kier Salmon
Lori Walker
Lorna Toolis
Lorraine Fletez-Brant
Margot McLennan
Michelle Rudd
S M Stirling

cast of characters
in no particular order

* historical person
in parenthesis: mentioned, not met

(Christian IV of Denmark, Norway etc) *
Queen Anne, wife of King James of Scotland *
Sir Robert Carey *
Sorrel, his usual hobby
(Henry Carey, Baron Hunsdon—Carey's father) *
Lord Scrope, Warden of the English West March *
Sir Richard Lowther, Deputy Warden of the English West
    March *
Lady Elizabeth Widdrington, Carey's love *
Sir Henry Widdrington, her husband, Deputy Warden of the
    English East March *
Alexander Lindsay, Lord Spynie, the King's ex-Minion *
Lord Maxwell, Scottish Border lord *
Henry Dodd, Land-Sergeant of Gilsland, Carey's henchman
Whitesock, his favourite horse
Sir Robert Cecil, Privy Councillor *
Margeurite Graham
Jonathan Hepburn or Hochstetter

Sir David Graham of Fintry, Groom of the Bedchamber to James *

Wattie Graham of Netherby, Border reiver *

Young Hutchin Graham, nearly a Border reiver *

Archie Fire-the-Braes Graham, Border reiver *

Sooks Graham

Bangtail Graham, man-at-arms, Carlisle castle guard *

Red Sandy Dodd, man-at-arms, Carlisle castle guard

Sim's Will, man-at-arms, Carlisle castle guard

Bessie's Andrew Storey, man-at-arms, Carlisle castle guard

Andie Nixon, man-at-arms, Carlisle castle guard (Kate, his wife)

Pringle, Garron, East, Perkins, Leamus—Earl of Essex's deserters, now new men-at-arms

Nick Smithson, leader of the Earl of Essex's deserters

(Ritchie Graham of Brackenhill, gangster) *

(Sim's Jock Graham, Border reiver)

(Solomon Musgrave, gate guard)

George Gordon, 6th Earl of Huntly *

Father William Crichton SJ *

Francis Hay, 9th Earl of Erroll *

Sir George Kerr, Groom of the Bedchamber *

Bessie Storey *

Nancy, her wife *

Thomas the Merchant Hetherington, businessman *

Hughie Tyndale or Elliot, Carey's valet

John Tovey, Carey's secretary

James Stuart, King of Scotland, 6th of that name *

Janet Dodd née Armstrong

Bridget, her half-sister

Ellen

Mary, her sister

Katherine, her gossip

Willie's Simon Amstrong

Ekie, 8 year old boy

Mrs Hogg, midwife

Mary Leaholm

Big Clem Pringle, blacksmith
Geordie and Cuddie Armstrong, Janet's brothers
Wide Mary
Cousin Rowan
Penny, Shilling, Angel, horses
(Samuel the donkey)
Jack, a lymer dog
Teazle, a more experienced hunting dog
(Buttercup, Jack's mother)
Richard Bell, Scrope's secretary
Wee Colin Elliot, headman of the Elliot surname
Simon Anricks or Ames
(Rebecca, his wife)
(2nd Earl of Bothwell) *
(Mme Hetherington)
(William Douglas, 10th Earl of Angus) *
(Lord Howard of Effingham) *
(Sir Francis Drake) *
(Sir Francis Walsingham) *
(Medina Sidonia, Spanish admiral) *
(Mrs Grainne O'Malley) *
(Goody Biltock)
(Thomas Digges) *
Dixon
Roger Widdrington, son of Sir Henry *
Young Henry Widdrington, eldest son of Sir Henry *
(Lord Burghley) *
Big Archie Carleton
Maitland of Thirlstane, Lord Chancellor of Scotland *
(Dr Dee) *
Herr Kauffmann Hochstetter
Peter, Mick, Harry, gunners
(Young Hutchin's Aunt Nettie and Uncle Jim)
Annie
(Jamie Dodd, headman of the Dodd surname)
Widow Ridley

Andy Ridley, her grandson
(Dunstan Ames, Simon Anrick's father) *
(Dr Hector Nunez, Simon's uncle) *
(Joshua Ames, one of Simon's brothers)
Chancellor Melville *
Mrs Proserpina—Poppy—Burn
(Sir John Forster, Warden of the English Middle March) *
(John Carey, Carey's elder brother) *
Little Archie
Matthew, Eric, Jeremy, Paul, Peter, Sandy—Spynie's henchmen
Skinabake Armstrong, Border reiver *
Mrs Elliot, wife to Wee Colin

Letter from Sir Robert Cecil to the King of Denmark.

Draft.

To His Royal Highness, Christian IV of that name, King of Denmark and Norway, etc etc. *[His Highness is but 16 years and still under regency, be very sure we have all his titles here]*

Your most Royal Highness, *[check correct address]*
You have asked me to make some description and account of Sir Robert Carey and his henchman Sergeant Henry Dodd, of whom you have heard little but rumours and the varied accounts of your spies at the Court of Scotland, which it is my pleasure to supply, being hopeful of your Royal Highness' favour and regard, and being also certain that when once you have been apprised of Sir Robert's character and circumstance, you will view him with as much favour as I do, no less and perhaps no more. *[be sure the Danish translation is accurate here]*
You say that your royal sister, Anne, Queen Consort of King James of Scotland, has written to you of the man, wherefore I will unburden myself perhaps a little less discreetly than I might otherwise have done.

Sir Robert is the seventh surviving son of my Lord Chamberlain, Henry Carey, Baron Hunsdon. It is worth making some explanation of Baron Hunsdon's antecedents since they are material to the character of Sir Robert.

To be blunt, Your Highness, it is more than likely that Baron Hunsdon is in fact Henry VIII's natural son, by his erstwhile mistress, Mary Boleyn, older sister of the more famous Ann. *[a little touch of scandal may entertain His Highness]* Thus Baron Hunsdon is both cousin and half-brother to our most revered Sovereign Liege, Elizabeth of England, Wales, Ireland, and France.

The royal bastardy means that Baron Hunsdon has no claim whatsoever to the throne and nor do his numerous children. Happily, My Lord Baron is not in any way ambitious but serves his mistress the Queen a great deal more faithfully and effectively than most people realise, who think him but a Knight of the Carpet. *[perhaps excise, not relevant]* Most of his children are or have been at Court and often high in favour.

Sir Robert first served Sir Francis Walsingham as a youth in embassies to Scotland and France. During the Scottish embassy he received great favour from the young King, your brother-in-law, James of Scotland. During the French embassy, he seems to have disgraced himself through his carnal appetites with some of the most puissant ladies of the French Court, which ended in a debtors' prison from which he was extricated with some difficulty and more expense by his esteemed father. I am aware of at least two probable bastards and there may be more. *[more to entertain His Highness! Nb. One possible bastard may be a Guise instead.]*

He returned to England and served the Queen at Court, although not without incident. There was a fistfight with Sir Walter Raleigh over a tennis match before either of them had become knights, and several duels. He became an MP and gave satisfaction therein.

Against the Armada, he served with his friend, the Earl of Cumberland, on the *Elizabeth Bonaventure*, where he was able to render incidental but important service to the Queen before succumbing (although not fatally) to a jailfever on board ship. He had also served the Queen in an unusual manner, during the final days of the Queen of Scots, but I am not at liberty to disclose details. *[excise?]*

He has been to war several more times and acquitted himself well, most notably under the Earl of Essex in France in 1591. There he was knighted by Essex for help in turning aside the Queen's just wrath with her unworthy favourite.

Last summer in 1592, he decided to become his brother-in-law Lord Scrope's Deputy Warden in the English West March, despite there already being an incumbent called Sir Richard Lowther. Certes, he was restless at Court and in need of knightly exercise, since he has proved to be an able soldier and a very much better captain than *[deleted]* many. He also owed considerable sums of money, in particular to his tailor, and there was an entanglement in London from which he urgently needed to flee. However there is also the matter of his extraordinary affection for his cousin, Lady Elizabeth Widdrington, née Trevannion, who lives in the north with her elderly husband, Sir Henry Widdrington, Deputy Warden of the East March.

I am not entirely clear about the progress of this love affair, but as Lady Widdrington is, by all accounts, a woman of principle and determination, it is yet possible that he has not breached her citadel and intends to marry her as soon as her husband is dead. This would be a very foolish mistake on his part because the lady only has a jointure of five hundred pounds and he currently owes three thousand pounds at least. It goes without saying that Sir Henry Widdrington regards him with considerable suspicion, jealousy, and loathing.

On arriving on the Borders, Sir Robert was immediately embroiled in an incident with the Graham surname, the upshot of which was that he somehow prevented the kidnapping of the King of Scots from Falkland palace by the 2nd Earl of Bothwell. Unfortunately, the precise circumstances are murky. Later that summer, after showing his capacities at a coroner's inquest in Carlisle, he journeyed to Dumfries to meet with the King of Scots while His Highness was on his Justice Raid against the Grahams.

Precisely what transpired at the Scottish Court, I have not been able reliably to make out, except that Sir Robert became involved with an Italian spy and had an affair with her; somehow earned the enmity of the King's favourite and Minion, Lord Spynie, and also Lord Maxwell, current Warden of the Scottish West March; took extremely foolhardy and potentially treasonous action in the matter of some firearms; and emerged with quite severe injuries to his hands but the renewed favour of the King.

In the autumn, he was ordered to London by his father. There he became involved in a riot at the Fleet Prison during which Sir Thomas Heneage, Vice Chamberlain, had his nose broken [by Sir Robert]. During the ensuing lawsuits, he decided to leave London and head for Oxford, which was then expecting the Queen on her Progress, leaving his mother Ann Carey, Lady Hunsdon, and his henchman, Sergeant Henry Dodd, to deal with the consequences of his dispute with Sir Thos. Heneage, which they did ably and with dispatch. In the course of these events, I was able to be of some service to Lady Hunsdon, a matter of great satisfaction to me.

At this point it is worth mentioning his henchman, Henry Dodd, Land-Sergeant of Gilsland who is serving as one of the sergeants of the Carlisle Castle guard.

I have had the pleasure and interest of meeting Sergeant Dodd in his own person and he is considerably more than the simple dour Border reiver he appears to be. It seems he should be the headman of the Tynedale Dodds but is not for reasons that are obscure but connected with a feud between the Dodds and the Elliots in the 1570s. *[too much admission of ignorance?]*

While he was in Oxford, Sir Robert was commissioned by the Queen to investigate a very delicate matter. During the Queen's Entrance in State into the City of Oxford, Sergeant Dodd saved the Queen's life, for which he was well-rewarded.

Shortly after his return to the Borders, with some ex-soldiers of my Lord Essex's, Sir Robert was involved in an incident at a tower known as Dick of Dryhope's, in which he called out the Carlisle trained bands, but honourably and skillfully avoided the bloody pitched battle that seemed inevitable.

This has made his name on the Borders and the Queen has now been pleased to grant him his official warrant as Deputy Warden.

He is close to the Queen, who sometimes calls him "her Scalliwag": to be given a nickname by Her Majesty is a signal of highest favour, so that I am proud to be known by her name for me, slighting though it is. However he has not yet successfully turned her favour into offices nor a pension nor a monopoly, from which I conclude he is either remarkably inept, unlucky, or else as unambitious as his sire. He seems mainly concerned with his affair with Lady Widdrington and with bringing peace to the Borders, rather than profiting personally by his office, a very remarkable and unusual circumstance. *[can you think of another instance?]*

I am now extremely concerned at the state of politics at the Scottish Court, particularly with regard to the Catholic earls. I beg of you, Your Highness, if you have any information at all on the King of Spain's intentions in Scotland, I pray you will tell me it. I have already dispatched a particularly effective and able pursuivant to the Borders and I am considering a journey north, which is not a matter I undertake lightly, owing to the infirmity in my bones from which I suffer. But I believe Spain is plotting against Scotland and England and would give my right arm to know more.

It goes without saying, all of this information is strictly private and not to be shared with anyone.

I remain Your Highness' most assiduous and secret *[?]* servant,

Sir Rbt Cecil, Privy Councillor.

[not sent]

late august 1592

Their dalliance had progressed in a stately fashion from whispers and stolen kisses in corridors, to dancing while the musicians played for them alone in crowded sweaty halls and banqueting tents full of unimportant other dancers, to light-fingered explorations of stocking tops and codpiece and stays, to this. Marguerite was heavy-eyed and languorous and, thank the Mother of God, not inclined to talk too much. Meanwhile the man who said his name was Jonathan Hepburn and that he sometimes worked for the Earl of Bothwell, was lying flat on his back, utterly spent, letting the sweat dry on his skin.

She yawned, stretched like a cat, got up and went to the door of the little servant's chamber, where the man whose chamber it actually was, waited patiently and counted his cash.

"Do you have any wine?" she asked in a voice that was tinged with a foreign language. For a wonder, it turned out that he did, and for a paltry English shilling would give them some. She brought in two pewter goblets of white wine. Hepburn sat up on his elbow and took the goblet, toasted her, and drank.

It was dreadful, acidic with a suspicious fishy aftertaste, but he got it down.

Of course, Marguerite was a married woman and it showed in the stretchmarks on her stomach and the dark aureoles of her very nibblesome nipples. She had given her lord at least one or probably more children. But her hair was blond and so was her crotch and she had a luxuriousness to her that Hepburn associated more with Southerners. It was business, all business, but, by the God of the World, sometimes you could mix business with pleasure. The fact that she was married to a very dull conscientious man by the name of Sir David Graham of Fintry was what was important. He was not a Border Graham, not one of the notorious clan of five brothers who had gone south in the 1520s, kicked the Storeys off their lands, and helped turn Liddesdale into the complete thieves' kitchen it now was. He was from the northerly respectable Grahams. There were interesting rumours about him but the most interesting thing about him was a stone-cold fact. He was a Groom of the King's Bedchamber, by hereditary custom.

"My dear," Hepburn said in the caressing voice he used for all women, "what if your husband catches us?"

She frowned and plumped down next to him on the narrow servant's bed with the sour sheets. "He would be very angry," she said with a sigh, chewing her bottom lip, "He might kill you and hurt me. Or kill me as well."

"Surely not, so old-fashioned?"

She shrugged and her voice took on a tinge of bitterness. "He killed a young man I looked at—only looked at, honest to God—and he was very cruel to me. The King hushed it up. He locked me in a storeroom where it was very cold and dark and there were many spiders."

Hepburn nodded. That was what he had heard. Now, was the other rumour true?

"Perhaps we should not see each other for a while," he said sadly, "so he doesn't get too suspicious."

She shrugged, quite French although she wasn't French, started billowing linen over her head. "If you are already tired of me…" she said, her voice muffled.

Hepburn jumped up from the bed and embraced her. "How could I be tired of you?" he whispered and she tweaked him where he was demonstrating that he was not tired of her at all, which made him gasp and her giggle. No help for it, he had to take the risk. This last detail was simply too important to go on mere hearsay. "I'll have to go to a priest this afternoon, but I don't care…"

"What will he give you for penance? Fasting?"

"Perhaps," said Hepburn who had fasted for religious reasons but not on any priest's say-so. "Will you too have to find a priest? Or are you a Protestant…?"

"What? And now be utterly damned forever? I would never be so silly. I am a Catholic." She grinned impudently at him. "I have found a very nice tame priest called Father Crichton who never gives more than a decade of Aves, a Paternoster, and a Gloria."

Just for a moment, Hepburn had to hold his breath. Was Crichton actually here, in Scotland? He had had no idea, thinking the man was still in northern Spain. "Is he a Jesuit?"

"Yes, but he is nice," She giggled and wriggled at the way he was stroking her breasts through the fine linen of her smock, "Not as nice as you, but nice."

"He isn't supposed to be as nice as me…" He was busy nuzzling her neck. "When did he arrive?"

"He came with my Lord Maxwell and his Italians in April or May, I think, to help with the new Armada but stayed at Caerlaverock. Now he is at Court and everyone who is not a stupid Lutheran or Calvinist goes to him."

That Armada, too, if it existed, had been wrecked by storms.

"My priest is old-fashioned and strict. Perhaps I could confess to your nice Father Crichton?"

She giggled again. There was something so relaxing about a feather-headed woman with stunning blond curls down her back. "Why not?"

Emilia had been dramatic and very sexy and had been completely resistant to his plan, which she thought stupidly risky. And then she had suddenly gone off with the Deputy Warden of the West March, Sir Robert Carey, so she could buy his guns and take them to Ireland, as if that was less risky.

"Wherever did he find you, Sir David Graham?" he wondered to himself in the Deutsch of his childhood and she answered him in Low Dutch. "In the Spanish Netherlands, of course, where I was living in a very boring village full of very boring Protestants."

"But you are from Antwerp," he guessed shrewdly and was rewarded by a kiss on the mouth which he enjoyed immensely. "Originally."

Her face suddenly crumpled like a child's. "I don't want to think about poor Antwerp," she whispered, her mood changing like a cloud crossing the sun, "I never want to think about it."

Hepburn looked at her carefully. She must have been a child at the time of the Spanish Fury in Antwerp. Had she been there?

"My dear…" he began.

"Never! I never want to think about it!" she shouted in Low Dutch and hit him in the chest with her fist, as if he were another man entirely. Hepburn put his arms around her to quiet her and found she was kissing him greedily, desperately, scratching his back. After one second of hesitation—what had brought this on?—he went with it and took her again, like an animal, while she moaned and tears pushed their way out under her eyelids and finally she screamed so he had to put a hand over her mouth. He took it away when she bit him and she then looked at him with old eyes and said, "Never say that name to me again."

"All right," he said. He managed a light smile and she smiled back at last. Jesu, who could fathom women? It was beyond him.

There was an anxious knock at the door.

"Sir, my lady, I must go serve the Queen in half an hour," came a voice.

"Give us ten minutes," said Hepburn, picking his hose up from where he had folded them and laid them down carefully. Marguerite was already at her petticoat forepart, buttoning and pinning with a will.

They came out separately, went in different directions. Marguerite hurried to the Queen's chambers where she sat on a corner cushion and gossiped with one of the Queen's plump Danish women. Jonathan Hepburn went down to the buttery to get himself a quart of ale to help him recover and with thinking out the next stage in his very elaborate plot that would end with James VI of Scotland dead, and Scotland and England in murderous chaos.

CARLISLE, EARLY DECEMBER 1592

The Grahams took up position under the Eden Bridge at about four o'clock in the morning, as near as anyone could guess, with the sky perpetually leaking rain. The water was freezing cold and high as well and the horses all protested about it as they splashed in and stood there sulkily, huffing and puffing.

"He'll be back before five, I guarantee it," said Wattie. "Naebody'll want to be oot in this any longer than they have to."

The bridge itself would not keep you dry, because it had been raining long enough for the stones themselves all to be leaking in the places where they had worn and there were potholes going right through. It was an old bridge. Some said the builders of the Giant's Wall had made it for a sort of warm-up for the Wall itself.

Archie Fire the Braes pushed another man called Sooks Graham out of the one remaining dry spot there. Well dryish. His pony was wet obviously and so were his legs and boots. There was a whispered sequence of snarls, and then Sooks shoved another man out of a slightly drier spot and so on down the line to the youngest one there who philosophically stayed under the last bit of parapet which gave no shelter at all but did conceal him from anyone crossing the bridge at night.

"And ye're sure *he'll* not be there?" said another man.

Wattie grinned and scratched under his helmet rim. "Ay, certain sure. He took offence at the doings last month and he'll no' come in wi' us, but he willna help the Courtier, see ye."

The youngest had a rough iron cap over his golden hair which was lent him by his cousin Sooks, since the colour was such a liability at night despite being dirty. He lifted it and scratched like Wattie at a place where it rubbed.

"He'll have the other men of the guard, though."

"Ay," said Wattie cheerfully. "It's Sergeant Dodd I worry about."

Young Hutchin nodded and wondered what it was about Sergeant Dodd that made everybody so careful of him and wondered how he could get some of that stuff himself.

"What about the new men from the South he's brung in?" he asked.

"Och," laughed Wattie, "who's worried about a bunch o' soft Southerners? Not me."

Everybody sniggered a little. They stood in silence for a while, as the dripping eased off.

Wattie put a hand out. "Damn, it's stopped raining," he said thoughtfully.

Young Hutchin moved his hobby out a couple of feet and back in again. "Ay, it has." It was still raining under the bridge, as the puddles on the bridge dripped through slowly, but outside it had eased off to basic miserable dampness.

Wattie sighed. It would have been a lot better if the rain had carried on but you could never rely on the weather, except to be as thrawn and contrary as it could. They would have preferred rain, so it had stopped raining. Well, the night was still as black as pitch and that would have to do. The men they were waiting for did not usually carry torches.

◇◇◇

Carey was wet and uncomfortable but in good spirits. He had brought the four Southerners who had learnt to ride well enough, and started teaching them the finer points of Border life. For a wonder, nothing very much was happening on either side of the Border, and just on the off chance and on impulse he had forayed into Liddesdale a way and found a remarkable number of cattle and horses penned up in a narrow little valley. He had taken a close look at them on foot by the light of his only dark lantern and found three different brands in four animals, grinned wolfishly, and given his orders.

Dodd was not there, being safely at home with his wife in Gilsland. To be honest, Carey was quite glad to be rid of him because from being a naturally dour and taciturn man, since the incident at Dick of Dryhope's tower, Dodd had become… well, sulky was too weak and nebbish a word, really. If Carey got more than four words out of him in an evening, he was doing well. He had not expected Dodd to like what he had done but it was now more than a month in the past and he was getting tired of the whole thing.

Still, this would be good practice for the new men and the other Borderers would enjoy teaching them the arcane art of cattle-driving with the four-legged treasure they had found.

It being so dark and raining, of course the herds had protested loudly at being moved and gone in dozens of different ways, while the loose horses trotted about uneasily. A couple of calves got free and went exploring, and Perkins fell off his horse when he went after one of them, which entertained Bangtail, Red Sandy, and Sim's Will no end. Bessie's Andrew, no longer the youngest and least important man, started shouting, and then someone else's horse stood on its hind legs while his rider cursed and beat about with the ends of the reins until he calmed down again.

"We should have brought the dogs," said Carey, making a mental note to bring Jack and Teazle next time and see if Jack might make a better herding dog than he did a hunter. The men of the guard were now circling the cattle, making little yips and yarks until they finally got the cattle moving out of the valley and into the main run of Liddesdale, southwards. The horses went with the cattle, not liking to be alone and shying at everything.

Yes, it would take at least an hour longer to bring the stolen cattle in, but it would be well worth it and Carey felt he needed something to cheer him up. He was probably going to lose his place when Lord Scrope finally went south to his estates, and he could turn his share of the booty into much-needed cash.

He spotted two cows and a heifer making a break for it northwards and went after them with a high *yip yip*, galloped his pony round them and turned them about so they were running back to the main herd. He whacked the lead cow with the butt end of his lance and found Bessie's Andrew there on the other side to encourage them a bit more.

The herd heaved itself together again and started moving west at a dignified lollop with a lot of question and response in the lowing. Most of them were English kine from the brands and it stood to reason they would prefer to go south to more familiar fields, so it was sheer obstinacy that was sending them west. Bangtail and Red Sandy galloped their ponies into the path and turned them with more shouted yips and yarks. All the cattle stood and bumped each other, lowing questioningly.

There was a bony old screw up near the front, with a crumpled horn, tossing her head and barging other cows when they went the wrong way. He could almost hear her, "Ay, this way, ye lummocks." Just for a moment he tried to imagine the cow politics that had made her the leader but his usually vivid phantasy could not cope with this, and he found himself laughing quietly at himself. Still, what was it Dodd had said about even goats having degree in their herds and refusing to follow an underling?

"Sim's Will," he said, "get that animal with the crumpled horn and bring her to the front. No, not that one, the bony one."

It took a moment for Sim's Will to get a rope round her neck and then Carey took the rope's end and forged his way through the pungent beasts and the mud until he and the old lady were at the front. She bellowed loudly and set out for the South with decision, sniffing the air and mooing and, for a wonder, the others followed her at last in mostly the right direction.

An hour later, as they came over the last hill, he could just make out Eden Bridge and the Sauceries beyond and relaxed because they were nearly home.

◇◇◇

Wattie cocked his head, accidentally tipping a helmet's brim of water down his neck.

"What's that?" he asked uneasily. "There's a herd of cows there..."

"Bringing them in for market?" said Fire the Braes, who knew less than most about such things, as he had been at the horn since he was in his teens.

"At this time? The gate's aye shut and will be for another two hours, whit's the point of it?"

They hushed as the mixed lowing and sound of hooves came closer and closer. Suddenly the noises went up a notch with anxiety and the sound of hooves became confused, the drumming stopped just before the bridge. Wattie signalled the other Grahams to stay still and quiet.

"What the devil's got into them?" demanded a Court voice just above them. "They were moving very nicely a moment ago, why won't they go onto the bridge?"

A single horse's footsteps rang above them, and Wattie was sitting his mount like a stone fountain, with the puddle water still running down, his head tilted and his mouth open.

That was when Hutchin's mount, which had been bad-tempered all night, straddled his legs and let fly with a long stream of pungent shit, right into the water.

Dinna let him notice, Wattie prayed to his nameless god of reivers, *go on, yer flash Court sprig, ye dinna ken…*He glowered at Hutchin who couldn't really be blamed.

There was a scuffle as Carey turned his horse on a sixpence and galloped back to the herd, while his voice bellowed, "Bring them on!" They stood still while the hooves went around to the back of the herd and then came the boom of a dag being fired into the air.

The lowing went up to near panic levels. The kine had heard gunfire before and didn't like it. They tried to go back, found men with lances and ropes in the way, turned about and found the bridge was clear, but more frightening men on horses with lances and swords and bows were coming up the riverbanks on either side as Wattie's relatives decided to take a crack at the valuable Deputy anyway, seeing they had come so far and spent two hours standing in the wet in the river. And seeing the Deputy was worth fifteen pounds on the hoof, dead or alive. Fire the Braes was shouting something incomprehensible about the kine, Wattie was bellowing purple-faced at them to stop. And there was Carey in a panicking sea of cattle, finishing reloading his dag, putting it in its case and drawing his sword, whacking the arse of the cow with the crumpled horn with the flat of it and charging forwards.

She let out a moo that was more a battle cry and lurched forwards, tossing her head and looking for something to gore in revenge, found a pony in front of her and stuck the crumpled horn in, found a space clear of men and horses and barged into it, followed by all her sisters, nieces, cousins, and second cousins plus the strange cows and the strange horses, all following her in a chaotic bunch because she was in front and moving.

The press of them running onto the bridge barged the next horseman backwards, so the hobby lost his feet and the rider fell off, the third was ridden by Fire the Braes, who was laying about him with his lance, so they went round him and then took him with them. Another boom from behind confirmed their feeling that they did not like loud bangs and they wanted to get away from them, so they went up to a speedy trot and then a run and bowled over another horse as they stampeded over the bridge, their eyes rolling and their horns tossing.

And there was the blasted Deputy in the middle of it, plastered with dung from a nervous heifer, swapping blows with the still-shouting Wattie Graham and another cousin who came up from the other side, until Carey bent with a wicked look and tipped the man out of his saddle, then turned to deal with Wattie again. He found the kine had shoved him in the opposite direction and took a shot at him with his other dag, missed but hit somebody else.

Somehow he still had hold of the old cow's rope, so he kicked his horse to keep up, and went with her while yet another Graham tried to go the other way to Liddesdale and got shoved off the bridge into the river while his horse did the sensible thing and scrambled to stay with the herd.

Just as the other Grahams turned to run, Carey caught sight of golden hair and bellowed, "Hutchin Graham, I want to talk to you!" but couldn't go after him because he, too, was being carried along in the flood of animals. He kept his seat, caught up with the old lady again, as the cows came off the bridge and galloped down and into the Sauceries and trampled down the fences…And then they stopped because there was lovely soft rich grass there, nurtured by some of the town's nightsoil, the meadows being kept for the garrison's horses. And so they fanned out and started to enjoy the feast while the sun notionally came up behind the clouds.

Carey's legs were a bit bruised from the crushing, but, for a wonder, nobody had stuck him with a horn. He rode up to the old cow, took the rope from round her neck and gave her a slap on the shoulder in thanks. He got a glare that reminded him of his mother, which made him want to laugh.

All eight of his men came trotting up, some of them with prisoners who would ransome very nicely. None of the prisoners was Wattie Graham, but Fire the Braes was furious.

"They're ma ain cattle ye've reived from me, ye bastard!" he shouted and Carey looked mildly offended.

"They've got a wonderful range of brands," he said, "Pringle, Storey, Ridley, I think that one is an English Armstrong."

"They're mine, damn ye!"

"No, I think you reived them, Archie."

"Ay," bellowed Archie, his hands tied behind his back in fists. "Ay, Ah worked hard to reive them and they're all mine, stolen fair and square!"

He realised that Carey was laughing at him and so were some of the men, especially Andy Nixon, the square Carlisler who often now was second in command. "Och, piss off, ye lang streak o' puke."

Nixon lifted his fist but Carey shook his head. "Well now," he said conversationally, as Perkins and Garron and East, commanded by Nick Smithson, tried to do something about the fences so the cows wouldn't wander off again. "What were you doing waiting in ambush under Eden Bridge like a bunch of god-damned trolls, only not so pretty? How many of you were there?"

"At least forty…Ah'll tell ye nothing."

"Well, you will after I've put you in the Licking Stone cell for a bit," said Carey, his voice oozing sympathy which made Red Sandy and Bangtail start snickering again. "It's not much fun, I'm told. It'll be much harder for you to talk to me once your tongue has swollen to twice its size with licking a few drops of water off the rough stone wall." Although from the way it had been raining recently, Carey rather thought Fire the Braes' real problem would be not drowning. However Fire the Braes was not to know that.

"Och," Fire the Braes said as Nixon attached him to the other two prisoners by a rope and jerked on it. "Ay, it was all Grahams, for the brave ye put on us last month, taking and hanging our cousins and guests…"

"For murder. And mentioning Lord Spynie."

Archie shrugged, "So what? And Ritchie of Brackenhill put the price up on ye, tae fifteens pounds and a helmet, so we'll no' be the ainly ones…"

"Forty men?"

"Mebbe thirty."

"That's what I thought. And someone had a try at me last week in Bessie's, only Bessie's wife saw him and cracked his skull with a jug."

"Ah dinna ken," said Fire the Braes sulkily.

"They say your tongue bleeds as well and then clots and so it cracks open…"

"Jesus, will ye stop? I came in wi' Wattie for the money and the fun of it, and now ye're threatening me wi' the Licking Stone cell and I'll no' have it, any of it."

"It's been busy all month and then in the last week it's gone silent as the grave, what's that about?"

"Ah dinna ken!" shouted Archie and tried to lunge at Carey who backed his horse a couple of paces while Andy Nixon and

Bangtail hit the reiver a couple of times to quieten him and teach him manners.

"So, let's see, we've got Fire the Braes, Sim's Jock Graham…"

Bessie's Andrew Storey hurried up to him. "There's one shot dead, three of them got trampled by the kine, one's still alive and the other two died, four ran intae the town, the rest forded the river upstream and ran for Liddesdale, Wattie Graham with them."

"Where's young Hutchin Graham? I swear I saw his hair."

"Dinna ken sir, probably ran intae the toon as well."

"They'll be at the postern gate arguing with Solomon Musgrave by now. Separate out the horses, we can always find a use for them and some of them have no brands on them."

He trotted to the northern town gate, the Scotch gate, where he found it shut, the postern gate shut tight and the gate guards denying stoutly that they had seen any Grahams, that there had been any Grahams anywhere—that Grahams existed, that there was a postern gate at all, and if there was, that it had ever been opened all night and certainly that there had ever been five people who might have gone through on payment of an irregular toll and certainly weren't Grahams….

Carey sighed, trotted back, brought in the three reivers on their feet and one slung over a pony's back, along with the eight men who were all looking very pleased with themselves, as well they might, except for Perkins who was protesting at being nicknamed Falls off his Horse Perkins.

august 1592

The Maxwell castle of Caerlaverock was tucked away in a part of Scotland almost nobody ever went to, except the people who lived there, near Dumfries. It was beautiful, certainly, in the opinion of the owner, the current eighth Lord Maxwell, ably backed by the Maxwell surname and their Herries cousins. When they weren't nose-to-nose with the Johnstones for the leadership of the Scottish West March, Maxwells had been known to make quite good West March Wardens, for a given and small value of "good." Now the old feud had broken out yet again and nothing mattered, save killing all the bloody Johnstones in whatever way seemed most expedient to the Maxwell.

He had had a splendid idea and was in the process of selling it to George Gordon, Earl of Huntly, the Earl of Erroll, and the Earl of Angus.

They were at a private supper in his private parlour where the silver loot from his and his ancestors' raids going back to before Flodden, shone softly in the candlelight. Father William Crichton squinted at the plate sometimes, recognising the chalices and patens robbed from monasteries during the Reformation, and some that looked to be English work, too.

He said nothing about any of it. He was a Jesuit and they always took the long, the educated view.

He was also the Maxwell's house priest, because Maxwell, like most of the northern earls, held to the old Faith, not the new ridiculous religion that had swept the country in 1560 when Crichton had been a pious young lad.

"*Benedicat vos omnipotens Deus...*" he intoned, letting the beautiful Latin carry him along. The polished table was spread with the first remove, and the lords had their heads bent. There was haggis, though it was really a peasant dish, a vast salmon from Maxwell's river, a haunch of beef, quite possibly from the Maxwell's own herds, venison from a hunt a week and a half ago, hung to perfection, quails, and some potherbs like turnips and neeps. Oh, and a sallet dressed with vinegar. Maxwell had an Edinburgh cook who had once worked in the Royal kitchens.

Unusually, once the venison had been broken, the lords served each other and the servants filed out. One large young man with freckles pulled the door firmly shut behind him. Father Crichton heard him draw his sword and his two feet stamping down on the floor as he took up position.

For the first ten minutes there was silence apart from the sound of knives and spoons scraping the occasional silverplate, napkins thrown over shoulders being applied to fingers, more manchet bread being asked for, silver spoons being used to sup the gravy made with red wine and a piquant sauce made of capers and lemon.

For the next half hour everyone talked about hunting, with occasional diversions into fishing and golf, Edinburgh tailors, fishing, hunting, golf, and the feud with the Johnstones which the Maxwell claimed was going exactly as he wanted it to, despite the setback caused by the stupid interference of the Deputy Warden.

The first remove was cleared by the servants filing in, and the second remove brought in with spitted chickens, blankmanger, more pathetic lettuce, quince cheese, and sheep and cow cheese with a magnificent cartwheel tart with twelve flavours of jam in it like a clock. They drank to Maxwell's wife in thanks, although of course she was not present, having tactfully gone to visit her mother.

"Well," said Father Crichton, who was very full, "perhaps we could begin?"

"Ay," said the Maxwell, rubbing the continuous eyebrow that went from one side of his face to the other. "Ye all ken why ye're here...?"

"Och," said Huntly, leaning back and loosening his belt, "ye're thinking of bringing the Spanish in again, are ye not?"

The Maxwell was a little taken aback. "Well, I am, but..."

"Ffft," said Erroll, as he pulled out his purse and gave Huntly a handful of debased Scotch shillings. "I thocht sure it's the French."

"The French are busy," said the Maxwell primly. "It has to be the Spanish King."

"Ay," said Erroll sceptically, "he's sending troops, is he?"

"He will," said the Maxwell positively. "He will because..."

"He willna," said Angus. "He disnae know nor care where Caerlaverock is, nor Lochmaben and..."

"He sent another Armada aginst the English again this summer..."

"Where is it?"

"Well it met some bad storms in the Bay of Biscay and they're refitting in the Groyne..."

"Ay, like the last one," said Erroll, drinking wine gloomily. "I swear the Queen of England's a witch."

There was a chorus of agreement about the unnaturalness of storms in Biscay in summer and they drank confusion to the old bat who had England in her grip and seemed to have a personal hold on the stormy weather as well.

"He might send another Armada next year, but..."

"Willna do nae good, she'll scatter that one too..."

"Will ye listen?" shouted the Maxwell and they quieted. "Father Crichton here has a canny scheme that will help the King of Spain to win England and incidentally wipe out the Johnstones by the way."

Everybody laughed except Maxwell.

"Ay, I thocht that would be in there somewhere..." said Huntly cynically.

"Ay, and why not? Ye've some feuds yerself, Huntly..."

"Hush," said Erroll who had noticed Father Crichton stand up.

He stood there for a moment, plain and unassuming, in a good suit of brown wool. "Ye recall the paper written by the King a few years back on the pros and cons of the Spanish having England?" It was obvious nobody did but this did not matter. "His Majesty of Spain has now seen a copy and finds it interesting."

"Ay, but King James isnae a Papist, is he?" asked a shocked-sounding Huntly, who was a Papist himself. "He's a sodomite, sure, but..."

"He isnae reformed neither," sniffed Angus, which produced a laugh. "He's neither one nor the other." More sniggers.

"My lords," said Father Crichton with a small proud smile, "I think the one thing that we can be sure of is that the King is a...Jamesist."

There was a pause and then a lot of laughter at this dangerous witticism. Father Crichton waited it out.

"The proposition is this, my lords," said Father Crichton, "that we take the usual assurances and bonds of manrent from our tenants and families while the King of Spain sends men quietly over the winter months, in hundreds here and there, some via Ireland, until there are at least four thousand *terceiros* based around Dumfries."

"How will we feed them?" somebody asked.

"The King of Spain will send food and money as well. While they are waiting they will need martial exercise and so my Lord Maxwell will lead them out..."

"To wipe out the Johnstones?"

"To deal with any disaffected elements in the area. Then when the spring storms have abated, the King of Spain will send a small Armada up through the Irish sea, using Irish and Cornish pilots, to meet us here. And in the summer of 1593 we march on England, down through the Western marches of Wales to Gloucester and Oxford. So the English willna ken they've been invaded until we're at Oxford perhaps, and London is open to us."

Father Crichton had been thinking about this plan for many years. It had some features he did not plan to share just yet, but as a peaceful man who had never been in a battle and dealt amongst the high abstractions of maps and orders, he was modestly proud of it. He thought of it as invading the soft underbelly of England and he rather thought the English would surrender and do a deal, once they realised how rotten their land soldiers were. Their frighteningly able sailors would not be able to do anything once the *terceiros* were ashore. There were hints that some of the men at the Queen's Court would be happy to do deals with the King of Spain and return to the arms of Mother Church. It was also said there was nothing an Englishman would not do for money.

"Hm," said Huntly, "what about King James? He's allus looked forward to getting the throne of England."

"He may not be disappointed," said Crichton carefully, because King James was indeed a problem, not least because nobody knew which way he would jump when it came to it—Catholic or Calvinist? "The King of Spain may prefer to rule through a vassal King, although he is the true heir through John of Gaunt and also his late wife, Queen Mary, not the bastard Elizabeth Tudor." Father Crichton didn't mention that Scotland could be swallowed later and converted back to the True Religion. "After he takes London, he will be King because everything flows from that, but there is more than one way to rule a conquest."

"It's a long way to go, Dumfries tae London."

"The Armada will resupply from the Irish sea," said Father Crichton, who had never seen Wales except in maps and assumed it was basically flat with some rolling hills.

They discussed the plan and Father Crichton brought out some specially drawn maps that showed as clear as day that it would be easy because nobody among the English would expect to be attacked from the northwest. The Queen would be guarding the south coast and the Cinque Ports as usual, not the approaches from the north. She trusted James and knew that he was considerably less martial than she was herself.

"Ye know," said Maxwell, "Queen James might even give his permission, seeing as the Spaniards would be only on the west coast and well away from Edinburgh and he disnae like a fight."

"Why should he give permission?" asked Huntly.

"Well the King of Spain's awfy rich, is he not? Why not bribe King James? I know he's annoyed with the Queen of England because she's cut his subsidy this year."

They all nodded thoughtfully.

The Maxwell spoke up again. "And besides," he said with a grin, "think of the plunder."

Father Crichton sat down again and listened with satisfaction as they talked about the rich pickings from the fat and easy lands of England. In a little while he would bring up the idea of assurances that they could give the King of Spain to convince him that they would do what he wanted, because the King of Spain had made a point about that. Philip II didn't trust the Scottish nobles as far as he could notionally throw them, which wasn't far since they were all fit young men and he was old and spent his days sitting at a desk.

Father Crichton made a quick prayer that the Lord Jesus Christ would bring the holy work to a satisfactory conclusion, with the Mass once more being said all across the sad, spiritually thirsty lands of England and Scotland, and of course, himself as Lord Chancellor.

autumn 1592

Sir David Graham of Fintry was feeling tired and sad. His back hurt from standing too much, his knees hurt from kneeling, his ears hurt from the howls of drunken laughter coming from the King's privy parlour where the King was entertaining some of his favourite nobles with a late supper. The pheasant and partridge were in pieces and a custard had been thrown for no very good reason that Sir David could discern although everybody found it very funny and the King was saying "Splatt!" at intervals, with tears of laughter rolling down his dingy face.

Lord Spynie was now prancing about with a tapestry wrapped around himself, imitating one of the Queen's fatter ladies in waiting. The Queen wasn't there of course, but in her own apartments with her ladies. Now Spynie had the tapestry as a cloak and was guying the Earl of Bothwell who had once been a friend of the King's, and was now at the horn. Sir David had to admit that Lord Spynie was a very good mimic, if you liked that sort of thing. Personally, he didn't.

He sighed and shifted from one foot to the other. As one of the King's Grooms of the Bedchamber, he was waiting to help His Highness to bed when he finally finished his hilarity and, since the King was in the room, he couldn't sit down like Lord Spynie and put his feet up on the table. Or, no, to be fair, Spynie was still pretending to be Bothwell, flirting with an invisible witch with his feet up.

He shifted again. He had a lot to think about, some of it connected with a highly intelligent and ingenious engineer who was also properly respectful of Sir David, unlike a lot of the young men at Court. He hadn't really noticed the man until he had some particularly bad news about the thirty years a-building of his castle near Dundee. He had been upset and was telling one of his few friends at Court about it in an antechamber. Sir George Kerr hadn't been able to do more than sympathise but a curly haired gentleman with pale grey eyes had stopped leaning against a wall and asked, with nice courtly respect, what the problem was.

"Part of the curtain wall is falling down again," said Sir David, mournfully. "I've turned off the masons but that didna stop it falling down again."

"Have you surveyed for running water?" asked the man.

"Eh?"

It turned out that the man's name was Jonathan Hepburn, he had been the Earl of Bothwell's man until the recent problems, and he was, among other things, a mining engineer. And so, the following week when Sir David was off-duty again, Hepburn had ridden to Dundee with Sir David and spotted that there was a small stream under the wall where it kept falling down. He had spent a few days organising the cutting of a small culvert to take the water away and all was immediately well. The rebuilt wall stopped falling down.

Sir David couldn't help liking Jonathan Hepburn, he was so respectful, so interested. All the other Grooms of the Chamber, even Sir George Kerr, thought he was mad building a fortress with a tower at Fintry, when fortified houses were now all the fashion.

"Ay," he told Hepburn over dinner in his parlour, with his pretty young wife, Marguerite, mercifully silent with her eyes modestly cast down, though her pale skin was looking oddly pink. "See ye, I'm old enough to mind the sights I saw in the Rough Wooing of Henry VIII, when we looked out from our old wooden tower and saw all the land speckled and pecked with fire from the English men at arms."

"They didn't come to Dundee, did they?"

"No, though they burned Edinburgh, so they did."

Hepburn shook his head disapprovingly. Sir David waved his silver spoon.

"And they might have burned us, they verra well might have, and that was when I swore to do anything in my power to make Fintry strong. I was only a wee lad but I remember it as if it were yesterday, I swore to rebuild Fintry of stone so it could keep out the English."

Hepburn nodded. "A noble aim," he said. "What can be more important than a strong castle where a man can put his feet down and know that it is his, and everything within it?"

Marguerite suddenly made a coughing noise into her hanky, coughed quite a lot and went quite red, then stood, curtseyed to her husband and retired to the hall to finish her coughing fit. Hepburn didn't even follow her with his eyes, as most men did.

"Ay," said Sir David, his heart swelling. "Ay."

Young Hepburn had had many excellent ideas for strengthening what had already been built and improving what was planned. They rode out and checked for more streams undermining the walls and found another unexpected place that needed dealing with, this time by diverting the stream so it fed into the moat.

Sir David had never known his young wife to be so well-behaved—there were no quarrels, no incomprehensible shouting matches. She was often impertinent and frankly too lively for his nearly sixty-year-old body and she had even protested when he dismissed two of her women when he felt they were plotting against him. But on this occasion she had behaved herself perfectly, almost as if she wasn't regrettably Flemish and a merchant's daughter.

It turned out that young Hepburn was also a Catholic, since his family came from a part of the Holy Roman Empire that had a Catholic prince and so was Catholic. Sir David approved of that: he couldn't bear the way starveling peasants in homespun and clogs would start haranguing their betters, even the King, on the wickedness of vestments and the importance of salvation through Grace alone. That kind of thing was simply none of their business.

Sir David had built a little chapel in the main Keep at Fintry, of course, and it gave him immense pleasure to bring young

Hepburn proudly to Mass there, where he promptly availed himself of the opportunity to go to confession. Sir David's priest was elderly, but Hepburn even knew of a Jesuit that was new come over from Spain and introduced Sir David to him.

And now Hepburn had confided to him that he was worried about Sir David's wife, the pretty and feather-headed Marguerite. She was certainly quieter, a welcome change.

Well Sir David knew that Hepburn had no opportunity for dalliance—he was very careful to keep his wife by his side all evening, and at night at Fintry, of course, she was his bedmate. She had much to do with the household during the day and occasionally she couldn't be found anywhere, but then she would reappear in the dairy or the wet larder while Hepburn might be on quite the other side of the castle, checking the mortressing. And of course she was often with their children, who had two nurses and a tutor for the eldest son who would inherit, in another part of the castle so they wouldn't disturb Sir David nor get entangled in the building works. He visited them occasionally.

The new corner tower was nearing completion—young Hepburn had been interested in how Sir David could afford to spend so much on masonry.

"It's nae secret," said Sir David, as they sat on ponies at a couple of miles distance from the castle so they could assess the whole of it. "I'm Groom of the Bedchamber to His Highness and offer him his nightshirt or his wine—not the cap, just his night-shirt—and help him dress in the morning. There's rarely fewer than ten petitioners at any levée and they all want to pay me."

"So there are compensations for having to stay up so late…"

"Oh ay, all the other grooms do the same, more than me in fact, it's quite traditional, ye ken."

"Of course. We must have traditions."

Sir David was glad Hepburn thought that. He had hated the disruption caused by the silly girl who had been briefly Queen and had been very happy to see a male Stuart on the throne again, even if he was under two years old and nominally a Protestant.

Hepburn smiled a little. "Does the King actually take the nightshirt?"

"Eh, no," said Sir David, "we generally can only get him to change it when he's been sick on his old shirt."

"Ah," said Hepburn, looking away and studying an unremarkable bush very fixedly.

At last Sir David had asked his wife if she was well, not ill with anything female, perhaps? He knew she wasn't pregnant again; he would have known at once because she was infallibly sick and cross. She said she was perfectly well but still looked worried.

And that was when he had started to wonder. Was it happening again? Did this wife too have a lover? He had of course dealt with the young man-at-arms who had looked at her, dealt with him very satisfactorily with a knife in the kidneys. But this was different; he knew no blame had attached to her with the man-at-arms, despite her blond hair. Had she taken another man into her bed, was she unhonest? It was a horrible thing to think of, it made his whole body shiver and go cold; he couldn't bear to be fooled again.

Young Hepburn had spotted him looking pensive, boiling internally with fear and rage, and asked him respectfully if he was well—just the same question Sir David had asked her. Sir David had passed it off—a little dyspepsia after a big post-hunting dinner for the Earl of Huntly, that big red-headed man with the bright blue eyes and the slow canny smile, whom the King seemed to like so well, he could do no wrong. Not even knifing the Earl of Moray to death was wrong when done by the Earl of Huntly, it seemed. Hepburn had been all solicitude and recommended a powder to ease the acid stomach, which had been bitter but had worked.

Sir David thought it was a tragedy that women were such fickle, flighty, unreliable creatures. You couldn't talk to them about anything interesting like architecture or hunting or even golf. And what if she was untrue?

"Maybe I could send Marguerite to Fintry," Sir David wondered. "Perhaps the Court is too wild for her, encourages unsuitable…er…thoughts."

Hepburn thought that would be a bad idea—she would be bored at Fintry, and everyone knew where idle hands led. And Sir David had to admit, though not to Hepburn, that there was another problem with that: What if she did in fact have a lover and invited him to Fintry? He didn't think he could bear that, just the thought made him tremble: his beautiful, safe, beloved castle, violated by the violator of his wife. If she did have a lover. He had no evidence, only a feeling.

So he watched her covertly, paid one of the Queen's chamberers to keep an eye on her and suffered silently, wondering. Sometimes he thought she did have a lover, sometimes he was sure she didn't. Sometimes the tension of not knowing made him sweat as if he had a fever.

It didn't help that Hepburn was now not so available, he was deep in plans with the King for a masque—one of the newfangled Court entertainments that encouraged such deeply unsuitable behaviour in the Queen's women. This one was a Masque of the Seasons with the ladies of the Court risking lungfever in the draperies that almost but not quite hid their nipples. He liked seeing a bit of nipple, did the King, and had been known to take a suck on them when very drunk.

Being an engineer meant you could design scenery and toys for masques as well. It was wonderful what the young man could do—he was even designing fireworks, with the help of the Frenchmen with their mysterious slitty-eyed demonic looking assistants.

But did Marguerite have a lover? Did she? Why would she need one? Sir David tupped her every Friday night, regular as clockwork, whether he felt like it or not because he knew she was prone to attacks of the mother—and the King's own physician, no less, had advised him that regularly swiving her would help. So why would she take a lover? If she had? Why?

He had a new Court suit made for himself, green brocade trimmed with gold velvet. It had been a while since he did that and he thought he looked very elegant and manly in it, and young Hepburn had thought so too. Sir David was quite proud that he had kept his figure and only had a little potbelly; he wasn't going bald at all though his hair was grey; he had the long lantern jaw of the Grahams which always aged well; he was wealthy, though most of his money went on building his castle, of course. All in all, he was as suitable a husband as you could find anywhere in Edinburgh. So why..?

Hepburn had listened to him friendlywise in the same ante-chamber where they had met, waiting for the King to finish playing cards with his nobles. Perhaps Sir David had rambled on a bit, for Hepburn had then coughed and asked the extraordinary question "Sir, have you considered buying your wife some new gowns?" Sir David just blinked at him. "Only both her Court dresses are five years old and have been remade twice and relined three times and I couldn't help overhearing..."

"Why would I do that?" asked Sir David, genuinely baffled. "They are not worn out yet."

Hepburn went into such a paroxysm of coughing that Sir David was quite concerned for him and told him to help himself to the wine.

"Some firework fumes must have caught in my throat," wheezed Hepburn. "Of course, it's a matter for you, but I have found most women are happier for a new gown."

Sir David thought about that for a long while because he now valued Hepburn's opinion and normally took his advice—but in this case, he decided, Hepburn was wrong. Why should he waste money on Court gowns for his wife when she had two perfectly good ones, plus everyday kirtles for when she was not on show? There was nothing at all wrong with the old gowns, except they were not designed in the foolish style with the Spanish farthingale that made women look as if they were standing in a barrel. In any case he had the corner tower to complete which was taking all his ready cash but would last for generations.

And then something very odd happened. The King suddenly caught sight of Marguerite in her oldest gown and gave her a twelve-yard dresslength of rose-coloured velvet, with six yards of white damask to make her a new gown that would also do for the Masque of the Seasons as Spring. Marguerite was ecstatic.

"Oh, the King, he is so kind," she bubbled to her husband, while she was brushing her beautiful golden hair that evening, something he normally enjoyed watching. "He saw I have noss-ing to wear…"

"Well, my dear, you do have your perfectly respectable cramoisie damask…"

"…and pow! Just like that, he gives me beautiful velvet and say, I must be sure and show him when the Queen's tailor has finished it. I will have it trimmed with freshwater pearls which are not at all expensive, Sir David, and perhaps some mother of pearl…" And so she went happily into a long explanation of styles which Sir David found painful in the extreme although he said "Yes dear" every so often.

It was painful because he had a thought about a possibil-ity so outrageous he couldn't quite believe he was thinking it at all…And yet Henry VIII of England had scattered his seed with abandon, and hadn't Maria, James' foolish mother, been touched with scandal? The disgusting English Queen had been tupped by everybody at her Court, including her horsemaster and a hunchback. It was a fault of royal personages: they could, so they did. Yet surely James…preferred men.

Sir David had witnessed many horrible and disgusting things while serving the King as Groom, like the times when the painfully young and spotty King and the corrupt French Duc D'Aubigny had gone to bed together like a married couple. Sir David did his best never to think about it, just as he did his best never to think about Lord Spynie's young pages, who often had red eyes and a reluctance to sit after a party.

But then the King seemed to have grown out of it and had a Queen now and as far as anyone could tell had consummated the marriage. And surely a girl as beautiful as Marguerite might tempt even a God-rotted sodomite.

When Sir David consulted Hepburn on the matter, all he would say was that he was sure Marguerite was honest, that he had never seen the King make any improper suggestions to her and he was sure that the matter of the dresslength of rose velvet and the six yards of white damask was just the well-known and foolish generosity of His Highness.

Yet the thought came between Sir David and his food, between Sir David and his sleep. When he closed his eyes, he saw the King kissing Marguerite, fondling her breasts with his greasy dirty hands, sweating between her legs...It turned his stomach to lead and made him feel desperate because even if he sent her home to Fintry, who knew what she might get up to, and if he kept her here at Court...Well, he couldn't watch her all the time. The chamberer hadn't reported anything but perhaps she had been rebought by someone with longer pockets than his...

He asked Hepburn again and saw Hepburn's eyes become opaque.

"Sir," he said, "I can but do my best, but if a woman of the Court is being pursued by the King, there is not a lot she can do about it."

And that was even worse. It had honestly not occurred to him that she might not be willing (though she had been happy about the gown, women were flighty), that James might be using his Kingship in so ugly a way. To be honest, he wouldn't put anything past the man since he was so deep-dyed in the sin of sodomy and, worse still, a Protestant.

It was only when he went home to Fintry on his weeks off and could see the tower and the walls that he felt a little better.

And then James began one of his fits of economising and started talking about reducing the number of his Grooms from eight to six.

It was obvious. The King would send Sir David home to Fintry, where he would not be able to do any more building without the daily influx of shillings and crowns from hopeful petitioners. And Marguerite would be defenceless in the King's power.

ÐECEMBER 1592

Carey took off his jack with the help of his servant, Hughie Tyndale, who made faces at what the jack was plastered with. "Don't clean it yourself," Carey said. "Get Young Hutchin to do it if you can find him." Underneath was a worn old hunting green doublet trimmed with velvet that was just about respectable enough for Bessie's. He also left his fighting boots with Hughie, who was getting quite good at cleaning off horrible things.

He didn't have another pair of long boots, but he had a pair of shoes which could cope with the mud, pulled them on, put a new tall-crowned hat on his head and walked quickly down the covered way to Bessie's. He was starving, and Bessie and her wife had set up their usual glorious breakfast for the men of the guard.

And at least he could eat the bacon now. He felt the healed gap in his back teeth with his tongue and shuddered. God, he had felt so ill.

He was having an argument with Sim's Will about which would win in a fight, two rats or a badger, when Bessie's wife, Nancy, sat herself down next to him in the common room and refilled his leather jack for him. In London he would have had his own pewter tankard behind the bar but Bessie didn't allow any such things in her house on account of the fact that they got damaged when you hit people with them—unlike leather jacks which weren't quite so bendable or expensive. Carey felt that reflected the irrationality of women.

He tipped his hat to her since she had curtseyed first before she sat down and raised a quizzical eyebrow.

"There's something I heard about ye, Deputy Warden," she said, "that there's been two letters come fra the Queen for ye. Have ye seen either one?"

He sat up at once. "No, I haven't."

"Ay well, one came wi' the regular postbag from Newcastle the day before yesterday."

"Did it now?"

"Ay, and there's another package for ye at Thomas the Merchant, but he'll tell ye about that as he wants the shilling."

"And the other letter? Who's got it?"

"Ay well, all the post is supposed to go to the Warden, but it often gets stopped by Lowther."

Carey smiled at her and lifted his ale in toast.

Once his belly was full of bacon, sausage, egg, black pudding, mushrooms, fried apple, and some interesting fried roots from New Spain via Newcastle, he felt quite sleepy but knew better than to take a nap yet. So he called Nixon to back him and strode on down into the town to the more respectable English Street, where Thomas the Merchant had his quite impressive three-storey house with carved beam-ends and smart saffron-yellow paint.

Thomas the Merchant was in front of the house talking to the Carlisle steward.

"I'll take the kine without brands that ye dinna want to slaughter, of course, and what about the horses?"

"We're keeping those. We always need more horses."

"Ay well, I'll come up and look at the beasts later..." That was when Thomas the Merchant spotted Carey and his face took on its normal wary expression.

"Ay, Deputy Warden, can I help ye?"

"You can," said Carey, doing his best not to beam at Thomas. "I heard tell you had a letter for me."

Thomas nodded and led Carey inside to his hall, where the plate was locked tight into two large cupboards chained to the wall. There he gave Carey a large official-looking packet stitched into double thickness canvas and addressed in old-fashioned Secretary hand "to the Deputy Warden of the West March, Sr Rbt Carey, Carlisle Castle."

He stared at it for a few seconds, wondering where it could have come from since most official correspondence (and there was a lot) was addressed to him as plain Sr Rbt Carey, Carlisle.

He flipped the packet over and saw the red portcullis stamp on the back and sudden joy lifted him up and he nearly gave a little jig of triumph right there in front of Thomas the Merchant. He didn't of course. He caught himself, bestowed an alarmingly sunny smile on the suspicious-faced old miser, and strode out into English Street which was crowded with people going out to work in the fields while the weather held.

All the way back up to the castle, with Nixon at his back, he had to stop his feet from breaking into a volta and also stop himself sprinting up the covered passageway. Once he had left Nixon behind and gone into the keep, nobody was watching and so he ran laughing up the stairs of the Queen Mary tower and did his jig on a landing where there was nobody to see except a tabby cat, watching sparrows from the windowsill, who didn't care. At the top of the narrow spiral staircase to his chambers he found his secretary, John Tovey, was still snoring and wasn't at all offended. He was on the palliasse—the two of them, Hughie and John, had come to an agreement where each alternated between the truckle bed and the floor.

He was still at a jog when he went through into his study and sat at the table that did duty as his desk, piled high as it always was with papers. Tovey's clerk's desk was in the corner with a candlestand next to it.

He turned the packet over and over in his long fingers, excitement still rising in him. Was it? At last? The Tower mark and the address. Could it be? Had the old bat finally...?

He pulled out his poinard from the scabbard at his back and slit the red stitching at one end, took out the inner packet and slit that stitching as well, which was yellow—which meant the Cecils. Inside were several sheets of paper.

The first he saw was odd—a passport to go into Scotland, dated from a week ago and no expiry date. But the second...

It was his warrant as Deputy Warden of Carlisle. It made him as official as illegibly small Secretary script and impressive seals could achieve and it was also signed and sealed with her Privy Seal by the Queen.

With it there was a private letter from the Queen, written by a Secretary in Italic but signed by herself as his affectionate and loving cousin and aunt. He skimmed the letter, which was short and only filled half the paper—she had heard of his standoff with the Elliots and thoroughly approved of the way he had resolved it, and that there had been no effusion of blood between her aggressive Border subjects.

"Yes!" he shouted, punching his fist into the air and kissing the letter. John Tovey woke up, groaned and turned over, then sat up looking embarrassed.

"Sorry, sir…" he began.

"Run and fetch me some wine if you can find any. Scrope may have some," Carey said and punched the air again. Then he sat back down in his uncomfortable chair and shut his eyes. He suddenly realised that a knot of tension that had been in his stomach for a month or more had magically dissolved away. The Queen was a woman, you could never be sure how she would react to anything and there had been a part of him that thought exactly the same as Sergeant Dodd. Another part had insisted that if you wanted to make any headway with the Borderers, you had to get away from blood repaying blood through the years.

It had been very hard to sit there and let more than five hundred Elliot reivers escape but he knew it was right. It was not just a clever or politic or Queen-pleasing thing to do, but the right thing. Dodd had violently disagreed and made his displeasure known, so now Carey felt he had lost the man. It was a pity. Andy Nixon was loyal and almost hero-worshipped him, he knew, while Nixon's new wife was always bringing him pastries and pots of jam. Perhaps Nixon was as good a fighter as Dodd, and a better wrestler, but he didn't have half the brains.

He read the Queen's letter again, more carefully, which was enough to delight any courtier, although typically it said nothing about the Deputy Warden's fee. And it said nothing about the passport into Scotland either, which was a little odd. Perhaps the letter she had sent to Scrope confirming the choice of Carey for Deputy Warden would explain it. Carey did not plan to go into Scotland at all if he could help it, although he had recovered completely from the last time.

Tovey came back with wine and Carey poured him some, explained why and they toasted the Queen. Tovey was pleased once he understood the importance of the warrant. It was official. Nobody could turn him out without the Queen's permission. God, it would be fun to watch Lowther's face when he showed the warrant to Scrope. Maybe Lowther would fall into a conniption fit with rage and die and save Carey a lot of trouble. He hoped so.

He read the letter again, folded the whole packet back up and put it in his doublet pocket where it warmed him like a hand-warmer full of coals.

autumn 1592

Sir David Graham was in a terrible state, a state he had been in before with his first wife, and he knew of only one way to feel better. And yet he felt utterly horrified by the idea and at the same time grimly vengeful, because hadn't the King betrayed him first?

He was sure that Marguerite had a lover now, he had found lovebites on her shoulder and he never gave her lovebites. He had said nothing. She seemed to have no idea she had them and continued prattling away about the beauty of her new kirtle with its Spanish farthingale and the pink velvet and the white damask until he could have screamed. But that was not his way. He had always been a quiet man, not given to displays of temper. That did not mean he had no feelings, only that he chose not to wave them around in public.

Finally he got Hepburn to himself on the links opposite the port of Leith. The weather was bad, blustery and raining, but he had needed to get out of the Court and blow the cobwebs out of his ears and Hepburn had agreed to come with him and play a little golf. Not a proper game, only practising.

He teed off and struck the ball well, it flew away, avoiding the trees, and landed in some long grass. Hepburn had hit his ball well too, but shorter.

They ended closer together on the green and while Hepburn lined up his putt, Sir David struggled with himself and finally burst out, "If he were not the King, he would already be dead."

Hepburn stopped for a moment. "Sir David?"

"The man who debauched my Marguerite. If he were just a man, even an earl, I would have killed him by now."

Hepburn looked straight up at him. "How? In a duel?"

Sir David snorted. "No, why should I honour him by fighting him? He's scum. He laughed at me yesterday morning, asked me if I was well, and all the time...all the time..."

Hepburn sighed. Then he straightened up and leaned on his golf club, the wind blowing his falling band sideways. There was no one else on the links and they hadn't brought a boy to find the balls.

"You believe it truly is the King?"

"Yes," ground out Sir David. "He can go to the Queen's apartments any time he chooses and swive anyone he likes. And Marguerite has a lover's bite and the kirtle...I'm sure it's the King."

"It could be some other man. It could even be me."

Sir David laughed indulgently at that. "No, no, Jonathan," he said. "You're not a God-rotted sodomite, but you are more interested in your alchemy and engineering than you are in women. I can tell."

"Ah," said Hepburn. "Well then, perhaps it is the King. But what can you do about it? I have said this before, he may be a coward but he is clever. You can't carry so much as an eating knife in his private apartments where being a Groom of the Bedchamber might help you, as there are always at least five other people with you..."

"Poison, in his first cup of wine in the morning. He's always thirsty in the morning, knocks it straight back."

"They will know who gave him the cup."

Sir David smiled wolfishly. "Not if I don't give it to him. I serve it out, taste it, and sometimes he takes it from me, sometimes a chamberer gives it to him, sometimes the Groom of the Stool gives it to him..."

"Who is that at the moment?"

"Sir George Kerr does the office at the moment, but I don't want him to give the cup because he is also one of our Catholic association."

"Yes," said Hepburn, "the association with Huntly and Erroll?"

"Of course. It's a very good idea from your Jesuit, Crichton, about bringing in Spanish troops to the west coast."

"I had heard something about it."

"Well, I'm not supposed to tell anyone. Anyway, sometimes, if a petitioner pays a lot of money, sometimes he can give the King his cup of morning wine. So we find someone who wants something big and he can come into the King's levée and as he will give the cup, everyone will blame him."

Hepburn looked at Sir David with real respect. "That's ingenious, Sir David. Brilliant."

Sir David twirled his golf club roguishly. "I think so. Of course it's not just any levée that petitioners can actually take part in. Usually they stand and watch at the other end of the bedchamber and come forward after His Highness is dressed. The next is the New Year's morning, but I can wait for my satisfaction if I have to."

"Yes," said Hepburn, chipping his putt and missing the hole by a mile. "We will need to choose the man to do it very carefully."

They talked for a while about who could do it, came to no conclusion. Hepburn rode back to Edinburgh with Sir David Graham who was now somehow happy, as if making the decision had helped settle his uneasy soul.

Hepburn was awed at how well his plan was going: he had hardly had a plan when he started, only he had heard something about Sir David and his first wife, how jealous he was, how the lover and the wife had both died quite suspiciously, how there had been a man-at-arms that had fallen for Marguerite and who had died also in mysterious circumstances in which he had somehow stabbed himself in the kidneys.

Hepburn knew he himself was a killer, although generally he didn't do the actual killing, he...facilitated it. He could see through people so easily, their jealousies and their ugliness, he felt he was providing a vermin-killing service. Sir David did not know what he was, which made him easy to control. Spynie was another one like Hepburn, they got on well and Hepburn facilitated him as well. He was even making friends with the King he had come to kill on behalf of the Spanish Most Catholic Majesty, and he could do it while still looking for the best way to end him. It was exciting and satisfying. It excited him to fool everybody into thinking he was a helpful respectful man with engineering skills and good address, when in fact he was so much more. He felt he was looking at the Court from a great height and laughing as the ants below him ran around excitedly while he pushed them one way and another with twigs and bits of paper and carefully killed some here and some there. Out of policy he normally liked to have two different and separate attempts running at the same time, one a little earlier. Then, if the proposed victim discovered or fought off one, he would relax and be easy meat for the second attempt.

It had taken so little to get the King to give Marguerite the pink velvet and the white damask; a mention of how mean her husband was, a wink, the idea planted in the King's mind that he could somehow shame Sir David into treating his wife better through royal largesse. The King was always clumsily trying to get the courtiers around him to treat each other better, as if they were not there through greed and ambition, as if they were all friends really. It was ridiculous but very useful. Then a couple of careful lovebites on Marguerite during one of their trysts in the storerooms at the back of the court and the thing was done.

Hepburn shook his head. He had made his peace with the demiurge of this World, with the Aeon who ruled everything. You had to choose: either the Demiurge, the Power of the World, or the Christ who had foolishly tried to oppose him and been crushed. Some called the Demiurge, the Devil. He called him God and felt the power run through him when he called on him. Fools called them Anabaptists: he had taken the trouble to read some of the difficult sacred texts in Latin and his conclusions had been rational, not emotional. He had no interest in the Sophia, the female expression of God. Women could worship her under the guise of Mary the Mother of God, the Theotokos, if they wanted. He thought they were fools of a different kind, but they were women and inferior. Sure, the Albigensians had tried to bring the Christ into the World by what they did and they had been crushed as well, by Saint Dominic, the Demiurge's servant. He chose not to be crushed. He would follow the Power of the World and when he died, he would go to His side to serve him more.

In the meantime he would obediently go to Mass and confess what he chose because as far as he was concerned, the Catholic Church was clearly the main tool of the Demiurge, not at all His enemy. He had travelled through the Netherlands, making himself useful wherever and whenever he could, and he had been recommended at last to San Lorenzo where he had actually met the Spanish King and talked to him of his ideas. He had the precious copy of the paper outlining his ideas with Philip's *Fiat* written on it and he thought that when Scotland descended into chaos with the death of the King, he would certainly become a lord at least, possibly a King. The Spanish King didn't know about that part of it, but thought Hepburn was another Catholic fanatic, as he was himself. Another fool.

He was careful and he was clever. He would survive and conquer and perhaps in a year or two, he would be running Scotland.

late autumn 1592

Janet Dodd née Armstrong was wondering if it would really be such a sin to murder her husband. It would be a sin, obviously, and petty treason moreover, but surely she had justification?

Henry Dodd had never been the happiest of men but there was something solid and dependable about him. Yet since the Deputy Warden had let the Elliots escape from Dick of Dryhope's tower without a battle, he had gone from taciturn but essentially friendly to a stone-faced silent man she did not know.

Even love-making didn't help, which it always had before; he seemed somehow abstracted as if his thoughts were far away and nowhere pleasant, until their tussling under the bedclothes while Bridget snored in the truckle bed became more like a fight. Not once since the Elliots had he asked to count her freckles, not once had she shucked her shift so he could admire her and love her breasts and hips, not once had she felt that blessed sensation halfway between a sneeze and utter joy that made her feel warm and happy all the next day. Not once. It was as if a stranger got into bed with her wearing Henry's shirt and Henry's face and tupped her as if she was an ewe.

She was seeing to the vegetable garden and she dug angrily. She had got a couple of her English Armstrong cousins to come and dig in two ponyloads of manure which she had obtained for nothing from the Carlisle stables. Henry was off on his precious big horse, Whitesock, checking the northern boundaries of Gilsland for moving marker stones. Gilsland was now theirs but she couldn't feel happy about it any more. She felt lonely, despite being surrounded by people, most of them some sort of cousin and one, Bridget, her half sister.

Suddenly one of the women holding poles for the men fixing the fencing over by the infield, clapped her hand to her side and doubled up. Janet dropped her spade and ran over.

"What is it?" she asked, "When is the baby due?"

It was Goody Ellen, a cousin, married for five years to Willie's Simon and proudly pregnant, but not fully gone yet. Was it six months?

"Not till Candlemas," gasped Ellen, tears of fright in her eyes. "Och it's bad."

Ellen hadn't had a baby before. Maybe these were ghost pains and she was just making a fuss...

"Oh...Oh, God, I canna hold it..." gasped Ellen, trying to grab her crotch round her belly. Janet lifted her wool kirtle and saw her petticoat was suddenly wet and stained, mainly water but blood and brown stuff there as well.

"Ekie!" she shrieked to one of the boys tidying beanvines. "Ride for Mrs Hogg, off ye go now. Say Ellen's gey early and her waters have broken."

Ekie was quite a young boy, maybe eight, but had a good head on him. He stood and stared for only a second before he sprinted for the tower and the stables.

"Take Angel," she shouted after him. "He's a good galloper and ye've ten miles to go."

Mrs Hogg lived near Carlisle and was the best midwife hereabouts, a tough flinty woman who had faced down drunken husbands and, it was rumoured, raiding Grahams.

"Och, God!" shrieked Ellen again, "Oh God!" Janet got Ellen's arm over her shoulder and helped her over the ruts in the field, onto the path, waiting for another set of shrieks to quiet, urged her along. "Willie's Simon, fetch me my aqua vitae, quick as ye can, lad." Ellen's husband had been running towards them from the wall at the far end of the infield but Janet had never heard good of husbands at a birthing and in any case he knew where she hid the stillroom key.

Janet found Rowan Leaholm on the other side of Ellen and they helped her along until they saw Big Clem the blacksmith come running up the path from his forge. He caught Ellen up and held her in his arms like a baby while she twisted and clutched her belly and cried out. His face was sad: his own wife had lost a wean in the upset of a raid that summer.

Janet saw young Ekie come trotting out of the courtyard and, good lad, he had tacked up Angel properly and was giving the horse a chance to warm up before his gallop, that was good sense and nice to see. The lad was cantering as he went over the hill in the direction of Carlisle.

They got Ellen up into the tower and into the little room Janet used as an infirmary and still-room, laid her on the bed where she sat up and shrieked again. Willie's Simon was there with a horn cup of brandy which she gulped and then gasped again. Clem thundered downstairs in silence with his broad kindly face troubled and sad.

More brandy went into her and then some more. Sometimes you could stop a miscarriage with brandy, Janet had heard, and at least it helped with the pain. Bridget was there as well. "Will ye go ben and tidy away any tools and such?" Janet said, thinking of the valuable sickles and spades getting ruined by the rain. "I'll stay with Ellen."

Janet sat and waited as patiently as she could, trying not to think of all the things that went wrong with having a babby. She liked Ellen and didn't want her to die. Although in ten years of marriage she had been barren, there had not even been a missed mense, yet she had seen plenty of her women go through birthing. Once, the baby had stuck in a girl's narrow hips and although Mrs Hogg had killed the baby, which was already blue and spent, and taken it out in bloody pieces, the girl had been too exhausted to live after three days of struggle. What was her name, that poor blond slip of a thing? She couldn't remember, it was back when she was new to being the mistress. The curse of Eve the pastors called it, and it was a curse, but if it all went well and the woman was successfully churched, it didn't seem to matter about the pain or the mess, the baby paid for everything. Providing it didn't die, of course.

Ellen shrieked more quietly and turned restlessly. Ah, the mess. There were plenty of women who went down to the stables to have their weans so they wouldn't have the trouble of washing the sheets after. Also it was considered lucky, since hadn't Jesus Christ Himself been born in a stable? With the ox and the ass kneeling to Him?

Janet fetched the coarse hemp sheets from the back of the linen press that were already a little stained with other people's blood since you often couldn't get it all out once it had set. She sat Ellen up to take the other sheets off and took her kirtle off as well. It didn't seem to have taken much harm, her underpetticoats were slimy and horrible but it hadn't soaked through. She and Bridget undressed Ellen down to her smock and Bridget took the kirtle and the sheets off to soak the sheets in water and try and see if she could sponge the stains off the kirtle.

Then she uncovered the birthing chair and brought it out from its corner, wiped the dust off it. Ellen saw it and started to cry again.

"The baby's coming too early."

"Ay, it is," Janet said.

"Do ye think it might live?"

"Do ye know when ye quickened?"

"It was May…No, July, late July when he quickened but I'd been feeling awfy sick before that, couldnae eat nor drink."

"He's just in his seventh month." Janet found she was shaking her head.

"D'ye think Mrs Hogg could put it back in and sew me up, do ye think? Oh God."

Janet waited. "I think once the waters have broken the babe's got to come out, will he or nill he."

Ellen cried harder and Janet shouted for someone, found Willie's Simon at the door and ordered him to fetch the brazier to keep Ellen warm and some ale for her to mull. It was going to be a long day. At least the wean hadna decided to come in the middle of the night, that was something.

Mrs Hogg arrived riding pillion with Ekie on Angel and clattered up the stairs in her hobnailed boots. Janet leaned out of the staircase window and told Ekie to walk Angel and rub him down and give him a bran mash and Ekie said "yes, missus" politely, despite the fact that he clearly knew all that. Mrs Hogg was a plump, comfortable-looking person until you got on the wrong side of her, and then watch out. Janet found herself wondering if the midwife knew any good spells or potions to help with her barrenness, but she would ask later.

The midwife had her big leather bag and took her sleeves off and rolled the sleeves of her shift up to her shoulders, tied them there with a tape, and put on a wide hemp apron. Then she smeared her hands with tallow and put her hands up Ellen's smock and felt about for what seemed a long time. She stood up and came to Janet saying, "Can I get a pottle of ale, missus? My throat's fair dry fra the ride."

Janet poured her a cup of ale over in the corner.

"It's breech and very early," she said. "When's it due?"

"Candlemas."

"Ah." Mrs Hogg's chin went down on her chest. "Ay, a May baby. Well, she'll need to go a-maying again."

There was another loud shriek from the bed and Mrs Hogg went over to her, took her hand. "Now then," she said, "save yer shrieking, hen, it'll get worse before it gets better."

A new thunder of feet on the stairs and there were the nearest two of Ellen's gossips at last, her sister Mary and Katherine from the dairy, in a bustle of kirtles and aprons. They sat down next to Ellen on the bed and hugged her and then held her hands while she twisted and tried not to shout.

Katherine had a good voice and she started singing a spinning worksong, all about spindles and pockets and in very poor taste, if you listened the right way.

Janet trotted down the stairs to see that things were going along. She and Dodd had decided to hold a pig-killing for the last survivor of the boar piglets, since he was showing signs of temper and he was racketing about in his pen, trying to dig his way out. Pigs always seemed to know what was in the wind but she wouldn't be sorry to see this one die. He was a nasty piece of work, too much of the wild boar in him.

She made her rounds, looked in on the horses—Penny, Shilling, Angel and Samuel the donkey. She considered where she could put a goat pen if she decided to keep goats which were a new-fangled idea for the Borders though she liked the sound of an animal that could eat anything, she checked the stores of grain and hay and straw and found as she always did this year that there wasn't enough.

Her mind started circling and worrying on the problem. She thought she would have to sell or kill one of the horses and Dodd wouldn't like that. Really she should have sent old Shilling to the knackers last year, but she was fond of the old gentleman and couldn't bring herself to do it. But she had to do something.

The cattle were all in the well-guarded infield, eating the stubble, the sheep were in the nearest outfield, away on the hill crossed by the Giant's Wall, which was horribly muddy from the rain. The soil was so waterlogged she wasn't expecting much from the winter cabbages. All the men were tired and cranky from having to keep a guard, and starting to come in for their dinner.

She delegated serving the men and the boys to Bridget, who was already stirring the large cauldron of pottage and slicing the bread to go with it. She hadn't eaten since breakfast but wasn't hungry.

Back in her little infirmary, Mrs Hogg had just finished another rummage under Ellen's smock and was drinking the last of the ale. Ellen was hiccupping badly and her gossips were getting drunk. There wasn't really room for her but Mary budged up on the bed to let her sit down. Then Willie's Simon appeared at the door, his face like a cow in calf himself.

"Is she gaunae be all right?" he asked Mrs Hogg desperately. "Is she?"

"It's in the hands of Our Lady," said Mrs Hogg.

"What can I do?"

"Naething, this is women's work."

"Can I rub her back for her? She likes it..."

"Her gossips can do that, out ye go, get yer pottage."

"I dinnae want it, I'm a good stockman, I've helped cows and sheep give light to their weans, I can..."

"Men fight, women birth, so get oot," said Mrs Hogg, who had a brisk way with husbands. Ellen stopped panting and reached her hands out to her husband. "It's best ye go," she said kindly. "The babby's too soon and the wrong way up, so mebbe he'll die, but we can try again once I'm churched, hinny."

Willie's Simon looked confused. "Too soon?"

"Ay, he's not...he's not properly cooked yet, see ye..."

"But.."

"It's all right," said Ellen softly, "we'll make another baby, eh?"

Willie's Simon's face cleared a little. "Oh, but..."

"And this one might live…Ooorgh…ooorrgh…Ah shit, I need tae shit…"

Janet shoved the young man bodily out the door and slammed it, while Mary and Kat jumped off the bed. The last thing she needed was somebody fainting.

"Ayaaergh!" howled Ellen and Mrs Hobb felt her quickly and then nodded. So they moved her between them to the birthing chair where she sat with her legs apart and her smock up and Mrs Hogg knelt like a priest at an altar in front of her with her hands slick with tallow.

Mary and Kat helped keep Ellen steady from either side while Janet put her back against Ellen's back and her feet on the wall and supported her while she bore down.

"Ay," said Mrs Hogg coolly, as something that looked oddly like a plum appeared between Ellen's legs. "Go with it, hinny, wait for the wave to come and then go with it. Aright, get yer breath. Can ye say an Avvy?"

"Dinna ken…" panted Ellen, tears and sweat pouring down her face. Janet wiped it with her apron.

"Well say it wi' me, Avvy Maria, grass a plenty, dominoes take em, benedictus two in mules and arybus…"

Ellen screamed and her face turned purple, the plum between her legs got bigger, then smaller, then much bigger and turned into a very small baby's bottom. Mrs Hogg took hold of it and pulled, pulled out one little foot and then another and they dangled, looking strange. Mrs Hogg was tutting.

"Aright, hinny, yer doing fine, let's have another Avvy Maria…"

Janet turned and braced her feet against the wall again while Mary and Kat held Ellen's shoulders.

"Et benny dictus fruit venter twee…" sang out Mrs Hogg. "Come on hinny, ye're a good strong lass, give it all ye've got, let's get the head out." Ellen went a darker purple, her neck corded as she bore down, and slowly Mrs Hobb pulled and there were shoulders and pulled and pulled and finally, there was a tiny baby with a big head, dark blue, very tiny and skinny with something funny on its back.

Mrs Hogg held it to one side, christened it with water from the bucket beside her, muttering the words as fast as she could as the little chest fluttered. Yes, there was something red and ugly on his back, in his back, was that bone..?

Janet craned her neck to see and as the water touched his forehead he struggled and fought but couldn't get his breath, as if the air was made of steel for him, and he gave a little sigh and went limp. Mrs Hogg was already bundling him up in a cloth, hiding the strange wound on his back and she glared at Janet to stay silent.

"He's not...he's not supposed to be blue..."

"No, hinny, he's not. He couldna breathe. He lived till I christened him, but he's just too little and he's deid."

Ellen clutched the baby and howled like a dog while her gossips wrapped their arms around her and cried. Mrs Hogg left the cord and just patted Ellen's back. Janet said quietly through the noise, "What was that on his back?"

"I'll tell ye later, it'll do her nae good to know."

Janet went and opened the horn-paned window wide and then they waited for the afterbirth, which came plopping out a little while later. Mrs Hogg caught it in a bowl and cut the cord and there was no blood. She took the bowl to the light of the sunset and moved the liverlike thing about, checking it closely.

"Ay," she said in a pleased voice, "that's all there. Ye'll be well enough in time."

Ellen's face was covered in snot and tears as she held the tiny bundle to her chest and sobbed deep wrenching sobs that came from her belly.

"Ay," said Mrs Hogg, not a tear on her face, "ye cry, hinny, cry away the sadness." She mopped Ellen's legs and quim and belly with cloths from the bucket. "Now let's get ye back on the bed."

Janet, Mary, and Kat carried Ellen bodily to the bed, where they pulled her dirty smock off over her head, one arm then the other arm, so she could still hold the baby and she shivered suddenly. One of Janet's own smocks went on over her head and a pair of breeches to hold the cloths. Everything went immediately into a bucket of cold water to soak for the night. And all the time she cried and cried for the tiny unbreathing baby, that was paling now.

Mrs Hogg put a knitted shawl from Kat around Ellen's heaving shoulders and then sat beside her and waited for the worst of the storm to pass. Eventually she asked gently, "Will ye let me lay the little one out for ye?"

"Why did he die? Why didn't he stay inside me? Why did he come too soon?"

Mrs Hogg shook her head. "Naebody knows why anybody lives or dies, ainly God and His Mother. But I'll tell thee, child, he was baptised whilst his little heart was still beating and he'll go straight to God, so he will, straight to heaven he'll fly and he'll be an angel there."

Ellen's tears were thick and slow now. "But why did God want him?"

"Ah dinnae ken, hinny, but perhaps He wis short of they smaller angels ye see in books, ye ken, the fat babies wi' the little wings. And maybe the baby was helping ye, so he came too soon while he was little so ye wouldna have too bad a time of it. So he wouldna hurt ye too bad."

There was a disbelieving giggle in Ellen's throat between the tears. "It can be worse?"

"Oh ay, it can be worse and longer. A breech is allus bad but ye only took a couple of hours. Next time it'll be much easier, I promise ye."

Ellen was no longer clutching the little bundle, she was holding it as if her baby had gone to sleep. "What did you christen him?"

"I christened him John, I allus do. John or Mary. That's why there's so many Johns and Marys hereabouts because sometimes the water of baptism wakes them up and they live."

Ellen nodded.

"Will I lay out your wee Jock for ye now?"

Ellen looked down at the baby's grey face with the open grey eyes. "Ay," she said, "he's deid, isn't he?" She gave the baby into Mrs Hogg's arms and she took him away.

Janet went and got an old sheet to do as a shroud and helped hold the floppy little thing while Mrs Hogg washed him down quickly and swaddled him tight and then laid him on the windowsill. The wound in his back was shocking, laid open down to the backbone.

"How does that thing happen? With the back?" whispered Janet.

Mrs Hogg shrugged. "Naebody knows. I think the Devil gets his lance and stabs the baby in the back and sometimes the heid, too, cos the Devil's a coward of course. Isnae a thing anyone can do about it, although the midwife I 'prenticed with, old Mother Maxwell, she said that if the mother likes beer that makes the babby strong enough to turn the spear aside. And if she sleeps with a horseshoe in the bed, that keeps the Devil and the faeries away anyway."

Janet nodded. She would pass the medical advice on to Ellen later. "Have you eaten, Mrs Hogg? Can I get you anything?"

"Ay, I'm tired, I could take a sup to eat."

They passed Willie's Simon squatting against the wall in the passage, crying into his hands. Mrs Hogg bent down to him and touched his shoulder. "Ye can go to her now, if ye've a mind to," she said.

"Is the babby...?"

"Ay, son, the babby's dead, it was too little to breathe. Ye go and comfort your woman, she's a brave strong lass."

Willie's Simon shut his eyes and breathed out hard, then stood up. "Will we have more...?"

Mrs Hogg laughed. "Well that's up tae ye and the lassie, eh? But yes, ye will and they willna come too soon."

Willie's Simon braced his shoulders and went into the infirmary and Kat and Mary came out, complaining that they were hungry. They all went down the spiral stairs to the warm hall where Janet had pestered and pestered until they had a modern range in the corner for charcoal as well as the great fireplace for lumps of cow, that always had a stockpot hanging over the fire and bubbling away.

Janet sent the girls for bowls and decanted platefuls, though it was very late for dinner, and served Mrs Hogg herself with the best maslin bread. Mrs Hogg ate with a will and so did Janet and she sent a lurking boy up to the infirmary with bowlfuls for Willie's Simon and Ellen.

The girls went off to tell what happened to the other girls and Janet fixed Mrs Hogg with a gimlet eye. "What was that ye were saying about May babies and maying?" Mrs Hogg had a peculiar expression on her face, a mixture of regret and determination.

After a while she spoke softly, "It's the mumps."

"Mumps?"

"Ay. If he's nobbut a child when he gets it, he just looks funny for a while and has a sore throat. But if a young man gets it badly his…"

"Balls swell up."

"Ay they do. Now they sometimes turn black and then he usually dies but more often they'll swell up and hurt and then go down again and he thinks he's none the worse. And he isna, except his woman will never get with child."

"*What?*"

"It was Mother Maxwell noticed that too and she told me." Mrs Hogg was avoiding looking at Janet. "All I can think is that the stuff that's in his balls gets soured somehow so the little mannikins he plants in his woman are dead or hurt or something."

A lot of young men had got the mumps in 1582 before the execution of the Scottish Queen, for it had been a while since there had been mumps on the Border. Including one Henry Dodd who had been in the castle guard at Carlisle for good and sufficient reasons connected with the Elliots.

Janet remembered it, how she had gone to visit him at the castle barracks and found him in his little bunkbed, his feet hanging off the end and he had been in terrible pain and terribly frightened and finally told her why in a whisper and she had fetched cold water and cloths and a raw steak and made him more comfortable.

She had loved him already, already chosen him to be hers and putting wet cloths on his poor hot swollen balls had been like the most natural thing in the world: it was only later that she had been astonished at herself. And that was why he was so terrified of illness, of course.

She stared at Mrs Hogg. "Henry…"

"Ay," said Mrs Hogg, "so I heard."

After a moment Janet let out a kind of cross between a laugh and a sob. "So that's why none of the potions nor the Lady's springs nor anything has worked and there's never been a babe."

"Ay."

"Jesus!"

Mrs Hogg leaned forward over her clean and polished bowl. "That's a fine pottage, missus. May Ah have some more?"

Janet moved like someone who had been hit on the head, got the soup, brought the bowl back. There was a large lump of rabbit in it. She didn't bring any for herself.

"So..?"

"So," said Mrs Hogg, scooping up beans, "ye've a problem, for a man that's nobbut a tenant may want to keep his tenancy and pass it to his son, ay, but he canna know if his lord will say yes. But the man that has the freehold of a place must have a son to inherit."

Janet swallowed. Was that why Henry had turned so sour? Was he wanting to get rid of her because he thought she was barren?

No, surely not. Not Henry. They hadn't talked about it…but no. She thought of the wicker basket wrapped in linen under her bed, that she took out carefully every Sunday to wear the green velvet London hat to church. She knew that word was spreading of Henry's stroke of luck in the South, when he had somehow persuaded the Queen to give him Gilsland's freehold, and none of the stories about it were half as wild as the truth.

"Mrs Aglionby told me about the freehold," enlarged Mrs Hogg. "She was quite amazed at it. And the Carletons are fit to be tied, so I've heard."

Janet grunted. She didn't care about the Carletons.

"There's no chance of him making a babe in me? Or anyone else?"

"None. Willie's Simon got the mumps too and he's made no babes."

"But…"

"Ellen came to me for a potion last year."

"I was wondering did ye have anything…"

"…and I told her to go a-maying," said Mrs Hogg, dipping her spoon. "Go a-maying, jump the fire on St John's night, light Lammas torches, scare off the Devil on All Soul's night, dance on Christmas night, and light the candles on Candlemas. Do ye follow, missus?"

Janet didn't know how pale she had gone, her freckles were stark on her milk white skin. She only felt the wild whirling in her stomach.

She didn't want to go with another man. She hadn't even looked at another man since she clapped eyes on Henry, for all his dourness, for all his silences and the ridiculous way he would never let himself laugh at anything and the strange shy sweetness of his smile when he let it happen…She didn't want anyone else.

Yet if Dodd couldn't plant a babe in her, that was a disaster. A disaster for them both.

"That's what I said to Ellen," said Mrs Hogg, "and she greeted for she's an honest woman and she didna want to, but I told her it didnae count when the man couldn't make a baby. It seems she saw the sense."

"Ay, and lost the baby. Is that not a punishment from God?"

Mrs Hogg paused thoughtfully. "It may be," she allowed, "but God also said go forth and multiply to us and if your right husband canna make a baby in ye, what are ye to do? Eh?" Janet said nothing. It depended how much you believed of what the pastors said God was like. "Besides, ye could say that Our Lady herself played St Joseph false when she went with the Holy Ghost, eh?"

Janet had never heard it put like that, was that some kind of heresy? Yet it made sense. You could say Jesus Himself had been

God's bastard. She was shocked at herself for thinking such a thing but…

"I know plenty of women who have gone a-maying to find a babe, and plenty of them have their babes safe and well, ay, and growed up too," said Mrs Hogg. "I say, think on it and do what seems to you to be right."

Janet wasn't aware she was nodding.

"Well that's a very nice pottage, missus," said Mrs Hogg in the same tone of voice. "Thank ee kindly for it."

"Your fee is five shillings?"

Mrs Hogg shook her head. "Nay, missus, I only take half for a dead baby. 2/6 is fine."

"Five shillings," said Janet firmly.

◇◇◇

Carey was whistling a little ditty that explained how autumn was mellow and fruitful as he went to find his brother-in-law, Lord Scrope.

As usual, the overbred ninny was in the stables. Today he was preparing to take Buttercup's litter out in couples on a hunting expedition and there was Jack with his yellow coat and enormous clumsy paws and floppy ears, shoving past his brothers and sisters to get patted by Carey.

"Good morning, my lord, and what a very pleasant morning it is, too…And Sir Richard, I'm delighted to see you too," breezed Carey loudly. He smiled at everyone. This was joyous because Sir Richard Lowther was scowling at him suspiciously from over by the kennels. Carey favoured him with an especially bright smile and let him stew for a while.

He looked over the dogs, agreed that they needed exercise, opined that perhaps it was too blowy and damp to fly the hawks and then allowed himself to be persuaded to take one of the merlins. That was really a woman's bird, but Philadelphia had gone south to serve at the Queen's Court again. She hadn't been happy in Carlisle but her hawks still needed exercise. Would it be possible to send her favourite hawks south to London so she could fly them in Finsbury Fields? He would need to find a good cadger for the journey; it was a long way.

"You seem very happy, Robin," said Scrope pettishly.

"Oh, I like it here in the north, my lord," Carey told him. "And of course there's the letter from the Queen that I received today." Oh, it was fun, the way Lowther glowered and stared to move away. "I'm sure you've seen it, my lord, there is always a copy that goes to the Lord Warden, isn't there, Sir Richard?"

Habet, thought Carey, *I've got you*. Scrope stood there, his scrubby little goatee not improving his face by adding chin at all. The hawk on his fist looked twice the lord he was. "Oh," he wittered, "And what did she write?"

Carey could not help himself, he practically crowed. But he kept his voice casual as he explained, "She's pleased with me, my lord. She thoroughly approves of the way I dealt with the Elliots and she has kindly sent me my warrant as Deputy Warden of the English West March." He paused theatrically. "Surely you have your copy of it, my lord, I'm sure Mr Secretary Cecil is very careful about such things."

Scrope stood like a halfwit with his mouth open for at least a heartbeat and then he frowned at Lowther, who seemed to be trying to find an exit from the stableyard where there wasn't one by the kennels.

"How peculiar, I should have got it by now. I'll ask Richard Bell about it."

"No need, my lord," said Carey, very helpfully, "Here's my copy and the Queen's letter as well."

Scrope scanned the letter, checked the warrant and said, "Er...yes, I wrote a report about the incident at Dick of Dry-hope's tower to Her Majesty, saying that you not only prevented what could have been a very nasty battle but you made Wee Colin Elliott look like a fool and a coward, which has done his reputation no end of harm. I heard from the King's Court that two of his cousins have come in and composed with His Highness and given hostages. I was both surprised and pleased, Robin."

Despite his instant irritation at being called Robin by Scrope, Carey bowed to him. "My lord, I am exceedingly obliged and grateful to you."

A long liquid snort was Lowther's only comment on this as he finally found his way round by the door and stalked away from the stableyard.

In the end because the western sky was looking ominous with rain, they only went out to Eden meadows to fly the hawks at the lure and they brought the young dogs to run alongside the cow-shattered fence which was still being mended. The herd of kine was penned in the upper half of the racecourse because there were a couple of hundred of them, and no wonder Archie Fire the Braes Graham had been upset. The real owners would have to come in and identify their animals and pay the Warden's fee for the finding of them and were slowly doing so as word spread.

Carey flew the little merlin at the lure and laughed to see how fiercely she flew and how much she looked like his sister. She even had the same way of cocking her head impertinently. He would write to her about the birds with the next dispatch bag.

He also took the time to tell Scrope what he thought had been going on with the ambush under the Eden Bridge. His theory was that the Grahams had been intending to ambush and kill him before he could receive his warrant so he would still be unofficial, which begged the interesting question of how they knew about the warrant before he did.

Scrope looked shocked and worried. "I'm sure you don't mean that Lowther purloined the warrant and then set the Grahams on to kill you? I'm sure he wouldn't do a thing like that, Robin."

Carey, who had been about to suggest that Lowther was doing exactly that and worse, stopped and stared at his brother-in-law. Surely nobody could be that obtuse, could they? He absentmindedly fed bits of meat to the merlin and nearly got his finger bitten. Jack was staring at a distant figure on a pony with a packpony following. Suddenly the dog gave a joyful bark and galloped off, pulling along the older dog he was coupled with to teach him hunting, busted through a part of the fence that had just been mended and ran across the Eden Bridge. "Anyway," said Scrope, his reedy voice taking on an admonitory note, "you simply have to get along with Sir Richard while I'm away at my estates because both of you will be in charge."

"Surely Lowther can't still be Deputy Warden…?"

"Of course he can, his warrant is during pleasure, as yours is, and Her Majesty has said nothing about him quitting the office."

"Well I am sure the question slipped her mind when she…"

"It's not like the Wardenry itself, where there is only one warden at a time. Theoretically I can have as many Deputy Wardens as I like."

Carey was furious and frustrated and trying to think of something he could say to squash the ridiculous idea, when Jack came galloping back, wagging his tail like a flail and still pulling the older dog along who was looking martyred.

Carey gave the merlin to the falconer, took his hawking glove off and dismounted to uncouple Jack who barked happily, ran off for a couple of yards, came back, barked, looked at the slowly approaching horseman, barked again, galloped away, came back and barked. "Seems very excited about something," commented Scrope.

"Yes, my lord," said Carey. To get away from the idiot before he said something unwise, jumped back on his horse and sent it uphill to the road where he let the horse go to a full gallop after Jack.

He soon recognised the smallish plain-looking, balding man and while he wasn't quite as delighted as Jack, he was pleased to see him. "Mr Anricks!"

"Sir Robert," said Anricks, taking off his hat and making a shallow bow in the saddle, which Carey acknowledged with a tip of his hat. "I am very pleased to see you, sir."

Carey grinned at the expectant Jack who was looking up at Anricks with an expression of such hopeful pleading on his face. "Jack never forgets any man who feeds him. You are forever his best friend."

Anricks shook his head at the dog. "I'm sorry," he said to the dog, "I have no food left."

Jack continued to look hopeful and Anricks sighed, produced half of a small pasty from his doublet front and threw it to Jack, who caught it with a single snap and gulp and went on looking hopeful.

"Come and meet my brother-in-law," said Carey. "I don't think you have yet, have you?"

Anricks shook his head and so Carey accompanied him to where Scrope was flying a tiercel falcon at the lure and introduced him as a scholar and sometime-toothdrawer and by way of being a merchant as well. Anricks made a very competent bow, though it also said to anyone with an eye for such nuances that he had been a royal clerk as well. He added with a cough, "Sir Robert, how is your tooth and jaw?"

"Very well, Mr Anricks, nearly healed up completely."

"I should like to inspect it later, I prefer to do that if the tooth was very bad…"

"Oh don't worry, I…" Anricks gave Carey a hard stare and Carey thought of the warrant the man carried from Sir Robert Cecil. "Of course."

Anricks included both of them in another tidy bow and then kicked his pony and continued into Carlisle, with the packpony sighing and plodding along behind and Jack running up and down a couple of times and looking surprised.

Scrope's huntsman caught the dog and coupled him up with a different and sturdier hound and they went after hidden rags and jumped stiles until the short morning had already turned itself around the low noon and become afternoon. Carey was suddenly beset with tiredness. He yawned for the fourth time and remembered that he hadn't had dinner, breakfast was hours in the past, and he hadn't slept since the night before last.

He made his excuses and went back to the keep, came into the Queen Mary tower whistling again because at last he had his warrant and the fees from the herd of kine and all was right with the world, trotted up the stairs and went into his chambers.

John Tovey was in his study at his desk, coping with the routine correspondence that Carey hated so well whilst Hughie Tyndale had gone down into the town to work with the trained bands. He was a good pikeman, was Hughie, which was no surprise when you considered his size and the breadth of his shoulders. There was something else about Hughie, something oddly off about him, as if he was a lutestring not tuned aright, but Carey hadn't worked out what it was yet. Hughie gave satisfaction as a tailor and was big enough to back Carey when he needed a henchman. Carey was sure he was being paid by somebody to give news reports of his doings, which was no problem at all—he was the son of Lord Hunsdon and used to being spied on by servants. Was there anything more than normal bribery? He wasn't sure.

Carey shucked off his nearly respectable arming doublet at last, took off his shoes, canions, and stockings—the stockings needed darning again—and got into bed with a sigh. "Will you draw the curtains for me?" he called out to John, and his secretary came and did that, pulling cautiously, for the curtains were at least fifty years old. According to legend, that spectacularly silly woman, Mary Queen of Scots, had slept in that very bed, probably under the very blanket, when she came south on the run from her own subjects.

Carey always wondered where her ghost was and then fell asleep at once.

◇◇◇

Hughie Tyndale was coming back from the muster feeling happy. He had tripped that bastard Hetherington and then blamed it on someone else, he had drunk a lot of beer afterwards. He had called in on Thomas the Merchant Hetherington to give in his usual letter and receive his shilling. The letter went to the mysterious hunchback in the south called Mr Philpotts.

When was he going to kill Carey? It was a good question, complicated by the fact that Carey seemed to have a lot of people queuing up to kill him and didn't care. Of course, if somebody else succeeded in doing it, Hughie could always claim it was him really, but he wondered if Mr Philpotts would know the truth.

There was another complicating factor which he had not seen fit to tell anyone since it was his business. Henry Dodd, the most evil man in the world. That wasn't business like Carey was; Hughie had no feelings one way or the other for Carey. He would get thirty pounds in his hand for killing the Deputy Warden, according to the man who said he worked for the Earl of Bothwell. Mr Philpotts' money made him pause, but in the end he would kill his man and get his money. He liked killing, and the fact that he could tailor, often made people forget that he was not weedy or round-shouldered the way his late uncle had been. And hadn't that been a satisfying life to take, his uncle choking on the garotte and never knowing who it was killed him?

But Dodd? Hughie knew that Dodd was the man he had been put on this Earth to kill. That was personal, that was family, that was vengeance sweet and late.

So should he do Dodd before or after Carey? Either of them was hard enough, for they were both right fighting men. Together they would probably be impossible unless he could get Wee Colin to attack them.

So it had to be separately. Poison for Carey? Since Oxford, Hughie had more respect for poisoners—it was ticklish to get the right dose into the right man—hadn't the dose intended for Carey gotten into him and nearly killed him? Although white arsenic was always good, odourless, tasteless, slow-acting. Yes, he would have to investigate where he could get arsenic. He thought he could buy it from an apothecary to kill rats. Not in Carlisle, though. Too much risk of a busybody finding out. And Carey didn't have any routine food for himself: he generally ate in Bessie's or even in the castle if he was short of money. So maybe not arsenic either.

Hughie shook his head with all the thinking which was giving him a headache. He wanted to kill somebody soon. It was more than a month since he had last seen the pretty sight of the red on the white.

And Dodd? Well, Dodd would be a big swordblade through the head or crossbow bolt in the back or better yet a knife in the guts so he would die slow and screaming to pay him back for what he did, or all of them, or torture. Hughie made pretty patterns of red and white on the defenceless chained white body of Henry Dodd in his imagination with Dodd naked in a dungeon somewhere, or even just one of the Elliot towers in Tynedale, chained, hurt, weeping. Maybe Hughie would chop his fingers off one by one and his toes or better yet use the Boot on him and the pinniwinks and then chop his mashed fingers off...

It made Hughie feel warm and happy but he knew it was unlikely and risky and he would probably have to settle for a knife in the guts, but that would do. That would do perfectly well.

He was sitting in a boozing ken by then, its red lattices quite newly painted and he asked for double ale because he was feeling rich. Not as rich as he would feel after he got the thirty pounds but quite enough to afford double. Like most lords, Carey paid well in theory but barely at all in practice.

He hadn't noticed the little man when he came in, but he noticed when the man came up to his table, bold as brass and asked if he was Sir Robert Carey's valet. "Ay, I am," he answered breezily. "Would ye like to buy me a drink? Ah'm fearful thirsty." It was a bit cheeky, but nobody asked something like that right out if they weren't after something.

The balding man smiled and went sliding his way to the bar and back again with a quart jack for Hughie and a pint for himself, being so short and weedy.

"Cheers tae ye!" said Hughie and then grinned. "Whit can Sir Robert Carey's man do for ye?"

"Nothing hard," said the man who had a fearful Southern accent, "I just want you to stay here for an hour or so."

"Stay in this boozing ken for an hour?" said Hughie. "Nay, I cannae do that, I'm due to go and help him with his..."

Sixpence appeared in the man's scarred palm and twinkled there.

Hughie beamed at it. "Now ye wouldna be after thinking of killing the man, eh? For if ye do, I'd need tae hunt ye down and kill ye yerself for spoiling everything, see ye? And that'd be annoying for baith of us."

"It would," agreed the man. "How would it be if I swear not to kill the man nor rob him?"

Hughie looked at the man with his weak squinting eyes and round clerk's shoulders and laughed. Some chance there. "Ay, that's fine," he pronounced indulgently, picking up the sixpence. "Now awa' wi' ye, ye're interfering wi' my drinking."

And just like that the man was gone and Hughie supped his second quart and leaned back and looked about. With sixpence extra on top of the shilling he felt rich enough to go to Mme Hetherington's and wap one of her whores. That was a luxury he hadn't been able to afford since he had done the job for Hepburn in the spring, certainly not while he was chasing Carey in London and while in Oxford he hadn't felt well enough anyway. He sighed happily. Life was good.

CARLISLE DECEMBER 1592

Carey slept for two hours and then came to feeling much better and also uneasily aware that there was an unknown man in the room. He slipped his hand stealthily under the pillow, waited a couple of seconds, grunted, turned over on his belly and then erupted out of the bed with the knife in his hand and his teeth bared.

Simon Anricks blinked at him with interest from where he was sitting on one of the three clothes chests cluttering up the room.

"Yes," he said, "the situation with the Grahams is worrying, isn't it?"

Carey's heart was galloping and he went to pour some wine for himself and his guest.

"How may I help you, Mr Anricks?"

Anricks was staring at the wall with the expression of someone who was thinking of how to explain something to a half-witted

A Clash of Spheres   65

nobleman. Carey had seen Anricks' warrant but still didn't like it that the man had come into his bedchamber while he was sleeping. Where the devil were Tovey and Tyndale? He wondered where the key to the bedchamber was, since he should probably start locking it.

"Of course, if I had had a pistol or a crossbow—a crossbow, for preference—then I could have just shot you where you lay and you none the wiser until Judgement Day," said Anricks coldly, "which would ill repay your parents' care of you, nor Mr Secretary Cecil's concern, nor indeed the Queen's manifest affection for her cousin and nephew."

Carey stared at him. "There is," continued Anricks quietly, "a certain dash and fire about you that makes you so careless of your safety—and indeed a very gentlemanlike courage—yet, I put it to you, Sir Robert, that sooner or later the dice will come down snake eyes and you will die."

For a moment Carey was too astonished at being told off by a mere toothdrawer to do more than stare open-mouthed at the man. Then he got angry.

"Well sir, I do not know why it concerns you, nor why you believe you can rate me for going to sleep…"

Anricks stood up. His voice became metallic. "I do not rate you for going to sleep, sir. I rate you for going to sleep in an unlocked room."

"My servants should be…"

"They should but they are not. It took me two minutes and sixpence to persuade your valet to delay coming to your chamber for an hour—although he did at least have me swear I would not kill nor rob you since he had never seen me before in his life—and Tovey went down ten minutes ago to get bread and cheese and beer at the buttery, since he can no longer see to write, which anyone could guess. I watched you snore for those ten minutes and no one has come in nor asked why I am here. It will not do, Sir Robert."

Anricks crossed his arms and stared at Carey. He had cold pale brown eyes which seemed to amount to more than he was, because in appearance he was unimpressive in his worn brown wool suit, the fashion ten years past, and a stuff gown with velvet trim and his bald head shining under his ancient cap.

"In fact I came to discuss the Queen's letter and proposal with you, but I am now wondering if you have even read it yet?"

Carey scowled and took out the packet. "If you mean this, I most certainly have read it and am very happy that she thinks so well of me as to send me my warrant…"

"Then you have not in fact read the secret section." Anricks looked as if not rolling his eyes was costing him considerable effort.

Carey blinked at the packet, pulled out the Queen's letter and sniffed it. His eyebrows went up and he sniffed again, went to the watch candle, lit two further candles in the stand on his table and held the letter carefully close to the flames until the paper warmed up and the brown letters showed on the blank back of the letter.

Anricks twitched slightly at the shout of laughter that came from Carey.

"Good Lord, Mr Anricks," he said affably, "you must think me a fearful dullard as well as foolhardy. Now does this stay or will it fade?"

"It will fade."

"Then excuse me while I note down Her Majesty's words to me." He dipped a pen and scribbled on the back of a bill for horsefeed. Anricks managed not to sigh at this further careless-ness and sat back down on the clothes chest. He ached all over from the ride to Carlisle.

"Well," said Carey as he finished and the lemon juice words faded. "Her blessed Majesty is full of surprises."

"Yes," said Anricks. "May I read it?"

Carey hesitated only a second before handing over the horse-feed bill and starting to pull on his stockings and canions again.

Anricks scanned Carey's scrawl, then handed it back. "It is important you find an excuse to go to Scotland and talk to the King about the lords Huntly, Errol, and Angus who, it appears, are plotting treason."

"Again?" shrugged Carey. "They're always doing it. They're Catholics. Luckily they are also rotten at it."

"The Queen and Mr Secretary Cecil are concerned that this time it's serious. There have been various oddities going on in Spain this year, activity in the Irish sea. They have been concerned for some time, in fact, which is why I am here."

"You in particular?"

"Unfortunately, yes. The Queen has an exaggerated idea of my abilities due to some adventures I had in 1588…"

"1588? During the Armada? Anriques?"

"Er…yes, sir…"

"Mr Anricks, I believe I may once have met your…your extraordinarily courageous and beautiful lady wife, Mrs Anriques. It was while I was serving under my Lord Howard of Effingham and Sir Francis Drake. In fact I may even have been a small part of bringing her to an interview with My Lord Howard in which she explained the Armada's true purpose and which inspired Sir Francis Drake to the stratagem of the fireships."

Anricks came to his feet. "You! You were the Court sprig who got her to the Admiral?"

Carey bowed. "I was, sir, and I heard more about it later from Sir Francis Walsingham."

"If you had not got my wife to the Admiral, sir, I believe we would now be fighting the Spaniards in England, or dead."

"Dead certainly, or I would be. Well…I believe this calls for something better to drink than the usual Carlisle rotgut." With a courtierly flourish he unlocked a small cupboard and brought out an unassuming bottle and two small Venetian glasses, poured, and gave Anricks one. "Sir, if you will permit, a toast to your brave lady wife and to yourself, sir, since Walsingham told me that without what you did, we would have lost the Battle of the Calais Roads."

Anricks flushed, tapped glasses and drank, paused, looked quizzically at the booze and then drank some more. "Did he tell you any of the details?"

"Not many. I would delight in hearing the tale from your own lips, if it please you to speak about it. Sir Francis was eloquent in his praise of you and your family and he was not a man who praised easily or at all. I think I myself earned two or three grudging words in several years' service to him."

"Sir Robert, is this…is this drink made of bacon?"

Carey chuckled. "No, it comes from the Highlands of Scotland and they call it in their barbaric tongue 'whishke bee,' which means exactly the same as aqua vitae. It is smoked in some way, but it's made from barley and distilled like a brandy."

"It's good," said Anricks, smelling the liquor and sipping again. "Very good." He shut his eyes and rolled it round his mouth and seemed to put his whole being into tasting the stuff, as if it was holy.

Carey watched with interest and when Anricks had swallowed, he opened his eyes and smiled a little. "On the occasion we were speaking about, for various reasons, I was captured by the Spanish and sentenced to the galleys, in fact to a galleas in the Armada itself. Up until then, I often didn't pay attention to my food, but just before my arrest, I had eaten some particularly fine membrillo paste—quince cheese, you call it here—with goat's cheese which was so good I *had* noticed. The remembered taste of the cheese and the membrillo somehow sustained me while I was a slave. So when I was free again, I swore that I would always notice the food I ate, for not to notice is in fact ingratitude and insult to the Almighty, maker of the Universe, who gives us all that we eat and drink."

Carey bowed a little. "Amen, sir," he said.

They drank more whisky.

"So," said Carey, "Walsingham said that you had retired to be a merchant in Bristol. If they have winkled you out of retirement, what's the reason?"

"What do you think?"

"Yet another Armada?"

"Precisely."

"Aimed at Scotland?"

"Perhaps."

"There was a rumour of one last summer but it was scattered by storms."

"As I remarked earlier, sooner or later the dice will come down against us and I am concerned lest 1593 be the year when that happens."

"Surely even the King of Spain can't afford another Armada so soon after…"

"That Armada wasn't destroyed. They lost some ships, sure, and others were damaged but more put into La Corunna—the Groyne—and are being refitted as we speak."

"So why Scotland?"

"Well, Sir Robert, the west coast of Scotland is wild and empty and the people there are Catholics insofar as they are anything. In fact the same is true all the way down through Cheshire and the marches of Wales, Gloucester, even Bristol… Well, Bristol is Protestant like most ports, but still there are a lot of Catholics. The Jesuits have been running missions into the West Country for ten years and it's starting to show."

"My mother says most of Cornwall is still heathen with a lacquering of Rome. I was born in the Marches of Wales and I don't recall much religion there at all. Most of them only went to church at Christmas and Easter, if they went at all."

"And sir, how many of your neighbours were enthusiastic Protestants? Any? Most of the nobility in the area is Catholic from sheer inertia, with the exception of my Lord Earl of Essex and he is a courtier."

"Would they truly fight for the King of Spain against the Queen?"

"Perhaps not. Perhaps they would revert to the noble English instinct to hate the foreigner. But who knows? Put an army of thirty-thousand in the field, led by the *terceiros*, the best troops in Christendom, offer the young men the choice of being killed or marching with them…"

Carey nodded slowly.

"Nobody understands how close a call it was in 1588," said Anricks. "We were so lucky. If Medina Sidonia had been less seasick, if Drake had hesitated to use the fireships when he did, if…Well. I think it true that the Almighty, for reasons best known to Himself, thwarted the Spanish, for I can scarcely think of any other reason for our luck. But how long will He favour the English? The Scots of the West Coast and the Highlands are fine soldiers, if undisciplined, and the kerns and gallowglasses are from Ireland of course, and they can run for days barefoot through the forests and bogs…"

"Carlisle?"

"I could take Carlisle in three days."

"Treachery?"

"Of course." Anricks gulped the rest of his Scottish drink. "Then you have the castle cannon to knock at the doors of Chester, Gloucester, Bristol, and then you take Oxford, and the Thames valley lies before you. London would fall a week later."

"It couldn't be that simple," protested Carey. "How do you feed your men?"

"Personally I would put a force into Bristol early on a surprise and send supplies up the Avon."

"Thank God you aren't King Philip's admiral."

"He has cleverer men than me to do his bidding, believe me. But thank the Almighty by all means, Sir Robert. In England we think ourselves very fine soldiers but we are woefully untrained, underequipped, and inexperienced. Our sailors are the best in the world but our soldiers…" Anricks shook his head.

Carey, who had seen some shocking things while fighting in France with Henry of Navarre, made no answer to this.

"In a way of course," muttered Anricks, "the Spanish have been battering at the locked front door of the Cinque Ports, when all the while the yard gate has been banging in the wind and the kitchen door kept by a little girl."

"But King James would never allow…"

Anricks had taken his old-fashioned velvet cap off and was

kneading it between his hands. His bald head had a little island tuft of hair in the middle.

"If he was offered a lot of money, gold, to look the other way whilst Caerlaverock and Lochmaben and Dumfries filled up with Spanish soldiers?"

Carey scowled as he considered the point. "Well, His Highness of Scotland is of course as easy to buy as any man, possibly easier, but…no. I think not. His Highness has spent most of his life dreaming of how easy that life will be when he succeeds, as he surely will if he is spared, to the throne of England. Would he take the risk of allowing thousands of foreign soldiers to build up in the West, waiting to march south? No."

"What if he didn't know?"

"Don't be ridiculous. It's fifty miles east to west and the comings and goings from so many men, the supplies, the food…no. Maybe you could keep the secret for a week or two but sooner or later His Highness would know."

Anricks nodded unhappily. "Or they go east first, take Holyrood House and kill the King, then go south down through the rich plunder of the Merse. Once they have a good handgrip on any part of this island, they can go anywhere they want."

Carey said nothing, his strategic imagination working. That was the key, of course. Once the…the virginity of the blessed land of England was breached, troops such as the *terceiros* would be unbeatable at first, simply because none of the trained bands from the cities and the counties would have the faintest idea of what to do. By the time they had learned, it would probably be too late. It was true what Anricks said, unpleasant but true. The Borderers would be better at the fighting as light mounted troops, but even they were used to the dance of reivers, not a disciplined killing machine like the Spanish King's 3rd legion.

As it had in 1588, the thought made Carey feel cold and hot at the same time, hot with rage, cold with fear. The fear was colder now because he had served in France and seen war at close quarters.

"Mr Anricks," he said, "I agree with every word you say, sir. But what do you want me to do? I know the Maxwell unfortunately. Huntly, Erroll, and Angus, I have only met briefly, years ago, at Court. I would love to give the Maxwell a set-down, I admit."

"Mr Secretary Cecil feels that to begin with, if we know which way King James is likely to jump, we will be in very much better case. If he is for the King of Spain, we will need one kind of action."

"What?"

"A Warden Raid from the English West March into Dumfriesshire early next year to find out if any Spanish troops are there or preparations being made for them."

Carey nodded. "And if His Highness is against the King of Spain?"

"Well then, King James can run his own Justice Raid into the area, find the troops if they are there and deal with them himself."

"He will need help," said Carey. "He's a very peaceable prince is His Highness."

"I don't suppose anyone has the least idea what the King thinks?" Carey laughed and Anricks smiled. "No, he is verbose and liable to go into print at any moment, but somehow it all adds up to rather less than nothing."

"What about the Earl of Bothwell?"

"Has anybody seen him recently? I know he is at the horn but where is he?"

"Last heard of," Carey said, "he was playing football in Liddesdale. He is now rumoured to have gone to the Highlands."

"I'm not surprised, this Scottish drink is very fine. I would go to its source if I were him."

Carey poured again from the bottle and toasted Anricks.

"There's one good thing about the bloody man," said Carey.

"What's that?"

"He's a Protestant. He says he was not engaging in witchcraft a couple of years ago, which may or may not be true, but at least he is not a bloody Catholic."

For some reason Anricks smiled at that while Carey paced up and down the room.

"Well, but, Mr Anricks, this is all speculation, isn't it? Are you sure it isn't all some phantasy that we are frightening ourselves into fits with?"

Anricks sighed. "No, I am not sure," he said. "It could indeed be all moonbeams and mist. Mr Secretary is doing his best to find out from Spain, there are little straws in the wind...A very interesting recent letter from your lady mother, for instance, saying that the Spanish had kidnapped three Irish pilots whom she freed in her ship..."

"Oh, God," said Carey hollowly, "what's she up to now?"

"She says she visited Mrs O'Malley to lay in some Irish aqua vitae and heard that four more had gone to Spain voluntarily for a lot of gold and the promise of land."

"Where?"

Anricks shook his head and spread his hands."Nobody knows. New Spain perhaps? There is so little to go on. Conclusive proof that this is all a phantasy and the Spaniards are not planning to put troops ashore at Dumfries would be most welcome to me, for then I could go home to my wife and children and enjoy the blessed tedium of life as a middling merchant in Bristol. But..."

"Yes," said Carey, "but..."

He came over and sat on one of the other clothes chests, facing Anricks. He still had the Scotch drink in his hand, so he split the remnants between them.

"Well, Mr Anricks, I put myself at your disposal as the Queen asks. What would you like me to do?"

Anricks inspected the floor which had some very elderly rushes on it since Goody Biltock had gone south with Philadelphia Scrope and there was nobody to terrorise the castle servants.

"I want you to come with me to Scotland, to Edinburgh and the King's Court."

Carey's eyebrows danced upwards. "Good Lord, has His Highness invited you?"

"He has indeed." Anricks felt in his doublet pocket and produced a very official letter asking him to come to philosophise for the King at Court as soon as he could.

"Latin not Scots, eh? Very philosophical."

Anricks gave a small smile. "It appears that Lady Widdrington told him of something I had mentioned to her and now he is all afire to have a proper dispute about it."

"Oh? What about? Nothing theological, I hope."

"Why?"

"Because His Highness considers himself a first-class theological brain and I don't think I could stay awake long enough to cheer his victory at the end."

"He is that good a theologian, is he?"

Carey smiled. "He is the King."

Anricks smiled back. "I don't think it is a theological matter, precisely. It is the question of the heavenly bodies like the Moon, the Sun, and the stars, and so forth. Do they move and if so, how?"

Carey squinted as he dredged his memory. "Something to do with crystal spheres? And they move around the Earth like a complicated onion. I'm afraid I was usually absent playing football when I should have been studying the globes."

"Quite so. My opinion of it comes from Thomas Digges, his preface, where he refers to the theoretical suggestion of a Polish priest called Copernicus, oh, about fifty years ago."

"Oh yes?" said Carey politely.

Anricks leaned forward with the enthusiasm he could never hide for the beautiful simplicity and rightness of the new thinking, which blew away all the ugly epicycles and epi-epicycles of Ptolemy and Aristotle's system.

"You see if we place the planets around the Earth in the traditional er…complicated onion arrangements, some of their movements are crazy and make no sense. Why, for example, do Venus and Mercury reverse themselves every so often, in what is called by astrologers, movement retrograde."

"They are dancing? There is a very complicated Court dance which claims to follow the movements of the planets…"

"Er…no." Anricks couldn't understand why nobody seemed to care about the sheer untidiness and ugliness of the old system. "Well," he said, "perhaps I am a little crazy myself for setting such store by it. Briefly, Copernicus, his idea is that all the heavenly bodies move around the Sun—with one exception—which produces a scheme of exquisite order and righteousness." The glass cups became planets along with a penknife and a couple of stones, the bottle the sun. "Here is the Sun, at the centre of everything, very befitting. First around him goes Mercury, which removes his retrograde quite, then Venus which removes hers. Then comes the Earth and around her flies the Moon. Then Mars, then Jupiter and Saturn and then we are at the fixed stars."

Carey was staring fixedly at the cups, frowning. "The retrogrades?"

"Well sir, see, if this glass is the Earth and this Venus and all spins around the Sun thus, for some of the year Venus moves to the other side of the great circle and, from our perspective, she is moving backwards. But all is as it was, it is just a trick of perspective."

Carey was still staring.

"Do you see, sir? Do you see how the Earth moving and the Sun being fixed answers?" Anricks' voice was timid. It was normally at this stage that people started to laugh at him.

Carey blinked owlishly. "Yes!" he said. "Yes, I do."

Anricks was astonished. "You do?"

"Yes. But Mr Anricks, what holds them up? The crystal spheres?"

"Certainly. We can keep our onion, it just has the Sun in the middle and the Earth moving…"

"Clean contrary to how it looks."

"Of course. I sometimes wonder if the Almighty is having a little fun with us."

"What about in the Bible where it says that Earth is flat like a shield and the sky a tent?"

"That cannot be true, for didn't Magellan sail all the way round and now Sir Francis Drake himself? Again it is a trick of perspective."

"God is fooling us?"

"I prefer rather to think," said Anricks quietly, "that the Almighty is gently testing us, giving us riddles to solve to entertain us."

Carey laughed a delighted boy's laugh that said he had gone looking for a beetle and found a frog. "Doesn't it make you queasy to think that the Sun is still, whilst the Earth moves?"

"No, I rejoice in it…"

Suddenly Carey clapped his hand to his head. "Good God," he said, "you're the madman."

"I beg your pardon?"

"A long time ago, nearly ten years now, I had a swordmaster who complained of a friend of his who had a crazy notion about the Earth going round the Sun and how it made him feel seasick."

"Was he a big heavy man with black ringlets, who yet could move lightly and featly?"

"Yes, and he made me lose my temper and knocked me on my arse for a demonstration of how temper could undo me. How is he? Is his name Mr Tucket?"

"No sir," said Anricks quietly, "his name was David Becket and a truer friend did never live, I think. Alas, he died fighting in 1588."

"I am sorry to hear it." They had a couple of drops left of the Scottish drink.

Anricks raised his Venetian cup. "Then I give you, David Becket."

"David Becket!" answered Carey, tipping his glass to get the last drop. "But it's clear then, you are the madman."

"I am. And here I am planning to go to Edinburgh to dispute with a King about whether the Earth goes round the Sun. Quite, quite insane."

"Maybe not" said Carey judiciously. "I think the King of Scotland will love the idea if you put it to him right. We'll be there over Christmas."

"I hope not."

"We will. How many followers are you planning to take to Court?"

"I don't know…Maybe one for me and one for you?"

"Quite, quite woodwild, Mr Anricks. I will need both my servants and at least four men-at-arms if we are not to look very paltry. And also we will be crossing the Middle March at the height of the raiding season. Unless you prefer to take the Giant's Road east and then go up the Great Northern Road through Berwick to Edinburgh."

"Although I have begun to build quite a practice at tooth-drawing in the West March, I would prefer not to dare the Middle March again at this season," said Anricks primly.

"So would I. So the Giant's Road and the Great North Road it is then."

"When should we leave?"

"It depends. Do you have any better clothes?"

"Better clothes?"

"Yes, Mr Anricks. The Scots King may be a barbarian who has never to my knowledge washed his body, nor shifted his shirt more than once a month and barely wipes his face and hands, but you are an English philosopher and must at least appear civilized."

"Well…I…have some brocade doublets and hose and a velvet gown or two that my wife had made for me, but they are in Bristol and with the best will in the world, I doubt they could be here in less than a week."

"Hm. We must see what the Carlisle tailor can do for you— we may catch him before he shuts up shop if we go now."

And Carey swept Anricks off down the stairs, pausing only to lock his chamber door with newly rediscovered conscientiousness.

December 1592 Carlisle

It turned out that Anricks had plenty of money and could afford a brocade far too rich for a philosopher, especially one who was also a part-time toothdrawer. He had no idea of fashion at all, so Carey chose a nice fine wool in a dark cramoisie, since black and green accentuated his yellow complexion and made him look liverish. He put his foot down firmly on Anricks' diffident hopes for tawny taffeta trimming and lining and settled on a narrow black brocade trim that only the expert eye would be able to discern as coming straight from the Low Countries. It was quite a surprise to find it in the Carlisle mercer's shop.

At the tailor's, he ordered a shell made and the suit cut out by the master tailor himself, found a perfectly respectable shirt with blackwork on the cuffs in the depths of Anrick's pack and had it and a couple more wrinkled grey horrors laundered. Hughie agreed to do some of the sewing of the doublet and the journeymen did the rest.

In return Carey agreed to read Thomas Digges' preface at least, which Anricks lent to him. He came back to Anricks with some questions. Anricks had been to visit the son of his patient, James Tait, who had nearly survived a knife in the guts, but had finally died, a week after the stabbing, of fever and pus in his intestines, to the extent that they swelled up until Tait looked pregnant. Strangely the external wounds had already healed. It had been a painful death and Anricks had been glad when the man had mercifully died. He had not had the chance to talk to Jimmy Tait since then and found him a little sad and thoughtful but also delighted with the metrical psalms he was learning and beginning to play the lute. Anricks got the impression that James Tait had not been an ideal father and would not be greatly missed, although the boy was anxious about his mother and determined to bring her and his sister and brother to Carlisle. But Anricks needed cheering up and so Carey did his best.

"Did you know that cannon don't shoot straight?" Carey asked.

"They don't?"

"No. Everyone thinks they do, but they don't, nor bullets. When you are laying a cannon to fire at a distance, you must always allow for some curve. Just like with an arrow, but much less. Why is that?"

Anricks stared at him. "I don't know."

"But why don't cannonballs go in a straight line until they run out of wind from the gunpowder and then drop?"

"I have no idea. What has that to do with the Earth going round the Sun?"

Carey smiled a little boy's rueful smile. "Nothing. I was just wondering about it, all those circles. How about looking at the planets through spectacles? Could we see what they are made of?"

"Certes, there are people who are studying to grind the glasses fine enough, though at the moment there is a problem with rainbows and clarity."

"What about the Sun? Is it a planet?"

"No, it seems it really is a huge great fiery ball in the sky."

"What is it made of?"

"I don't know. Sulphur, perhaps, since it is yellow."

Carey nodded. "This is all part of your speech."

"Why does it matter?"

"Because you have to make the truth sound good to the King, otherwise he will turn it into a joke and get drunk. Or drunker."

"And is the naked truth not good enough?"

"No, Mr Anricks, it isn't. This is a public dispute, a species of theatre, and he may have some good scholars ranged against you to make you look foolish."

"Is that so bad? Then he can defeat me and feel reassured at how clever he is."

Carey laughed. "Yes, a good point. But you must give him a good show. If you do, he might make you his pet philosopher and keep you at his Court and that will give you the chance to find out what is going on with the Catholic earls."

Anricks smiled. "I see."

"Yes. You are the dancing bear and I am the bearmaster and whenever this dispute happens, whether at Christmas or New Year, you will give such a dance that King James will want more of it."

"I do not want to be at Court for Christmas."

"Who asked you, Mr Anricks? Nor do I, but I suspect we must."

"You don't want to spend Christmas at..."

"The key word is 'spend'. Christmas at the Queen's Court means at least one new suit and possibly some outrageous costume for a masque, although she is not as addicted to them as His Highness. Plus, I will certainly have to get His Highness a gift for New Year's Day which will cost a fortune and completely wreck my finances…"

Anricks leaned over and touched him. "As my bearmaster, I believe I can finance you to a limited extent…"

Joy struck Carey's face. "You mean I could have a new Court suit?"

"Well…"

"My old one is with my father in London and really it's growing a little out of fashion now it's more than a year old—I haven't completely paid for it yet—but perhaps I could have something in the Scottish style with the padding King James likes…"

"Well…"

"Now the question is whether damask, brocade, satin.."

Anricks had the feeling he had somehow carelessly unleashed a monster, but thought Carey deserved something for the way he had instantly backed him—and, although he didn't admit this to himself, for being one of the very few people who didn't laugh at the new Cosmology. Considering the dangers and the difficulty of the Scottish Court, it was praiseworthy how quickly he had agreed…Was that suspicious? Sir Robert Cecil had been concerned that Carey might have done some kind of deal with King James on his own account. That could be one interpretation of the mysterious doings at the King's Court while James had been on his abortive Justice Raid to Dumfries in the summer, although there were plenty of others.

Carey himself was happily burbling on about the different kinds of brocade that might be available and Anricks watched him, sitting at his ease in Bessy's common room with the remains of his pie on the pewter plate beside him. Chestnut-headed of the dark red not the carrotty kind like Her fiery Majesty, Anricks thought the portrait of him he had had painted for his knighthood had done him no favours. It showed the tense cautious courtier with the fashionable shaved forehead in honour of the Queen, not the expansive, very slightly drunk Deputy Warden in front of him.

Sir Robert Cecil had spoken about Carey when he came personally to Bristol to ask…perhaps better the word "beseech"… Simon to come out of retirement and find out what was happening in Scotland, if anything. He had spoken of Carey with surprising respect, that he was no more a Knight of the Carpet than his father, that he was a remarkably able soldier and also had the ability that Walsingham had, of being able to winkle the truth out of complicated and opaque circumstances.

Cecil's hunched back always pained him when he rode long distances, something he had never allowed to stop him. A jolting carriage was no better. He had sat uncomfortably on a pile of cushions in Simon's parlour, eating the wonderful crisp wafers that Rebecca could prepare, and drinking the rich dark sweet red wine of Oporto. Cecil tilted his head so it was straight, even if his body wasn't. Every so often he would stand and pace about, full of nervous energy.

"I have read all the secret reports on you, Mr Anricks, and I think there is not a man in England as well fitted to the work as you."

"But I do not want to come out of retirement. I like being bored."

Cecil closed his eyes a moment and smiled his remarkably sweet smile, then moved again, easing his back.

"I suppose money…"

Simon spread his hands, palms down. "I have plenty of money, far more than I need and if I were ever in want, my respected father, Mr Dunstan Ames, Deputy Comptroller of Her Majesty's Poultry, would help me and if he failed, why then my uncle Dr Hector Nuñez would step into the breach."

"Is that the Dr Hector Nuñez who is importing boatloads of tobacco from New Spain to London?"

"Yes."

"And you would not be interested in a knighthood which you certainly deserve for your actions during the Armada…"

"No. I am a Jew."

Cecil smiled again. "I know no legal nor chivalric reason why you may not be knighted, but admit that a Herald might correct me on that point. But there is always a first time for anything."

"No, it would be ridiculous."

"If money and honour don't move you, what might?" Cecil asked almost playfully. "Safety? The safety of your people? It moved you before?"

Simon narrowed his eyes and looked at Cecil in silence for a long moment. Cecil at last moved uneasily.

"Sir," said Cecil, "I could tell you that your people's continued quietness rests on your continued service to Her Majesty, but you would know it for a black lie. Her Majesty has told me that you are all of you forever her own Jews, and yours and your wife's service to her at the time of the Armada was of such an order that she will not again blackmail you."

Anricks tilted his head in acknowledgement. "That is good to know," he said, his pale brown eyes still cold.

Cecil sighed. "However, the Queen will not, no matter how we pray that she may, live forever and after her comes, we hope, King James, VIth of Scotland, Ist of England. God willing and if his luck holds."

"Yes," said Anricks. "Or the King of Spain, of course, which I would prefer not to see."

"Amen," said Cecil. "There is at least no Inquisition in Scotland."

"Are there Jews?"

"I don't know. Nor does anyone know what the King thinks of Jews."

"Hm." Anricks was thoughtful. "Well, Mr Secretary, you appear to have found the key that will unlock my retirement."

"It does you honour that you will do for your tribe what you will not do for money or honour."

Anricks made no answer to this. He seemed depressed and poured a large glass of Oporto wine and drank half of it.

"Ah…would you care to see some of the documents I have had copied or would you…?"

"Tomorrow," said Anricks firmly, "Today I am going to get drunk on this excellent booze and mourn my shattered peace."

"Would you prefer me to leave, sir?"

"No, Sir Robert, my wife has had the guestroom cleaned, swept, piled high with pillows, and new candles arrayed everywhere. She is at this minute in camera with the cook, devising a dinner of spectacular opulence in your honour. She would kill me if you went to an inn."

"That sounds delightful…Er…the dinner, I mean…"

"And besides, I don't hold it against you, for I am sure you are at the orders of that red-haired…"

"Termagent? Amazon?"

"Careful, Sir Robert, we are skirting treason here."

"Witch, perhaps. I would give a great deal to know how she is always one step ahead of me in intelligence-gathering."

"She has her own intelligence service, mostly of women, commanded by her *muliercula*, Mrs Thomasina de Paris."

"Good God!"

"I thought you knew."

Cecil laughed. "No, I was blind."

Anricks refilled his glass and Cecil's with Oporto wine, lifted it. "Then to the redhead, long may she reign!"

"To the redhead, Mr Anricks! Hear hear!"

Anricks knocked back the wine, then paused. "Oh, all right, Mr Secretary, let's see these documents."

It had been worth it although as with most raw intelligence there were a lot of documents and very little pattern. A couple of reports on the activities of a Jesuit called Father William Crichton who seemed the dangerous kind, since there was nothing suspicious about him except that he had been in northern Spain and was now in Scotland. An incoherent tale told by a Herries cousin who had guarded a private supper for the Maxwell, the Earls of Huntly, Erroll, and Angus at which Crichton had said grace and then talked for a long time. Some accounts in Spanish, copied by someone Simon suspected might be one of his brothers, detailing the kind of refitting going on at La Corunna. An account from a mad Irish chieftain that his two best pilots, expert in the Irish sea and its wildly treacherous currents, had disappeared from Ireland and reappeared in Spain where someone had stuck a knife in one and knocked the other on the head so hard that he could remember nothing any more, and thus had returned. Anricks smiled: that was definitely one of his brothers, probably Joshua.

"Not much to go on," said Anricks, putting his spectacles down and refilling the glasses again. He wondered what sort of hangover you got from Oporto wine.

"Straws show which way the wind blows," said Cecil owlishly.

"Or they don't."

It had been a very bad hangover and Anricks had resolved never again to get drunk on Portuguese sweet red wines.

In the name of the Almighty, thought Anricks, coming back to the bacon-smelling fug of Bessy's common room, *Carey is still burbling about his Court suit*...Anricks stared in honest amazement and was caught.

Carey laughed and clapped him on the shoulder.

"Ah well, Mr Anricks, we all must have our enthusiasms. Mine for fashion and making good clothes, yours for the new gospel of the heavens according to Capricorn..."

"Copernicus, as explained by Thomas Digges."

"Yes, quite so."

"Have you come to a conclusion about your new Court suit?"

"Indeed I have." There followed a tirade of quite extraordinary detail and dullness, in which it became clear that while the Carlisle tailor was good enough for a mere philosopher, and indeed for Carey's ordinary clothes, he was not at all adequate for Carey's outfit to wear at Court at Christmas and so they would take Carey's best black silk velvet doublet and hose with a few trifling alterations, but that when they arrived in Edinburgh, Carey would have the Edinburgh tailors make a proper Court suit for him in the very highest fashion and all that remained to be settled was the fabric, linings, trim, and buttons, particularly the buttons.

Anricks wondered aloud how much high Edinburgh fashion might cost, heard the sum of eight hundred pounds mentioned which nearly made him faint until he realised Carey was speaking in pounds Scots, which were only worth a quarter of an English pound because the Scottish King debased his money, while the English Queen was very particular about her money and its fineness.

Two hundred pounds English was still a substantial sum and Anricks darkly suspected that Carey might be very good at telling good clothes, but might not be very good at knowing what they cost on account of not wanting to know.

However the clothes certainly had given Carey enthusiasm for going to Scotland and he had the excuse that it was politic for the new official English Deputy Warden of the West March to introduce himself as such to the Scottish King and councillors and ask for a Warden's Day after sixteen years without one.

At any rate that was what he said to Lord Scrope when the ninny got querulous about not being able to go to his estates just yet.

"What am I supposed to do while you're away? The Grahams are riding and the Armstrongs and Elliots and the Maxwells are hitting the Johnstones…They all seem to have gone mad."

"Yes, my lord," said Carey, "It is because of the harvest."

"What? Why would the harvest make the surnames raid?"

Was it possible he didn't know, Carey wondered. "The harvest was very bad and so they haven't much barley or oats and so they're raiding to get the animals to sell so they can buy some. The trouble is, prices everywhere in the north are high because nobody in Scotland has much barley either."

"Oh. Well, why don't they ship some in?"

Have you looked at a map recently or ever, Carey wanted to ask. It's hard to get ships here from anywhere. Ireland is in as bad case or worse than Scotland. That means you have to bring it in from the Hansa or even further south. Anricks had said something about writing to his family about the dearth, but the seas were closed for winter and it would take a week for a ship to travel all the way up the Irish Sea from Bristol, even if the weather stayed calm, which it wouldn't.

"Yes, my lord," he said because he couldn't be bothered to explain it to his idiot brother-in-law. He added an outright lie. "I hope I'll be back before Christmas."

ᕍecember 1592 Gilslanᕍ

Sergeant Dodd was comfy in his old jack, with the padding worked in the Dodd pattern, though he had been thinking that maybe now Janet had a new hat, he could buy a new helmet, maybe even a morion, with some of the money from London. He would talk to his wife about it when he got back...

Then he remembered their quarrel and his long face soured. It hadn't been so very much, all things considered, it was just...

She had asked him why he was so silent and miserable, and he had finally told her, venting his fury at Carey for letting Wee Colin Elliot and all the bastard Elliots get away. He could not understand why the man had done it, could not, when he had them so nicely in a trap. He had tried to put it down to madness, plain and simple, since the Courtier did many things that were crazy, but in fact Carey had not been acting as crazy as usual and had in fact run the whole encounter beautifully, right up to the moment when he had casually swept the world from under Dodd's feet, and let them go.

Dodd still felt sick every time he thought about it. And then, what had his wife said about it, when he told her why he was upset? She had said that sure, it was annoying, but wasn't it grand that Wee Colin Elliot had taken such a blow to his credit with no one having to die, especially Dodd. And he had stared at her and stared at her, thinking, where's the woman who kicked Bangtail in the balls last summer for betraying them to the Grahams?

"Whit does it matter about dying," he had managed to say, despite the shock, "so long as the Elliots do too?"

"Matter?" Janet had said. "Weren't ye telling me about how fat the South is where they have nae feuds? It's over ten years since the Dodds and the Elliots were at each other's throats, ye beat 'em fair and square then, let's leave them be so long as they leave us be."

Dodd had sat by the fire with his mouth too full of what the Elliots had done to his dad and his mum and his uncles and his cousins, too full to say a word and she knew the story anyway. Wasn't she an Armstrong, English branch, but still, they had a plenty of feuds. And what you did in a deadly feud was you wiped out the other side, if you could, first chance you got.

She had kissed him lightly on the head, not noticing his stillness and gone out to make sure everything was locked up tight and the girls upstairs, and Ellen still recovering in the stillroom and the men downstairs on the first floor of the tower or out guarding the outfield and the boys in the stables and each animal where it should be.

She came back, went up the narrow spiral stair and still he sat, howling winds flying through him and the black ball of rage filling his chest. His wife agreed with Carey, the arch traitor. Why?

At last he had gone upstairs and lain down next to his wife in their proud half-testered marriage bed, and then when she turned to him and snuggled up, he had turned away silently, turned his shoulder to her again, shutting her out completely.

He hadn't slept much that night and rose in the morning early, feeling even worse than usual. God, he wished there was a potion that could wake you up.

Janet was already up of course, and that was when he had decided to ride out on Whitesock again and continue inspecting the boundaries of Gilsland, making sure no boundary stones had gone wandering and checking were the ditches clear and the fences strong around the coppices to stop the deer eating all the new shoots. He would also take a look at the large sections of the Giant's Wall that ran right through Gilsland, and think whether they were ready to be mined for more stone. He had meant to do it weeks before but had been busy.

Whitesock was a friend at least, a horse with a steady commonsense most unusual in any beast. Dodd had not found anything yet that could make Whitesock shy or bolt and he let the big brown head nuzzle his chest and fed him some carrots. All horses were mad for carrots and they also liked apples.

Out on the bare hills, he felt a little better again with the wind blowing and no actual rain for a change. The land was as dour and ugly in winter as he felt himself to be and even pushing Whitesock up to a gallop on the top of the wall and jumping the broken parts didn't make him feel happy for more than a minute or two.

He had not taken any men with him, although now he thought of it, Willie's Simon needed distraction because of the dead baby after years of trying to make one. At least Willie's wife wasn't barren like Janet, though. Dodd had his sword and his lance but that was normal, he wouldn't have felt dressed without them.

So he loosened his sword and took his lance in his right hand and had Whitesock jump down to the Road from the Wall when he saw two men riding towards him in the direction of his tower.

They were wearing cloaks which in Dodd's opinion was a waste of time in the wind and there was one in the front with a clever canny face and loose brown curls, while the other man was clearly a bodyguard of some kind, with the battered face and lance to prove it. His jack looked Scottish, East March, perhaps he was a Dixon or a Trotter.

He slowed Whitesock to a walk and then stopped where the Wall would give him some shelter to his back if it came to a fight and Whitesock nickered and stood silent, all four hooves planted, also staring hard at the strangers.

They picked their way down from the higher bit of road by the Wall and also slowed down. Finally they came close enough to be heard.

"We are looking for a man called Sergeant Henry Dodd," the foremost one said loudly, "Land Sergeant of this place." That one was wearing a hat and no helmet, whereas his bodyguard had an iron cap. The hat had a small brim and was tied to his head with a scarf.

"Ay," said Dodd after a moment's thought. "Ye've found him."

The first man untied the scarf, nearly lost his hat immediately, took it off and bowed in the saddle and then tied it back on again.

"My name is Jonathan Hepburn and I work for the Earl of Bothwell. I'm pleased to make your acquaintance, sir."

Dodd leaned slightly, not feeling in the mood for courtliness. "Ay," he said.

"Well," said the man brightly after another moment of silence, "This is lucky. I was expecting to have to go all the way to Gilsland to find you, sir. I would like to talk to you if I may, if we can find a place to get out of the wind and perhaps get a bite to eat and something to drink…"

Dodd sighed; he didn't want to talk to anyone. And why was the man calling him "sir", when it should have been "Sergeant." For a moment Dodd thought of taking both of them back to Gilsland tower but then thought better of it. "Well," he said reluctantly, "there's a Widow Ridley keeps a little alehouse not far from here. We could go there."

Half an hour later they were at a cottage in a little knot of cottages a little way into the Middle March, only different from the others because it had the statutory red lattices, last painted ten years before and almost invisible in the grey dusk. An old woman with white hair like a dandelion clock exploding out from under her cap was sitting just inside the door, out of the wind, knitting a stocking at a startling rate. She came out as they dismounted.

Dodd, she knew of course, and she bobbed a curtsey to him which always made him feel uneasy, so he tilted his neck in return.

"Widow Ridley," he began but the stranger interrupted him.

"We were hoping for something to drink, Goodwife Ridley," said Hepburn with a charming smile. "And would ye have aught to eat for we've not eaten since this morning?"

Widow Ridley's eyes travelled up and down both of the strangers and then she bobbed a tiny curtsey and led them into the small front room where the Thirlwall drunk was asleep in a corner, and sat them down on the other side of the fire from him. The curfew was taken off, the peat turves brightened up though they put out more heat than light, and Widow Ridley went to tap three quarts from a barrel into leather jacks.

"Is this double beer?" grunted the bodyguard.

"It's ale and it's good," said Widow Ridley snippily. "Ye can have water out of the well if ye want."

"Not beer? Ale upsets ma stomach."

Widow Ridley looked outraged. "This wilnae do ye anything but good, ye great lummock, d'ye want it or no'?"

"You want it, Dixon," said Hepburn, looking amused. "Do you have any stew or pottage, goodwife?"

"Hmf. It's no'got saffron in it, wilna be good enough for the likes of him."

"Please mistress, I'm very hungry," said Hepburn.

She went into the little kitchen and brought back three bowls of what was probably her own supper, a thick bean pottage. Dodd accepted his which had a lot of bacon in it, Hepburn said thank you and Dixon got the bowl without any bacon and what looked like a big gob of spit on it. He started eating it anyway. She disappeared again and they heard her clogs in the mud. A moment later she was back with two hunks of bread and a burned bit of crust, all probably borrowed from a neighbour, and, of course, Dixon got the crust.

"Will there be anything else, sirs?" said Widow Ridley haughtily.

"No thank you, mistress," said Hepburn obsequiously and was rewarded by a complex sniff. She went and sat down in the kitchen again and they could hear the furious clicking of her needles.

"Well," said Hepburn with a smile, "I expect you would like to know what this is all about, Sergeant Dodd."

Dodd didn't answer. He would, but why admit it?

"I am under the orders of my Lord Earl of Bothwell to make you a certain offer." Another inviting pause which Dodd didn't bother to fill. He liked silence.

"We understand you work for Sir Robert Carey?"

"I'm Sergeant of the guard at Carlisle, ay."

"And we know you've fallen out with him over the very foolish way he let the Elliots go in October. Anyone would, really. My Lord Earl is also annoyed with him over the way he spoiled the raid on Falkland palace last summer."

Dodd said nothing. Then "No," he said.

"No?" asked Hepburn, looking puzzled. "You haven't fallen out with him?"

"I have, ay. But I willna kill him and there's the end of it."

Hepburn smiled yet again. God, he was greasy. "No, no, we wouldn't ask anything like that. Just a certain absence."

That was different. The Grahams had asked him not to be there a few nights before, when he was due to go on patrol and had been willing to pay him ten shillings, which he had taken. He hadn't yet heard how that had played out, but judging from the deafening silence from Carlisle, not too well for the Grahams. One of the lads would have ridden out to tell him if Carey was dead, if only to bid him to the funeral.

"Ay?"

"We think Carey will soon be going into Scotland."

Dodd shrugged. "I doot it. And if he does, he may not ask me, he kens I'm mithered with him unless he's a stupider man than I tek him for."

"If he asks you, we want you to say yes."

Dodd sighed deeply. More travelling into foreign parts, more sleeping who knew where. At least he would understand the people, his Scots was quite good.

"Ay well, if he asks. And then what?"

Hepburn handed over four crowns, a pound, not Scots but sterling.

"At some point I will ask you not to accompany him and that is all."

"Ay?"

"That's all."

Dodd stared hard at the man. He was wearing a plain wool suit, some dark colour hard to tell in the firelight, with the indefinable look of having been tailored. His plain white falling band was clean and his cloak was a thick prickly grey wool with the oil left in it, you could see the way the damp dewed on it and didn't soak, from hill sheep clearly. It was a nice cloak, densely woven, perhaps from the herds near the lakes to the southwest. His face was square and the beard neatly trimmed, somehow neutral. If it wasn't for his unruly curly hair, it would be hard to remember him.

"Ay," he said, wanting to hand back the pound but somehow the money stuck to his hand. It was enough for a plain morion helmet. "We'll see."

"Oh, Sergeant Dodd," said the man softly, "not a word to Carey and don't play me false, d'ye understand? We ken where yer wife lives."

Dodd said nothing. Of course he did, if he knew Dodd's name. He didn't like being threatened, although you had to expect it when you took money. He wasn't worried. God help the man who took on Janet Armstrong in a fight. Perhaps Hepburn caught this for he smiled again.

"It's only a little thing we're asking ye to do," he said. "We're not going to kill him. Just teach him a lesson and send him back to London."

Dodd said "Ay," again and that seemed to satisfy Hepburn because he settled back on the bench and started asking questions about horses and the harvest like a normal man and Dodd didn't feel like answering. The conversation petered out as Hepburn got tired of trying to hold up both ends of it. They finished their pottage and Hepburn paid a ridiculous amount in sterling because Widow Ridley had quadrupled her prices just for him.

And that was all wrong because Dodd knew that the Earl of Bothwell was at the horn and he would have heard about it if the Earl had robbed a town or raided Lord Maxwell's cows and insight which was the only way he could have laid his hands on so much cash.

Gimlet-eyed, Widow Ridley watched from the door as Hepburn and Dixon mounted up and rode on the way they had come if they came from Edinburgh. Anyway, their horses were Edinburgh animals from the brands. Her knitting became louder as she spat after them.

"I wouldnae trust them further nor I could throw them," she snapped and Dodd nodded slowly.

"Missus Ridley, can I sleep on yer bench here like your ither guest…?" The Thirlwall drunk hadn't moved all the time he had been there. "Only it's dark and the rain…"

"Ay, ye can, Sergeant," said Widow Ridley. "Mebbe ye'd like to bring in yer great tall horse if he'll fit, since it's the raiding season."

Dodd looked at her in astonishment. "I take that verra kindly, missus," he said. "Ah'm fond of the beast and he'd make a good raid of a poor one."

Widow Ridley smiled a little for the first time, so her face wore the ghost of the way she looked forty years gone, before her teeth fell out and her wild hair went white.

She did more than allow the horse in the house; she brought in some straw to lay in the corner and Dodd carefully walked Whitesock in through the door—he had to put his head down to get through though there was space under the rafters once he was in. Not even that spooked him, he just neighed curiously and then stood still to be untacked and whisped down and then she brought in a bucket of mash for him. He nickered his lips in thanks and she patted his strong brown neck.

"Once upon a time, I'd ha' got on my pony and ridden out into the rain to tell my father of such a horse," she said. "Come quick, Da, I'd say, it's a good one."

"Not now, though," said Dodd, suddenly worried.

"Nay, not now," she laughed at him. "They're a' deid."

It made Dodd feel unaccountably better to know that the great London horse was in the same room with him, as the Thirlwall drunk snored and Whitesock blew and whickered in his sleep and eventually Dodd slept on the bench with an old homespun blanket over his shoulder and his saddle under his head.

Ten miles away by then and following the wall carefully to Haltwhistle, the men were walking their horses and wishing they had stayed as the weather closed in.

"God, he's a dour one," said Hepburn. Dixon grunted.

"Do ye think he'll do it?" Hepburn asked a mile later when they had realised they had overshot Haltwhistle and would do better heading for Hexham. Dixon shrugged.

"What does it matter?" he asked. "When do we kill him?"

"Probably after Carey's been arrested," said Hepburn thoughtfully. "Once the King is dead. Then we do Dodd."

Dixon grunted again. "I'm bringing my brothers in for that job," he said. "I dinna like the looks of him."

sometime in autumn 1592

Father William Crichton looked at the pieces of paper that had cost him such a lot of time and work. They were blank and at the bottom were the careless signatures of the Earls of Erroll, and Angus, also lesser fry like Auchinlech and even two Grooms of the Bedchamber. Not one of them was a forgery. Huntly had promised to sign a blank piece of paper too. Above the signatures, Crichton or anybody else could write anything he chose. As a guarantee for the Spanish King and a test of good faith, they were a triumph.

He had met all the men when he was at Court, at Falkland, very secretly. One of his reasons to be there was that he had been meeting the King and doing his best to persuade him to join the scheme. His Highness had even invited him to a small hunting lodge in the park and then seen him alone except for a page, in the evening after the hunting was finished and the King was at his ease eating a light supper of partridges and venison.

"Your Highness," he said while the King drank wine by the pint. "My liege the King of Spain…"

"Mr Crichton, ye are a Scot, are ye not?"

"Yes, Your Highness."

"Then I am your liege, not the King of Spain."

Crichton had coloured up at that, embarrassed. "Your Highness," he said humbly, dropping to one knee off the little stool he had been given, "I apologise, of course you are temporally. But I see the King of Spain as my spiritual liege because he is a Catholic."

"Surely then that's the Pope?"

"And the Pope, Your Highness."

"A man should have one, perhaps as many as two lieges. I canna tolerate three."

Crichton did not know what to say.

King James smiled and beckoned a redheaded lad with a crumpled ear to pour some more wine for him. "Och, dinna fret. I'm no' Her Majesty of England to have your bollocks off and burned and your guts intae the light of day and yer body cut in four parts so the angels will be at their wits' end to put ye back together on Judgement Day."

Crichton, who had nightmares sometimes about being hanged, drawn, and quartered, made a little noise in his throat which had gone dry. "I'm very glad, Your Highness," he managed sincerely.

"Nay, the Boot and the pinniwinks will do for me," grinned the King, buttering some manchet bread. "And then a nice rope."

"Ah…"

"So get off yer poor aching knee and tell me about yer idea," said the King. "Ye'd have the King of Spain land his troops at Dumfries and such like western ports and stay here over winter, then in the spring they march south and take England. Yes?"

Damn it, thought Crichton, they weren't supposed to spill the whole plan, Huntly was just to feel him out…

"Well…"

"Or is that no' the plan?"

"Not quite. For instance, problems with supplying the troops means they will likely bring them in the New Year to shorten the time of them being idle."

"Tell me all about it," said the King with an expansive gesture. "That ye know, anyway."

"Well that is the plan, I don't know all the bureaucratic details but the King gave me his *fiat* at the beginning of this year. He has read your paper about the possible benefits of Spanish rule which you wrote at the time of the Armada and liked it and asked that you be apprised of his…er plans. You see, I thought, and the King of Spain agrees with me, that perhaps it would cause less effusion of blood all round if the landing were not contested nor the troops troubled while they were in Scotland and perhaps we could buy some supplies from you at good prices and arms as well and…er…so on…"

"I've got an idea to prevent the effusion of blood," said the King, waving a partridge leg. "How about the King of Spain doesnae land troops anywhere in Scotland, doesnae keep sending Armadas for the storms to scuttle, and we all settle down and start trading and making money out of each other. Eh?"

Crichton looked at him in bewilderment. Had he really just implied that trade was better than war? "But Mother Church…"

"Ay, the Church," said the King. "Now I've allus longed to be a Catholic."

"You have?"

"Oh ay, it wis the religion of my dear martyred mother so it was, and I feel a great spiritual longing to be part of the great Universal Church again."

Crichton was nearly trembling with excitement. "Your Highness, this is wonderful news! I can…"

"I've often thought of getting baptised into the Catholic Church and leading my poor benighted subjects back to their spiritual Mother," said James, turning his eyes up to heaven. "The trouble is, at the moment if I did any such thing I would be in battle the following week and at the horn a week later. Which wouldna suit me, ye understand."

"You truly believe your subjects would revolt…"

"Ay, they would. Some would not," said the King, splitting another partridge with his black-nailed fingers, "but Edinburgh, Aberdeen, Fife, even little Leith, the cities would be up in arms. Ye recall what happened to my poor mother."

"But John Knox is dead and in Hell now."

"Ay, but Chancellor Melville of Aberdeen University isnae and he's a strong puritan, he thinks of only one thing which is the advancement of Calvinism. I've just had tae sign a dreadful law that removes bishops in favour of presbyteries. Presbyteries! God save us, wi' the poor silly creatures having tae decide for theirselves what's right, which they mostly dinna want to nor cannot."

"Shocking!" said Crichton sincerely.

"Ay. So any clue to anyone that I'd like to make a change in religion and I'd be oot, ye follow?"

"Of course," said Crichton, wondering if the King was actually talking treason. But no, he was the King. If he said it, it could not be treason.

"So ye see, Father—I can call ye that?" Crichton nodded faintly. "Let's take all this a little softly, a little quietly. And in any case, how can I possibly agree to troops building up fifty miles from Edinburgh? Even if I'm all for this plan to take England and cast down the auld bitch who's docked ma subsidy this year, and if I'd be willing to form an alliance wi' the King of Spain—which would be in the nature of a minnow forming an alliance wi'a perch, d'ye not think?—but even if I were... Thousands of soldiers and not mine running around the West March, I dinna like it."

"I can talk this over with Huntly and Angus. Perhaps we can find another place to land the soldiers, perhaps in the Highlands?" said Crichton, who loved maps but had never seen an accurate one.

"Good idea," beamed James, who had stalked deer all over the Highlands.

Crichton dipped his head. His mind was racing. If the Scottish King would declare himself a Catholic that would change everything. *Cuius regio eius religio* was the maxim all over Christendom because it worked: as the King, so the religion.

And of course a large number of Spanish troops in the West would certainly encourage the King to declare himself a Catholic, would give him a perfect excuse in fact. And then perhaps the King of Spain's general, yet to be decided, could indeed join forces with James and then both of them could invade England from the north. The strategic possibilities were breathtaking.

"Just tell 'em their old dad disnae want Spanish troops bothering him, eh?"

"Yes, Your Highness," said Crichton. "I am very honoured that Your Highness has seen fit to explain so much to this poor priest." *I'll be a Cardinal,* some part of him was singing, *for a coup like this, a Cardinal's hat at least!*

"Ay, ye should be. They'll credit ye with ma conversion and make ye a saint, I shouldn't wonder."

"Oh, I doubt that," said Crichton with smug modesty while all the time the back of his mind was singing, *Cardinal's hat! Cardinal's hat!*

"And not a word to anybody, eh?"

"Of course not."

"Besides, I don't want war with Spain. Why not wait until I inherit England so I'm King there by right and then make the change? Surprise 'em all one morning? What's all the hurry?"

Having been in Spain, Father Crichton could answer this. "His Catholic Majesty is not a well man and I think he reasonably fears to go to Judgement with his great failure to take England back into the fold on his conscience."

"Ah," said the King, nodding wisely, "I see. I see. So tell my naughty northern earls, Huntly and Maxwell especially, no Spanish troops in Caerlaverock, not even to wipe out the Johnstones, or I'll run the Justice Raid of all time into the west and burn it down."

"Yes, Your Highness."

"We'll meet again, Father Crichton, I've enjoyed talking tae ye."

Father Crichton bowed himself out, with a couple of partridges wrapped messily in a handkerchief to keep him going on the road back to Edinburgh. In fact, as soon as he was out of sight he had headed west again. He knew Huntly and Maxwell would instantly reject the idea of putting troops ashore anywhere other than Dumfries, no matter what the King thought, but he thought he could sell the rest to them.

At the hunting lodge, the King, who was mentally drafting a very careful ciphered letter to Sir Robert Cecil in England, spotted that his young page was looking troubled.

"Whit's the matter, Rob?" asked the King.

"Well, Your Highness, when ye met Chancellor Melville here last week, you told him how much ye love the precious word of God and that you would always protect and save the church of Calvin and Knox in Scotland and that the Catholic earls are a thorn in your side…"

James laughed, wiping his fingers on the napkin over his shoulder and dabbling them in the waterdish, wiping them sketchily again. "I'm caught," he said. "Yes, I did."

"And then today you said to that priest that ye'd like to be a Papist?"

"Ay, that's true."

"Well, which is it, sir?"

"What?"

"Which one were ye lying to?"

The King stopped laughing and looked grave. He beckoned the boy to him and the boy came and stood there with a frown of puzzlement on his face.

"Now, Rob, ye know what a King is?"

Rob opened his mouth and left it open. "He wears a crown."

"On special occasions, ay, I do."

"And he goes hunting and signs papers."

"Yes," James laughed. "Anything else?"

Rob scowled in thought, which James had already discovered didn't come easily to him.

"People do what you tell them to, usually."

"Sometimes," said James, with a touch of bitterness.

"And that's it," said Rob looking triumphant.

"Well there's an important bit about being a King that ye've left out."

"Och, and ye've a Queen…"

"Ay, though that's not it. The thing is, Rob my dear, God chose me to be King. God protected me all through my childhood when many ill-affected men kidnapped me and might have killt me. God made me King. Now when ye meet God on Judgement Day, He'll say tae ye, 'Rob, were ye a good boy and did ye allus tell the truth and did ye allus do whit yer elders and betters tellt ye to?'"

Rob thought carefully, his handsome brows bulging with the effort. "Yes," he said at last.

"Well that's verra good, lad, I'm pleased tae hear it. Whit do ye think He'll ask me at Judgement?"

"James, were ye a good man?"

James shook his head. "Nay Rob, me dear, that's whit he'd ask if I wis just another man. But I'm no' a man, I'm a King. So I get another question. 'James,' He'll say to me, 'James me lad, were ye a good King? Were ye a King like David or Solomon or Hezekiah, did ye do yer best for every one of yer subjects, Catholic or Protestant? Did ye keep the peace as far as ye could? Were ye a good King?'"

Rob was staring at him. "Oh."

"And I hope I'll be able to answer tae Him and say, like ye, 'Yes, I was good.' But to be a King is a position that comes to ye fra God and is sacred. And sometimes you have to do things that would be bad if you weren't a King. Which is why when I spoke to both Melville and Crichton, I told them what they wanted tae hear."

The poor lad was standing with a napkin between his raw-boned hands and was frowning again. "But which one did ye lie tae?"

James ruffled his hair. "Both, me dear, I was lying to baith of them."

δECEMBER 1592

They rode out of Carlisle on a cold morning. The blustery weather had stopped and after that it had turned suddenly cold, so cold Carey wondered if it might snow. The winds were all from the northeast and cut to the bone like a knife.

At Carey's suggestion, Anricks had written back to the Scottish King, also in Latin, thanking him for the invitation, accepting the challenge to a game of planets, a battle of the spheres, a duel of philosophers, and explaining that Sir Robert Carey would provide him with an escort because the Deputy Warden had business with His Highness as well. The note that came back with the same messenger said that Sir Robert would be very welcome and King James added a scrawl in Latin which welcomed his good cousin and hoped they would get in some hunting if the weather permitted.

With them went Red Sandy Dodd and Bangtail Graham, Tovey and Tyndale, Leamus the Irishman from the Earl of Essex's deserters, and the sixth man was Dodd. Carey had written to Dodd in Gilsland, a letter politely allowing the possibility of a refusal, but Dodd had written back on the back of the letter saying he would meet them at the Wall in Gilsland around nine o'clock. There were also two lads from the castle guard to act as messengers and grooms which made ten, enough for respectability. Everyone was rationed to one remount maximum and there were five packponies, two of which were for Carey and Anricks. It bore out the saying that if you wanted to send one man from *A* to *B*, then you needed one man. If you wanted to send two men, then you needed four men, and so on.

Dodd was there at Gilsland, sitting on Whitesock with another pony on a leading rein, his lance pointing to the sky, his new morion polished and his face slightly harder than the stones of the Giant's Wall behind him. He lifted his fingers to his helmet to Sir Robert and Sir Robert responded with a nod, and then Dodd joined their party at the back. Nobody said anything.

They made good time along the Giant's Road and reached Newcastle by evening, stayed the night in the great carting inn there, and then went up the Great North Road and by a strange coincidence found themselves in the little post village of Widdrington as the quick evening came down.

Carey had sent one of the lads ahead to warn Sir Henry Widdrington. As they rode into the courtyard there, they saw Roger Widdrington come to meet them, whom Carey hadn't seen since the last time he went to Scotland. Roger Widdrington had some trouble meeting Carey's eyes and took refuge in pomposity, as only a seventeen-year-old can.

"Yes, we have space for your horses, Deputy Warden, though the hobbies will have to double or triple up and for your men, as well, though some might have to sleep in the stables. Mrs Burn is still here and she has taken her chamber, which is why we are one room short. Her baby is due any day now. Perhaps you would care to be introduced to her, Sir Robert. I know Mr Anricks and Sergeant Dodd have already met her."

"If the lady is well enough to receive me," said Carey with a slight bow. "I heard something of her sad tale from...Well... er...I heard it."

"Where are Sir Henry, his wife, and your elder brother?" asked Anricks as he let himself carefully down from the horse and staggered slightly.

"Sir Henry and his lady wife and Young Henry were invited to Scotland by the King a few days ago," said Roger. "It's most inconvenient, what with the raiding season. I was out on the trod last night but one, though we didn't catch anyone."

"Did any of that big herd of cattle we brought into Carlisle last week have East March brands?" Carey asked Red Sandy, speaking a little loud because Dodd hadn't been there and so would get none of the fees.

"No," said Red Sandy stolidly, "West or Middle March only."

There was the usual flurry as the horses were bedded down for the night and the men sorted out where they would sleep, mostly by tossing coins. Meanwhile Roger Widdrington bore Carey and Anricks off to introduce Carey to Poppy Burn.

Elizabeth had done her best to make her small guest chamber suitable for a lying in, with the walls hung with cloths and the window carefully sealed to stop bad airs coming in.

Poppy was even bigger than before and moved very awkwardly with her legs apart. She had on an old let-out English gown of Elizabeth's and was reading a book when Roger knocked and opened the door. She was a bookish woman; there was a pile of other books on the little table, including a couple of books of chivalric tales, and Ascham's *The Schoolmaster*, an old and worn copy lying separately from the others.

Mr Anricks went in first and she greeted him with delight, struggling up from her chair. "Why Mr Anricks, what are you doing here? I think you've drawn all the loose teeth in the village. Are you going back to Scotland?"

"Yes, Mrs Burn, I am now officially a philosopher. May I introduce Sir Robert Carey to you, ma'am. Sir Robert, Mrs Proserpina Burn, Mrs Burn—Sir Robert."

"Well," said Poppy holding out her hand with a smile, "I have heard so much about you from Elizabeth. I am delighted to meet you at last."

Carey bowed over her hand with every Court flourish available to him, because she was a pretty woman even if she was nine months gone. She managed an adequate curtsey.

"I am sorry for your loss, ma'am," said Carey, "however I am very happy to be able to tell you that I hanged your husband's murderers personally last month, from Dick of Dryhope's tower, both of them, father and son."

She clasped his hand. "Thank you, sir, I heard that you had, but thank you so much for coming to tell me personally. Now I have had my revenge, I can think of the babe." Carey bowed again. "I heard there was nearly a terrible battle but that you convinced the Elliots to withdraw with no loss of life."

"Almost none, yes," said Carey. "Although we would have won the battle, it is the way of these things that good men's lives will be lost. Much better the Elliots ran away which has made a laughingstock of the whole surname. And I had what I had come for, the murderers."

"You risked a pitched battle just for my husband's killers?"

"Say rather that I risked it for the sake of justice, ma'am," said Carey very courtlywise. "Justice for him and for you."

There was a pause and then Poppy Burn said something odd. "It is a dark and terrible world I have come to. Thank you, Sir Robert, from the bottom of my heart."

Carey bowed again and then Poppy looked sideways at Anricks.

"Sir, although Mr Anricks is not a man-midwife, he is, by way of being a medical man. I wonder if you would leave him with me so I can consult with him?"

"Of course," said Carey, and went out, thought about sticking around just in case, but then caught the smell of roasting pork from the kitchen and went down to investigate.

"Mr Anricks, you know how I am placed," Poppy said to him familiarly as he brought up a stool to sit on. "I have decided that the minute I am delivered and if spared, churched, I desire to go home to my family in Keswick."

Anricks nodded.

"A very suitable place to go, since the manse is no longer yours," he said, "although I haven't heard yet that a new minister has been appointed to Wendron."

Poppy bowed her head and then looked up at him. "Please, Mr Anricks, I have no right to ask this, but would you accompany me?"

"I'm sure," said Anricks judiciously, "that if you want him to, Mr Roger Widdrington will accompany you to the mouth of Hell itself."

"Ah." Poppy smiled a secret smile. "Well. But will you do it if I need an escort?"

"If I can. I may of course be dead."

"Why? Are you going into danger?"

"I am going to King James' Court to dispute with him or possibly his wise champions as to whether the Earth goes round the Sun or vice versa as popular superstition will have it."

"Earth goes round the Sun...Oh no, Mr Anricks, I am sure you are mistaken."

Anricks sighed and resisted the temptation to explain why it made such better sense. She was a woman and very close to her time. He didn't want to do or say anything that might upset her.

"Perhaps I am," he said peaceably. "However, His Highness wants a proper academic dispute about the matter."

"Well, I hope it goes well for you. Can I ask if you would take a packet to Edinburgh for me?"

Anricks bowed. "Certainly," he said, and she brought out one of her usual packets, double sewn in canvas and sealed. He took it, felt it, and smiled.

"Not so thick as usual."

"Yes, although it was hard to write," she said, her eyes quite feverish. "I hoped you would come back or perhaps I would have given it to the carter in the end."

"Sometimes the more prosaic messenger is the safest."

"Do the usual thing with the packet, leave it in the jakes, behind a brick, at the Maker's Mark in Edinburgh."

"Of course," said Anricks, who took the package and put it into the breast of his old woollen doublet. "Can I help you in anything else?"

"It was Lord Spynie who ordered the death of my husband, wasn't it?"

"Please, ma'am, I beg you will not trouble your mind with..."

"It was." Tears were glittering on her eyelashes.

"Yes, it was. Though you know the circumstances. For that crime, I do not entirely blame Lord Spynie."

She nodded and for a moment she shuddered as if she was doing something that needed huge effort. "You are saying I should not think of pursuing him."

"Yes," said Anricks baldly. "God knows, the man is evil but in the rough and tumble of Scottish Court life, it was fair enough. Also, vengeance is mine, saith the Lord, I will repay."

"Indeed," said Poppy, "though Mrs Sterling the midwife says sometimes the good Lord needs a bit of prodding, being infected with His Son's notions about forgiveness."

Anricks inclined his head. He could say nothing to Christianity with its very laudible and peaceable scriptures on the matter and its total ignoring of them. Also his opinion on vengeance had changed over the years.

"Now, serious matters are done," said Poppy, clasping her hands round her belly and giving a big smile. "Tell me about your wonderful wife and children, Mr Anricks."

So Anricks smiled and spoke about Rebecca and how the latest child had been born while he was away, which he found both a relief and a worry: a relief since he didn't have to hear the cries and shouts of his wife in labour, but also a worry since he couldn't know until several days after if his wife had survived and if she was well, which, thank the Almighty, she was as of her last letter. The eldest boy was nearly nine now and a clever lad who already spoke Portuguese, Spanish, and English and…

He left her dozing and passed her woman coming up with supper on a tray for her, recognised the smell of pig and sighed.

In the parlour where the family ate, he saw the first remove laid out. Politely they had waited for him, which did him no good at all, so he claimed stomach trouble and picked at the pot herbs and the remains of a chicken and also had to turn down a liver sausage that smelled good even to him.

Carey was probing Roger Widdrington for more information on why Sir Henry, his wife, and eldest son had also gone to Court.

"Well, I think His Highness took a great liking to Lady Widdrington last time they met and it's quite normal for Sir Henry to spend a lot of time in Scotland," said Roger.

"Oh. Is he getting a pension from the Scots King?"

Roger again took refuge in pomposity, his downy chin scraping his small ruff. "I'm sure my father's loyalty to Her Majesty the Queen is absolutely unimpeachable…" he began, looking worried.

"Of course it is," said Carey, waving away the tempting quince sweetmeats in the second remove. "I asked because I know Sir John Forster in the Middle March certainly gets something from

His Highness and has for decades. And James of course has his three thousand-pound subsidy from the Queen to keep him on the straight and narrow."

Anricks thought he would rescue poor young Roger and also he was genuinely curious. "Are you looking for something similar, Sir Robert?"

Carey smiled sunnily. "Who knows? Of course, I wouldn't turn His Highness down if he offered me a pension. That would be rude. And I wouldn't like to break tradition now I have my warrant. I can always use the money to pay my men."

"Ahum," said Roger. "Well. Tradition."

"Really, I'm more curious as to whether Sir Henry will be seeing Lord Spynie again."

"I'm afraid I have no idea..." said Roger, looking panicky.

"Ah," said Carey, "I thought so. How is his gout?"

"A little better," said Roger, grasping at this safer subject. "He has started taking an empiric dose made of crocus bulbs which does seem to help."

"The same as my Lord Burghley," said Carey. "He was suffering badly when I saw him at the Queen's Court in Oxford. I'm sure the crocus bulbs will do the job. And how is my esteemed elder brother John?"

"He is still having trouble with the Berwick town council..."

"Of course he is, he's a pompous ass and so are they..."

The gossip about the doings in the East March went on and on and eventually Anricks could not stomach any more candied eringo root nor quince cheese and took his leave to go to his bed in the other guest bedroom. It was a familiar room, with a couple of palliasses on the floor, a truckle, and a testered four-poster, so he modestly took the truckle. He got ready for bed, carefully used his silver toothpick and toothcloth, said his prayers and then looked at the packet Poppy had given him.

He looked too long for he soon heard Carey's step on the stairs and had to put it away half unpicked.

Carey nodded at him, undressed, knelt to say his prayers, and rolled into the bed with his shirt on and his long legs poking out under the blankets. Five minutes later his firm snoring started echoing through the night and Anricks understood why neither Sergeant Dodd nor Red Sandy were using the palliasses and were probably happily asleep in the stables with the horses.

Anricks sighed and looked up at the handsome coffered ceiling, sighed again, turned over, sighed once more and turned over again. His body was aching from the two days' brisk ride with only changing of your horse to break the monotony and from the lumpiness of the bed at the inn at Newcastle. He was very tired and while he tried not to think of the time when he had slept like the dead, lying naked on naked boards with a hundred other men's snores rumbling around him, he seemed to have lost the trick of it now.

◇◇◇

Dodd had almost enjoyed the various kinds of pork they had been given in the hall, along with a savoury bag pudding full of herbs to soak up the gravy, and excellent beer. He had listened to Red Sandy and Bangtail arguing the old question about whether Scotsmen had tails. Leamus the Irishman had said in his soft foreign accent that he had been quite sure that Englishmen had tails until quite recently, and Bangtail ended the matter by saying that he didn't know about the Scots men but the Scots women definitely didn't have tails the last time he banged one, which caused everyone to howl with laughter.

The two lads were both called Archie so they had some fun with that and hit upon calling the one who was as tall as Carey with wider shoulders and much bigger feet, Little Archie, and the one who was a bantam with thick black hair standing straight up and generally took messages, Big Archie. That would do for the moment, until they had done something that would make a better byename.

"Is it true that the Deputy is still sweet for Lady Widdrington?" asked Red Sandy, munching the chewy bread.

"Ay, it is," said Dodd and his mouth turned down at the thought of it. Was that why he had let the Elliots go? Because he was sweet over a woman? And she wasn't even an Elliot, she came from Cornwall with one of those weird names.

Red Sandy tried again. "D'ye think he'll get her or no'?"

Dodd shrugged. He really didn't care one way or the other. Red Sandy poured him some beer which he hadn't asked for and exchanged looks with Bangtail.

"So," said Red Sandy, "are ye still sorrowing over the way we let the Elliots go or is there aught else bothering ye, brother?"

"What?" staid Dodd, looking at him as if he had gone wood.

Red Sandy repeated the question word for word.

"Are ye having me on?" Dodd replied and the black anger expanding again until it felt like all his body was tight with it.

"The Elliots, right," said Bangtail, looking anxious and being ignored by the Dodd brothers. Leamus swung his lanky legs over the bench and wandered off.

"Only ye've bin a right sour streak of shite for the last month," said Red Sandy loudly and slowly, "and we're a' getting tired of it so I wondered had something else happened?"

"What more d'ye need?" hissed Dodd and found he had hold of Red Sandy's shirt collar. "He let them go!"

"Right, fine," said Red Sandy, not even trying to take Dodd's hand away. "Tell ye what, brother. I dinna care how sour and thrawn ye are wi' the Deputy, but will ye not treat us the same, eh?"

And Red Sandy stared Dodd in the face until he let go of the collar. Dodd didn't know what to do or say, but in the end he stood up and walked to the stables where he dossed down next to Whitesock who nickered welcomingly to him and then laid his great head down in the straw next to Dodd's.

Dodd's chest felt full as if it was going to explode and for a moment he almost put his arm around Whitesock's neck. But then he stopped himself and forced his eyes shut against the burning in them and somehow went to sleep.

In the morning he found that his own arm had betrayed him by creeping around the horse's neck in the middle of the night when he hadn't noticed, which made everything worse, not better.

δeCeMBeR 1592 eδINBURGh

For the first time ever, Lady Widdrington found she was enjoying herself in Edinburgh. She made sure Sir Henry had plenty of time to chase Lord Spynie by making herself scarce and she did that by following the King's suggestion and meeting the ladies of the Queen's Court, and sitting with them or walking in the gardens of Holyrood Abbey with them or sitting sewing with them or going out on a hawking expedition with them on days when it wasn't raining.

She had now met Queen Anne and usually found her with her Danish ladies, playing card games and singing songs in Danish that sounded rude and certainly made them giggle. Queen Anne was a plump fair-haired girl who seemed quite sad and worried about something. She had been Queen of Scotland for two years, but there was no baby yet and of course tongues had already started to wag about it so that was probably the trouble.

She was a friendly woman, quite informal, with her attractive Danish accent and after Lady Widdrington had made sure she lost to the Queen a few times at Gleek, she was looked for by her and often called to Her Highness' apartments in the older part of the palace that still looked very much like an abbey, and had beautiful carvings on the walls and in the window niches and Gothic arches. After a little, she was invited to share a bed, sometimes with one of the fatter Danish ladies and sometimes with a pretty empty-headed wife of one of the King's Grooms, Marguerite Graham. She was more than happy to be in the world of women and save Sir Henry the trouble of thinking up excuses for why he didn't want to sleep with his lady wife. And it even pleased him a tiny bit, because her being associated with the Queen gave him more status. What could be more unexceptionable than a Danish lady-in-waiting or a Flemish chamberer?

Often she couldn't sleep as she lay in bed next to the great pink snoring pillow of a woman, and then of course her thoughts wandered to Carey, which she tried to stop because that hurt her, and then her thoughts usually wandered back to the ugly interview with her husband at Jedburgh.

They had been in the remains of the once mighty and beautiful Jedburgh Abbey, and the King had not at first been present in the room. Nosy though the King was, he respected proprieties usually.

Lady Widdrington had been all across the March, into Scotland, back down to Jedburgh and she was still shaking from the encounter with the young Lord Hume on the church tower.

Her husband had not come up to the tower because he was afraid of heights. The King had arrived in the middle of it all and pronounced that Lady Widdrington must come to Edinburgh and meet his Queen. Of course she had agreed and then gone, her heart pounding, to meet her husband in the old abbey warming room.

He had been angry with his usual smouldering rage which she had spent such effort and pains when she was younger to understand and find something rational in it.

"Well, wife," he had sneered, "what have ye to say for yerself?"

Elizabeth considered this as an opening gambit. She was long experienced in this kind of discussion. Whatever she said would be wrong, she knew that. If she apologised for going into Scotland without his permission, that would be wrong. If she told him her reasons why she had gone, which she felt were perfectly rational, and excused herself, that would be wrong. Whatever she did or said would be wrong because she herself was irredeemably wrong because she was a woman.

She also knew that whatever she did or said, at the end of all the words and the shouting, she would be beaten because beating her made him feel better about everything else. She didn't understand why, but it did. Temporarily.

So she said nothing. She knew he hated her silence too, but that wasn't why she did it. Nor was it because there was after all nothing to say. She simply couldn't be bothered to fight him because not only was he an old man always in pain from his gout, but he was also a man in love with somebody he couldn't ever have and she felt sorry for him. She probably couldn't ever have Robin Carey either, so she knew exactly what her husband went through every day of his life, poor man.

She was careful not to smile at him, though strangely she wanted to. There back in the old abbey warming room with its pungent smell of socks and rarely washed old men, she took off her damp velvet gown, unlaced her kirtle unfashionably down the front and heaved it off over her head, left her petticoat and bumroll, undid the top of her smock and let it fall down so her shoulders and upper back were exposed above her stays and then went and knelt at his feet, so he could beat her and get it over with.

She shut her eyes and waited for the belt to come whistling down on her shoulders, crushing the internal child that always wailed and wanted to know why. She thought that the last set of welts had healed up but there were scars on her shoulders that often opened up again when Sir Henry felt particularly poisonous.

He was taking his time and she sighed. She crossed her arms over her chest to protect her breasts and waited for the onslaught. *Come on,* she thought, *you've given me time to get nervous, get it done and then I can go home and sleep.*

A draught caught her and a different sweaty smell and she realised that the door was open behind Sir Henry. She looked expecting to see one of the Widdringtons and what she saw astonished her.

The King was standing there, in all his soft-edged glory, staring with a very peculiar expression on his face. Not lustful, as she might have expected, seeing her smock was down over the top of her stays, but extraordinarily compassionate. She was steadied by that. She stayed on her knees where she was, since she might as well.

At last Sir Henry turned to see the King, his unused belt dangling from his thick knotted fingers. He bent his neck and said thickly in Scots, "Can I no' be private with my wife?"

"I came to say farewell, Sir Henry," said King James in a reasonable voice, "and this is what I find?"

He brushed past Sir Henry and raised Elizabeth. "Madam," he said, "put yer clothes on." So she pulled up her smock and tied the laces, fought her way into the damp and muddy kirtle and then put the gown round her shoulders. Her hat she had taken off when she dozed and her cap was firmly pinned to her head with a dozen long pins as usual. She sighed because now it was all to do again so Sir Henry could satisfy whatever it was in him that thirsted for her pain. Her skin was shrinking again from the remembered pain of blows, leaking into the future.

She sighed again and turned to go, found King James there again.

"Lady Widdrington," he said very softly, "d'ye mind what I tellt ye of George Buchanan, my tutor?" Yes, she did. She had been shocked. She nodded. "Buchanan liked to beat me too, said it would make a better King of me if all the sin fra my mother had been beaten out of me. My scars are on ma bum, see ye, and it was only when my dear friend D'Aubigny wept over them that it occurred to me there might be any objection to them. I will see what I can do again."

"Thank you, Your Majesty, but I'm afraid there isn't much you can do," she told him. "I just wish…"

Sir Henry was still standing there like a post, only his eyes flickering between the King and his wife.

"Ay, what d'ye wish?" whispered the King.

She found her eyes suddenly full of tears and tried to push them back. "I just wish he could have Lord Spynie and be happy," she said in a rush, not knowing until she heard the words what she was going to say.

Oh God, Sir Henry was right there in the room. What would he do to her now?

Suddenly the King embraced her, which nearly knocked her out with the smell. "Och Lady Widdrington, ye're the kindest woman I've ever met. Will ye go ben whiles I speak to your husband?"

She found her hat with shaking hands and put it on, then went out to the remnants of what had once been a fine set of cloisters and got her shaking knees to walk about until she stopped quivering like a hunted deer and could think straight. She was wrung out. Now what would happen to her? She wondered exactly how angry Sir Henry would be with her at what she had said. Had he heard it? Had he been listening? Would the King be angry with her? Maybe not, since he had said she was kind.

She was a little surprised about George Buchanan, that leading light of the Reformation in Scotland, that stern beacon of righteousness, though not very. She was old enough to know that the more righteous a man seems the more ugly his private life tends to be.

So she walked until Young Henry came and found her and walked with her, his head bent and his spotty face grim and strained.

"If he ever beats you again, ye're to tell His Highness," said Young Henry. "By letter or messenger or whatever. Sir Henry isna a Scot and he is the Deputy Warden of the East March but King James says he willna have it."

"Young Henry," she said to him, "I know Sir Henry hates me and blames me for all his ills. So what happens if he can't vent his spleen on me? Do you think he'll start to like me?"

Young Henry stared at the ground for a while. "You should go home to your mother and father," he said.

"In Caerhays castle?" she said, "In Cornwall? At the other end of the country, hundreds and hundreds of miles away? Don't be ridiculous."

Even now she still thought it ridiculous, though deep inside her she longed to see her mother again. She had stopped writing to her because Sir Henry read the letters which meant she could not tell the truth. Sir Henry had not the wit nor the acting ability to hide his feelings as she did, he was a constant boiling presence beside her, even when he wasn't there, of rage and dull fury and somehow she couldn't help feeling compassion for him in her heart, for how sad and unhappy he must be. She knew this could only annoy him and it did. Yet there it was: she was still very afraid of him, although he hadn't actually beaten her since Jedburgh. She was afraid of his ire and yet she couldn't keep the compassion out of her voice whenever she answered him, which made him all the more furious. So generally, as much as she could, she avoided talking at all, or just said gently and humbly, "Yes, my lord," or "No, my lord," which he hated even more. If only he could just divorce her. Unfortunately that was impossible short of a private Act of Parliament and they were not peasants just to part and not see each other again. Poor man, he didn't even know what he wanted from her.

So at the King's winter Court in Edinburgh she was more than happy to sleep next to big pillowy Danish girls or silly sweet Marguerite, who was often not in her bed when she should have been. She started learning Danish to pass the time which made the poor Queen cheer up and giggle at her terrible pronunciation.

CAERLAVEROCK, DECEMBER 1592

William Crichton was sitting in a stuffy little wooden box with a grill to one side on a very uncomfortable seat with a thin cushion on it, his breviary open in his lap although he didn't really need it. There was a lot of noise of someone arriving and then the other door opened and shut and a man knelt down in front of him on the other side of the grill. Despite the darkness, Crichton knew exactly who it was since he was the lord and the lord goes first. As far as Crichton could make out, Maxwell was wearing a black damask doublet with black satin trim and a small ruff and that made his permanent scowl from having eyebrows that met in the middle even more forbidding. He cleared his throat and coughed, which was understandable since the little confession booth was left over from the days before the Reformation when Holy Mother Church had held them all in her hand. Which was to say, it was old, full of woodworm and, as far as Crichton could judge, had been frequently used as a jakes by desperate serving men and probably dogs.

"Bless me, Father, for I have sinned..." intoned the Maxwell and then went into a baroque recital of sins of the flesh, including many instances of fornication, impurity, impure thoughts and actions. Maxwell did not mention killing in battle or on a raid, since to his mind only a fool would call them murders, though he grudgingly included plenty of assaults and two actual murders, if you could call them that since one had been of a Johnstone found alone on the hills and the other had been when he was drunk. When the regrettable tale finally wound itself to the end, Father Crichton wondered what would happen if he refused the Maxwell absolution for the continued habitual feast of sin which no doubt was the same as last year and doubtless would be the same next year. Nothing good, he suspected, and he would shortly be sold to the English authorities.

He gave a rosary as penance, to be prayed at the Maxwell's convenience. Then "*Ego te absolvo...*" he intoned in the sacred washing of the black soul of the Maxwell and tried not to dwell on the more outrageous bits of the confession. Was it really possible to do that to two women or had the man just been boasting?

After the Maxwell had gabbled through his prayers, crossed himself, and risen from the kneeler, let himself out again, his household came in with the same grubby stories, although his lordship had made a better tale of it. His wife came in last with a prosaic tale of anger and envious thoughts and one beating of a servant girl she suspected, correctly, of bedding her husband.

George Gordon, the Earl of Huntly, was due to come to Caerlaverock soon and then the two of them would travel to Edinburgh with at least half of their households for Christmas.

Crichton would rather have stayed at Caerlaverock to receive the first *terceiros* once the seas calmed down in the spring. But Maxwell wanted him in Edinburgh and as he was Maxwell's house-priest, that was that.

The night before they set off they were sitting by the fire in Caerlaverock hall and roasting chestnuts and Huntly said, apropos nothing else, "Well, what if we kill the King?"

It's the sort of thing you just don't say, thought Crichton, *unless you're lord of thousands of acres and an entire clan and regard yourself as a prince in your own right.* "I think it would be a bad idea," he said.

Huntly laughed at him, said that the King was a pervert and a sodomite as well as being a goddamned Protestant and surely he deserved to die.

Yes, but he's the King, thought Crichton anxiously. *And he might become a Catholic.* Aloud he said to Huntly, "Well, my lord, he showed good favour to ye after ye murdered the Earl of Moray…"

"Ah didnae murder him, I killt him and he deserved it."

"Then killed him."

"Ay, the King fancies mah bum, allus has," explained Huntly, throwing a chestnut in the fire to watch it explode, "and I'm married to one of his precious D'Aubigny's daughters and he's aye sentimental…"

"Ye got away wi' it," said Maxwell. "I wish I could do the like to that bloody man, John Johnstone, the bastard."

Crichton thought about telling the two lords some of the things Jesus Christ had said on the subject of enemies, vengeance, and forgiveness and he knew he would never do it. It was just as well that neither Huntly nor Maxwell could read since they had spent their teens learning more useful things like swordplay and the names for different groups of animals. It was also just as well that neither knew any Latin except for rote learned prayers.

The Protestants were so set on everyone knowing scripture, everyone reading and hearing the Bible in their own language at church, insisting that everyone should know the Word of God. It was foolishness and irresponsibility—the Word of God was like gunpowder, apt to blow up people's lives if not treated with due care and in particular, kept away from peasants.

The lords were still sitting by the fire, surrounded by a hairy carpet of wolfhounds and currently discussing the best way to murder the Johnstone without getting caught for it.

"Ye could do it," said Maxwell to Huntly, "Ye'd get away with it again, ye know ye would…"

"Why should I?" asked Huntly as a chestnut cracked like a pistol. "Johnstone's no' my blood enemy, he's yours. Ye do it."

"Ay but the King disnae fancy mah bum and I'd get warded somewhere cold wi' no women…"

"Ah cannae help that," said Huntly. "And forebye it wad be a sin for me to kill a man I had nae blood feud with, would it no', Father?"

Crichton hesitated and said, "It certainly would be a sin for ye to murder the Johnstone…"

"There ye go, ye're trying to get me to commit a sin, Maxwell, so shut yer trap about it, eh?"

"For God's sake, killing the King is a wee bittie of a sin," protested the Maxwell. "Why are ye so fussy?"

"I'm not gonnae commit the sin of killing the King," said Huntly. "Somebody else is, isn't that right, Father?"

"Well…er…"

"And forebye somebody else will get the blame," added Huntly, laughing a lot. "That should make ye happy, Maxwell. That's funny, is that…"

Maxwell was struggling to look as if he knew all about this. "Ay," he said also laughing, "that's hilarious. Will he greet, d'ye think?"

Crichton desperately wanted to ask who was planning the outrage but didn't dare because then they would know he didn't know. Instead he kept his countenance and blinked down at his hands. Who could it be? Not Spynie, the man was gimcrack, totally dependent on the King and he knew it. The Ruthvens weren't allowed close enough to the monarch and he couldn't think of anyone else who would dare. Was it one of the other lords in the association, perhaps? Erroll, maybe?

Suddenly Crichton had to get out of there. He had the awful feeling he was going to weep because something he had set up with loving care was suddenly twisting out of his hands. Did the King of Spain know about this plot, whatever it was? Had he given it his *fiat* as well? Couldn't he see that for all his faults, King James was more useful alive than dead?

He stood up, bowed to the company who ignored him, went out of the hall and found the narrow staircase that led up to the battlements. Up he went and up, getting breathless and finding his fear and horror burning out of him, until he could look out into the long cold night and the stars above him. It was freezing and he had brought no cloak, but he stood there and stared up at Orion marching across the starfield with his little dog behind him.

He wanted to pray and so he prayed for King James' continued health and he also prayed for the souls of the lords who were trying to bring in Spanish troops. If King James had been excommunicated like his appalling and scandalous cousin of England, of course, he would have had no qualms. Well, not very many. But James had not been excommunicated, he had been very careful about that—and had he not said in so many words that he wanted to be baptised a Catholic? Hadn't he? Directly to Crichton himself? That would make it doubly a sin to kill him since he would have had no chance to purge his sins and would thus go to Hell for being a Protestant.

And there was the paper he had written in the 1580s before the Armada sailed the first time, looking at the pros and cons of the Spanish invasion from the south. How that paper had got into the King of Spain's hands, Crichton didn't know, but it had. Was it all just coneycatching? Had King James himself arranged for the paper to end up in Spain, to keep the Spanish off his back while they got on and conquered England?

Crichton sighed. He had to find out more about this plot, if it existed. Maybe King James is a Protestant through and through and would never turn to Rome, but he's a man and it's a sin to kill anyone, even in Scotland where life is so cheap.

He said the *Pater Noster*, three *Aves* and a *Gloria*, and went down the stairs to see if there was anything left for his supper.

EDINBURGH DECEMBER 1592

Their little procession was now within five miles of Edinburgh, coming up the last bit of the Great North Road, which wasn't in as scandalous a condition as the parts further south, with the big green and brown mound of King Arthur's Seat on their right. Carey had sent Little Archie ahead to warn the King's majordomo of their arrival. He and Anricks were wearing their best available clothes, him in the black velvet doublet and hose, Anricks in his new suit and a gown borrowed from Scrope without asking, looking very self-conscious. The cut was good and Carey was particularly pleased with the way the doublet pulled Anricks' shoulders back since he had a tendency, like many clerkly men, to round shoulders.

He looked critically at everyone else, riding politely in twos, all reasonably smart and wearing newly cleaned jacks and polished helmets.

Now that was interesting. Dodd had a brand new helmet, a nice plain morion with the curves and peaks that kept the rain out and made it hard to knock off. Carey had seen it but had not noticed it, which was embarrassing.

Carey had himself and Anricks riding after Bangtail and Red Sandy, then behind him Tovey and Tynedale, then Dodd and Leamus who ignored each other, and then the final lad, Big Archie, the small man with a shock of black hair, leading all five of the packponies and the remounts. Now that was also odd. Big Archie looked different.

Other than that, they were looking good. Carey let his favourite hobby, Sorrel, drop back until he was next to Dodd and smiled across at him.

"I like your new helmet, Sergeant, where did you get it?"

Oddly Dodd's neck flushed red at that and he said in a strangled voice, "Aglionby in English street."

"Oh, is that the mayor's brother?"

"Ay."

"Well it's a good one then." Carey wasn't wearing his helmet, it was packed with his jack on the last pony, ready for the journey back. He didn't need it this close to Edinburgh, even in barbaric Scotland. Instead he had a high crowned hat that he hadn't been able to resist in Oxford and Mr Anricks had his old hat since Anrick's usual hat was an ancient soft bonnet, twenty years out of fashion, that a London beggar would have disdained to wear, a little too horrible even for a tooth-drawer, let alone a philosopher.

Dodd was staring woodenly to the front now and so Carey contented himself with dropping back once more to take a look at Big Archie, the groom who was leading the packponies. The ponies all looked fine, being unshod. None had gone lame, for a wonder, their packs were carefully stowed and nothing was on the point of falling off. Even the groom was wearing a respectable black doublet and a bonnet pulled down on his head and...

Carey slowly took another look at the groom. He would have sworn that the sprig of the Carletons now known as Big Archie was smaller and didn't have the length of jaw or those piercing blue eyes though his hair was in tufts and sooty black...

"Goddamn it," he said wearily, "it's bloody Young Hutchin Graham again."

"Nay sir, I've the look of him, sir, but I'm a Carleton..."

Carey swiped the bonnet off the lad's head and found that the sooty black hair was in fact plastered with some combination of soot and grease, underneath which was Hutchin's golden hair, unmistakeably.

He swiped sideways with the revolting bonnet, back and forth, whacking Young Hutchin with it so the young devil had to lean over to the other side of his pony and cling like a monkey, all the while protesting that he was a Carleton, sir. The others were staring and trying to hide their grins, except Dodd, still looking grimly ahead.

"Do I have to strip you and put you under the pump to get that disgusting stuff out of your hair...?" bellowed Carey, and Young Hutchin finally put his hands up and shouted, "A'right, sir, a'right, I came with ye to make sure ye was all right..."

This so astonished Carey that he stopped hitting the boy with the bonnet and said, "What?"

"To mek sure ye was a'right…"

"Ballocks, Young Hutchin, you came with us either to sell your arse in the best market…"

"Nay sir," said Young Hutchin indignantly, "I'm no' that way…"

"Or to get your revenge for last time."

There was a pause. "Ay sir," said Young Hutchin, with a crooked grin, "Ye've the right of it."

"Dear God! This is Edinburgh, you blithering nitwit, King James is King here, do you understand and…"

"Ay sir, but I'm not here to dae it, see ye, I'm spying oot the lay of the land and seeing what's here and what the strengths are. Do ye like mah hair? Ah did it masen…"

"Your hair is simply disgusting, Young Hutchin, but it might put Lord Spynie off for long enough so you can run crying to your mother….

"Nay sir, I canna do that, she died birthing me," said Young Hutchin with some dignity. "And I've growed a lot since last summer, see ye, all me breeks is too short and I've gone through two pair o' clogs…"

It was true that puberty had clearly hit the beautiful boy that Young Hutchin had been with unusual force. His legs and arms were four inches longer than they had been, while his feet were in a man's pair of boots, very old ones, and his hands were rawboned and large. On the logic of dogs with big paws, he had a considerable amount of growing to do yet.

"And you've come to scout out the King's Court, no more?"

"Nae more, sir," said Young Hutchin glibly.

"What about that ambush you were in with your wretched uncle a few days ago?"

"Och that was in the way of business, sir—poor Uncle Wattie, he's fit to be tied again and ye got maist of the kine he reived in the autumn and Archie Fire the Braes is gaunae be expensive."

Carey nearly cracked a smile at that. "When did you make the swap with Archie Carleton?"

"Ay, I sold me funeral suit cos it's too small for me and I got the new doublet and breeks cheap…"

"You mean you stole them?"

"Nay sir, and then I had enough money to bribe Big Archie, and I shadowed ye all across the moors and we swapped last night while ye were in the inn at Berwick. That bit wis fun."

Grudgingly Carey nodded. "Well, that was very good work shadowing us," he admitted. "I had no idea."

"Thankye sir. So I can come wi' ye sir."

Carey sighed heavily. "I could send you back…"

"Ay, and ye ken very well, I willna go…"

"…in irons with an escort…"

"Och sir!"

"But very well, Young Hutchin, you may accompany us. Maybe my Lord Spynie won't remember you."

"Nay, he willna wi' me hair like this."

"God Almighty."

Carey returned to the front of their little column where Anricks was waiting expectantly. Carey explained some of what had happened in Dumfries in July and Anricks nodded.

"So that was what was at the root of your trouble with Lord Spynie, I did wonder. And he's an ill man to cross."

"Mr Anricks," said Carey heavily, "in all my life, I have never crossed a man that wasn't an ill man to cross."

For some reason Anricks started to laugh at that, a creaking kind of laugh and eventually Carey started to laugh as well.

Soon the walls of Edinburgh were frowning on them from their left, but they didn't need to enter the towngates at all since Holyrood House was a converted abbey a little way outside the Netherbow Port. They met the Vice Chamberlain at the end of the Cowgate and were directed through the old Gothic gatehouse into the abbey grounds.

Of course the King's palace in Edinburgh wasn't anything like as enormous as Whitehall nor as much of a labyrinth. Carey had spent nearly a year there in his late teens in the train of Sir Francis Walsingham's embassy. They found themselves lodged in the oldest part of the palace, on the back wall, in the monks' old storehouses and infirmary. Sir John Maitland of Thirlstane, the Lord Chancellor, had come away from his beloved Thirlstane for Christmas and the New Year and he bore Carey and Anricks off to feed them venison pasties for supper.

They ate privately in a parlour and since Maitland was rich, the food was very elaborate and often unidentifiable, so Anricks simply said a prayer and tucked in. Carey was being updated on some very complicated politics to do with the northern earls, Huntly, Erroll and Angus, and Anricks found himself sitting beside a large fleshy man with a big nose, a few years older than him.

"Ah, yes," said Maitland, waving a hand at the two of them, "Mr Simon Anricks, Mr John Napier, pray be introduced to each other since ye are both by way of being philosophers and ye baith have opinions on Thomas Digges."

Almost unable to believe his luck, Anricks turned with interest to Mr Napier and within five minutes was deep in conversation with him about an astonishing addition to the *Ars Mathematica* which he had invented. They switched to Latin and went at it hammer and tongs, with bits of paper being produced and scrawled on and Anricks looking more and more delighted and impressed. It took quite a lot of work to separate him from Napier when the supper and the music finished.

◇◇◇

Alexander Lyndsay, Lord Spynie, was sitting at a late supper in his own private parlour at Holyrood House. There were four young men with him and two boys, all dressed in elegant livery with a nice variation in the styles, the same damask handled differently for each boy by Spynie's own tailor.

Spynie was drinking excellent French wine and eating some delicious goose liver sausage with toasted manchet bread. But mostly he was just enjoying watching his youngsters argue and brag and wrestle with each other, vying for the honour of being his bedmate that night. Occasionally Spynie thought sentimentally about young Christie Hume who had died in the summer, drowned while drunk in a river. He also thought wistfully about the beautiful young Lord Hume. He always wanted the next thing, the new thing, someone fresh.

It was clear to him that she had thwarted him again, that bloody woman the old man was married to, Lady Elizabeth Widdrington. She had thwarted him in the summer when he had wanted revenge on the new English Deputy Warden who had dared to come after him with a sword when all he was doing was offering that remarkably handsome Graham boy the chance of bettering himself. She had now thwarted him again at the top of Jedburgh tower and that was not to be borne. That needed action. He didn't know or care whether the bitch had let Carey into her hellmouth, though he assumed that she had, but he did know that they were sweet on each other which made them both nicely vulnerable.

He was trying to bring the threads of his plots together and his high forehead wrinkled as he looked into the fireplace. Like many blond men with fine clear skin, he was ageing rapidly, not helped by the white lead he used to hide his occasional pimples.

The oldest young man, a doddering greybeard of nineteen, noticed and glanced across at the two fifteen-year-olds, matched twins, bought from the slums of Edinburgh. They moved into the corner, picked up two lutes and started to play softly.

Spynie liked music and he liked being catered to, but what he was about was taking some serious thinking.

First, of course, there was Hughie Elliot, or Tyndale as he called himself. So far he was the best of the lot. That eminently useful and helpful man called Jonathan Hepburn had found him and used him for a couple of little jobs and found he was good at both his trades, the tailoring and the killing. Hepburn got him to London where Carey had been embroiled in some family problem, but had failed to insert him into Carey's service. However when he sent Hughie to Oxford, Carey had snapped up a tailor who could also fight like a trout a fly.

The brow wrinkled again. According to Hughie, somebody had nearly succeeded in killing Carey at Oxford, which Hughie had regarded as a personal insult. Spynie wondered about that: he didn't mind who killed the man or how, he wasn't fussy that way, he just wanted him dead. Now Hughie had gone a bit quiet despite being quite close in Carlisle and in Carey's sevice, which gave him multiple opportunities. Perhaps a visit was due? Or no need, because Carey was bringing his servants to Edinburgh with him, according to rumour. That was for the very fine opportunity of the Disputation. The King had thought that up for himself, but when Spynie learned that Carey had invited himself along, he was overjoyed.

So he could be sure to twist the knife in Lady Widdrington, he had enthusiastically backed the King's desire to invite Sir Henry and his wife to Edinburgh as well as the enormous spotty lump of Sir Henry's eldest son. And now Hepburn had reported by letter that he had just suborned Sergeant Dodd, Carey's best henchman, so it was looking even better for Spynie.

There was a loud knock on the door and Sir Henry came in when one of the younger boys opened it for him.

Sir Henry was becoming a bore in Spynie's opinion, though he still found it tickled him to get such doggy looks from the old man. He came into the parlour wearing his Court suit of black brocade with a ruff, his corrugated ears and bulbous nose making him look troll-like.

"My Lord Spynie!" said Sir Henry delightedly, as if there could be any surprise at finding him taking his ease in his own parlour. "D'ye want to go hunting with the King tomorrow?"

Spynie brightened up. The weather had been terrible, so bad you couldn't even play golf.

"Yes," he said, "is he asking for me?"

"No," said Sir Henry, "he just said anyone who fancied some sport could come with him."

Spynie did his best not to look disappointed. Gone were the days when His Highness would tickle his ear and invite him by name and then they would sneak off from the usual disorderly throng and go and disport themselves in the coverts.

"Ah, well," he said, trying to be philosophical.

Sir Henry came and sat down near Spynie and took the cup

of wine from the littlest boy, drained it, held out the silver cup for more.

"I'll go," he said. "He's hunting *par force de chiens* and I love that, though it plays merry hell with my gout."

Spynie really didn't care about Sir Henry's gout but smiled at him anyway. "It's certain Carey is on his way with this tooth-drawing philosopher His Highness is so excited about?"

"Ay, he's just arrived. Reason for the hunt, in fact."

Suppressing his annoyance at not being told this first, Spynie said "Good. Then I'll come."

Sir Henry grinned wolfishly. "When are you going to kill him?"

"I'm not sure yet, I want to make sure of him," lied Spynie because he never told anyone that kind of thing.

"Poison?"

"Possibly. I haven't decided yet."

"I want my bitch of a wife to be watching."

"Sir Henry," said Spynie, quite annoyed, "do ye want the man dead or do you not? So long as he dies, I dinna care how it happens and if he falls off his horse and breaks his neck tomorrow I will be just as happy as if I had put white arsenic in his wine myself. Happier because no one will think to blame me."

Though now he came to think of it, that might make a good end for Carey, even better than having Hughie do it. He tapped his teeth and stared vaguely into space while he thought how you might achieve a tragic fall while riding to hounds for one particular man and no one else. There were ways and means. Which would be best?

Sir Henry's fond smile at him annoyed him though he didn't show it. "Ay, ye're right," said Sir Henry with a sigh. "It's a good thing ye've got the brains."

"Yes," said Spynie, slightly mollified. "Where is she, your wife I mean?"

"Buttering up the Queen, so I heard," said Sir Henry with the scowl his face always wore when he thought of his wife. "And learning Danish, God save us. I've not missed her."

"Just so long as she doesn't interfere again," said Spynie, also scowling. The stupid bitch's interference in the summer was a large part of the reason why Spynie was not now drinking the King's wine in the King's Privy Parlour and kissing the King long and lingering on the mouth. For some inexplicable reason the King had not liked their proceedings at all. You would think the disgusting Englishman was some kind of relative. Worse, it had somehow turned the King personally against Spynie as though it was all Spynie's fault. He still hoped to get back in the King's good graces and in his bed, but the old delightful intimacy was not there any more and nor did the King laugh at Spynie's jokes, which annoyed him because he worked hard at them.

Just for a moment Spynie toyed with the idea of seducing Sir Henry. Probably he would have to get him drunk first because Spynie suspected the old man was still a virgin that way and then…But his stomach always rebelled because Sir Henry was such an ugly old man. Useful but old and gouty and might well turn squeamish too. No, tonight it would be Jeremy, who was in the full flower of his so-temporary masculine beauty and was not at all a virgin, nor squeamish.

Also recently Sir Henry had started smelling of old piss which Spynie didn't approve of at all. The King smelled terrible too but there was something exciting in that, an animal smell like a boar.

Still Sir Henry was useful, remember that, and while Spynie was not the King's Minion any more he needed useful people totally devoted to him and his interests. He wondered again who was the King's latest—or did he have one? Spynie hadn't noticed anyone new at Court who was pretty enough despite the way powerful nobles brought likely boys and lads in their family to Court to see if they could catch the King's eye, just as they would with their daughters if he had been interested in women. They were wasting their time with the boys, James was not interested in children either.

Spynie smiled at Jeremy, beckoned him over and kissed him on the mouth, a sign that the choice of the evening was made.

Some naughty spirit made him say to Sir Henry, "Would you like to take one of my boys as your bedfellow, Sir Henry?"

And bless the old man, he looked puzzled and said, "No, I prefer to sleep alone because of my gout. Thank you." Was that a look of panic under the puzzlement?

The twins were still assiduously playing the lute but the two new boys, one only eight, looked at each other and the eight-year-old shuddered. Poor ugly old man, no one wanted him.

Spynie beckoned the youngest two boys over and told them to clear away the food but leave the wine.

He had the beginnings of a plan now and he decided to ask young Matthew, one of his henchmen, to fetch him Jonathan Hepburn. He thought the plan quite a good one and felt a tickle of excitement at the base of his stomach, the feeling he got when he was removing someone who stood in his way. Carey would be dead in a couple of days.

◇◇◇

Early next morning, Carey took Anricks off with him to the best mercer in town where he dallied for what seemed to Anricks like several hours over different kinds of damask and taffeta and velvet. Then he went to the best tailor in town, as recommended by Maitland where Anricks made good on his promise to buy Carey a new Court suit in the latest Scottish fashion, despite the eye-watering price of nine hundred-ninety pounds Scots, including the cloth.

Carey then was very completely measured and since he hadn't used that tailor before, Mr Arbroath the Master tailor, promised him a shell in coarse linen by the following day, before they even spoke about the fabric or the trim which Carey hadn't been able to decide on at the mercer's.

And it was on the way back from the tailor with Carey still burbling on about some damask from the Low Countries which had taken his eye and was even more wonderful than some other damask and leafing through about twenty swatches that all seemed very similar, when it happened.

The first thing that Anricks noticed was that the tailoring related burble had stopped and the next thing he noticed was that Carey had also stopped in the middle of the Linenmarket.

In fact he was standing stock still so the Edinburgh crowds had to part for him, his face shining with happiness.

Anricks followed where he was looking and found a little group of richly dressed ladies, who had just come out of the milliners' street and were talking in a mixture of a Germanic-sounding language Anricks didn't know, and broken Scotch as they walked along.

In the middle of them was Lady Widdrington, gravely repeating something like a verse, her face relaxed and remarkably pretty, in her usual severe doublet-style bodice and kirtle and with a fur trimmed black velvet gown over the top, her cap covering her hair and a not quite fashionable hat on top.

She felt someone's eyes upon her, looked round and saw Carey.

First she stared back and her face too lit up so it was as though two invisible sunbeams were spearing down from the grey sky to light their faces alone. One of the maidens with loose fair hair elbowed another blonde in a married woman's cap and hat, and the whole gaggle of them also stopped.

Carey was the first to recover the use of his wits and he bowed low and elegantly to all of the ladies, who of course curtseyed back in a group, except for Lady Widdrington who was two seconds behind the others.

Then Carey strode over and asked Lady Widdrington to introduce him to so many beautiful ladies, and were they the Danish Queen's ladies and how wonderful it was that they were and how did they like Scotland?

It was well done, thought Anricks, for he did not really speak to Lady Widdrington at all once the introductions were made. Yet he found out that Lady Widdrington was currently staying with the Queen's household, and where that was and regretted that the Queen wasn't a good rider and so would not ride to hounds in the hunt the day after, and finally dragged Anricks into introductions as the philosopher who would be disputing on the movements of the heavenly spheres. Most of the girls shuddered at the idea of the Earth moving instead of the Sun, except for one who remarked that she knew of an astrologer living on an island who was studying that very thing.

And then Carey made his bows again and the girls all curtseyed, the maidens all made eyes at Carey, and off they went. The minute they turned the corner, Carey scowled and led the way to a boozing ken where he sat and called for double-double ale for both of them.

Anricks was agreeable and took a pull of his ale which he found quite strange tasting now he was used to hopped Bristol beer. Carey stared into space, then turned to him.

"You know of course that Lady Elizabeth Widdrington is the woman I am going to marry?"

"Yes, I know, Sir Robert. If I didn't know before, which I did, I would have known at once from your faces."

Carey smiled briefly. "However," he said, "the fact that Lady Widdrington is here in Edinburgh means that her foul husband, Sir Henry, is also infallibly here, which is very bad news for me and quite a problem for you."

"How so?"

"Sir Henry and Lord Spynie are normally in cahoots as the Scots say and they want…"

"To kill you. Yes, I had surmised something of the sort."

"Do you not see that as a problem?"

"Sir Robert, I don't. If they succeed in killing you, I shall be sorry but I will continue with my disputation as a means of getting close enough to King James to find out his thoughts on the Catholic plan against Scotland, if it exists." Carey smiled. "And if they do not succeed in killing you, why then, I shall continue with my disputation with your help. I don't see your putative murder as affecting me greatly, one way or the other."

Carey chuckled. "Philosophy?"

Anricks smiled too. "And if I should unfortunately get killed in mistake for you, or die of plague or in a bear attack or some such, then I expect Sir Robert Cecil will find some other poor fool to dig into the matter. I doubt we are as important as we think we are."

Carey raised his jack to Anricks and they both drank.

"However it is also philosophical to take precautions and this puts a different complexion on tomorrow's hunt."

Carey raised his brows. "You think Sir Henry and Lord Spynie will try something?"

"Of course they will, it is a golden opportunity. Men such as you, Sir Robert, break their necks while hunting every day of the week and I would imagine, Lord Spynie's men are prospecting for a convenient place as we speak."

"Yes."

"We should sit and draw up a list of likely ways they might try to kill you at the hunt—I would also advise a gorget under your doublet."

"It'll be infernally uncomfortable."

"Not as uncomfortable as a wire snare pulling tight on your bare neck, which I regard as second only to a rope between two trees in likelihood."

"True."

Anricks finished his drink and smacked his lips judiciously. "I see this not as the kind of murder where they come after you mobhanded—or not yet. More a sneak attack."

"Well neither of my servants can ride well enough so it will have to be Sergeant Dodd at my back, despite the fact that someone has bought him."

"Perhaps I could do something to the purpose as well," said Anricks, "although I am not sure what."

"Will you come hunting, Mr Anricks?"

"Certainly not, sir. I am a philosopher and it is a well-known fact that philosophers do not hunt. Mr Napier does not either."

"Why is that?"

"Chase after a pack of hounds, all day, on horseback, risking your neck although no one is trying to kill you—most unphilosophical. And besides philosophy is in itself a kind of hunt as we follow the tracks of the vagrant thought and search the coverts for the scent of the white hart of truth."

Carey applauded. "Nicely put," he said. "Will you use that in your speech?"

"I might," said Anricks, "but I was going to start with a disquisition mathematical on the differences between the Ptolemaic and the Copernican systems. Mr Napier was helping me with it yesterday evening."

"Mathematical?"

"Yes, you know, if there is a language of the universe, a language of the angels as Dr Dee calls it, I am certain it is mathematics. Sure, that's the language the Almighty speaks, as Maimonides says."

"And there I was praying in English. Or should it be Latin?"

"There is an argument for speaking Latin or Greek or even Hebrew to the Almighty so we remember He is unlike us, being eternal and all powerful, whereas we are short-lived as mayflies in comparison, and puny. Normally I think English is as good a language as any to speak to the Almighty in and comes as easily to my tongue as the Portuguese."

Carey nodded. "Personally," he said cautiously, because philosophers are notoriously sensitive, "I would keep the *Art Mathematica* to an absolute minimum since His Highness understands nothing of it, and use words."

"Oh," Anricks looked crestfallen, "are you sure? They say he's very clever. I wrote something of my disputation late last night, inspired by Mr Napier's wonderful new numbers, with the mathematics laid out very simply and clearly…though indeed there is something odd about…"

"May I see it?"

Anricks pulled some crumpled sheets of paper out of his sleeve pocket and handed them to Carey, who squinted, frowned, tried the sheets the other way up and focussed on them for a while.

"I'm sorry," he said at last, "my arithmetic is good enough for siegework and artillery and playing cards, but I can't make out any of this."

"Really?" said Anricks in a huffy tone of voice, "I thought it was all a bit easy."

Carey coughed. "Well maybe for you, but I am certain that His Highness will make even less of it than I did and if you try to win your dispute with mathematics, you are doomed."

"But Sir Robert, as Dr Dee says, the world is written in mathematics…"

"Yes, but His Highness doesn't speak Mathematics. You would be better saying it in Dutch."

"But that is the point, number is a universal language that needs no translation, once you understand the concepts…"

"Mr Anricks," said Carey gently and firmly, "since I may have my neck broken for me tomorrow, take heed of me today. Trust me, His Highness will be at best bewildered and at worst bored. Find a way to translate it into good Scots at least."

"But…Oh, very well!" And pettishly Anricks went out and threw the sheets of paper into the kennel running down the middle of the lane.

They stood and walked down through the town to Holyrood House—nobody but a fool would try to get a horse through the streets of Edinburgh just before Christmas. It was like London.

Back in the street they had just left, the boy who had been shadowing Carey and Anricks, carefully picked the sheets of paper out of the kennel, wiped the worst of it off on his breeks and trotted after them into the palace and gave them to one of Lord Spynie's men.

"I'm certain sure it's in cipher, sir," said the boy excitedly, completely forgetting Carey and Anricks' prior conversation, "like the Pastor was telling us, or maybe alchemy or astrology cos it isnae normal, is it?"

Lord Spynie's man gave the boy a Scotch shilling and put the sheets away in his wallet. It looked like witchcraft to him. He didn't think Carey was anything except a good Protestant, but you never knew with philosophers.

◇◇◇

Dodd was in an old storeroom that still smelled faintly of cheese and was made cramped by multiple shelves, but already had a bed and truckle in it. He gave Bangtail and Sandy the bed and took the truckle for himself, because he didn't want to sleep next to his brother who was a notorious kicker and roller-over and besides, he was still annoyed with him. Leamus, the Irish deserter, looked around, clearly decided against asking to sleep with Dodd, wandered out in his loose-limbed way and wandered back with a palliasse, a pair of sheets, and a blanket. He cleared a bit of floor of rushes, inspected the wall and floor minutely, put the rushes back and placed the palliasse equally carefully on top, tucked in the pair of sheets and blankets and then wandered out again. Dodd put his doublet and hose from Oxford on a shelf, hoping it wouldn't get too cheesifyed, got into the truckle and turned away from the bed so he could sleep.

But he couldn't. Bangtail and Sandy talked for a while and then went to sleep. Leamus came back with a loaf of bread and a pottle of ale which he put on another shelf, undressed quietly, folded his jerkin for a pillow, muttered to himself for a while and then got into his bed and fell asleep. Had he been praying? Dodd shrugged. He didn't care if the man was Catholic or Protestant or both, so long as he did what he was told, which so far Leamus always had.

However he had a problem because Carey had bidden him to the hunt tomorrow and Hepburn had stopped him around the back of the stable block and said he could go but must drop back once the silver trumpets began to blow. It added more bad feelings to the brawl inside him because it went against his grain to betray a man like that. It was as if the dependable black ball of rage was still familiarly there but on top of it sat something green and growing like grass that said he shouldn't do it, despite Carey being the man who let the Elliots get away—despite all that, he shouldn't do it.

Next morning, Leamus was up first and brought in a bowl of water for them to wash in. He carved the bread into four hunks, produced a round cheese from Bessie from his pack, and poured out ale into their horn cups. Everyone was astonished at this and said thank you to him, at which he smiled a little and said, "My da' always said that any fool can be uncomfortable. It takes a clever man to be comfortable." That was the longest sentence anyone had heard him say since the silly comment about Englishmen having tails, and then he went silent again.

Dodd took the largest hunk of bread and cheese and drank the ale but said nothing, feeling ill. It wasn't just the morning being morning, he had slept badly. So he was even more wooden and silent when it came time to go and meet Carey, found both of them had been given one of King James' Arab crosses each to ride in the hunt, and almost forgot himself to talk about the beautiful bay animal, which annoyed him again.

She was beautiful, though, and he patted the arched neck and blew into the nostrils which horses liked, and admired the compact shape of her body and her delicate hooves. Would she be nimble enough in the forest—the shape of her and her short back promised speed, but how would she do with loose footing?

Carey was inspecting his chestnut gelding too, passing his hands down the legs, lifting the hooves, feeling the hindquarters and getting nudged a couple of times for carrots, which he hadn't got. "Oh you *are* beautiful," said Carey to the horse, patting his neck and grinned delightedly across at Dodd. "These will go like the wind, Sergeant, you'll see."

He couldn't help a small smile in return, because this was a horse of a completely different nature to a hobby; even Whitesock would look awkward next to her. So it was true that the King had a wonderful stud at Falkland palace with Arab stallions and the Grahams hadn't got the best of the herd.

At the meet, there was a milling confusion of men and horses and servants and mounted attendants like Dodd, a cart full of musicians and a train of packhorses with the vittles. Spynie was there in his smart intricately cutworked black leather jerkin worn over a red doublet to show off the cutwork to advantage. There was a looming redheaded man in a feathered bonnet and a velvet doublet on a large handsome horse with some charger in him, whom Carey pointed out as George Gordon, the Earl of Huntly. Dodd knew the Lord Maxwell with his monobrow of course, and three more Maxwells at his back who were arguing loudly about whether a buck could be got to fight a horse and which would win.

Typically Carey, who was wearing his second-best suit, the hunting green, rode straight into the middle of them, bowed all around and asked after Lord Maxwell's beautiful Irish wolfhounds.

"Och, they're somewhere about," said Lord Maxwell, looking for them. "They're the best deerhounds in the country, of course I'd bring them. There they are!" He whistled and a boy ran over holding the four leashes with the wolfhounds trotting gravely behind him. They smelled Carey and let him lean right down from the saddle to pull their ears, smelled Dodd and left him alone. Lord Maxwell's smile changed from honest pride in his dogs to a courtier's smile, and Carey smiled back so all was as dishonest as could be.

"How's the West March of England?" asked Maxwell.

"Remarkably peaceful for the time of year," said Carey with a knowing grin, "which is to say not peaceful at all since it's the raiding season. I found a lot of cattle in Liddesdale on patrol last week and also saw off a Graham ambush."

"Ay, I heard," said the Maxwell dismissively. "Any of them mine?"

"We found no Maxwell or Herries brands," said Carey blandly, since he knew that Maxwell was careless about branding his beasts, "So, no. I am surprised to see you here at all, my lord."

"Oh? Why? The King likes me again."

"Of course, my lord," said Carey very smoothly, "but didn't the Johnstones just raid a lot of your horses from near Lochmaben?"

Lord Maxwell scowled. "Ah hadnae heard that," he growled.

"Oh, my mistake, probably just a rumour. Could I trouble you to arrange a Warden's Day, my lord? It's now sixteen years since we had one in the West March and well past time for one."

The Maxwell, who had only agreed to be the Warden so he could use the office against the Johnstones, nodded vaguely, "Ay, we should, o' course."

Trumpets sounded at the King's approach with his own attendants and Carey turned his horse to face in that direction.

"How's the Deputy Warden, Sir Richard Lowther?" asked the Maxwell, with heavy meaning.

"Well, I know he has gout, poor man," said Carey with false sympathy, "which never improves any man's temper, and of course for some reason he is not at all pleased that I have just received my warrant from the Queen as Deputy Warden and so we have to work together." Carey favoured the Maxwell with a particularly happy smile and trotted away, glancing back once to see the Maxwell impatiently beckon another Herries cousin and send him off with a verbal message.

Dodd knew it wasn't true about the Johnstone raiding the Maxwell's horses and thought Carey had said that purely to spoil the man's sport for him. He trotted after Carey and set himself behind him to the left, glad he hadn't worn his jack or helmet as no one else had one.

The King rode into the clearing and everyone took his hat off and at least bent the neck to him. The King was in a dark purple doublet and hose and high leather boots which disguised the fact that he had had rickets as a child—quite mildly compared with Sir Robert Cecil—it just meant he was shaped like a tadpole with broad shoulders and puny legs.

"Och, what a goodly show!" he said to the assembled company. "We'll have some sport today." His sweaty grubby face with traces of breakfast egg in his beard beamed upon them because King James was never so happy as when he was pursuing deer across country at a gallop.

If he had been inclined to talk to anyone, Dodd would nevertheless have been struck dumb at the beauty of James' horse, a wonderful grey with a high arching neck and a high pace, a pure Arab and perhaps the father of Dodd's own mount, since he was a stallion.

"Och," he said, struck to the heart at it. It was too much, he almost had tears in his eyes as he watched the beautiful beast prance and sidestep while the King spoke to each of his nobles in turn.

"I think His Highness calls his horse Whitey," said Carey quietly in his ear. "Something about not letting him get too big-headed."

Dodd almost cracked a smile, but remembered and just said "Ay," and carried on staring hungrily at the animal. Carey shook his head in amusement and moved away.

To start with it was all milling about as the dogs cast around for the scent and the younger ones became excited about rabbits and snapped at other dogs they didn't like and the Master of Hounds used his whip to break up a dogfight that broke out over by the musicians' cart.

Carey sat his horse and watched patiently. If he had been riding Sorrel he would have let the reins loose so the horse could cast around in case there was anything a hobby could eat in the bare winter forest. However he was riding a horse he didn't know, so he kept them tight and discouraged any messing about by the horse. He didn't really need to: the horse had been beautifully schooled. Dodd was nearby on his own part-Arab and Carey had to admire the way his body went with the horse and controlled her without even thinking about it. He didn't even know what a centaur he was.

Yet Dodd's face was stony and dour, and not from its natural set. Silence and rage breathed out of Dodd like a smell—maybe it was a smell, since the wolfhounds hadn't done more than greet him. It looked like he wasn't going to forgive Carey any time soon.

Suddenly the hounds all moved together and gave tongue, and they were off across country, streaming out in a long comet's tail around the King, a couple of trumpets calling. It was a short run; they caught some young rascals with just a couple of points against a deerfence, and the forward hounds pulled them down and killed them and then the whole pack gave tongue again and went after something new.

Carey was keeping up with the King, a few ranks back as was suitable, with Dodd sticking to his back like an ugly limpet. He was watching all the people around the King, had seen Spynie quite a long way from the centre and found a shifting population of tough Border earls. There went Kerr of Cessford, and Earl Hume, and one or two handsome young men, but no one figure staying close to the King.

So the King hadn't found a new minion yet, eh? Carey thought back to his own youth without regret—Lord, what an innocent he had been. He looked around behind him, saw Dodd as usual behind him, saw the beaters running behind the horses and thought he glimpsed Bangtail running among them, but then lost him again behind some trees covered with ivy.

There was a knot of nobles all shouting at each other and the Earl of Huntly burst out of the middle of them, his face alight, and galloped hell for leather after the King whose white horse was floating ahead like a speedy cloud, ripping through undergrowth and leaping brooks as if his hooves didn't quite touch the ground. It was easy to forget, but in fact the King was a superb horseman and not at all shy when in the saddle hunting, although he was notoriously frightened of knives and guns, which his aggressive subjects thought very strange. As a result of this eccentricity, none of the nobles were armed with anything more than hunting knives, nobody had any kind of gun, swords were absent, of course, even crossbows were only in the hands of a few men-at-arms to finish off anything more dangerous than a deer.

Huntly had caught up with the King and shouted something at him and the King turned his mount on a sixpence and came back to the stand of trees where everybody was waiting for the hounds to find the scent again. He happened to be near Carey and brought his horse prancing alongside and beamed at him.

"Sir Robert Carey, what a pleasure to see ye again, cousin, how is Carlisle?"

"Still there," said Carey drily which made His Highness laugh.

"Ye've brought yer tooth-drawing philosopher, have ye not?" Carey bowed. "Ma Court's in need of a philosopher. Lord knows, we hae a sufficiency of dominies and ministers but not a whiff of a philosopher, apart from a couple of mathematicians. How's he shaping?"

As if Anricks was a hunting dog, thought Carey, highly amused. "Well, Your Majesty," he said, "he is working on the first part of his dissertation."

"Ah, excellent. He's no' here, is he?"

"No, Your Majesty, he says it's a well-known fact that philosophers do not ride to hounds but spend their time hunting in mental coverts, pursuing the white hart of truth wheresoever he may flee."

King James laughed again, he loved flights of rhetoric, which was why Carey had unblushingly stolen Anricks' trope. "Och, that's pretty. I havenae got a proper philosopher to dispute wi' him so I'm thinking I may take the job maself."

"Your Majesty is an extraordinary prince," said Carey, his heart sinking. "Is there another ruler in Chistendom that could be able to do such a thing?"

"Mebbe, mebbe not," said King James complacently, "but I dearly love a good intellectual argument so...Och, my Lord Huntly, are ye back, what did ye catch?"

"Only a few does, Your Highness," said Huntly, some twigs in his hair and his hat over his ear. "I let them go. There's a full crop of staggards and rascals in this forest and no need for killing the women." He turned and winked at Carey for some reason and laughed.

"Ay, ye're right."

They were waiting for the hounds to take the scent again and Carey imagined the frenetic activity behind the copses and deerfences as previously captured deer were released from cages and driven towards the King and his party.

And then the King spotted something himself and they were off again, a little group of stags running before them, flashing their rumps in and out of the trees. There went the King, Huntly, shouting and singing, the Maxwell, Spynie…Spynie was looking over his shoulder at something and Carey looked over his own shoulder to see what it was. Nothing there was more interesting than holly bushes. He kicked his horse to a gallop and followed the leaders, heard the clear cold tones of silver trumpets in the distance, felt rather than saw that Dodd had suddenly fallen back. There were two attendants on either side of him, keeping pace with him, forcing him slightly off course. He was headed for a copse that was clear of undergrowth. Spynie was still breaking his neck to look back at Carey and now Huntly was as well. Suddenly Carey went icy.

The wonderful horse was galloping too fast to stop quickly so as he passed between the first two trees, he hunkered right down to the horse's neck, felt something swipe his hat off, tried to slow the horse, took his feet out of the stirrups, felt rather than saw something else and felt the horse lift in a desperate effort to get over whatever it was, but wrongfooted and the back legs tangled in something. With a panicky scream the horse went over sideways and Carey just managed to jump clear out of the saddle and roll into a hollybush.

As he lay there winded and surrounded by prickles, Carey saw Bangtail run past followed by Red Sandy, straight into the holly patch and into a fight, which bashed to and fro until Bangtail's head and shoulders suddenly appeared between the bushes, dealing a wonderful headbutt on his opponent's face which produced a fountain of blood from a mashed nose. Red Sandy emerged from the prickles on the other side and caught the man nicely behind the ear with a cosh that he then politely put away in his jerkin. The two of them dragged the man out between them with holly leaves in their hair.

"The other one ran," said Red Sandy breathlessly as he passed.

Somehow the King was there, looking thoughtfully down at him from his grey.

"Sir Robert, ye've lost your hat."

Then he looked at the crashing in the brambles where the horse was trying to get up and a strange look of terror crossed his face. "*T'il est haut!*" he shouted and galloped off immediately to the group of nobles, including Huntly, trotting up behind him, galloped between them and rode on ahead as they turned their horses and whipped them to a gallop behind him. If he hadn't been the King, Carey would almost have thought he was fleeing from something terrible, fleeing for his life. But no, surely not. Kings don't do that.

Carey was still crowing for breath but started picking his way out of the hollybush which seemed determined to hang onto him like something out of a ballad about the Faeries, and made half a dozen holes in him every time he moved.

Wheezing, he fought clear of it and staggered over to where his horse was flailing about in the winter brambles, both his hind legs caught in some kind of thick wire. One leg was at an ugly angle and another of the attendants was standing there, staring but not doing anything.

Carey caught the panicking great head and put his weight onto the forequarters which weren't injured although the hooves were kicking. He held the head, muttering sweet nothings until the animal had calmed a little and then looked along the beautiful ruined body to where one of the foresters had come up and was examining his hindquarters carefully. Scored in two places by what had tripped him, both his back legs were still tangled in the wire and one of his legs was clearly broken. The forester looked up and shook his head slowly, reached in his pack and pulled out a crossbow.

Carey had only met the horse an hour before, but still his heart hurt for the stupid destruction of such a lovely animal. He didn't even know his name. So he held the horse's head tightly, whispered more endearments in his ears and put a hand over his eyes as the forester came up, aimed the crossbow at the centre of the chestnut forehead and loosed the bolt. After that there was only a shudder and the usual smell of shit and the glorious horse was knacker's meat.

Carey's heart was still thumping and so he waited a minute before he let go and stood up and found Dodd standing nearby with his statute cap off in respect.

His hands were shaking too, more for rage than for fear because he knew exactly who had caused the fall and how. He went over to the man Red Sandy had coshed who was still unconscious and kicked him to check, then went back to where the rope had been and finally discovered his wounded hat. He also found the rope still there, tied at neck height between two trees and looked very carefully at it before he untied it and took it down.

"Och," said Dodd a little way away, his face stricken for a moment. He still had his mount, who was tethered to a tree a little way off and neighing anxiously in the direction of the knacker's meat. Mother and son, perhaps?

"Here we are," he said, the rope under his arm, as he untangled the wire from the horse's legs. He chucked the rope at Red Sandy. "Nice little trap, rope first which I ducked under and then a double wire at the horse's chest height. He tried to jump it, but…" His voice suddenly seized up and he stopped, had to breathe carefully in and out a couple of times. "Not possible," he finished bleakly, staring straight at Dodd who was examining the ground in front of him.

"All right, ye!" said Red Sandy to the man he had caught, whose hands he was roping behind him. The man was coming to but was still googly eyed. "Who paid ye?"

"S…Spynie is m…my good lord…" came the mutter which only confirmed what Carey already knew. Who else had been craning his neck, looking to see him fall? No one. Apart from the Earl of Huntly whom Spynie could have told.

More attendants were coming up with a cart, and a slide. They roped up the dead horse's back legs and dragged the body onto the cart and then closed the back, touched up the carthorse and trotted off in the direction of Holyrood House and the kennels most probably. It wasn't so unusual for a horse or even a man to be killed in the hunt, what was unusual was the means.

"Sir, are ye hurt bad?" asked a gruff voice, and there was another attendant, an elderly man with a bag full of bandages.

"No, no, I'm not," admitted Carey, after a look all over himself. Holly scratches aplenty and bruising on his shoulder and back where he had hit the ground when he rolled, but nothing worse. "Do you have another mount for me?"

"Ay sir," said the man, beckoning up a young groom with a fresh horse for Carey. Not an Arab this time, but a perfectly respectable hunter. What Carey wanted to do was have a drink but that seemed out of the question. Or maybe not.

"Do ye have any brandy?" he asked the man who seemed to be some kind of surgeon. A shy smile lit the man's face.

"Ay sir, would ye prefer aqua vitae or whishke bee?"

"I'll have the whishke bee, if I may, goodman."

There was a look of approval and a small flask was produced which Carey drank from and nodded because it was very good, though not as smoky as the stuff he had drunk in Carlisle. More of an earthy taste.

"All right," he said to the young groom, checked the bit, the girth and then swung himself up and adjusted the stirrups. "Sergeant!"

Dodd was already mounted again and his face returned to its usual granite.

"We'll see if we can catch the King again," said Carey. "Bangtail and Red Sandy, thank you very much for catching that bastard... Was it Mr Anricks that suggested you come along as beaters?"

"Ay," said Red Sandy, "and he paid us forebye, he's a nice man and sensible. Said we wis tae try tae stop ye breaking yer neck."

"Well, take the man back to Holyrood House and put him in a storeroom for the moment. I don't think my Lord Spynie is likely to try anything more against me now."

Bangtail knuckled his statute cap and they started trotting the man back to the palace. "Och, ye can run or we'll set light tae yer breeks," Carey heard one of them say at the man's protests as they disappeared between the trees.

Carey looked long and hard at Dodd who said nothing. And so he put his heels in and galloped off after the King and his nobles who had left a trail behind them.

◇◇◇

The man who said his name was Jonathan Hepburn was extremely angry. As far as he could tell from a couple of foresters he had paid, the idiot Lord Spynie had made an attempt on Carey's life, botched it, and then left the English Deputy Warden with a prisoner who could say who had arranged for a rope and two wires to be stretched across the man's path. Worse still, Spynie had asked Hepburn to tell Sergeant Dodd to hang back at the silver trumpets but had not explained why. As he had done as he had been asked, that meant that Dodd could say Hepburn had been part of the plot against Carey, which in fact he hadn't, since he had come up with a new use for the mad Courtier and needed him alive for the moment.

He was tired of working for Spynie in any case since the man was often stingy and ungrateful. He didn't need the ex-minion any more, since he was now working directly for his Catholic Majesty, and had two bills of exchange from the King of Spain, one of which he had turned into a tidy sum of money at the Steelyard, where they gave him a better rate. He had got rid of Dixon as well, since the man was stupid as well as aggressive.

Spynie came back from the hunt early and found him and begged him to do something about the man Carey's men-at-arms had just captured. Hepburn was tempted to tell Spynie to do it himself, but didn't on the grounds that information was like gold and you didn't give it away. Instead he looked through the maze of old abbey storerooms, disturbed a clerk at a standing desk who said Hughie would most likely be in Sir Robert Carey's rooms working on his clothes. So he went to find Hughie Tyndale who was sitting crosslegged on a table in the old infirmary, sewing away with a will on Carey's new Court suit. Hughie lifted his head and smiled as Hepburn came in.

"Och," he said, "it's nice tae see ye again, sir, though I've not killt Carey yet…"

"No, that's fine," Hepburn answered, "I don't want you to kill him at the minute, I've got another job for you."

"What's that, sir? Will I kill anybody else for ye?"

"Yes," said Hepburn and saw Hughie grin and smack his lips. "I need something tidied up."

They talked for a while about how best to do it and after a while, Hughie came back from a poke around and said he'd found the locked storeroom but didn't have the key. He picked up a leather bag from the corner as he went. Hepburn took a quiet look around the place, found no key, but had some skeleton keys he had found useful in the past. Hughie was curious and interested and so they both went to the storeroom. Hepburn banged on the door, heard a doleful, "Yes, sir."

"We've come fra Lord Spynie to help you," said Hughie, grinning.

"Good," said the man in relief.

Hepburn went through a few of the keys, found one that worked. Hughie Tyndale unlaced his sleeves and rolled his shirt-sleeves up, opened his bag, put on a voluminous blue butcher's apron over his clothes, went in with his favourite thin wire with wooden handles. There was a brief struggle and a glottal sound and then Hughie came out again, showing thumbs up. Hepburn took a glance and saw the man's head almost off and blood everywhere, didn't see the need to check any further, and locked the place up again. Hughie carefully took his butcher's apron off and wiped his garotte with a clean corner. Then he left the apron stuffed into a hole in the wall they passed where there was an airbrick. There was not a speck of blood on Hughie's clothes anywhere, which was quite impressive and so Hepburn paid him and Hughie put his wire back in his pocket and sauntered off whistling tunelessly, to the tiny suburb around the northern corner of the Edinburgh walls which was apparently where the tarts could be found.

And then Hepburn went to the main hall of Holyrood House, slipped in at the back and drank some wine, watching as some of the servants rolled around completely drunk, just like the King of an evening, and some of the henchmen got in a dagger-stabbing game that they were all very good at, stabbing between their fingers faster and faster. Idiots.

Most of the Court was off hunting with the King, but the Queen didn't hunt. And killing excited him, made him feel the power of the Demiurge flowing through him, made him want a woman.

He went into the gardens where Marguerite often walked in the afternoons. Usually they met late at night when everybody was asleep, but he needed her now. So he walked in the gardens, taking a tiny risk, passed Marguerite as she walked with some of the Queen's women, laughing and giggling, paused to wink at her once and then passed on, pretending not to know her.

Twenty minutes later she was trotting through the storerooms right at the back of the palace, where there were stables for visitors filled with ugly hobbies and a couple of good horses. Hepburn had spent the time waiting for her in checking his precious leaden tanks for leaks and found nothing, which relieved a worry. When he heard Marguerite's quick footsteps, he hid behind a door, then stepped out and caught her and she squeaked once, then melted into him and said things to him in Flemish which made him more excited.

He half-carried her into the unimportant looking storeroom where he had put the leaden tanks and the lead half globes when he had brought them a few weeks before. Then he unlaced himself with suddenly clumsy fingers, lifted her skirts and impaled her like a fish on a hook, set her back against the wall whilst she wrapped her stockinged legs around his kidneys and bucked and threshed until he bit her again and she cried out behind his careful hand over her mouth.

Hepburn and Marguerite stood like that for a few minutes while Hepburn got his breath back and Marguerite felt the glorious happiness washing through her that cleaned away Antwerp and made every risk worthwhile. Then Hepburn set her down and kissed her again with that smile of his that she loved, that said he was cleverer than anybody.

They were too experienced to speak. Hepburn picked up his hat which had fallen off in the heat of the moment, laced himself again, gave her one more kiss and walked out of the storeroom. Marguerite counted conscientiously to one hundred, made sure that she was tidy and had no telltale smears on her, and also walked away.

Behind them both, high up in the rafters and lying full length along one of the main beams was Young Hutchin, in a state of some excitement himself. He had to wait and deal with it before he could climb down from the place he had scrambled into when he had heard Hepburn coming. He jumped down onto one of the lead tanks which had given him a useful leg up to the rafters, straightened his clothes and went out, looking extremely smug. She was a pretty one, the blond woman, a bit old maybe, but juicy and she was wearing pretty clothes of brocade and velvet which meant she was important. He had been impressed with the whole thing. Could he hold a woman up like that and swive her? Not yet maybe, but he would one day. He let his imagination work on this for a while and had to visit the jakes on the way. God, the courtiers were a randy bunch—Carey had been at the women too, the Italian lady, when he had been at Court in Dumfries. One day, Young Hutchin promised himself, he would do it too and sooner rather than later because he honestly thought he might explode if he didn't.

◇◇◇

Anricks was still standing at his clerk's desk a couple of hours later with papers spread out in front of him. He had carefully unpicked the sewing on his packet from Poppy Burn, and then tried a number of different decoding methods on the carefully ciphered pieces of paper. Anricks still wasn't sure whether the text came from Poppy herself or somebody else but couldn't think who that somebody else could be or how they could meet with a woman who had taken her chamber. He had remembered to ask Roger Widdrington about Poppy's gossips and found she had no gossips in Widdrington and had only the girls in the house to look after her. No man had come near her since Sir Henry Widdrington had left.

So the text came from Poppy. Who had taught her to cipher and why? There was a dull itching of frustration under his breastbone because so far her cipher had utterly defeated him.

With the previous packets he had copied out the whole ciphered text very carefully and then delivered them where Poppy asked, sending the copy south to London to try if Sir Robert Cecil or Mr Phelippes could get any more from them than he could. As far as he knew, they hadn't.

He sat back and stretched his fingers. What was the index book? He shut his eyes and tried to imagine the shelves of books in Minister Burn's study, but no, that was the wrong place to look. Poppy Burn would need the book to hand, would need it now, in fact. He thought back to her chamber at Widdrington, thought of the book in her hand...No, that had been a book of sermons and quite new. The book she used would be older and well-worn...There was something. He pictured the little table with the pile of books, the one book lying off to the side, open...What was the frontispiece? A man with a bush over his shoulder...No, it was a schoolmaster holding a birch which was quite funny because Ascham argued eloquently that to get the best out of the pupils, the schoolmaster should not birch his charges too often.

His heart was thumping with excitement as he delved into his pack and found the book. Ascham's *The Schoolmaster*. A different copy and he hadn't read it yet, but he thought it was the same edition since it had the same picture at the front. His hands shaking slightly, he settled down to try what that would do.

Half an hour later he paced around the room stretching his fingers. He was sure it was the right one, even though it still didn't make sense because it didn't make sense in a way that wasn't random letters, there were repeated words—"und" for instance. She had used the book to give letters, not just words, page number, paragraph, word then the individual letters. Sometimes she used the same sequence of numbers for the same word which was bad practice but understandable if you were in a hurry.

At the end of the letter where you usually found the words that gave you your start was no name but a short word "liebe." He knew Latin, French, Italian, Spanish, Portuguese but no Allemayne and that was what he suspected the letter was in. Deutsch. Or perhaps a Scandinavian language since the Queen was Danish. Why Allemayne? He didn't speak it even badly which now annoyed him. He scowled at his careful copying, then sighed and packed up all the sheets of paper, put them back into the packet and sewed it up again with the same thread in the same holes, reattaching the seals with a knife heated in a candle. He would take it to the place Poppy had said, the Maker's Mark, Edinburgh, and see if he could catch a glimpse of the man who picked it up. He hadn't yet, because the man didn't come at a regular time.

Now he had to find someone who could translate the Deutsch for him, someone he could trust. That would have been simple in London or Bristol, but were there Deutschers in Scotland? And how was it Poppy Burn came to be using Deutsch? Surely the letter came from someone else? On one point he felt he could relax—most Allemaynes were Lutherans so, apart from the question of why packets of ciphered letters were going to and from the Scots Court at all, surely there wouldn't be anything too deadly in it?

So when Carey came back from his day's hunting, muddy and carrying his half-bent hat rather than wearing it, Anricks was eager to tell him the whole tale of the secret packets.

Carey was looking tired and sad, which was odd after a day spent hunting and had eaten in hall with the King so Anricks sent Hughie Tyndale down to the buttery to get him some ale and bread. Hughie was by contrast very happy and smelled of drink, but did the errand willingly enough.

"Yes," said Carey as Anricks cut the bread, said grace and thanks to the Almighty for it, and tucked into a slice of liver sausage he hoped wasn't pork and some pale winter butter. He didn't think the liver was pork, it was too strong flavoured, more venison. "Spynie had exactly the attempt at me you predicted, but two traps, a rope at head height for me and two wires at chest height for the horse who had done Spynie no harm that I can think of."

Anricks tutted. "But you survived?"

Carey smiled faintly. "Clearly. The horse didn't, though. Broke his damned leg."

"Oh." Was that why Carey was subdued? Remarkable.

Then Carey brightened. "Oh, but Bangtail and Red Sandy were there as you arranged and caught one of the men who pulled the wires tight at the right time. Shall we go and interrogate him?"

They went down to the storeroom as soon as Anricks had finished, Carey produced a key and flourished it open, marched in and stopped immediately. His boots were sticky soled with blood and there was a strong stench of shit.

Anricks brought a candle and examined the corpse carefully. He had been garrotted and there had not been a fight because his hands were still roped together.

"Damn it," said Carey, "Damn it to hell."

"The door was locked…"

Carey examined it and tried a couple of other keys in the lock. Two worked. "It's the old abbey, I suspect that the monks weren't too particular about locks except for food, drink, and money. Anybody could have come in and done it."

They locked up the corpse again and left him there until they could decide what to do about him since there was no way of finding out who had garrotted him. Clearly Lord Spynie was the man who had given the order, but there was no way of proving it and Carey didn't want to take the blame. There was always the Lough in the north of the city, if necessary.

It was already getting dark but the gates to the city weren't shut yet, since it was close to Christmas and, more importantly, New Year, when everyone always gave presents. Carey was down in the dumps again, so they took a walk through the crowds and after Anricks had checked carefully for followers, he broke the matter of the Deutsch letter with Carey. Carey listened carefully, his head cocked, his old hat pulled down on his head and the wounded hat in a sack in case they could find a milliner who could cure it. The torches on the walls and shops along the main street leading up to the castle flared and caught in the wind and the shop windows were bright with lanterns.

Anricks didn't say where the letter had come from and Carey didn't ask, which showed as nothing else did that Walsingham had had the training of him. Anricks finished by saying he was not now so concerned, since most Allemaynes were Lutherans after all.

"Not all of them," said Carey, surprised. "The southern Allemaynes are Catholic and under King Philip's cousin, the Holy Roman Emperor."

Anricks was embarrassed. "I should have remembered that," he admitted, "although it's out of my field. So we are back at the beginning. Do you speak any Deutsch?"

"No, only French. But there must be some Hansa merchants here. Shall I take your copy of the letter for you, Mr Anricks, so you can work on your dissertation?"

Anricks coloured. He had not worked on it since Carey had told him not to use mathematics. All the fun had gone out of the project now—how could he say anything to the purpose without using mathematics, the language of the angels?

Carey smiled at him and wagged a finger. "Mr Anricks, if you want the King to adopt you as his pet philosopher, then you can be eccentric, your hair can stand on end…"

"I wish I had that much hair."

"You can quote Greek and Latin to your heart's content but…"

"Yes, I know…"

"Translate it into Scotch. I can help with that, my Scotch is reasonable but you must write it first."

Andricks sighed. "But..."

"Find a way. Or no pet philosopher, you. Ah, this is a good place."

They were in the milliner's lane, in front of a shop with glorious highcrowned beaver hats lined up on its shelves, the torches at the front flaring backwards from the wind and the lanterns making ominous shadows.

Carey dived into the shop, having to duck his head once he was inside. Anricks waited outside, anxiously thinking of beginnings for his dissertation, watching the little puppet play in the shop. Carey brought the wounded hat out of the sack, the hatter took it sadly in his hands, turned it round, examined the ropeburn mark across the front and slowly shook his head. Carey looked unhappy and came out.

"He says it can't be mended," Carey said, and stood there with the hat in his hands, turning it.

"I never thought it could."

"Well, but..." And Carey fell silent and looked at the ground.

Suddenly Anricks understood. "You need a new one, don't you?"

Carey smiled the smile of a boy who has dropped his sweetmeat in the mud and is now offered the possibility of a new one by his nurse. "Yes, I do, Mr Anricks, but what with the new Court suit..."

Anricks was married to a wonderful woman of character who combined intelligent economy with judicious spending on important items. He rarely had to think about money at all, except when he bought another large load of books, or occasionally an entire library that had been sitting in someone's barn since it was robbed from a monastery. And Rebecca was usually good-humoured about those purchases. Books were sacred to her too, as to all Jews. As he had said to Cecil, he had plenty of money, although he thought Carey could beggar him in a year. Never mind, he thought, it's an investment.

"I don't see how you can wear Court duds and not get the right hat to go with it," he said, reverting to the London speech of his childhood. Together they went back into the hatshop.

◇◇◇

Janet was counting bushels of grain again while spinning with a dropspindle. She found it soothing, the spread and twist of the oily wool between her fingers, the twirl of the spindle as it went down, pulling and twisting the fibres behind it, and then winding up the wool onto the spindle and repeat. It was one of those handcrafts, like knitting, that you could do with your hands without troubling your mind, once you got the way of it. But she was still worried. She couldn't make the bushels add up to any more than they were, which was not enough. Was it poor old Shilling's death sentence?

At least the weather wasn't as wet and muddy as it had been. It had turned cold in the last few days and there had been a frost the night before which meant they could start harvesting the Brussels sprouts, strange new-fangled things they were but they were tasty and a welcome change from cabbage. She left the grain in its wickerlined pits and went out of the store shed and up the ladder to the barnekin wall, where she could walk all along the creaking fighting platform with her thick shawl over her shoulders, her cap pinned on tight against the wind, and think.

She tried not to think of Henry who was off in Edinburgh with the Courtier. She couldn't help thinking of him and his soulsickness but really she needed to work out what to do about the Widow Ridley who had come to Gilsland the night before with her grandson and was sleeping in Janet's trucklebed.

The Widow Ridley said she had two tales to tell but had only told one of them. It was confused but it was about Henry and how he had brought in two mysterious bad-mannered strangers, man and master, eaten and drunk, talked for a long while and then gone. Money had changed hands, from the strangers to Henry. Henry had spent the night in her commonroom, along with his great tall horse. There was more but Widow Ridley had been tired and nodding off and so Janet sent her to bed.

"I cam to tell ye, missus, because I thocht ye'd want tae know what yer husband was at and that they were apothecaries or wizards or both and because I'm short of grain maself and could do with some money and I know ye're a fair woman."

Janet considered. Widow Ridley had walked all day to come and tell her and she didn't like the story at all. Who were the men and what were they doing and where were they going and did the money that changed hands have anything to do with the new helmet Dodd had bought a day later? He said he had found the extra money in his doublet pocket after London, which she knew was a lie because she had checked the doublet for money before she brushed it and hung it up filled with sprigs of rosemary and wormwood to clean it out.

She could give Widow Ridley a shilling and she would, but she didn't know what to do. There was nobody to ask. The Courtier was in Edinburgh with her husband, she couldn't ask Lord Scrope because he would patronise her and then forget about it, she couldn't bother Sir Richard Lowther who would probably refuse even to talk to her, Lady Scrope was now with the Queen in London and Lady Widdrington with her odious husband. Janet knew that most of her gossips, like Ellen or Bridget or Rowan or Kate Nixon or even Mrs Hogg, would know no better than herself what to do, while the other women around were mostly young and daft, or old and set in their ways.

She felt very lonely. Surely Henry was doing something dangerously stupid, quite possibly he was betraying the Courtier, possibly the Grahams had bought him completely to kill Carey. Possibly it was something utterly different to do with the Border.

If Dodd had been bought to kill the Courtier, what should she do? Henry was her husband. If the Courtier was her husband's enemy now, then he was her enemy as well, surely. Except she liked the Courtier and it wasn't just that he always called her Mrs Dodd, rather than Goodwife, or always bowed to her curtsey, and had helped all those months ago with her haying and had looked uncommonly pleasant in his shirt and breeks on her haycart. Well, not entirely.

She paced up and down the fighting platform with her spindle and suddenly realised she had filled it completely with a good thin, tight thread and needed to go down the ladder to get a new one and another couple of baskets of lambs-tails too.

She sighed and stared to the north and east. She could say she had come to Edinburgh to buy grain with some of the London money, because the prices in Carlisle were outrageous, and she could go to Richie Graham of Brackenhill and buy well-forged Scotch shillings at eight to the pound sterling, not four, which would help a lot even if the prices in Edinburgh were daft as well, which she suspected they would be. And she could be with Henry over New Year and maybe he wouldn't be as grim and silent as he had been and maybe she could find out what he was up to.

She sighed. It was a serious matter to go to Edinburgh because she had to take the Widow Ridley, which meant a cart, which meant at least four men and herself which wasn't enough for the Middle March, the state it was in. But she felt she must do it: inside her was something that was set like flint and said, "Go to Edinburgh with the Widow Ridley." She hoped it was an angel and not a demon, and then laughed at herself for her phantasy and stepped quickly down the ladder to fetch another spindle.

◇◇◇

Carey, or rather Anricks, had bought a high-crowned marvel of a beaver hat which he was now wearing and, Anricks had to admit, looked good in. This morning he had tried on the shell at the tailor's, asked detailed questions, suggested a different way of working the armholes to allow easier movement. The tailor promised the new doublet shell by the next day and Carey had narrowed the swatches down to ten, including two possible taffetas for the lining.

Dodd was nowhere to be found which meant Carey was very watchful, was wearing his swordbelt and poinard since he was not in the presence of the King. He and Anricks sauntered along, enjoying the rare watery sunshine although it was cold, and the crowds—not nearly as close-packed as London which was a proper city and Westminster as well, but still respectable. Carey was looking at the way the people were dressed and finding it fascinating. The style was subtly different, especially among the richer merchants, a more Allemayne look. Carey saw many men wearing the peculiar multiply-split cannion breeches called something like plunder-hosen which you now only saw on beggars in London.

On which thought he turned aside to ask something of a storekeeper in such braid Scots, Anricks had to ask what he'd said.

"I'm trying to find a Deutscher for you," said Carey, "but I think they're all at Leith."

As that was the seaport for Edinburgh, it made sense. Eventually they hired a couple of spavined nags at a branch of Hobson's livery stables, and rode out through the New Port, along the northward road for about three miles, past the golf-course. Leith was pretty much all port and soon they found the Hansa Steelyard with its stockade and small wooden tower and its waterfront and cranes and little church. They had some argument at the gate but were let in and led to a comfortable house where a grave-looking solid man with greying short blond hair and a beard sat behind a desk. He took the letter, refused payment, and gave it to his clerk who hurried off to translate and presumably copy it.

Carey and Anricks sat peacefully on the bench while Carey wondered what form the next attack would take. Man with a knife? Gun? Crossbow? He didn't like the feeling that he had a large white target painted invisibly on his chest, accustomed though he was to the Grahams' antics. For most of that family, it was simply business, perhaps with the exception of Wattie Graham. Spynie seemed more malevolent.

Through the open door he looked at the businesslike people all busy bringing in cargo from the round-hulled ships, packing it onto carts and sending it south on the main road, to Edinburgh. There was only one ship that was taking on cargo, hides, unfinished cloth, some barrels. That was the trouble with Scotland. They didn't make a lot that anybody wanted to buy. Everyone looked very respectable and serious and they clearly didn't let any poorly dressed people inside the gate, which Carey approved of. Even the men operating the walking wheels for the cranes were decently clad in good hemp shirts, jerkins, hose, and usually boots.

Anricks was scribbling something on some paper with a piece of graphite. Carey took a squint at it from the side and was disappointed. More mathematics, damn it!

"Why is it taking so long?" Carey asked, wondering if they could find any tobacco to drink the smoke of.

Anricks looked up and blinked. "So that they can get it copied to send to their masters in Augsberg or Frankfurt."

"Oh. You don't mind?"

Anricks shook his head. "What can I do about it? I need it translated." He paused and looked out the door. "Maybe I should learn Deutsch."

After a while a younger man in very splendid split plunderhosen in yellow and blue came and bowed to them both and invited them into another office to discuss their document.

That was a larger office, lined with handsome oak panelling that glowed yellow with the sun coming through a glazed window. They were brought wafers and wine while a blond heavyset middle-aged man in a magnificent dark brocade and fur-lined gown sat and read both documents and the young man stood near the door.

"I am Herr Kauffmann Hochstetter, from Augsberg. Vere did you get this?"

For answer, Anricks produced his warrant from Sir Robert Cecil and Hochstetter took it and read it carefully. He gave it back. Carey was starting to feel uneasy. Anricks seemed placid enough but there was something wrong. He started looking for avenues of escape. The prospects weren't good: the little office building was in a fenced-off enclosure around the docks, with one heavy gate, the fence was high and sturdy. He concentrated on looking as elegantly empty-headed as he could.

"Yes," Anricks was saying, "I am a pursuivant for Mr Secretary Cecil."

"And the document?"

"Is from somebody I believe to be a spy but I don't know who for."

"And vat is your interest in this, Mr…ah…?" Hochstetter said to Carey.

"Sir Robert Carey, cousin to Her Majesty of England," said Carey languidly, although in fact his ears were working hard. That had set the Allemayne back a little.

"Ja?" he said.

"I am accompanying my friend, Mr Anricks," added Carey blandly, "who is the real expert in these matters…"

"But vere did you find this?" asked Hochstetter with a frown.

"Herr Kauffmann," said Anricks, still patiently, "you already have a copy of it. May I have my own copy of the text back if you prefer not to translate it for me?"

Carey stood up. He had finally identified the sound that had been worrying him.

"Well well," he said beaming fatuously. "This is all very pleasant, but I'm afraid I must be going along now. You'll let us know about it when you've finished the translation, I'm sure, lovely meeting you Herr Kauffmann Hochstetter, very sorry but I must get back to Holyrood House where the King is waiting to play backgammon with me."

Anricks opened his mouth to argue and then stood and bowed to the Herr Kauffmann and let Carey sweep him out into the smaller office, whisking past the young man at the door, across the yard, towards the gate, gently talking all the time while Hochstetter followed them but seemed at a loss to know what to do.

"Don't look back," said Carey in French while he sauntered to the gate, which was open to let some more carts in, and slipped through behind the horses with Anricks in front of him. There was a sound of multiple running footsteps behind them and Carey speeded up to a run, propelled Anricks to his horse, gave him a leg up without asking him, leaped onto his own nag's back and whacked the reins across the animal's withers to wake him up. Moments later they were galloping back down the road from Leith, not very fast admittedly, but at least a bit faster than the running pikemen behind them who soon gave up. Carey laughed uproariously at them and gave them two fingers and a fig over his shoulder, before whacking Anricks' horse across the backside and speeding up. Anricks concentrated on hanging onto the saddle and trying to find the stirrups.

They got back to Edinburgh, returned the sweating animals to Hobson's, and went straight to Holyrood House and to the rooms Carey was using. At least Carey's room was locked, although seeing what had happened to Spynie's man, Anricks didn't place too much confidence in that.

He was still breathing hard and sweating as Carey unlocked the door, threw his brand new hat onto a chest, and poured himself some Italian red wine. "What made you…?"

"Marching footsteps in the distance, coming towards me," Carey replied, downing his wine in one. Anricks did the same. "I've never liked that sound."

"Me neither," said Anricks, paling further. His fingers on his wineglass were gripping too tight and shaking.

"Next time there's a riot against the Hansa, I'm going to be in it," said Carey. "How dare they try to arrest us?"

"It's urgent to find out what the letter says," said Anricks. "At least I had Tovey make another copy of it…"

"Of course you did, you're not stupid," said Carey. "Come on, let's find the King and break the matter with him."

That was easier said than done—the King was hunting again, but only with his favourite lords and had given strict instructions that he was not to be bothered. Anricks had painstakingly copied out the letter again twice and they stood in an empty antechamber where there was a wealthy-looking man, staring grimly into space and drinking. Carey thought he was one of the Grooms of the Bedchamber.

"Well," said Carey thoughtfully, "we go to the Queen."

"But she's a woman…"

"She's the Queen and she's Danish, which is almost Allemayne. Come on!"

Carey led the way with long impatient strides to the other wing of the palace, on the other side of the garden that had been the cloisters, where the Queen's apartments were. He asked humbly at the guarded doors if he could speak to Lady Widdrington very urgently. After a lot of argument, the man-at-arms agreed to ask the lady and after about half an hour, Lady Widdrington appeared at the door with a young Danish girl they hadn't seen before, wearing an informal pink English kirtle, who kept giggling.

Carey, of course, flourished a beautiful bow and Anricks did his best. Lady Widdrington curtseyed but the girl didn't, which Anricks thought was rather rude of her.

"I am very sorry to disturb you, my lady, but I have a very serious matter to put to you."

"Oh?"

Carey explained about the packet, the Deutsch text and the way the Allemaynes of the Steelyard in Leith had reacted. Lady Widdrington nodded and smiled. "Well, your…your Deutsch is good, isn't it?" she said to the girl who was staring straight at Carey with great curiosity.

"Not so fery gut, but I vill look," said the girl and took the paper from Anricks with a big smile. Anricks started looking anxious again.

The girl scanned the text, raised her nicely plucked eyebrows and read, "My dear bruder, quickly this is for say your…your plan, your idea of killing Solomon cannot verk and iss wrong and you must instantly stop. I know you my husband betrayed, which I do not forgive, but still my bruder you are and I must try. Do not kill Solomon. My love."

Lady Widdrington blinked at the page. "What does that mean?" she asked.

Carey was looking thunderstruck and also pale. "Solomon?" said Anricks, "Who is Solomon?"

"It could mean the King," he said slowly, "also of course, any wise man, but it could…"

"Solomon?"

"Well, the King is very wise, of course…"

"It iss zee old rudeness," said the girl, looking haughty, "Zat my Royal husband is truly the son of David Riccio, Queen Maria's secretary."

"Your…" began Anricks and then found Carey's hand on his shoulder, pressing him inexorably down to the rushes as Carey himself knelt on one knee.

"Your Highness," said Carey, with his head bowed, "please forgive my intrusion and my stupidity…"

"Stuff ond silliness," said the girl, looking highly delighted, "I made Lady Viddrington bring me with her for she should haf a woman and I vont see the man vat steal her heart and make her sad for she cannot haf you."

Both Carey and Lady Widdrington had gone bright red.

"Now ve should talk, yes? I vil go back, put on a robe and come out viss my dear Lady Schevengen Vot speak Deutsch gut."

She grinned at both of them and slipped through the door.

"We were playing cards," said Lady Widdrington, a little helplessly. "Unfortunately, I got a bit drunk on flowerwater last week and…"

Carey was smoothly on his feet again. Anricks stood up and then turned aside as Carey stepped across the space between himself and Lady Widdrington and took her shoulders gently in his hands. "Please…" he breathed. "Please…" The man-at-arms was tactfully staring into space.

Lady Widdrington put her hands up to Carey's neck and pulled his head fiercely down to hers. Anricks didn't know what happened next because he made sure he didn't see and stood staring at a painting of some Greek gods in the Italian style and thought longingly of his Rebecca with her plump belly and stretch marks and wonderful soft dark hair.

"Well," said Lady Widdrington half laughing, "that tastes much better than last time...mmmm..."

Carey hadn't spoken and they were busy again until Anricks heard some noisy thumps on the other side of the door and coughed loudly.

By the time the Queen came through the door—in a magnificent purple velvet gown with her hair up and her cap arranged to show some of her smooth blond hair, followed by a stout matron in cramoisie who seemed to be complaining at length in Danish—Carey and Lady Widdrington were again at a decorous distance. There was only a distinct nibblemark on Carey's lower lip to show that anything had happened at all.

"Now zen," said the Queen, looking even more pleased with herself, "ve go in ze parlour."

They went to a panelled room nearby, filled with chairs and cushions and some little tables and some of the Queen's women were there, disposed gracefully. Carey smiled at all of them and bowed, told them not to bother getting up to curtsey because he was only paying tribute to their combined beauty and virtue. Some of them giggled at that.

The Queen called for sweetmeats and some Danish drink, as well as candles as the sky darkened, and sat herself down in the chair with arms that had the Scottish cloth of estate with the Danish royal arms impaled.

Carey and Anricks went back on one knee but the Queen told them rather irritably to stop all that English nonsense. They sat on padded stools instead and a girl brought round a tray with little Venetian glasses on it, filled with a clear liquid. Everyone took a glass, including Carey and Anricks, and then stood and clinked the glasses together, the Queen shouted "To my lord and King and husband!" and tipped it back in one.

Everybody else shouted "Prost!" and also tipped the liquid back, so Carey did the same as did Anricks. Simon found his throat gripped by a fiery hand. When he managed to breathe out again, he found there was a delightful scent of peaches that came with the fumes, as if he had become a dragon breathing a summer day.

"Mm," said Carey appreciatively, "what is that wonderful drink, Your Highness?"

"Schnapps," said the Queen happily, and leaned forward with a black bottle. "You like?"

"Yes, yes, I do," said Carey and got another little glassful.

"Zo. Lady Schevengen is much better at Deutsch than I and she says viss me on the meaning. Zo. If Solomon is my Royal husband, zen he is in danger. How did you catch ze letter?"

Anricks explained carefully that he had left the original packet in a jakes at a Scottish alehouse, drunk a pint of good beer there and left. The alehouse was dark and crowded and he had watched but no one came to pick it up while he was there.

"You are a spy. Do you hef a varrant?"

Anricks handed over the letter from Cecil and again opened his hands to show the scars across his palms.

"Ah," said the Queen, "I know vot zet is, you ver in ze galleys."

Anricks bowed. "Your Highness is very perceptive."

The Queen looked at him beadily. "Ven?"

"1588."

"Ssank you Mr Anricks, I vil not trobble you about it again. Now, Sir Robert, do you haf a plan? Lady Viddrington says you alvays haf a plan."

"Not yet, Your Highness."

"You vill—zo Lady Viddrington says sometimes you plans go wrong, eh?"

"That's certainly true, Your Highness," said Carey with a scoundrel's smile, "for instance, last summer a plan of mine to scout out Netherby tower to find out why the Grahams were stealing so many horses went very badly wrong indeed."

The Queen put her head on one side and half closed her eyes.

"Go on!" she said imperiously.

So Carey told the story of how he had treed himself on the top of Netherby tower with the nefarious reiver Jock o' the Peartree Graham as his prisoner—and how that meant he found out that Bothwell and the Grahams were planning to raid Falkland palace and kidnap the King and that he had spiked Bothwell's guns by telling Jock all about the wonderful horses kept around Falkland palace.

He told it well, with becoming modesty and an eye for the ridiculous, even telling how Jock had tricked him. The Queen first giggled and then shouted with laughter. "I vundered how so few men ve had could beat off so many raiders. How fonny. Zey stole ze horses and not the King."

"Yes Your Highness. But my plans don't usually go quite that wrong."

Lady Widdrington stared at him severely when he said that and he reddened again.

"Not usually!" he protested.

"It's a fery fonny story," said the Queen judiciously as she poured herself more schnapps. "Now vot can ve do about zis maybe plot against my husband?"

"There are two things we must do," said Carey with decision. "Firstly, we must make His Highness of Scotland aware…"

"But he vill be so frightened," protested the Queen.

"Er…Your Highness?" said Carey, honestly nonplussed.

"He gets fery frightened about sings like ziss," said the Queen, "And he…vell, it iss not gut for him to be so frightened."

Carey was staring at her, his brows knitting. Anricks realised that he really could not understand the idea of an adult male and a King being frightened of anything, much less admitting it, so before he said something disastrous, Anricks put in, "Also, we don't actually know that Solomon means the King. But I feel you should increase the number of guards around him, double up the tasters in the kitchen and so on."

The Queen nodded firmly. "Yes, ziss I can do. I vill write to him and say I haf had a bad dream and he must be fery careful."

Anricks wondered if she had been listening.

"Well, perhaps…"

"Und I vill summon my Lord Maitland of Thirlstane, the Lord Chancellor, and put zis in his hands," said the Queen. "Ziss too I can do. Perhaps I vill ask my scryer as vell. Whose is the plot?"

"Oh, I think that's obvious, Your Highness," said Carey. "Ultimately."

"Yes?"

"The King of Spain is at his tricks again and this is also a plot against England."

"Go on."

"Her Majesty of England is now…ahem…over fifty years old…"

"Fifty-nine, I sink."

"Er…yes. She will not have a child of her body. Forgive me for my tactlessness, but the King does not have an heir of his body yet either."

The Queen looked down, coloured and nodded sadly. "Iss true," she whispered.

"No matter," said Carey with a shining smile, "By the grace of God I am certain you will soon have a lovely little prince— but there's the weakness. At the moment nobody in England is too worried about the Queen's age because they have got used to her childlessness. They know that no matter what she says, His Highness of Scotland will eventually inherit the throne of England."

The Queen nodded, her lips firming. "He iss looking forward to it fery much."

I'll bet he is, thought Carey but didn't say it. "Now imagine what would happen in England if His blessed Highness were to be assassinated?"

The Queen nodded. "No heir. Only Philip of Spain."

"And Arbella, God help us, and a few others. Here in Scotland it would be the most terrible, the most tragic blow, from which God preserve us, but in England…? Civil war. And then Spain comes in, perhaps from the north, and we are too busy fighting each other to fight the Spanish."

Suddenly Anricks realised something: the traces Cecil had seen *had* been a plot, the thing was true; the sea monster was sticking his head out of the water to show he was not a mere phantasy. In fact it was a bigger monster than they had realised, a shrewder and more dangerous secret blow against England and Scotland both. At least he was not wasting his time.

"Vould the English be so stupid?" the Queen was asking.

"Yes, Your Highness, we would," said Carey positively, "so we must assume that the person to be assassinated is His Royal Majesty and find out how the deed is to be done and who the immediate plotters are."

"Off course. Do you know how to do zat?"

"No, Your Highness, I don't. But I'm sure something will come to me. It usually does."

"Mm. Ass long as ve can, ve do not tell the King, understand? You do not know how he is, he gets so frightened and he remembers his fosterfazher assassinated and his beloved D'Aubigny poisoned, and all the people who haf been killed around him and zen he cannot be Kingly. He iss a merciful and gentle prince, but not a fighting man, understand?" Carey bowed to her from his stool. "Understand, Sir Robert?"

"Your Highness, I...yes."

"Ass long ass ve can, ve keep ziss quiet. Also it is better if the assassins do not know that we know."

"True. You will consult my Lord Maitland?"

"Off course. I vill do it now." She sent one of the younger girls off to fetch a clerk and dictated a letter to Lord Maitland, telling him of the problem.

"Will the letter be ciphered?" asked Anricks.

"Off course. Grigory is a good cipher clerk, he takes dictation straight to code."

Anricks looked at the finished letter and found a simple substitution code that he thought he could break in under an hour, but said nothing.

They drank confusion to the Spanish in more schnapps and then the Queen announced that she was tired and so there was a gathering up of embroidery and a piling up of cushions as the procession formed to go back to the Queen's Privy Chambers.

Carey escorted them to the double doors, bowed elaborately to all the women, even the fat ones, so he could bow as elaborately to Lady Widdrington. He went on one knee to kiss the Queen's hand and she blushed and giggled. She was eight years younger than the King and sometimes it showed.

At last it was all finished and Carey came over to Anricks and blew his lips out like a horse. Then he grinned like a schoolboy.

"I've just had an idea."

Anricks had not yet learned to be cautious when Carey said that and so he smiled back. "What is it?"

"Come with me, we can soon find out if it will fly."

And Carey started striding away on his long legs like a heron so Anricks was forced to trot to keep up.

"Don't you think it's a bit late…?" he puffed.

"No, this is the perfect time," said Carey blandly, increasing speed.

◇◇◇

They came to a new set of apartments, this time made out of the monks' old dorter, but quite a long way from the magnificently decorated apartments of the King. Carey sauntered up to the handsome lad on guard at the door and said to him breezily, "I want to see my Lord Spynie right now, in a matter of national importance. Go get him, there's a good fellow."

The lad scuttled off, his eyes big and Carey leaned against the wall where there was a tapestry. "He will keep us waiting," he said. "Do you want to go to your bed, Mr Anricks?"

Anricks would have slept on the floor to see this. He shook his head. "Do you think this is wise?" he asked and got the same look Lady Widdrington had got when she had asked him if scouting Netherby tower dressed as a peddler was wise.

"No, I don't think this is wise," said Carey, "if by wise you mean never doing anything out of the ordinary. However I don't want to try and protect the King while also having to look over my shoulder for more fancy attempts on my life. So this is expedient. Who knows what will happen?"

They waited. Carey started wandering around the antechamber looking at the paintings and sculptures, some of which were scandalous.

"How long will he keep us waiting?"

"Could be an hour if he needs to get dressed again."

Anricks wondered if he had made the right decision or if he would have to sleep on the floor after all. It was already past ten o'clock.

"Is his wife or mistress there?" Anricks asked naively and Carey laughed.

"He's probably sending the younger boys to bed."

"Boys?" asked Anricks and sighed heavily.

"Ay," said Carey, making a grimace of distaste.

They waited a while longer and then Carey found a backgammon set on a windowsill and they sat down to play.

After five minutes, Carey offered Anricks a penny a point, which Anricks insisted should be notional pennies only, for honour alone. This was just as well because Carey started losing heavily and by the time Spynie's guard finally came back, he owed Anricks several purely notional pounds.

The young guard cleared his throat and said that Sir Robert and his man might enter the parlour where Lord Spynie would meet him.

"One moment," said Carey and hopped his men along to what he was sure was a devastating triumph, only to find that he had been neatly trapped.

"Mr Anricks," he said, "who taught you backgammon?"

"An African prince named Snake. I taught him chess. He usually beat me at both games."

"You play chess? We must play some games."

"I prefer the game with no dice and the puissant queen…"

"So do I, especially as it is in compliment to Her Majesty…"

"No, it isn't. It compliments Queen Isabella of Castile on the occasion when she marched her men across country to rescue King Ferdinand of Aragon…"

Spynie's man gave an offended cough and Carey looked up. "Oh, yes," he said, "my lord is ready? How splendid." He unhurriedly put away the men, closed the box up and put it back on the windowsill. "By the way, Mr Anricks is not my man, he is a philosopher of independent means and he is here to take part in a learned dispute."

Spynie was waiting in the parlour, wearing a blindingly flashy suit of red and tawny velvet, slashed with yellow satin and around him were six youths in his livery, in varying attitudes of toughness, one actually paring his nails with a long poinard.

Carey took the scene in and smiled indulgently, while favouring Spynie with the barest shadow of a bow. "Dear me," he said softly, "were you worried I was going to come and take revenge for your ridiculously incompetent attempt at killing me during the hunt yesterday? Which did me no harm but killed one of the King's best horses?"

Spynie looked uncomfortable. "You aren't?"

"No, no, my dear fellow," said Carey with his eyebrows up, "it's all part of the game, isn't it? And you've had the man we caught in the forest garrotted, so there are no potential witnesses that can speak against you." The young tough who was using his poinard to pare his fingernails slipped and blood burst from his thumb. He rushed out of the room, sucking furiously at the wound.

"Such a palaver over one blond boy. Have you seen him recently? He's done some growing."

Interestingly Spynie flushed.

"No need for all your roaring boys," said Carey, waving his fingers negligently in their direction, "this is much more important."

"Sir Henry Widdrington…"

"I know, it's very sweet how you treat your elderly lover, poor old man. I'll deal with Sir Henry in my own time and at a place of my choosing. Now would yould like to hear something interesting that may be about your sometime lover, the King?"

Spynie shrugged.

"This is from a packet of papers uncovered by a friend of mine after all sorts of adventures," lied Carey. "We don't know who it is from or who it is addressed to, but the meat of it is as follows." He gestured at Anricks who started reading the translated letter. At the mention of killing Solomon, Spynie stopped looking deliberately bored and sat up.

"Is that about the King?" he asked.

"I don't know," said Carey, with interest. "Is it?"

"What do you mean…?"

"Well, it could be your own plot to kill the King, couldn't it?"

"Don't be stupid, of course Ah wouldna kill the King…"

"You're no longer his minion, are you? Maybe you are resentful. Maybe the King of Spain has bought you…"

Spynie drew his poinard and advanced on Carey who drew his sword and stood *en garde*. "Careful," he said very quietly, "I'm not manacled in a cellar this time."

Spynie stopped, breathing hard. "I would never…" he began, "Never. I love him. Do you understand? I love him. If he doesna love me, that's hard, but I still love him."

"Really?"

"Ay," said Lord Spynie bleakly, "really." He sheathed his poinard and took a cup of wine. "Ah would die for him." It was not said with any bluster, but quite matter-of-factly.

Carey paused and then put up his own weapon. "Then help me find the plotters and kill them," he said.

Spynie swallowed some wine and nodded once. "Read it again," he ordered Anricks who did so without complaint.

"The letter was written in Deutsch and was sent to Edinburgh," said Carey. "I can't tell you any more about it because it was collected from a jakes in an alehouse called the Maker's Mark and I don't know who collected it."

"Have ye told the King?" asked Spynie, biting his thumbnail.

"The King has been hunting all day. We have told the Queen who has written to Maitland. She asked us not to tell the King yet."

Spynie nodded. "Ay," he said, "that's better, much better."

Carey's eyebrows were almost at his hairline but he said nothing.

"Ye've nae idea who?"

"Of course not," said Carey, "or he would already be dead. Oh, speaking of that, we put the unfortunate servant you ordered to try and kill me, into the Lough. He was already dead from being garrotted, I assume by somebody you hired."

Spynie was abstracted and just nodded absently at this.

"I assume that's all right?" said Carey, not looking at any of the henchmen.

Spynie shrugged. "And it's not just another kidnapping, he's tae die. If Solomon is the King."

"Who else could he be?"

"I dinna ken another man named Solomon."

"Perhaps you could use your resources to find who is to do the deed?" suggested Carey in a thin voice. "After all, my lord, you know the Scottish Court much better than I do. Perhaps ask around?"

"Ay," said Spynie, "Ah can dae that."

"And tell me what you find. It's important to share information in these cases."

Spynie shrugged again. He was deep in thought, or what passed for thought in his case. Carey turned his back on the man and went to the door.

"Sir Robert," said Spynie in an oddly strangled voice, "Ah…"

"Yes, my lord?"

"Ah…thankye for telling me."

For answer Carey bowed shallowly to the company and left, followed at a trot by Anricks.

They hurried back through the sleeping palace to Carey's rooms. Carey needed help with the points of his doublet, gave up trying to wake Hughie, so Anricks untied them and then undressed himself without help since he had never bothered with a valet in his life, apart from when he was at home and wearing something complicated and civic. Then he spent some time using a toothpick and polishing his teeth with a toothcloth and salt.

"Is that a good defence against toothworms?" Carey wanted to know.

"Yes, I believe it is the only defence because it removes their invisible eggs," said Anricks who had worked up a very satisfactory theory about toothworms and desperately wanted to tell someone. And so Anricks must instruct him in the use of the silver toothpick and rough cloth while explaining his theory and he continued explaining while Carey got into the main bed, complained that his teeth felt peculiar, rolled over and fell asleep.

◇◇◇

Lord Spynie was lying awake in bed. His tussle with Jeremy had not been a success and the young man had finally given up trying, turned on his side and gone to sleep. Spynie was staring up at the tester while the voices ran round his head. Could it be? It couldn't be. But the Maker's Mark? No, surely not. But that was Hepburn's usual alehouse. Lots of people went there, Spynie did himself, it had good beer, and a very good ordinary, mainly pies with flaky pastry. Hepburn was so helpful, so respectful, so convenient. Look at the way he had dealt with Spynie's abortive attempt at killing that bloody man, Carey. Just because whoever received the letter must be a regular at the Maker's Mark, didn't mean…

But what if it did? What if Spynie was closely associated with a man who needed to be told not to kill Solomon? What then?

Spynie turned over for the fourth time and tried to think. What could he do? Maybe ask Hepburn, forbid him…No, don't be ridiculous. If he truly was trying to kill the King, why would he listen to Spynie? In fact, if Spynie had realised what he was trying to do, might he not kill Spynie himself? He was good at that, after all.

Spynie actually put his fist in his mouth to stop himself from crying out. He wanted to protect the King, but suddenly, now it came to it, his bowels had gone to water and his head was spinning. This wasn't what he had meant when he had said he would die for the King. He wasn't sure what he had meant, but whatever it was, it wasn't this.

And maybe Hepburn was innocent. Maybe he really was just a mining engineer from Keswick where a lot of them spoke Deutsch...

Oh, God.

Spynie turned over again. I'm ill, he thought frantically, I'm sick, I'm not well. I'll keep my chamber. I'm feeling sick and I need to shit, I'm ill.

Deep inside him was a better part which said he should get up, collect his henchmen, and arrest Hepburn tonight. He ignored it, as he always did, and soon the little voice quietened.

He couldn't sleep, though.

◇◇◇

Young Hutchin Graham had found a dairymaid at Court who would let him suck her tits and was very happily doing that in the back of the palace dairy while doing his best to sneak his other hand up under her kirtle. She spotted him, smacked it down and slapped his face. "I told ye, only above the waist!" she said, popping the tit out of Hutchin's mouth and stuffing it back into her stays. "No more fun and games for ye today, young fellerme lad."

"Whit about tomorrow?" asked Young Hutchin pathetically, and got another slap.

"Ah'm no' gaunae spoil myself for a reiver and that's that, so ye can tek what I gi' ye or go sell yer bum tae Spynie."

"I wouldnae do that," protested Hutchin. "Whit dae I want wi' a man? It's girls I like, two of them fer choice, in the one bed and then Ah could suck the tits of one and the other..."

The third slap resounded and Hutchin's head bounced lightly off the wall while Mary, if that was her name, flounced off. Hutchin sighed because Mary had very nice plump white breasts and enjoyed him sucking them.

He got up and limped out of the dairy towards the stables where he checked on the horses and found Dodd there as well, seeing after Whitesock for the night. Dodd grunted at him and kept on brushing the horse down, though his coat was already like satin.

"Whit's wrong wi' ye, Sergeant?" Young Hutchin asked cheekily, knowing he was risking a serious buffet and getting ready to dodge. "Ye've not said mair than four words all the time we've been here and none o' them wis thanks, yer face is like the rainy day they'll hang ye on, and ye punched Red Sandy yestereven for nothing mair than asking ye how ye were."

Dodd grunted again and didn't answer, so Hutchin took the precaution of climbing up onto one of the hayracks and added, "Are ye still sulking over they Elliots, eh?"

Dodd's face tightened and became even darker. "I am not sulking."

"Well, at least I've doubled yer count of words. And by the way, ye are sulking, my Aunt Netty used tae sulk jest like that, drove my Uncle Jim wild it did, for ye couldnae get anything oot o' her of why, jest grunts and a shoulder and sour looks, ay, like that one yer giving me now, though I ken verra well it's just the Elliots."

Dodd grunted and went to Whitesock's other side.

"And ye willna drink wi' anybody and when yer eating ye willna say anything and…"

The tail was taking Dodd's attention now. Whitesock snorted and tipped a hoof. Unusually among horses, he liked having his tail seen to and never kicked out over it.

"Ye shouldnae ha' punched Red Sandy," pronounced Young Hutchin from the very top of the hayrack. "It disnae matter if ye sulk at the Courtier, but Red Sandy's yer blood and he means well. And I know two more families of the Elliots came

in to compose as they dinna like the Courtier's fancy ways wi'
besieging and they don't want it tae happen to them and he's
got his warrant oot of it."

Dodd gave Whitesock a carrot. "Finished?" he asked.

"Nine," said Young Hutchin triumphantly. "I dinna wonder
at ye petting yer horse so, he's the only friend ye'll have left, ye
fool. How the devil will ye get yer surname to back ye if ye've
punched every one o' them?"

Dodd paused and then started fiddling with Whitesock's
mane. The hobbies doubled up in the two nearest stalls were
watching cynically, you could almost hear them tutting.

"Ye dinna understand," Dodd managed to say.

"Ye're telling me I've nae feuds? I'm a Graham, ye're telling me
I dinna ken about feuds and battle and killing? I'm a Graham."

"Have ye killed yer man yet, Young Hutchin?"

"Not sure," said Hutchin, his eyes like slits. "Mebbe. I stuck
him wi' me dagger, mebbe he lived, mebbe not, the bastard."

"Ah wis younger nor ye the first time I killed a man, I knowed
he was deid because he bent over and all red shining blood cam
oot of his mouth and ma friend got the ither one right in the
back and so we got away."

"Ay?"

"We were happy, laughing and then later Daniel said, d'ye
think he wis married? I said I didna know nor care and then
later...well, I thought about it."

"What was it started the old feud up again?"

Dodd sighed. "Three sheep and a cow that went missing fra
the Elliots' herds and so they raided us for our cattle and my
dad killed Wee Colin Elliot's dad wi' his lance."

"Good work," said Young Hutchin. "And then it was a bloodfeud, o' course."

"Ay."

"But ye won, did ye no'? They had to come in and compose?"

"Ay."

"So what's changed since then?"

Dodd wouldn't answer that and walked out of the stable, wishing he hadn't said so much to Young Hutchin. It was true. The Elliots had come into the West March of England as part of a trap to catch the Courtier, but so far as he knew, they had not raided the Dodds since the peace.

But they were Elliots. That was the trouble right there, they were Elliots and he hated every one of them, severally and collectively. They were Elliots and he could still hear them laughing as they cut the throats of his uncles and his cousins.

He would have given a lot for a pipeful of Moroccan incense and tobacco which made him feel so peaceful, as he stood by the door of the stables and listened to Young Hutchin trotting briskly about, talking nonsense to the horses, bringing them their nighttime buckets of water.

Good God, he had forgotten to give Whitesock his bucket. He went in and found Hutchin had watered the horse along with the others, and so he walked out again. The ball of black rage was still sitting there in his stomach making his meat taste of nothing, dust and ashes in his mouth, and for the first time in his life he wondered if he was the only one who had it. Did other men not have it? For example, the Courtier, did he have such a thing?

Well, I'm damned, he thought bleakly, *I know that, why wouldn't I have a black ball of rage in my gut? God, I wish I could have a pipe of tobacco.*

Hutchin wandered out and nodded at him. "Now then, Sergeant," he said, as if they hadn't had a conversation, which Dodd appreciated. He got his tongue and voicebox to work. "Good night, Young Hutchin," he said gruffly.

"I'm no' sure," said Young Hutchin, "but I think that makes fifty words." And he disappeared into the night.

◇◇◇

Janet watched Widow Ridley with her fluffy white hair around her grubby cap like a starburst as she put herself on the outside of a meat and onion pie with vigour, despite having only two teeth, one on each side of her mouth, to bite with. She managed with a great deal of mumbling and sucking.

"Now," she said, "I've minded me of the other tale I came to tell ye."

"Ay," said Janet absent-mindedly. She was thinking that this particular batch of meat pies wasn't one of her best and was wondering why.

"These men that spoke to Sergeant Dodd and gave him money, Ah'd seen them before, so I had."

"Oh?" Across the hall table, Janet caught the two girls' eyes and reminded them with her eyebrows that they were to clear the trenchers that hadn't been eaten, and the piecrusts, and clear the jacks and wipe the tables and take the leavings to the chickens. They sighed in unison and got up to do it.

"Ay," said Widow Ridley, taking another sup of her ale. She had a powerful taste for ale, did the Widow Ridley, for this was her third jackful. She didn't look at all drunk though. "They passed along the Giant's Road, west to east, a couple of weeks ago, with a cart and three more men, and in the cart were strange magical things. There were strange leaden tanks that sloshed and slopped and there were things ye use for distilling like pelicans and tubes and heavy leather gloves wi' chainmail on them, all wrapped in sacks."

"How do you know?"

Widow Ridley chuckled. "I wis curious, so I looked," she said. "Now one o' the tanks had sprung a leak at a corner and fra the hole dripped oily stuff that had a magic spell upon it, for it made steam and smoke arise fra the cart-bottom where it dropped. I just happened to dip my finger in it, by accident, ye ken, and then my finger was on fire wi' invisible flames so Ah had to wash it off wi' water and it wis covered in blisters for a week and more and it's no' right yet." She waved a red finger at Janet. "The men carefully poured this oily stuff into two round bowls they had with them, propped them on the cart and then set up a fire and mended the leaden tank and tested it wi' water from ma well, and then poured off the water and it had taken the magic for didn't it burn the weeds around my jakes so they havenae come back yet. And then they poured the oily stuff back in the tank and fixed the leaden lid upon it again."

"How long did all this take?"

"Two days and they paid me for it, five shillings I got, English, and then they went on eastwards and they didna tell me where they wis going but I heard one o' them say, Edinburgh. So now."

And she sat back and held out her jack for more ale.

"That's a very interesting tale," said Janet. "Are ye saying the men were up to mischief in Edinburgh?"

"Why else were they so close-mouthed about where they wis going? I asked 'em four times and they told me lies each time, until I wis sitting in the jakes and heard them by accident. What's they men that try to make gold?"

"Miners?"

"No," said Widow Ridley, her voice far away, "though..."

"Alchemists."

"Ay, that's it. Alchemisty things they were and, now I think of it, I've heard they furriners down in Keswick speak like that cos they wis all speaking furrin with coughs and gasps, but then he spoke to me in English, quite Christianlike."

"He?"

"The man that gave Sergeant Dodd money."

Janet waited for the inevitable. "And they had funny hose on and they had tails."

"Did they?"

"Ay, and then off they went along the Giant's Road, talking furrin again."

"And the alchemist..."

"Bought yer man, Mrs Dodd, ay."

"Are ye sure?"

Widow Ridley bent over with laughter. "Ay, o'course, I know the look of a man being bought."

It struck Janet that, placed where she was, the Widow Ridley may have had more custom than you might think and might also know a lot of smugglers.

Janet smiled very kindly at her and brought her a jug of her best ale. "Mrs Ridley," she said, promoting her from Goodwife, "I should have talked to you long ago."

"Ay. Cheers."

"Can ye think of anything else about this alchemist?"

"Ay," said Widow Ridley thoughtfully, "everything smelled nasty, kind of metal and sour. He was a nice-looking lad wi' curly brown hair and grey eyes, quite square of the face, calls hisself Hepburn."

What on earth did they have in the tanks? "And they were going to Edinburgh?"

"Unless I heard wrong. Which I might of, see ye, ma hearing's not what it was."

"Had you ever seen such things before?"

"Nay."

"Thank you for telling me all this, Mrs Ridley, though I'm not sure what to do with it."

"Yer man's mixed up wi' a witch and an alchemist. Ye should fare tae Edinburgh and fetch him back home before he gets in trouble. They're fools, men are, allus going after the latest bauble. Go after him and fetch him back, like Janet did in Tam Lin."

Janet smiled.

"Will you come with me, Mrs Ridley?"

For answer, Widow Ridley stretched out her hand. Janet put two shillings English into it. Widow Ridley examined the money carefully, then put it in her stays.

"Ay," she said, "Ah'd like tae know what they witches is at."

◇◇◇

Carey, faced with a mystery and nothing to get hold of, concentrated on the only thing he could.

He started by looking for Allemaynes. Apart from the ones at the Steelyard whom he didn't want to tangle with again without a squad of pikemen at his back, there weren't many. He had just come from the Tollbooth where they had the records of foreigners, mostly reputable merchants like Herr Kauffmann Hochstetter, or gunsmiths. He had followed up one lead and found a small house full of blond young men who invited him to join them for a beer and then gave him some extraordinary light-coloured beer which was weak as to flavour and quite weak as to the booze as well. It tasted…interesting. They were trying to start a brewery to make more but admitted they hadn't got very far.

"Ve haf gut beer but not enuf," said one of them seriously, and Carey agreed that it was a serious problem and went in search of more Allemaynes. For completeness he looked for Frenchmen as well and found a few and talked to them happily in French, enjoying the beautiful music of the language and the memories of the beautiful women who had taught him so much, some of it French.

He went back to the Court, found the King was hunting again and Anricks was talking to John Napier incomprehensibly about mathematics. He decided that Edinburgh was boring and he was bored and furthermore at a stand with the problem of who might want to kill the King and how, so he went out again to the best inn in town and decided to get as drunk as he could on the basis that this might make something happen.

He got into a game of cards with some men from the King's troop, they were gunners and talking about cannonball weights and mortars and the terribleness of the serpentine powder they were supposed to use. When he put the question to them of how do you kill someone specific with gunpowder, they loved it.

"Ay, it's easy to kill a lot of anybody," said one of the gunners called Peter, "but killing one somebody is harder."

"Nay, it's no'," snorted another gunner called Mick, "ye just use a lot and mek sure the gunpowder is under the floor of his bedroom."

"Didna work wi' Darnley, did it?"

"No, but they had it under the wrong room."

"What about the fuse?" asked Carey. "It might go out."

"Use several," said a gunner called Harry. "Ye'd need to anyway."

"So maybe your man is suspicious and they search the cellars."

Peter shrugged. "Naething better than a fireworks display—all the gunpowder there. People are strange. If it's labelled fireworks, naebody thinks it's gunpowder."

Now that was interesting. "Does the King like fireworks?"

"Ay he does, though he disna like guns, ye ken. There's allus a fireworks display at Court at Christmas or New Year's," said Mick. "The Queen loves 'em. Every Christmas if it's no' pouring wi' rain, or New Year's if it was, there's rockets and all sorts let off fra the gardens of the palace. The people come to watch fra outside though they can't see everything so good as the King."

"And he's not worried about the bangs?" asked Carey, betting on a chorus and losing to a better chorus.

"Och, he's nowhere near 'em, he's at the front looking over the courtyard and there's all mermaids and centaurs doing dances and the fireworks are just a part of it."

Changing his mind about getting drunk, Carey went and talked to the firework makers who were in the process of setting up the racks and cages at the other end of the garden, well away from anything that could burn. He watched the strange yellow family with slits for eyes filling tubes with gunpowder and paper and mysterious glittery powders, and watched some men measuring out the lawns and hammering in stakes where the benches would be.

He talked to everybody, trying to get a picture of how you could kill a nervous King who wouldn't have any kind of blade or weapon in his presence. It was surprisingly hard, now he thought of it, but it must be possible.

He even spoke to the Lord Chamberlain, and was thoroughly patronised. "Any man in the room, ay, and some of the women too would give their lives for His Highness..."

"Yes, of course, but..."

"That letter, which Maitland told me about, says dinna kill Solomon."

"Who else could Solomon be?"

"It is a foul calumny on the honour of Queen Mary…"

"Of course, but…"

"We've men doing naething but guarding him. We've asked at the Steelyard and Herr Kauffman Hochstetter has nae idea who it could be—they don't want the King dead either."

"Of course not. There would be chaos…"

"Ah dinna see what else we can do," concluded the Lord Chamberlain, with a superior little smile. "The King is safe."

You could try and use your imagination, Carey thought, considering what his own father, Lord Chamberlain Hunsdon, would be doing down in London if he had a warning like that. *Oh sorry, you don't have an imagination.* Based on something that had happened once at Kenilworth a long time ago when he was a lad, Carey went back and asked the firework makers if you could aim a rocket for the King.

"Well, ye could, if ye knew in advance where he was gaunae be, but the King likes to move around and so likely as not ye'd end up killing somebody else and ye wouldnae get a second chance."

"Could you not bring a gun into the Court and fire it under cover of the explosions from the fireworks?"

"Ay, ye could, if ye can get one in range, but he doesnae like anyone near him he doesnae ken and certainly naebody with a gun, he really doesnae like that and I heard tell he has armour under his clothes, which is why he willna shift his shirt."

"Really?"

"Ay, it's ainly chainmail they say, but it's good and fine and it'll keep knives and spears off. Not bullets, though, unless they're from a distance. And guns are terrible for accuracy. A pistol maybe, but ye'd need to be up close and it's verra hard for anybody he doesnae know to get sae close."

Carey was thinking of King James with new respect—he had clearly put some careful thought into not getting murdered like so many of his ancestors.

◇◇◇

Dodd found that Young Hutchin Graham had seemingly attached himself to him and so Dodd, who was bored at Court and really only needed to attend Carey when he went hunting, paced around Holyrood with the boy, who was interested in Lord Spynie's rooms—and while following Dodd was less noticeable and less vulnerable.

He found them, like most Royal apartments, to be a series of rooms leading into each other with an antechamber and a single set of double doors giving entrance at one end and a small spiral staircase for the servants at the other. He haunted the servants' end of the rooms and was kicked out twice and then came to Dodd who was waiting in the courtyard for him, shaking his head.

"Ay, it's too hard to get to him in his bed."

"Unless ye sell yer arse."

"I've been talking to Crispin, the youngest of his henchmen, down in the buttery, and they all have to sit around in his parlour of an evening, playing lute or cards or some such, and then he picks one of them tae gae to bed with, and it's usually different, though half the time it's Jeremy, the biggest one."

"Ay," said Dodd, considering, "are ye thinking of killing him or warning him?"

"Killing him," said Young Hutchin, "o' course."

"Well he didna kill you. Nor any of yourn."

"So what?"

"So mebbe ye could try warning him, or frightening him."

"Why?"

"If ye kill him, ye'll likely hang for it. D'ye want that?"

"Ah will no', I'll get away wi' it..."

"Ye might, sure. But this is Edinburgh and ye've a powerful long way back to the Graham lands and if ye kill Lord Spynie, I'm thinking the King will be a tad mithered wi' ye."

"I'm mithered wi' Spynie."

"Ay," said Dodd drily, "but it'll take ye longer tae die when they hang ye. Think about it."

"Well what else can I do? I've come all this way and spent a ton of money on this."

"Ay, and boasted about it."

Hutchin didn't answer that. "Well? Are ye saying I shouldna kill him nor knife him nor beat him up…?"

Dodd sighed. "I'm saying ye canna. Ye're nobbut a reiver and ye havenae the men nor the way of getting at him. He's got henchmen, ye havenae. He's rich, ye're not. He's the King's Minion and ye're the son of Hutchin Graham, that got caught and hanged two years ago for reiving the Fenwicks' cattle and killing two of their men."

Young Hutchin's face got longer and sourer. "Ye're saying I canna…"

"I am. Let it be. Come back when ye're older and…?"

"Would ye say that about the Elliots?"

"It's different."

"I may not get the chance again. Mebbe I'll be dead by next year like me dad?"

"Ay," said Dodd, staring into space, "that's likely."

"Ye're useless," snarled Young Hutchin. "I willna. I'll get him somehow."

He marched off with his head held high and Dodd shrugged and started whittling a piece of firewood with his knife.

◇◇◇

Nobody could just up and go a hundred miles to Edinburgh from Carlisle, unless you were a young man riding post. It took complicated organisation and a lot of people. First Janet called on her younger brother, Geordie, at a loose end at her father's tower, to come and run Gilsland for her in her absence. She gave him a long list of things he must do or not do: what if she wasn't back in a month, what if they got raided, although he protested he knew all about that—and made him repeat the list three times. Then she got hold of her sister-in-law, another Eliza, and gave her a longer list of things she needed to cope with, including getting the flax retted when it was ready because that was the only crop not ruined by the wet weather and she was very glad she had planted so much of it. Eliza was young but steady and seemed to have good sense, whereas her brother Geordie was as flighty as a maid, like all men.

If she had been a man she might have ridden over to Keswick where the Allemayne miners were and asked some questions, but Keswick was sixty miles in the wrong direction entirely and she didn't have the time.

Widow Ridley was charmed at the idea of going on a trip to Edinburgh for the first time in her life and sent her grandson ten miles there and back to her inn to lock it up properly and get her best kirtle and hat and some other things. She couldn't ride anymore, of course, but Janet knew they would need a cart anyway and she could sit on that. At least the weather was frosty, and looked set to stay that way, which had hardened up the mud. They would go on the drovers roads, winding through the hills until they got to Hawick and then they would continue over the main road from the south to Edinburgh.

Janet couldn't empty Gilsland in the raiding season, but she took as many of the men as she dared, six of them, all in their Armstrong jacks and helmets, one Ridley, and a boy to run messages. Widow Ridley was chatting nineteen to the dozen in the cart and Janet had managed some kind of horse for each of the men, and old Shilling for herself.

They needed at least half a stone of food a day for all those people and thriftily Janet took the oldest sausages still hanging on from last year's pigkilling, not the new ones that weren't properly smoked yet. That was one reason why she needed the cart and also for last year's linen as well.

She thought it might take as long as ten days to get to Edinburgh, considering the cart, and she quailed at the dangerous country they would be travelling through, and how much the whole expedition would cost. Or rather her head quailed; her heart was telling her that this was no impulse, she needed to be in Edinburgh. She needed to rescue Henry from himself.

On the cart, under all the linen and uninteresting loaves of bread, was also a carefully calculated three small barrels of her own flowerwater, distilled in the summer, of elderflower, of raspberry, of blackberry, when it had been too wet to go out. Around Janet's waist, under her stays, was Dodd's moneybelt with half of Dodd's money from London in it.

And so she set off, her face set, her hat pinned to her cap, her second-best kirtle on her back and a shawl over her shoulders that her mother had knitted, for luck, her best kirtle and spare shift and her London hat stowed in the cart as well. She had two ponies pulling it but she soon decided to put two more in the traces, for it was heavy.

It was dark, long before dawn, the winter stars across the sky like silver dust and Widow Ridley stepping out instead of sitting in the cart on the beautifully made and fulled linen. Janet was proud of that, it wasn't easy to find places to stretch the linen where it wouldn't get muddy but she had done it and she was proud of the bolts of cloth she and her gossips had spun and woven last winter. Maybe it wasn't fine enough to pass through a gold wedding ring, like in the ballads, but fine enough.

She had changed her mind about buying Scots shillings from Ritchie Graham of Brackenhill since Brackenhill was in the Debateable Land. Better not on the whole to alert the March to her existence. She would use the little smuggler's road through Newcastleton, to avoid the Debateable Land and Liddesdale, join the road that led through Hawick and so to Edinburgh. She hoped. Once she was past Hawick she should be well enough. It was seventy-five miles, she thought, or thereabouts, all the way to Edinburgh, nobody really knew for sure, and she hoped the weather would stay frosty and that they made the fifteen miles or more to Newcastleton before nightfall.

As the hours passed she moved back and forth on Shilling, seeing the tidied winter gardens, seeing the infield where they had plowed in the barley and the wheat since it had gone bad in the wet, seeing some outfield that had been abandoned to marsh grasses, seeing horses and cattle penned up away from the road. They got past Bewcastle and she thought of stopping there but they had made good time so she tried for Newcastleton. She knew there were eyes on the hills that were watching her little party and it was only a matter of time before...

It was almost a relief when a patch of hillside moved and became twenty men in jacks and helmets as the sun westered behind them and shot rays of copper and gold under the grey clouds. Who were they? Were they Elliots or Grahams or Armstrongs...?

Widow Ridley woke up from her snooze on the cart and began knitting again and the two men who were helping to push, mounted up.

Janet drove her heels into Shilling who had been stumbling along like the most exhausted horse in the world and the old hobby caught the scent of the other horses and sidestepped then drove forward. He even lifted his mane and whinneyed and she patted him to calm him.

Thanks be to God and Our Lady, she knew the man at the head of the troop. In fact he was her second cousin.

"Now then, Skinabake Armstrong," she said to him as he came towards her and he tipped his steel cap to her.

"Now then, Missus Armstrong," he said, using her family name not her married name. But still he knew who she was married to.

"Och," said Janet with a big smile, "I'm glad to see ye, Skinabake, there's terrible thieves and reivers hereabouts."

"Ay," said Skinabake, since in fact his troop of twenty were some of the worst of them.

He fell in on her left and his men paced on either side of the road, hemming them in. Under strict instructions, the men didn't look to right or left but kept on going, except for Widow Ridley's grandson, who peered nervously from one reiver to the other.

"Sergeant Dodd ordered me tae Edinburgh," she lied, "he wants tae buy some feed and so we've got the linen to sell, o' course. He's busy off somewhere at the moment."

"Ay, where is he?" asked Skinabake, his brow creasing. Sergeant Dodd in a known location was one thing, Sergeant Dodd roaming around anywhere was another.

"Ah dinna ken, Skinabake, d'ye think he tells me everything?" she laughed and the frown deepened. "Now I wis just thinking, it would be great to see some of my ain family for this part of the March is allus tickle and worse at the moment, and I could do with some right fighters to protect maself and Widow Ridley here."

"Ay," said Skinabake, looking back at the cart and seeing Widow Ridley waving cheerily from the top where she was driving.

Janet skewered Skinabake with another smile.

"How's yer mother, Mariam Ridley?" she asked, then over her shoulder to the cart, "is that a cousin of yours, Widow Ridley?"

"Ay, mebbe."

"Well enough," said Skinabake, not liking to admit he often hid out with his mother when Sir John Forster was on the trod. "Going on for sixty now."

"Is she, by God? I wouldnae have thought of her as fifty yet," said Janet. "So, Skinabake, could ye see yer way to protecting me and Widow Ridley and my people until we get to Edinburgh? Ye'll come well oot of it, I promise, I'll sell the linen and pay ye."

It was notorious that reivers didn't like cloth, although they took it, of course. It couldn't run.

The six young men in their English Armstrong jacks continued stolidly, as instructed and young Andy Ridley, Widow Ridley's grandson was well back and almost out of sight on a fast pony so he could ride for help if need be.

"Ay," said Skinabake, his brow frowning ever more deeply.

"Come on," said Janet, "Ye can do it—or are ye out on the trod yerselves?"

She knew that they weren't, nobody had a lump of burning turf on his lance and they had been heading towards England at sunset. That meant they were on a raid, she knew it and so did they, but she had some hope they wouldn't know that she knew it.

"Nay," said Skinabake, "ainly…ah…visiting."

Visiting Carletons and Tailors and Musgraves, I'll be bound, Janet thought but didn't say.

Skinabake licked his lips. She moved Shilling to block his sight of the cart and smiled. "Will ye dae it, Skinabake?" she said winningly. "I'd feel much safer wi' you and yer men guarding us."

Of course he could easily tell his men to take the cart and the horses and leave them to walk home. He could but she was his second cousin. If he did rob her he would have to kill all of them, especially Janet herself, and word might still get back to Will the Tod, Janet's father, which would be bad for him, and also to Sergeant Dodd, which would probably be fatal. Janet had just offered him a way to get money with much less risk.

His brow suddenly cleared and straightened and he smiled his gap-toothed grin at Janet.

"Ay, o' course missus, we'd be pleased tae."

"Ye will?" gushed Janet, "Och, that makes me feel so much safer, I heard there wis Elliots round about."

"Ay," said Skinabake wisely, "Ah heard Wee Colin's trying to rescue his reputation after Dick o' Dryhope's tower. Did ye ever hear the like?"

"Nay, I didnae."

Skinabake sent half his men off with instructions she didn't hear but could guess at perfectly well. They were to wait until whoever they were raiding had heard that Skinabake's troop was guarding Janet Dodd's expedition to Edinburgh and then they were to hit them hard and fast and drive off the prime stock.

Oh well, thought Janet, *at least he's guarding us.* He put five men ahead and five behind and rode alongside Janet until she took pity on Shilling's theatrical stumbles and dismounted to walk for a bit as the sun disappeared and the evening came on and it got colder. She really hoped she hadn't missed the drover's road and that Newcastleton was close and then she saw the little red lights of the village over a brow of the hill and put two of the men at the front of the cart to stop it going too fast down the hill. Widow Ridley hopped off the cart and walked next to her, making eyes at Skinabake who pretended not to see. With luck there would be a packtrain she could add herself to, and say goodbye to Skinabake, who could not be trusted.

At the tiny inn she found that the regular packtrain from Carlisle was a day ahead of her which was a pity but couldn't be helped.

She and Widow Ridley doubled up in one bed and half the men went in the other bed and the other half of her Armstrongs kept watch in the stables to see nothing surprising happened to the horses. Skinabake and his lot refused her offer of a room for them, on the grounds that the village was full of Liddles, and disappeared to somewhere on the dark hills, probably stealing chickens. And they were halfway through the most difficult part of the journey and the linen and the booze and herself and Widow Ridley were still intact and the weather was still frosty so the mud was hard as iron. *Perhaps only four more days to go,* thought Janet, as she dozed off with Widow Ridley snorting in her ear.

christmas week 1592

Carey was checking the kitchens as Christmas loomed and the Court filled up with holly and ivy. He was painstakingly wandering into and poking around each of the four different kitchens at Holyrood, talking charmingly to the cooks and finding out what manner of men were working there and who they were. He found that, as with the Queen's kitchens in Whitehall, their fathers and grandfathers had served the Kings and Queens of Scotland for generations and also none of them knew when or if the King would eat the food they produced. There were no new cooks except a boy of eight newly apprenticed and all of them were Protestants. Peculation there was in plenty, so that

King James was probably paying for three times as much food as the Court actually ate, but that was traditional.

He talked to the gardeners, he talked to the huntsmen, he made a foray with Lady Schevengen into the Queen's apartments and talked to her servants, and he found nothing. He checked among the holly and ivy hanging around the carvings and found no knives or crossbows there, he searched carefully through all the public rooms and found no weapons, he interviewed each member of the guard with Maitland beside him, and found again, no Catholics, only Protestants.

The King went hunting almost every day and when he could he went too, and found that the beaters and attendants were sometimes Catholics, coming as they sometimes did from the Highlands, but that the King was happy with this and that the kind of Catholics they were had barely heard of the Pope and generally gave their allegiance to some abbot or other.

Christmas was a worry to him so he went to the handsome St Giles' cathedral in Edinburgh and checked every inch. He was still looking for gunpowder and so he also checked the crypt; he drew a blank there as well. Carey thought that the King's constant hunting was paradoxically a good thing, so long as he didn't break his neck by accident, since a moving target is always hard to hit.

On Christmas Eve all the young men of the Court went out to the woods and found a magnificent oak tree to be the Yule Log, a large and heavy tree the foresters had already selected and cut down and trimmed. They sang songs around it and tied a ribbon round it and then roped it up and hauled it slowly but steadily to Holyrood House, across the empty winter fields, drinking very large quantities of lambswool and ale as they went. It took them several hours so everyone was magnificently drunk by the time they hauled it past the walls of Edinburgh.

Edinburgh's gates were closed because Edinburgh and especially Edinburgh's ministers did not approve of Christmas which they held to be a Papist feast. You could see the heads of children peering over the wall as the gentlemen of the Court sweated the

Yule Log the last half mile and a few gave cheers before they were hushed by their mothers. Carey was with them, hauling on a rope with the best of them, in his hunting doublet and drinking slightly less than everybody else. It took a lot of trouble to get the tree through the old abbey gate and across the courtyard, partly because nobody could pull steadily in one direction anymore. Some of the watching woodsmen and servants had to help at that point, smiling broadly.

Once they got the tree into the great Hall, the women were waiting to decorate the Yule Log with more ribbons and little cakes and nuts glued to string and they cheered as the sweating men hauled it in. Everybody danced then, except Carey who said he didn't know the measures. While the young men handed the women round and spun on the spot, he stayed by the tree and examined it minutely, tapping it all over to be sure there were no hidden compartments full of gunpowder. The King was there, next to the Earl of Huntly, clapping and cheering with the rest of them, but Lord Spynie was nowhere to be seen: he had caught a mysterious fever after Carey visited his apartments and was seeing nobody at all except Jeremy and the boys. None of the lads looked worried, though, and he was eating plenty. Carey had tried to get in several times but had been turned away each time, which irritated him immensely because it stood to reason Spynie knew something he wasn't telling.

Once they had the fire sharpened enough, they rolled the Yule Log into the fireplace with the tactful help of the woodsmen, and the enormous tree lay there, filling it nearly completely, and gradually its lower parts started to burn. The wood was dense and hard: it would take at least a week for the whole of it to burn through.

They all toasted the Yule Log in whishke bee and then they sang it another song, very ancient and with nonsense words in the chorus and a haunting tune, before some began leaving to go into the audience chamber with the King for a very late supper. Carey stood in the hall with the woodsmen for a while, looking at the tree and sipping his whishke bee. Would it be worth seeing the Queen's scryer to track down whatever was being plotted against the King? Carey didn't approve of that kind of thing, apart from astrology of course, which was perfectly scientific. Although with the new picture of the Heavens he was still trying to get used to, he couldn't think how astrologers would deal with the fact that retrogrades were just a trick of perspective. Did it mean that when your life went wrong, that too, was just a matter of perspective? Surely not.

Huntly was still there and seemed to be in an uproarious mood, a large pink faced, red-haired man in his early thirties, whose track record was lamentable: in only February of that year he had knifed the Earl of Moray and set fire to his house. He had been caught in active treason times without number but the King let him go...

Carey almost stopped breathing. Did he speak Deutsch? Surely he could employ a clerk if he didn't, since he certainly couldn't read?

Quietly, Carey moved through the people until he was close enough to the Earl of Huntly to hear him guffawing at something the Maxwell had said. The King had already gone to the audience chamber for supper.

"Och, that's funny is that," Huntly was saying and then he saw Carey and deigned to notice him. "How now, Sir Robert, how's yer bum?"

Carey's eyebrows lifted slightly. "Well enough, my lord," he answered, "Why?"

"Only I wis thinking of when ye took that fall in the hunt, did ye hurt yerself?"

"Oh no, only I got spiked by the jealous holly. The poor horse had to be killed for his leg was broken by my Lord Spynie's wire."

"Spynie's wire?" Huntly roared with laughter. "There's an excuse for yer falling off."

Carey smiled thinly.

"Why were ye tapping the Yule Log, were ye looking for sweetmeats?"

"Not exactly, my lord. I was looking for hidden compartments holding gunpowder."

"What?" More loud laughter. "To kill ye?"

"No, my lord, the King."

"What makes ye think that, eh, Sir Robert? We're no' at the Queen's Court here."

"Nonetheless, I have evidence that His Highness' life may be in danger and I would be exceedingly grateful to you, my lord, if you could tell me of any suspicious men at Court."

Huntly looked thoughtful and nodded, his eyes twinkling. "Ay, I can think of one man, right now, keeps creeping aboot the Court, asking questions in the kitchens and the Queen's rooms and he wis tapping the Yule Log not five minutes ago, looking for a secret compartment for to hide gunpowder in."

Carey sighed.

"Ay," said Huntly, with a fatuous grin, "he's English too. Ah wouldna put naething past him!"

Carey was annoyed but didn't show it. "I'm afraid I have no idea whom you mean," he said coldly, "apart from yourself, being such an excellent candidate."

"Och no," said Huntly, leaning over Carey, breathing alcohol. "I dinna need to kill the King, cos he fancies ma bum."

"Ah," said Carey, moving away, "how fortunate for your lordship." He had reached the other side of the hall by the time the earl had worked out the double meaning, which got him an ugly scowl to which he smiled blandly.

At least one thing was clear. The murderer, the man who was giving the orders, was clearly the Earl of Huntly. Who was working for him was not clear—perhaps he would do the deed himself, since he seemed to have a taste for murder. But Carey relaxed slightly. It's always good to know who your enemy is, and the Catholic Earl was certainly in it up to his neck, probably along with his usual friends, the Earls of Erroll and Angus.

He noticed Young Hutchin standing near, also gazing at the Yule Log and clearly thinking of something else, his horn cup of whishke bee empty. He hadn't seen him recently so smiled and nodded at the lad.

"How are you liking Edinburgh, Young Hutchin?"

"Ay," said the lad, now no longer a boy but not yet even a youth. "It's…interesting."

"Have you scouted out Lord Spynie yet?"

"Ay." The line of Hutchin's jaw hardened. "He's no' easy to get to and being ill means he's impossible."

Carey nodded sympathetically. "He didn't even come out to bring in the Yule Log."

"Sergeant Dodd said I shouldna kill him because he didnae kill nor hurt me, just insulted me. I should let it be or some such. I canna understand it."

"Ah," said Carey, "I can see why you're confused."

"And I've thought and thocht of a way to get intae his rooms and there isna," Young Hutchin said with frustration. "They're even on the second floor so ye canna get in by a window, if they were open, which they arenae, or big enough, which they are, just."

Carey considered this. He had seen Jeremy on the end of another rope, around the tree, with two of Spynie's henchmen and he knew all of them would be in the audience chamber tucking into venison pasties.

"What would you do if you did get in?"

Young Hutchin stared at him in mystification. "Whit?"

"All right. Just as an exercise, how would you get in?"

"Ay, the jakes is an old one wi' a hole that just lets out onto the wall and there's a nice bit of ivy…"

"It's a garderobe…"

"…I could climb but somebody might see me before I got ma head out the seat of the jakes, if ye follow."

"I do. May I suggest doing the climb in a shirt only so you can wash yourself off afterwards?"

"Whit?"

"And if you got into Spynie's apartments, what would ye do?"

Young Hutchin obviously hadn't thought about this. He frowned heavily. "Ah…mebbe I wouldna knife him, sir? Cos

Sergeant Dodd said I'd hang for it and it'd take me a long while tae die?"

"A very good point."

"So…ah…mebbe I'd tell him what a bastard he is?"

Carey looked at Hutchin with grave disapproval. "I'm disappointed in you, Young Hutchin Graham, surely you can think of something better than that?"

Hutchin stared back at him for a moment and then a slow evil smile lit his features. "Mebbe I could take him a little present, eh?"

"Hm."

"Like a knife stuck in an apple, ye ken, tae mean his heart or…"

Carey too had an evil smile on his face. "I have a much better idea."

◇◇◇

Spynie hated being cooped up in his apartments, he was drinking too much and the King hadn't asked after him once, which broke his heart. He had a few books but wasn't good at reading and anyway, he preferred hunting in one form or another. His henchmen did their best to keep him entertained but the boys had run through their repertoire of lute music three times and he was tired of it. He heard the celebrations in the hall and the audience chamber and longed to join them, but…he was frightened. He had let Jeremy and Paul and Peter go because if he hadn't, he knew they would just have gone anyway, so he had the two littlest boys with him and one guard.

So when there was a firm knocking on the door, it was almost a relief. Perhaps the King had come to visit, as he always used to do when Spynie took sick, even when Spynie had a dose of the clap after visiting the tarts to the north of Edinburgh, His Highness had come to see him and suggested all sorts of doses and arcane medicines. Not now though, and Spynie missed him.

When the door was opened by the youngest boy—was that Eric? Spynie wasn't sure—he was very disappointed when that bastard Sir Robert Carey strolled in, carrying a jug of lambswool and two silver cups. Carey set the tray down and served them both with the mixture of hot cider and egg, lifted his cup and gave the toast of "His Highness' good health and confusion to the Spanish" which meant Spynie had to drink. He only sipped, being cautious about poison in drinks he hadn't seen made or that had been made by someone other than his own servants.

"I was sorry to hear that you were ill," lied the Deputy Warden.

"A flux, that's all," lied Lord Spynie who in fact felt he was going mad with boredom.

"Do you have any ideas about who the Deutsch speaker might be, the one who received the letter about Solomon?"

"None at all," lied Lord Spynie. Carey watched him gravely for a minute.

"Who was the man who arranged the killing of the person who tried to kill me on my first hunt with the King?"

"Ah…I don't know what you mean."

"The plot was yours, and a remarkably clumsy one. The unfortunate servant whom we had locked up was dispatched efficiently and without leaving any clues, from which I conclude that the man who did it was not yourself, my lord, but a…a consultant."

"Sorry, canna help ye."

"And quite possibly the man who is planning to assassinate the King. Of whom you said, my lord, and I quote, I would die for him. At the least I would like to talk to your…consultant."

Spynie fixed a ghastly grin to his face.

"No idea."

Carey thought about drawing his poinard and using it on the ex-favourite until he bloody opened up, but decided that Spynie would just scream for help and he would end up arrested again. In any case, he was not going to kill an eight-year-old and a ten-year-old boy to cover his tracks.

"So what are your plans after the King is dead?"

Spynie didn't answer that.

Carey started wandering around the room, looking at the paintings and the statues and Spynie watched him, hating him, wishing he could come up with some clever answer, and deep inside him the panic was growing again, along with the paralysis.

"Of course, my lord, I know you're a good Protestant, so much less likely to be plotting against His Highness," said Carey, after contemplating a picture of Leda and the swan in which the swan seemed more enthusiastic than strictly necessary.

"I am," said Spynie, "I would never…"

"Then perhaps you could help me with the man I think is the most likely plotter of them all. He's a Catholic, first and foremost, he has done it before, many times and he…"

"The Earl of Huntly?"

"Exactly."

"Ah." Spynie thought hard and fast. Anything to keep Carey from thinking of Hepburn—and in fact there had been rumours of something in the wind, and the Earl of Huntly was in very high spirits this Christmas, which he normally was when plotting. "Ay, now ye mention it, I've heard rumours mesen."

"What kind?"

"Och, the usual, he's in with the Jesuits, he's in with the King of Spain, he's planning to bring Spanish troops to the West Coast…Nothing hard and fast, ye ken, just servants' talk."

Carey nodded and came and sat on a chair by the bed where Jeremy sometimes sat. "Is he staying at Court this Christmas or in Edinburgh?"

Spynie shook his head. "He hates Edinburgh and the ministers hate him back, so no. He's at Court with a few of his henchmen and the rest are at Falkland."

"Where?"

"Where what?"

"Where at Court is he staying, my lord?"

"Why do you want to know?"

Carey simply regarded Spynie gravely, like a schoolmaster wondering how stupid a boy could be. Spynie coloured up.

"He's on the other side of the courtyard, in the Queen's old rooms, before they refurbished the abbey for her."

Carey nodded. "And how many of his men will be there this evening?"

Spynie shrugged. "Most of them will be attending him at Court, he likes to make a good show."

Carey smiled at him, an alarming smile, all teeth and sparkling blue eyes. "Now, my lord," he said quietly, "I wonder if you could help me? Nothing hard. Just invite the Earl of Huntly to play cards with you tonight."

Spynie looked mutinous. "Ay, but then he might guess and he's awfy big and loud, is Huntly…"

"I'm asking very little of you, my lord," said Carey, "considering that I'm wondering if the Earl of Huntly is planning to kill the King somehow. Yes, I want to search his rooms while he's not there and you can make that easier. You don't even have to die for the King, just bloody play cards."

Spynie contemplated the floor with its smart white rushmats. Perhaps he could do that, perhaps that wouldn't be too difficult. And perhaps it was Huntly at that…Although…no, he wouldn't think about it. But he could play cards with Huntly.

"Ay," he said, "I'll do it. Tonight. I'll send Eric to him now to ask him, say I'm feeling better but I'm bored." And he beckoned Eric who came trotting over, looking nervous, told him the message, listened to him repeat it back and then watched him struggle to open the big door and trot off down through the interconnecting rooms. He was a pretty boy, though a little easily scared.

"Thank you, my lord," said Carey. "I expect I will see you tomorrow, since you seem so well recovered. His Highness was saying he would like to see you when he goes to church on Christmas morning."

"He would?" said Spynie and then calmed his beating heart because, probably the Englishman was lying again.

"He would," lied Carey. "He wanted me to tell you particularly. If he has to live through an interminable sermon by Chancellor Melville on the sins of the flesh and the sinfulness of Christmas, you can suffer too."

Spynie grunted. He had to admit that sounded like the King.

"So," said Carey, gathering the cup from the table at Spynie's elbow, putting all on the tray and picking it up, "Merry Christmas to you, my lord. And to you, young henchman as well."

Sandy, the ten-year-old who was showing regrettable signs of acne, opened the double doors for him and he tipped the lad a Scotch sixpence, paced out. Spynie scowled moodily at the fire. You had to admit, you could see what the King had seen in him. Thank God, he hadn't replaced D'Aubigny for whatever reason, or Spynie would have remained forever just another impoverished minor Scottish nobleman.

Half an hour later, the Earl of Huntly came bounding into the rooms, followed by a number of ruffianly Gordons. He made Spynie's elegant chambers suddenly look quite small, and stood with his fists on his hips demanding to know what game Spynie wanted to lose at, Gleek or Primero, and bellowing with laughter.

It was only when Spynie went to bed several pounds poorer at about three o'clock that he found the dead rat lying in its lifeblood between the sheets in his four-poster bed. It made his heart thud and was very upsetting, because what was a rat doing in his bed and did it have plague? He slept in the uncomfortable truckle bed and had the two boys with him but didn't even feel like doing anything because he was so frightened of the plague.

◇◇◇

Carey found Young Hutchin out the back of the horse yard, using the pump to get rid of some of the ancient shit covering him. He was naked and shivering but looked very pleased with himself.

"I have another job for you, Young Hutchin," said Carey, handing him a horse blanket to use for a towel. "Why didn't you keep your shirt on?"

"Ah've only g-g-got the one," said Hutchin, wrapping the blanket around himself. "Whit d'ye want me tae do?"

"I want you to break into another set of rooms for me," said Carey, pouring out the remains of the lukewarm lambswool and handing the silver cup to Young Hutchin. "Get that down ye and I'll give you one of my shirts so you can use your own when you climb up another guarderobe."

"Ye will? Whit d'ye want me tae steal?"

"Er…nothing, thank you. I want you to find the key and open the main door, so I can come in and search the chambers."

"Whose?"

"The Earl of Huntly,"

"Why?"

"For good and sufficient reasons, Young Hutchin."

"Ay, but I've never met him and he hasnae given me any insult…"

Carey handed Hutchin a shilling. "Half now, half when we're back here and everything has gone perfectly."

"Ay sir, I'm up for it."

"I've taken a look and I think the garderobe is in the same position but there isn't any ivy, so I'll boost you up…"

Young Hutchin's heart was beating hard and slow when he went out into the courtyard again with Carey, carrying horse-blankets. The sounds of music were coming from the audience chamber and they had to stop several times and he had to hide in bushes when drunken nobles and their henchmen went past. Carey did a very good impression of somebody too drunk to see and pissed into a flowerbed on one occasion.

At last they found the place in a smaller back courtyard where the garderobe hung over the back of the wall. It was a tricky climb, sure enough, and Hutchin felt scared. Carey was wearing his arming doublet which was just as well because he still had a bit of the shit on him as the water had been so cold. Carey had said, if you see or hear anything that frightens you, just run and get out of the place. He left the horse blankets under the garderobe just in case, which was nice of him, Hutchin thought. He stole a look at Carey as he looked carefully around the little courtyard and saw the man had a smile on his face again. Hutchin smiled back. It was exciting to be doing something so mad, as if the Courtier was an uncle and they were raiding someone dangerous for his favourite horse, to put a brave on him.

Carey half-squatted and Hutchin put his bare foot onto his thigh, got up to his shoulders and hunched there as Carey straightened with a quiet "oof" noise, and held the wall to steady himself. Hutchin had seen acrobats at Bessie's in Carlisle doing something similar, and he stood on Carey's shoulders and wobbled, holding onto his hair, put one hand up, then another one, found a ledge, found a hole with one toe, went up a little way, found another hole for his other toe, another ledge for one hand, slippery, broken, a staggering smell of fresh shit, got both hands up, muscles bulging, got one toe on the ledge, found a big stone to hold onto, it pulled out and fell while Hutchin gasped, but Carey wasn't there anymore, he had gone to find his way round to the chambers by the normal route.

Somehow that gave Hutchin strength, that Carey trusted him. He got his hand into the hole left by the stone, boosted up again, found another slippery ledge and the round hole of the seat above him, shoved at it one-handed, found it was nailed down, pushed, tried again, then lost his temper and punched it, breaking it, nearly slipped right back down again, braced his back against the front wall of the garderobe, punched again. It gave with a cracking sound that sounded like the trump of doom, and he got both hands up to the hole and pulled himself up, through it, thanking the god of reivers that his shoulders hadn't grown yet, and squirmed through the shit, piss, and a crusting of old sick and out into the garderobe.

Very carefully he opened the door and stepped out. Two men were asleep on palliasses, and a third on a truckle bed. They all sounded drunk. Were there any dogs? Most people kept their dogs in kennels but sometimes womenfolk liked to have little dogs in bed with them... Well, nothing was barking, so he padded through the Earl's bedchamber with its four-poster bed, through the inner chamber, through the parlour and found the double door which was locked. Where was the key?

Hutchin looked for hooks, looked in pockets, found nothing, felt under the bed, nothing. He was beginning to panic and his right knuckles were sore and bleeding. He went to the door, tapped on it, heard Carey's voice on the other side breathe, "I'm here."

"Sir, Ah canna find the key…"

"Look in the keyhole," whispered Carey and Hutchin looked, found the key, unlocked the door.

The doorhandle turned, the door opened. Carey came sliding through the door in his socks. "God, you stink," he said with a grin and Hutchin wanted to giggle. "Anyone there?"

For answer Hutchin held up three fingers and mimed sleep. Carey nodded. He crept through into the parlour, checked drawers very quietly, checked clothespresses, filled with velvets and brocades, went on into the bedchamber and checked under the mattress and the bed. At last he checked a clothes chest in the corner and found some sheets of paper.

Carey took them out, squinted at them in the light of the stars. "Hm," he said.

One of the servants on the palliasses turned over and snored loudly and Carey and Hutchin went still as statues. The servant got up, went blearily into the garderobe and took a long luxuriant piss.

While he was in there, Carey shoved the papers back in the clothes chest, grabbed Hutchin's shoulder, propelled him through to the parlour and out of the door, shutting it quietly. He picked up his shoes and hat in his other hand, crossed the floor and ran down the stairs to one side, two at a time. Carey paused at the service door, saw no one, and they sprinted across the small courtyard, then Carey stopped, turned, sauntered back, picked up the horseblankets under the garderobe, sprinted again. They took a back route to the stableyard and stopped at the pump and finally both of them laughed.

"You've left shitty bare footprints all over Huntly's chambers, he'll be upset tomorrow. Let's get ye clean and get rid of that shirt too."

"Och, sir, I like it."

"You'll have to launder it yourself then…"

"Och."

Carey had left soap there which he handed to Hutchin and manned the pump so the boy could wash in freezing cold water for the second time that night.

"My mam would say I'll get me death of lungfever…"

"Good thing she's not here then…" said Carey callously, pumping away, paused and then added, "God rest her."

"Ay," said Hutchin, with a grin, "It's a pity I didnae steal nothing, I'd like a souvenir."

"Too dangerous. When Huntly sees the shitty footprints he'll know you were there and I'm thinking he'll be furious. So better have nothing to hide, he'll probably get the King to search the whole palace."

"Ay," said Hutchin. "Did ye get what ye wanted, sir?"

Carey paused. "I think so. I found sheets of paper, some with numbers on them, though it was too dark to see them, one I think might have been a money draft on a bank in Antwerp and there was one with nothing on it and Huntly's signature across the bottom of the blank page. It's all very interesting."

"So his lordship is a traitor, eh?"

"That's already clear. I think he's plotting to kill the King too."

"So will ye blackmail him or kill him or what?" Carey didn't answer.

The boy was now much cleaner than he had been before he started climbing up garderobes and Carey went into his bed-chamber where Tyndale and Tovey were both snoring, but the truckle bed was unoccupied because Anricks was staying with Napier in Edinburgh. He picked his oldest shirt, brought it out and Hutchin put it on with a cheeky grin.

"I'll smell like a lord in this."

"Not for long, and try and keep it under your jerkin until it gets a bit grey." Carey took Hutchin's old hemp shirt, rolled it up and then thought better of it, sighed, took his sleeves off and rolled his own shirtsleeves up and then went and rinsed it out under the pump.

Hutchin thought this was very funny. "Ye'll not get rid of it?"

"No, if I was Huntly, I'd be looking for a shitty shirt tomorrow too. If I could, I'd burn it. I should have let you stay naked to get up into his chambers."

"Och, hemp disnae burn well, and the smoke stinks. Leave it wi' me, I've an idea though I'll wear your lord's shirt tonight, it's nice and soft, so it is."

Carey was unrolling his shirtsleeves, and lacing his sleeves back on just at the upper tabs. Ceremonially he handed Hutchin his shirt, a second English shilling and a Scotch sixpence. "That's for beer tomorrow," Carey explained. "I'm buying your silence as well, Young Hutchin."

"Ay, o' course. See ye tomorrow, sir."

Carey nodded. "Thank you, Young Hutchin. And Merry Christmas."

Hutchin knuckled his forehead to the Courtier, and trotted out to the stables where he usually slept in one of the horse's stalls where it was warm and smelled comfortable. Carey could hear him chuckling to himself as he went.

He prayed and got into his bed, thinking hard about the Earl of Huntly. In London, in Whitehall, it would have been so simple. If Carey had found anything like as incriminating in the chambers of an English lord, he could have taken the documents to his father and shortly after, the man would have been in the Tower. But in Scotland…The King liked the Earl of Huntly and also felt grateful to him for helping him get free of the Ruthven raiders all those years ago. Nothing was simple in Scotland. Carey would have to catch Huntly red-handed, but before he actually killed the King. God, that would be ticklish.

◇◇◇

As the Armstrongs plodded on northwards the next morning, the day before Christmas, heading for Hawick which was about twenty miles away, Skinabake and his men kept close. The road was much worse and all uphill so Widow Ridley was off the cart and walking along, knitting at a stocking with one needle in a case on her belt, her right hand clicking away with the other needle and her left hand holding the cart's side to help her along. The horses were blowing and complaining and every so often one of them would stumble on the icy mud. Janet took a look at the cart's axles which seemed firm enough, but she hoped the road wouldn't get any rougher.

"Ay," said Widow Ridley breathlessly, "ye'll need tae be rid o' Skinabake soon and I'm thinking he willna go easy."

Janet snorted and was answered by Shilling behind her as if they were having a conversation.

"O' course ye've got the barrels of brandy under the linen. That might help."

"Skinabake?" Janet laughed shortly. "He's got a head like a rock."

"Ay, how is he wi' valerian and wild lettuce?"

Janet smiled at her. "Have you got some?"

"Ay, 'appen I have," said Widow Ridley and chuckled. "I brung maist of my stillroom cupboard, allus do when I go to Carlisle, the herbs are wrapped in my best kirtle. Ye never know what you might need."

"Could you put some in the top barrel without Skinabake seeing you?"

"Ay," Widow Ridley giggled like a girl, "I use it to quiet the lads when they come in excited after a raid, don't want 'em busting my place up, do I?"

Janet couldn't laugh. She was afraid she had made a terrible mistake. Maybe she should have stayed safe in Gilsland and sent a message to Dodd—but in his current mood he would prob-ably have ignored it. And she thought the linens would sell well in Edinburgh, especially if she could get there before New Year's Day, when people looked for presents. And she wanted to see the Courtier and tell him about the alchemist and his magic water. She shook her head and sighed. She had gone too far to go back now, she had to see it through. Please God, the weather stayed frosty.

Widow Ridley elbowed her in the ribs. "Dinna be sae sad and sorry for yersen," she said. "Skinabake's no' the worst of them by a long road."

"Ye're enjoying yerself, Mrs Ridley, are ye not?"

"Ay, Ah am that. Never been tae Edinburgh afore."

"Me neither."

"Och, ye don't say."

"Carlisle, o' course, and Berwick once, but never Edinburgh." Janet paused. "So I'm relying on you tae keep me out of trouble."

Widow Ridley looked sideways at her, Janet managed to keep deadpan as the old woman started to heave and laugh until she began coughing and Janet cracked a smile.

In the end they made it to Saughtree at the top of Liddesdale, and were given a barn to camp in which was kindly of the Elliots there since the frost was a hard one that night. They had a little fire and didn't use the aqua vitae since Skinabake and his men seemed quite well-behaved, helped get the packs off the ponies and one of them even sang some of the old songs for them, and some new ones as well that Janet hadn't heard.

They took the night in two watches. Janet couldn't sleep, she sat up watching the fire for a long time, wrapped in her best cloak that she had woven and fulled herself, of black sheep's wool so it was dark brown and quite prickly for it was new. She dozed off at last and woke up in the blackest part of the night, knowing that something was very wrong. She listened and heard nothing. No snores. Or just a few.

She stood up, listened. There were sounds in the night, foxes barking, badgers snuffling through the gorse but...

She walked quickly to the large double doors of the barn and found no one there, not Skinabake nor any of his men. Her Armstrongs were still sleeping, and the two lads supposed to be doing the guarding, fast asleep with the barrel of Janet's aqua vitae between them. She stood there for a moment, honestly wanting to scream and go and kick both of them in the balls. But the situation was too serious for that.

She went back to the door, opened it a little and looked out. Her nightsight was well in since the fire had gone down to coals in its little bed of rocks—the barn was only half full of hay anyway. She looked and listened and smelled the cold air.

Nobody. Skinabake and his ten tough young men had disappeared as if the faery folk had happened by and kidnapped all of them.

She ran back to the fire, kicked earth onto it, kicked Cuddy her bastard half-brother awake, bent down to hiss in his ear, "Cuddy, wake up!"

His eyes blinked open, focussed and then he was awake. "Whit?" he whispered.

"Skinabake's gone and all his men," she hissed, "sometime while I wis asleep and Jock and Archie sleeping too."

"Och. Fuck," said Cuddy, sat up on his elbow, saw Archie and Jock with the barrel, scowled and laid down again on his side. She was about to rate him for going back to sleep when she realised he was listening to the sounds in the ground. She held her breath.

"Ah can hear horses," he whispered, lifting his head, "A lot. More than twenty. They're coming close quietly, their hooves are muffled."

"Och," said Janet and for a moment she felt murderous fury at herself and at the Borders where they would not, could not let a married woman and an old carlin take a trip anywhere, much less Edinburgh.

Cuddy was sitting up, putting on his helmet.

"A'right," she said, "Get the other lads up and ye're to ride for my father..."

"No, Janet, we'll fight for ye," he said, pale with fright. "They willna take ye without a fight..."

"Happen they might be on a raid..." said Jock's Jock Armstrong on Cuddy's other side, his own head pressed to the ground.

"They might, but this village is full of Elliots."

Cuddy and Jock's Jock looked at each other. "Well but..."

"I think they're Elliots and they're after me," she said coldly. "That would put a good brave on Sergeant Dodd, d'ye not think, his wife taken by Elliots?"

"Och, fuck," said Cuddy again. "I hadna thought of that."

"Please dinna use Scottish obscenities," said Janet primly. "Nor had I thought of that, to be honest, which I should have. We should ha' gone by the Giant's Road."

She stood awhile in thought while the young men got themselves together—they were all sleeping in their jacks so only needed to get their helmets and sometimes their boots on.

"All ye lads, leave the cart ponies and Shilling wi' me, take all the ither horses and ride for me dad's tower. He'll know what tae do."

"But ye'll be all alone…"

"I willna, I'll have Widow Ridley with me for propriety and whoever it is coming willna ken where ye are and that might make him cautious. Ye can have the Ridley lad hang back on the fastest pony to see what happens if ye like, and if they are on a raid, ye can come back to me."

"Ay," said Cuddy unhappily, "Ah dinna like it, Janet."

"Nor do I. Now do as I bid ye."

They were already up and tacking up the horses, and a few minutes later they opened the double doors and broke southwards down Liddesdale, galloping for the English Armstrong lands and Will the Tod's tower. Janet went and sat by Widow Ridley and listened to the beat of their hobby's hooves fading. She thought of something, went and collected the brandy barrel, put it back on the cart under all the linens wrapped in their hemp.

Widow Ridley was putting her cap on, grabbing handfuls of startling white hair and shoving it under the linen, while more escaped from the other side and then she drove a pin into the middle of it and grunted.

Out of the night materialised fifty more riders, the hooves muffled with rags, with the square quilting of Scotland on their jacks, Liddesdale helmets, their lances and Jeddart axes, led by a small nippy dark-haired man carrying a dark lantern, that she had never met but still knew at once.

Janet stood up. "Wee Colin Elliot," she said with magnificent contempt and curtseyed. "Welcome."

christmas day 1592

Anricks spent Christmas at John Napier's house happily playing with the wonderful toys mathematical he called his Bones.
After the Earl of Huntly had caused a fuss looking for someone
who had trailed smelly footprints all over his chamber and
failed to find anyone, the Court got itself together to process to
St Giles. The King and all his Court and his Queen and all her
ladies attended the Christmas Morning service at St Giles where
Chancellor Melville excelled himself in the length, complexity,
and tedium of his sermon, and gained the admiration of every
minister who heard it. Since church-going was always compul-
sory on Christmas Morning, Simon Anricks and John Napier
were there as well, giggling like a couple of schoolboys while they
wrote notes to each other in mathematics. Spynie was nursing a
hangover while the Maxwell, Huntly, Erroll, and Angus were all
at a Catholic Mass said by Father Crichton in a private chapel
at Holyrood, once used by the sainted martyr, Queen Maria.
The King blandly insisted to the ministers that he had no idea
where the Catholic earls went on Christmas Morning, silly boys
that they were, because he was busy listening to the minister's
sermons in Edinburgh town.

Afterwards His Highness returned to Holyrood House and
ate an immense dinner which included a swan stuffed with a
peacock, stuffed with a goose, stuffed with a duck, stuffed with
a chicken, stuffed with a pigeon, stuffed with a blackbird, stuffed
with a wren, which everyone admired.

Jonathan Hepburn was getting worried, he had to admit.
He had two plans in play, one covering the other, either one
could work. He had Marguerite to keep happy although she
was becoming terrifyingly adventurous, he had the complicated
and dangerous alchemical plot in hand, though not active yet,
everything was in a delicate balance and here came the Deputy
Warden, in long boots, trampling through, asking questions.

How the bloody man had laid hands on Hepburn's sister's
stupid and dangerous letter, he didn't know, but he had. The

worrying message from his cousin in the Steelyard had made that clear—it was a real pity they had muffed the opportunity to arrest Carey and his odd little hanger-on and clap both of them in irons until it was all over. There might have been a bit of fuss from the King, but it could always be smoothed over by nice thalers, after all. However, his cousin had failed to act firmly enough.

But the family firm of Haug and Company now knew something was in play and Hepburn had received another letter from his brother in Keswick, asking querulously if it was true that he was planning to kill the Scottish King—and in a simple cipher as well, as if it being in Deutsch was enough to keep it secret. He had responded immediately that he was not, that it was a lie, that his sister must be mad and that nobody should pay attention to the vapourings of a widow about to have a baby. Until he could get to Keswick, that was all he could do.

He had to assume that the Scottish *domus providenciae* was alerted, but that they had kept it from the King as they normally did because of his cowardice, so the *domus magnificenciae* would be racketing on as usual. It was inconvenient and annoying but he thought he had proceeded cautiously enough that his original plans could continue.

He worried about it, though; he couldn't help it. And yet, logic told him that the best thing to do was nothing. He avoided Carey as much as he could, until the man somehow caught him in the hall after the Christmas dinner and asked him if it was true that he was originally a mining engineer from Keswick.

"Ay, it is," he answered with his best boyish grin, "only I got bored with digging and went to seek my fortune in the Netherlands."

"Did you find it?" asked Carey lazily. "I mean your fortune?"

"Ah no," said Hepburn ruefully, "not yet. I was young and stupid."

Carey smiled. "I've often thought of taking ship to Flushing and selling my sword to the highest bidder. Whenever I get tired of being told what to do by idiots."

"Hah!" Hepburn laughed. "Do you think that stops in the Netherlands? It doesn't."

Carey laughed, poured them both some wine from the nearest jug, took a drink immediately. Hepburn did too and made a face. As usual in Scotland, it was terrible.

"So how did Allemaynes come to be digging holes in the hills around the Cumberland lakes?" Carey asked. "I know Allemaynes are the best miners in the world…"

"No, I'd say the Bohemians are, but anyway. The Queen invited us back in the sixties, and my family's firm decided that there were good signs that there might be metals there, so we came, my father Daniel Hochstetter and one hundred-fifty miners from Augsberg. Have you been to Keswick, Sir Robert?"

"No," said Carey, very friendlywise, "I haven't. It's only sixty miles from Carlisle so I'm afraid I have to make some excuse and my excuse is that all the cattle-raiders, robbers, and murderers are in the opposite direction. Why do you call yourself Hepburn, if your name is really…er…Hocksteader?"

"That's why," said Hepburn. "Who can pronounce Hochstetter? I find it hard to say myself and I've had plenty of practice. My Lord Bothwell gave me permission to use his surname when I was working for him."

"Ah." Carey was having some trouble drinking the wine. "And did you ever know a man called Hans Schmidt, the gunsmith?"

Hepburn didn't let his smile become fixed, allowed himself to look puzzled, then reminiscent, as if Schmidt had no importance. "Slightly," he admitted. "Not very well and it turned out he wasn't a gunsmith at all, didn't it? Where is he now? I've not seen him since the summer."

Now that was good. Carey looked away and his face twitched a little. "Oh, I think he's dead," he said. "He made an enemy of Lord Spynie after all."

That was what Hepburn had heard and it was good news. "He was a coneycatcher and not a very good one," he said callously. "Bold but stupid."

"Yes," said Carey. "Tell me, do you know a woman called Poppy—Prosperpina Burn?"

Hepburn paused for just a second, frowning in thought. "No, should I?"

"I don't know."

"She's not at Court, I think."

"No, she's the widow of a Scottish minister of religion who was murdered about two months ago—I hanged his murderers myself."

Hepburn lifted his cup in toast. "Well, I'm delighted that justice was done," he said respectfully, but saw no answering smile.

"Thank you," said Carey gravely. "Is it true that you are arranging the scenery for this year's New Year Masque?"

"Yes, I am," Hepburn said, happy to get away from areas where he had to lie, back to areas where the truth was the best concealment. "I can show you my plans, if you like. You see, I want the King to be in the middle with the Earth above him…"

"You don't hold with Copernicus his theory that all goes around the Sun?"

"Of course not," said Hepburn, a little testily. "Mr Anricks has worked up a very pretty theory about it, but in fact William of Ockham made it clear two hundred years ago that if we have two answers philosophical, we should always pick the simplest. Not in human affairs, perhaps, but certainly in philosophy. The Sun manifestly rises in the east and obviously sets in the west and appears to go around the Earth, which clearly seems to be the centre of all. Why not agree with the simple answer that that is in fact what it does, instead of some Papist flight of fancy that has every planet flying around the Sun and the Earth itself flinging itself through space?"

"Well…"

"Depend upon it, if we were rolling around the Sun, the seas would show it and the winds would show it and why wouldn't we ourselves feel the motion?"

"Well, Mr Anricks is very convincing…."

"Madness often is. He may be convinced himself but that doesn't mean it's true."

"No…"

"Are you watching the fireworks this evening?"

"Of course, if they're on…"

"It's looking like snow to be sure, but I think it will hold off until the last rockets have been fired."

"Oh, why? Scottish weather isn't usually so co-operative?"

Hepburn couldn't tell him that the Demiurge would see to it so he laughed instead, looking round at the small knots of gentlemen and ladies talking and some dice games starting up. "In fact I must ask you to excuse me, Sir Robert, because I'm helping with setting some of the fuses and suchlike, although the Han family have most of it in hand."

"The Han family?"

"The Chinese, who are the best firework makers in the world, and their French managers. We are lucky to have them. They are related to the family that makes the Queen's fireworks in England and they even say it was the Chinese who invented gunpowder—when everyone knows it was a Papist monk looking for a cure for constipation." Hepburn paused and grinned. "And he found it."

Carey laughed again at that and so Hepburn hurried out of the hall. He was sweating lightly when he met the French Master Artificer and went to look at the arrangements in the gardens in the deepening dusk. All through the evening he found himself arguing both sides: he should kill Carey, to stop him interfering; he should not kill Carey, because he had fooled him. He set the fuses, advised on more than one for each rocket, checked the metal cages and tubes were firm, while the war went on in his head. From the fireworks platform at the end of the garden, by the storage sheds and lean-tos, he looked out at the Court assembling on the benches in the cold evening to view the fireworks, saw the torches flaring and pages running around with jugs full of mulled wine and beer, saw the musicians gathering in their carts, their Chapel Master coming to make final arrangements, saw the lads from the stables gathering as close as they could get to the fireworks, held back by ropes and scowling men-at-arms. Should he kill Carey or not?

The King and the Queen arrived with the King's favourite nobles, including Lord Spynie, for a wonder, and the Queen's ladies-in-waiting. He had looked into using the fireworks to kill the King, of course. It would be a lot easier to kill Carey.

The music started, a new composition. On the beat, the Master Artificer lit the first fuse and watched as it burned towards the first array of rockets, before stepping back behind the metal shield. Hepburn took cover there too and found Carey standing there, talking to the Master Artificer animatedly in French as the rockets coursed their way into the pitch-black skies and burst into flowers of blue and white and gold and red.

Just for a moment, Hepburn was angry and then he relaxed. Of course Carey would come to watch the fireworks from the Artificer's shield; that was where he could make sure none of the rockets had been misplaced, nor the Roman candles pointed horizontally instead of vertically. That was why Hepburn had not used the fireworks, in the end. There were too many people involved, too many hands; it was not controllable.

So he laughed with Carey, listened with satisfaction to the "oohs" and "aahs" from the crowd, shared some brandy from his flask. Carey now seemed more interested in the Earl of Huntly and even asked Hepburn if he had seen Huntly anywhere near the fireworks. Hepburn was able to answer with complete honesty, that he hadn't and he thought the Earl would be very noticeable.

They stood surrounded by the peppery sharp stink of gunpowder and the smoke as the Scottish Court besieged Heaven with its ordnance of flowers and waterspouts and spinning wheels and a flag of St Andrew in blue and sparkling white at the end, all made of purest fire, all lasting a few seconds and then dying, unlike the mysterious stars hidden behind the sour-smelling clouds.

After the show was over, they shook hands and Carey ambled back to the main crowds of the Court where King James was drunk and shouting and the musicians kept playing until the falling flakes of snow sent everybody back into the hall.

Carey was thoughtful as he stood around in a group of other gentlemen, by a tapestry, watching the Queen's ladies dancing a charming Danish dance together, very like an Allemande, in fact. He felt he had drawn a blank with Jonathan Hepburn, the man seemed as honest as anyone at Court could afford to be and friendlier than most. He dismissed the man from his thoughts because he was now certain the man to watch was Huntly and he was trying to think how he could work out what the earl was planning. Sadly, being mainly illiterate except for his signature, Huntly had probably not written notes on how to kill a king.

Then he caught sight of Anricks, deep in conversation with John Napier again, and went after him, brought him to bay just outside the hall.

Napier continued down the corridor, heading for the gate, saying he was for bed and perhaps a little more calculating, as if it were something he did for fun to relax him. However Carey had urgent business with Anricks.

"You know that the Dispute about the Heavens is set for New Year's Eve and His Highness will dispute with you and Napier, as the defender of Ptolemy," Carey said to him.

Anricks had clearly forgotten everything about it and stared back at Carey, going paler and paler.

"His Highness?" repeated Anricks.

"Yes, indeed."

"Oh."

"So how is your own speech progressing, Mr Anricks? May I hear some of it?"

"Ah," said Anricks, reddening a little, "I own I have been studying mathematics and not writing my speech…"

"You only have a week," said Carey, looking very unhappy.

"Yes, but these mathematical Bones are so beautiful…" And Anricks launched into a long abstruse explanation about squares and square roots, during which he accidentally fell into Latin and continued in that language, so that Carey's eyes glazed over in minutes. To save himself from actually falling asleep in the face of Anricks' enthusiasm, he asked if Napier had published a book of his new numbers. Anricks looked annoyed as he reverted to English.

"No, he is much more interested in his book about the Apocalypse," said Anricks sadly, "which is worthy, of course, but still…He is far too modest about his new numbers, says they are only mathematical tricks to make calculating the Number of the Beast easier."

"Well, I suppose that makes some sense at least. Will he assist you in the speech?"

"Ah no. We have differing opinions on the celestial spheres and will be on opposing sides."

"Really?"

"Yes, Mr Napier is quite old-fashioned in some ways and seeks to keep some of Ptolemy: he avers that all the planets save the Earth do indeed go around the Sun, but then the Sun, and all the rest too, goes around the Earth."

"Oh. Is that possible?"

"It is possible if the Almighty were quite insane," said Anricks irritably, "but since the chief virtue of Copernicus is its simplicity and Napier's notion is even more complicated than Ptolemy, I think we can dismiss it."

Carey hid a smile. "Must things philosophical be simple?"

"Yes, Sir Robert, they must. Which is harder to do, complexity or simplicity? Which is more beautiful? Which makes sense? William of Ockham made all this very clear two hundred years ago."

"Ah…"

"Well, Mr Napier's fixed on it so he will speak about it. What happens after His Highness wins the Dispute?"

Carey smiled. At least Anricks was always realistic.

"There is to be a Masque of the Planetary Spheres and then all finishes with a dance of the Queen's ladies who will dance whichever pattern the King judges is true."

"Wearing very little?"

"Of course. And either they will circle the Earth, or they will circle the Sun or presumably they will circle Mr Napier's Sun while it circles the Earth. Personally, I hope Mr Napier's view prevails."

"What?" Anricks' face was horrified.

"I would delight in seeing the Queen's ladies dancing around the Sun as he dances around the Earth. I think it could be quite funny, with plenty of collisions, especially as the ladies will all be very drunk."

Anricks put his hand over his eyes and let out a low moan.

"And you've written your speech, have you?"

"Er...no."

"Nearly finished it?"

"Ah...not exactly."

"But you've started it?"

"Well..."

"Mr Anricks," said Carey, putting his hand on Anricks' arm and looking into his eyes very seriously, "you have six days. Get on with it."

"But..."

"I, your bearmaster, say, Hup, hup, hup! Write your speech, Mr Anricks!"

◇◇◇

Wee Colin Elliot tipped his helmet back on his head. "Mrs Dodd," he said, "I'm told yer husband is in Edinburgh."

"Ay," she said, proud of herself because her voice was steady and she was talking to Henry's blood-enemy. "Perhaps."

"Where are yer kin?"

"Run away," she said. "Gone home. They're not here now."

"Ay," Wee Colin looked about him. "Skinabake Armstrong's gone as well," he said. "That's lucky, is that."

Janet said nothing. She stood beside the cart next to the silenced Widow Ridley and heard the few winter birds hurting the air with their hope. Would he kill her?

"Well, Mrs Dodd," he said, leaning his arms comfortably on the saddlebow to talk down to her, "ye'll come wi' me."

"Why?" said Janet, "What use are we tae ye, an old woman and the wife of Sergeant Dodd? D'ye think ma husband will pay a ransom for me? He willna."

Wee Colin laughed, showing good teeth and a twinkle in his blue eyes. "Nay, Mrs Dodd, I ken that. He'd choke on it so he would. No, I want him to come to me, on his own."

"He willna do it."

"He will. Come on wi' us, missus, we havenae got all day."

Very slowly Janet hitched the unwilling sleepy ponies to the cart and then gave them nosebags as a reward. She hitched Shilling to the cart as well. Even more slowly she tidied up after them, found a glove, a sock, and two crossbow bolts left behind, and then went to the head of the lead pony and took off the nosebags. They got the cart out of the barn and started up the hill to get out of Liddesdale, the worst part of the March. Wee Colin and his fifty raiders paced beside and around her.

It was mostly Elliot country, she knew that, but wondered if there might be any Dodds or Armstrongs around—except Skinabake, of course. She wouldn't make that mistake again. If you're willing to sell out your second cousin, what else might you do? She didn't think there would be any Dodds, and if there had been once, there certainly wouldn't be any now. Besides, she was an English Armstrong and she did know that her father would be highly delighted to raid the Elliot herds with a cast-iron excuse.

Wee Colin would not let her be, asking her questions and seeming unoffended at her stony silence. "What d'ye know of our bloodfeud wi' the Dodds?" he asked once and she said, "I know ye lost."

"Ay, we did," he said, tapping his teeth with his thumb. He smiled easily, did Colin Elliot. "And what did ye make of the doings at Dick of Dryhope's tower?"

"Ye lost that too," she told him. "Worse, ye were outmaneovred and then ye looked frightened. Were ye?"

"Frightened? Ay, Ah was," said Wee Colin affably and she looked at him sidelong. "Yer Deputy Warden had us lined up for the slaughter between the pikes and the arquebuses. I fought in the Netherlands maself for a few years, I knew what he was at. Never expected to see it on the Border."

Janet made a short "huh" noise.

"Ay," said Wee Colin, "I didna fancy it. I hear Henry Dodd's offended at the Deputy for letting us get away."

She decided to go back into silence and anyway they were going steeply uphill on a very rocky road and poor Shilling was groaning and puffing even though he wasn't pulling anything. Widow Ridley had already got down to walk, her knitting needles clicking away.

"Tugger, Wattie's Watt, Blind Jock, and Eckie, come over here and help wi' the cart," ordered Wee Colin and four of the men came over and started helping to push the cart and get it over the worst rocks in the road. They complained about it but not very much, which was impressive.

"How far to yer tower?" Widow Ridley asked in a querulous voice.

"We'll see where we are come nightfall, Mrs Ridley. I'm expecting it to snow," said Wee Colin. "Why is the cart so heavy?"

"It's full of linen," said Janet. "We were taking it all to Edinburgh to sell."

"Och," Wee Colin shook his head. "That's a pity. I wis hoping ye had some food there."

"I have, but not enough for all your gang."

"I'd take it very kindly if ye'd share with us."

Janet sighed. It wasn't as if she had a choice and at least he was asking politely. "Bread, cheese, sausage, in the hemp bags. Help yerselves."

"Your kin have gone to fetch Will the Tod."

"Ay, my father," Janet said. "I hope so."

For some reason Wee Colin laughed again. "He'll be out in a day or two, barring snow, mebbe four days if he calls on William of Kinmount. He's got ten days for the hot trod."

Janet didn't dignify that with an answer. She could feel his eyes on her, shrugged. What would happen, would happen, and there was very little she could do about it now. The whole

expedition had been a daft idea. She had been wood even to
think of it, and if both she and Henry got out of it alive, she
wouldn't blame Henry if he decided to beat her black and blue.

Wee Colin Elliot was the headman of a large surname and
had been for ten years. His tower was the biggest of all their
towers but that was not where they went as the skies darkened
over their heads to purple. Instead they stopped at a little tower
a way from the road to Hawick, no more than a fortified house
with a squat keep and a strong fence around it. He didn't explain
whose it was and Janet didn't ask.

And yet Mrs Elliot was there to welcome them at the gate.
She was a Fenwick and Janet curtseyed to her since it didn't hurt
to be polite and Widow Ridley did the best she could with her
knees as they were.

They were led up the stairs in the tower, to the third floor
where the family lived. Janet caught a glimpse of a woman with
a veil around her face peering at her and another older woman
who smiled friendlywise, and she and Widow Ridley were led
into a little chamber with a truckle bed in it and a jordan and
nothing else. On the bed there was a tray of gritty bread, cheese,
and pickled onions and a pottle of ale which was very welcome,
for both of them were hungry. Nor did they lock the door on
her which surprised her but she was too tired to do more than
tiptoe to see out of the arrowslit. Dusk was coming on and the
ugly black clouds coming from the northeast made a sour smell
on the wind.

She sighed and sat on the bed next to Widow Ridley who
was unpinning her hair, taking her cap off, and attempting
to plait her hair. Janet watched her struggle for a minute and
then tapped her shoulder and took over the job. They ate their
supper in silence and Janet put the tray on the floor when they
had finished.

She wished she had her Bible to read. She was getting better
and better at reading though she still had to read it aloud to
herself, as Henry did too, and she was right in the middle of
the exciting bits about David. To her surprise, the linen was

still in the cart with the barrels and about half of the food. It hadn't been pillaged as she expected and she had seen it pushed into a storage shed. The horses had all been unhitched, given some feed and settled for the night in a stable nearby. Again that was a surprise. She would have expected them to be sent to the paddock to mix with their new stablemates, not given expensive grain.

"I wish…" she started.

"Ye wish I hadnae tellt ye about they witchy things and the man that bribed Sergeant Dodd."

"Yes," said Janet, annoyed at being so easily read.

"Ay well, he may surprise ye, Wee Colin, he's got a steady head on him." She was knitting again, turning the heel.

"If you told him…"

"Nay, how would I do that, d'ye think I'm a witch? But I think mebbe Wee Colin Elliot's been waiting for this day for a long weary while."

Janet nodded. It was a good answer to Dick of Dryhope's tower. Dodd's blood enemy now had her as his prisoner. Nothing good could come of that. All she could hope for was that her father would come for her but now she thought about it, why should he? There was ransom to be demanded and, depending on the price, paid or argued over. Henry wouldn't like that. He wouldn't like it that Skinabake had clearly sold her to the Elliots, and he wouldn't like it that she had been taken on her way to Edinburgh. He wouldn't like having to go so far into Elliot territory to rescue her. They had all heard and laughed at the tale of Geordie Burn in the Middle March being fooled when he took Lady Elizabeth Widdrington. She didn't think anything like that would happen to her. Why had Skinabake sold her? It had been going well enough until then.

She shut her eyes and bit down on her bottom lip to stop herself crying. Widow Ridley was already tucked up in bed, still knitting and powering through the foot of the sock.

"Och hinny," she said, "come ben tae bed. What can ye do about it now?"

◇◇◇

In the morning nothing was any better. It was cold and the clouds were still hanging low and threatening over the little valley with a sprinkling of sugar on the hillsides but it was too cold to snow. There was no fire in the room and so they stayed in bed and Janet dozed while Widow Ridley finished off the sock and cast on another one.

Eventually booted feet came up to the door and a spotty girl came in with a tray of more gritty bread, cheese, and ale for them both, and took the old tray away. Janet started pacing, facing the first day of inactivity since last winter but this time she hadn't even any linen to hem. It felt very strange to have her hands doing nothing and she found they got up to peculiar antics, twisting and knitting round themselves.

By an hour later she was enraged that the jordan was full so she tried the door and found it unlocked, since it was distance that imprisoned them, not walls. She took the jordan, fully prepared to throw it in the face of anyone who questioned her.

On the narrow stairs she met Colin Elliot's wife, the serious-looking brown-haired woman she had curtseyed to the night before. She curtseyed again because it was her tower and said, "Will ye show me where to tip this, Mrs Elliot?"

There was a pause. "I told Annie to empty it in the morning when she brought your breakfast," she said, her eyes narrowing.

"Ay, well, she didna."

"This way," and Mrs Elliot showed her out to the yard where she tipped it onto the dungheap and sluiced it in a buck of rainwater.

She went to go upstairs again and Mrs Elliot hesitated and then said, "I'd like tae speak tae ye, Mrs Dodd, if ye've the leisure?"

Well that was prettily put. Janet nodded. "I'll go and help Mrs Ridley to get dressed," she said, "then we'll both come down."

Widow Ridley was very happy to come down to the second-floor hall of the tower where there was a good fire burning in the great fireplace. They sat side by side on a bench while Mrs

Elliot took the chair with arms. Girls were running in and out with table linen and there was a large log sitting burning slowly in the fireplace and holly and ivy decorating the walls.

"Mrs Dodd," began Mrs Elliot, "Ah was niver so grateful in my life when my Mr Elliot came home two months ago and said he had escaped a massacre."

Janet nodded gravely. "I heard about it."

"Now I don't know why the Deputy Warden let them get away, but I'm grateful, believe me."

Janet said nothing at first, then said hesitantly, "Sir Robert Carey is a Courtier from London wi' strange notions. He wants tae stop feud here on the Borders. Ye cannae do that without some show of goodwill, I think. He had your man and his surname in the hollow of his hand, coming in for their friends the Grahams. And by not crushing him, he said, if ye want peace, I do too."

Mrs Elliot nodded. "That's what Colin thought. What did yer man think tae it?"

Janet paused a long time before she answered. Should she lie? If she told the truth, what should she say about herself? Unwillingly she found herself thinking of what Mrs Hogg, the midwife, had said and the war it had started in her chest.

"I'll tell ye straight," she said at last, "he's very angry. He still wants tae finish the feud the old way."

It was no secret, after all. Alone of all the men there at Dick of Dryhope's tower, Henry Dodd had wanted slaughter and death.

"Could ye convince him otherwise?"

Janet laughed. "It wad be a waste of time tae try," she said. "It's a new way of thinking and Henry's old-fashioned. He still loves bows when everyone else is mad for guns and pistols."

Mrs Elliot nodded slowly again. "Wee Colin has a plan," she said. "He thinks I dinna ken what it is but I've known him long enough and I got his brother to tell me." Janet raised her sandy brows. "He doesnae want ransome for ye. He ainly brought ye to this tower because it's gaunae snow and when it has, he'll take ye on to Edinburgh." Janet did her best not to look disbelieving.

"He's already turned down an offer of ain hundert pounds fra yer father and another of a hundred and fifty pounds fra Kinmont Willie."

"My God," cackled Widow Ridley, "that's a lot o' money for one thrawn ginger cow."

Janet found herself blushing. It *was* a lot of money and her father and uncle had made the offers quickly. That was a high compliment.

"So what's his plan?" asked Widow Ridley, leaning forward.

"He'll help ye both get to Edinburgh and you will carry a challenge to single combat to your husband. Just Wee Colin Elliot and Sergeant Dodd, alone, to try the matter on their ain bodies."

"Och," said Janet and sat back, feeling sick.

"Ay," chirped Widow Ridley, "I see his thinking. It's clever and brave. As long as Sergeant Dodd's alive, the old feud's alive, so with him dead, it will die. And if Sergeant Dodd kills Wee Colin, he may accept that as an end. He'll be at the horn in England in any case."

"Brave?" asked Mrs Elliot.

Widow Ridley was enjoying herself. "Och, Wee Colin may be a bonny fighter but Henry Dodd has got something special, he's a natural killer like Geordie Burn or Cessford, but halfway sane. Wee Colin's got no chance. Mah money's on the Sergeant."

In the distance, Janet thought that the book on that fight would probably be large.

Mrs Elliot frowned. "I think he could win, but I don't like it, I admit. They could both die of their wounds."

Janet thought but didn't say, that it didn't matter about wounds, Dodd would win. Maybe he would die later, but not before he had killed Elliot. Suddenly her eyes filled with tears which infuriated her. She had always known she was likely to be a widow, but she had always assumed she would have children. Now she knew she wouldn't, or not from Henry; it made her heart sick to think of him dying.

But if he fought and won the duel, perhaps that would ease the anger in him against the Elliots. Perhaps.

"Do you want me to carry the challenge?"

"Ay, that's whit I said. If ye say ye won't, Wee Colin will just use a messenger."

"Ah'll do it," piped up Widow Ridley with unseemly enthusiasm.

"Ay," Janet thought. "If I carry it, and Mr Elliot has helped me tae Edinburgh, Sergeant Dodd will still say yes."

Mrs Elliot sighed. "I ken that. Ay well, I've given ye warning." She laughed a little. "My man's pleased as punch wi' his idea, says it'll finish the feud whatever happens. Can I ask ye to see to that, Mrs Dodd? When they fight, if my Colin is killed, will ye hold yer man to the deal?"

Janet reached forward and caught Mrs Elliot's cold right hand with hers.

"There's ma hand, there's ma heart," she said. "I will, I swear it."

Mrs Elliot smiled. "Ye never know with a fight," she said. "But thank you. Now, I must get back tae my kitchen, see ye, I've a goose to bake."

Wee Colin Elliot spoke to her later as the skies dumped their snow in fat flakes that were soon falling so thick you couldn't see a hand in front of your face. He was standing in front of the fire in his Sunday doublet, not his workaday jack, the white linen of his falling band making a bold sight against his weathered face. He was a nice-looking man too, blue eyes, black hair, for all he was so short, about the same height as Janet herself.

She had to remind herself that it was Christmas, which she had all but forgotten with all the botheration. Here in the little lesser tower, they were a long way from any kirk and there was no feasting of the surname, although dinner had been good with a roast goose and breadsauce and some more of those Brussels sprouts, along with the cabbage and bashed neeps and fried sippets and a good smoked and boiled ham. The families round about had come in to receive the hospitality of the headman. They had all gone home early, with nervous looks at the sky.

"D'ye think he'll take my challenge?"

"Ay, o'course. Even though he's not the Dodd headman."

"I know Jamie Dodd, we've allied on a couple of raids and he's a sound man."

Jamie Dodd was about six or seven years younger than Henry, and his youngest brother, but they hadn't met for years. He was young to be headman of a riding surname but that was accounted for by the feud and the way it had taken so many of the fighting men.

"What does Jamie think to yer plan, Mr Elliot?" she asked.

"Ay," said Wee Colin, "he's no' agin it. He thinks I should use a champion."

"Then Henry will not come."

"I ken that. Besides, Mrs Dodd, that's not how I do things."

"A pity."

Wee Colin smiled. "Ye're so sure your man will win?"

"Ay," she said, and shut her mouth with a snap.

"Ye're saying I've no chance?"

"Ay, ye've a chance. It's a fight."

"I wonder what my odds will be in the book?"

Janet didn't answer this for a while. "Mr Elliot, ye're set on this?"

He looked down at his brown square hands. "Ay."

She sighed. "I'll take your message and we'll send a message back to ye. I think we may have to wait a bit, though," she added and went to peer out of the upper door, with the ladder below it to the ground. Snow was falling silently on snow that was already settling, a siege of feathers.

◇◇◇

The morning of St Stephen's Day brought them a new world in Edinburgh, everything made new and beautiful, all the dungheaps turned into respectable hills, all the roofs and walls and fences draped in white blankets, the young dogs running around barking, the cats touching the snow with disapproving paws and shuddering back to the fires.

Children were soon playing in the snow, throwing snowballs and building snowmen, while the dominies and ministers hurried about telling them it was idolatry and the work of the Devil and to take them down at once. By evening it was snowing again on half-swept streets and soon the footprints were blurred again.

King James went hunting the day after and Carey and Dodd went along with the mob of nobles and attendants. It was the most perfect hunt Carey had ever seen, bright and the snow dazzling in the forest where it hadn't been trampled, trees black against it and a long run after a most splendid hart of fourteen points that the dogs finally pulled down on the Leith links as the sunset echoed his blood across the sky.

They all rode home down the road from Leith, with the King talking animatedly in the middle about what he would do with the hart's antlers and then the Earl of Huntly started up an old song in his astonishing bass. Carey knew another version of it in English and answered him and then all the other nobles and attendants and foresters came in on the chorus. The sound of the powerful deep voices singing as they rode back through the snowy fields with the crows starting from their rookeries made the hairs on Dodd's neck stand up.

And the next day it froze hard again, but the day after that it was a little warmer and the icicles were lengthening and by that time the snow had become a nuisance, with great piles of it beside the main streets and all the alleys and wynds turned to deathtraps of ice and slush.

By then, true to his word, Wee Colin Elliot had taken Widow Ridley and Janet Armstrong across the naked hills and onto the main road from Hawick again. They stayed the night in Hawick where the innkeeper wouldn't take her money and then he and twenty of his men accompanied them all the way to Edinburgh, so they could see the walls and the great lump of rock that was Arthur's Seat, still cloaked with nearly virgin snow.

Wee Colin nodded to Janet then and rode back down the way to Hawick, leaving her with Widow Ridley and the cart and all of the horses, including Shilling, whom Janet was riding. It took them the rest of the day to get to Hollyrood House since the road was slippery and dangerous and they went at a slow walk, and even when they came to the abbey gate, there was a long argument to be had with the men there about who they were and where they had come from. They had to send someone to fetch Henry Dodd in the end.

eOINBURGh, new YeaR'S eve 1592

Young Hutchin Graham was talking to one of the hobbies while he got the knots out of the hobby's mane. Partly because he was bored with all the high doings at Court and now bored with the snow in which he had built a snowman, secretly because he wasn't a wean anymore, but also because he was feeling worried and upset and the stables were warm and dry and smellt nice of horses and hay and a little bit of horseshit. He didn't know where Sergeant Dodd was, which was just as well.

That was the problem. He had been in the small storeroom with the leaden tanks in it, the night before, despite the foul smell because he liked to imagine himself as the man he had seen swiving his woman there. Then he had heard voices in the passageway, and dived behind the tanks to hide, peeked out and seen the same man with the curly hair, but this time with Sergeant Dodd. They stood by the door and talked in low voices, and Dodd's face was sullen and bad-tempered as usual.

He thought he had heard the name Carey mentioned, at which Dodd's face darkened even more, and then, clear as a bell. "Kill him after New Year's Day."

"Not tomorrow?"

"He has a job to do for me on New Year's morning. Kill him if you can in the afternoon."

"Ay, I can."

"It may not be up to you. New Year's Day, in the afternoon? Understand?"

"Ay."

And then the man with the curly hair counted twenty gold angels into Dodd's hand, and the Sergeant tinkled them into a leather purse and put it in the pocket of his jerkin. Then they both went out, leaving Young Hutchin stunned and fearful.

"So, Sorrel," he said, "whit do ye make of that? Should Ah tell the Courtier or no'? Cos Dodd'll get another fifteen pounds from Ritchie Graham intae the bargain and…well, ye see ma trouble?"

The hobby sidestepped and swung his tail.

"Ye know the Courtier best," Hutchin said. "Whit should I do? If I dinna tell him, my family will ay be happy and if I do… there'll be mither wi' Sergeant Dodd and the mood he's in, that could be the end o' me."

Sorrel snorted and shook his head.

"Och…" Hutchin began and then stopped for there was a commotion outside in the yard.

◇◇◇

Carey stood at the door of the King's audience chamber, an addition to the abbey built by the King's grandfather, James V, and nearly as large as the hall. He was receiving the guests to the Disputation, many of them respectable merchants and ministers, some with their wives. After the Disputation, there would be a Masque by the Queen's ladies and the King's gentlemen, and the point of it was to give the Queen's ladies a chance to wear very pretty diaphonous semi-classical robes and to give the gentlemen a chance to show off their dancing and leaping and their outlandish and expensive costumes.

Anricks was standing on the other side of the door in his cramoisie brocade suit, looking very philosophical. Carey was happy because his own new suit fitted him well and looked magnificent, being of dark green damask and black velvet in the Scottish style with a peascod stomach and a ruff, trimmed with narrow gold lace, the canions daringly the same fabric as the doublet, with a set of wonderful buttons in gold which Anricks had also paid for without complaint. His new high-crowned beaver hat completed the look and gave him even more height. He thought that he alone of the entire Scottish Court had bothered to bathe early that morning after breaking the ice in the Lough, since there were no baths nor stews that he knew of in Edinburgh, thanks to the ministers closing them all down on the grounds of sin. But he could not contemplate the New Year without washing himself beforehand; that was what ten years of serving at the Court of the very nasally sensitive Queen did to you.

At one end of the audience chamber, on a dais, were the King and Queen's thrones, the King's of gilded wood with arms, the Queen's of whitepainted wood without arms, both of them with a cloth of estate over them, both empty at the moment. The King would take part in the Dispute in the audience chamber but then everyone would process into the hall for a banket and to watch the Masque. The Queen would take part in the Masque with her ladies and then join her husband on the dais in the audience chamber to say goodbye to the guests.

At last everybody was there, including Maitland of Thirlstane, the Lord Chancellor, and the Catholic earls as well, who were to play a prominent part in the Masque. The Queen and her women wouldn't come until the Masque so everyone could gasp at their costumes. Women couldn't be expected to take an interest in the planets or even know what they were. They were having a New Year's Eve party in the Queen's chambers.

At last King James, in his purple suit, now with a greasy stain down one side of the doublet, stepped down from the dais and paced into the middle of the audience chamber, smiling and his eyes gleaming.

"Guid evening, my lords and gentlemen," he said to the crowd. "I am here not merely as a King but in the guise of a Philosopher King as in Plato, to dispute a matter of true and vital importance—what do the planets or spheres do? Is it true that they dance around the Sun or is it true that they dance around the Earth, the centre of the Universe and the world created by Almighty God? We shall try this matter a little, important as it is, for do not the planets affect us and our lives through their influences in astrology?"

Carey leaned over to Anricks and whispered, "I hope you are prepared?"

"No," said Anricks, "I am not. I have struggled to write a speech and find I cannot do it without mathematics and so I have put the whole into the hands of the Almighty and rest content with whatever He decides to inspire me with."

Carey looked at Anricks with his eyebrows up. "Are you joking?"

Anricks smiled. "No. All is in the hands of the Almighty as it always is."

"Jesus Christ." Carey thought for a moment and then shook Anricks by the hand. "Well, you have more balls than I have ever had. Good luck."

King James had been making a few jokes about people who had found the planets thwarting them. Now he lifted his tones. "And to oppose me with his own plan for the Universe, I call upon Mr John Napier and to oppose me with the Copernican plan for the Universe, I call upon Mr Simon Anricks."

There was a sprinkle of ironic clapping as Napier stepped forward, clutching a sheaf of papers, wearing a new suit of tawny and a tight ruff. He bowed to the King and the assembled company, looked about and blinked.

Anricks waited for half a minute and then stepped forward himself, bowed to the company and genuflected neatly to the King. His face was looking interested and contented and not at all nervous.

"Now," said the King, "what order shall we follow, gentlemen?"

Napier seemed struck dumb by this, opened his mouth a couple of times and then shut it.

"Mr Anricks?"

"Your Majesty, my opinion is that as the King, the representative of the accepted order and, as it were, the reigning champion..." some people laughed at the pun "...you should begin and state the situation as it currently obtains among the planets. Mr Napier should follow you because he is Scottish and I should come last of all because I am only English and speaking for a revolutionary...yes, gentlefolks, a *revolutionary* theory." There was another light tittering. "And then Your Majesty should sum up all the arguments in the manner of a judge and make your decision."

James smiled gently at him. "You will not become nervous, waiting so long to speak?"

Anricks paused and then smiled back. "Possibly. But then I might gain some inspiration from your speech and Mr Napier's. Perhaps you may even convert me back to Ptolemy again."

Some more people clapped and the King stepped into the centre and began to speak. He spoke well, in his pleasant canny Scotch, describing the world as everyone knew it to be, immoveable and solid, in the centre of the Universe with the Sun and planets whirling round it in their complicated patterns. He quoted many authorities, including Lucretius, he dealt with the unfortunate epicycles and epi-epicycles as examples of the wonderful complexity of God's Mind, and in an hour he brought himself round to the conclusion that all is exactly as Ptolemy and Aristotle before him described—the crystal spheres in their appointed places and the Earth at the centre as the home of mankind and the Saviour, Jesus Christ.

It was a good speech, little touches of humour here and there, and quite short at only an hour. Everyone cheered and the King knocked back a cup of wine in one.

Napier stepped forward next, shining with sweat, his sheaf of papers visibly trembling in his hand. He began speaking in a mumble, got louder every so often and then softer and Carey soon lost track because Napier was doing exactly what he had warned Anricks against and speaking mathematics to an audience of mathematical virgins. The King drank more wine, stopped pretending to be interested and started gossiping with Lord Huntly and then, when he arrived at the King's elbow, with Lord Spynie.

The incomprehensible mumble continued until Napier turned a page, suddenly looked wildly at it, glanced up bewildered and said, "Alas, I have forgot the rest of my speech, which I think I may have left at home..."

"Our thanks to Mr Napier for his very learned explanation of how the planets all go around the Sun and then the Sun goes around the Earth," said the King and hiccupped. "Now Mr Anricks, what have you to add?"

Anricks stepped forward. "I am not a learned man, unlike the King or Mr Napier, I am only, as they say in France, an amateur of astrology," he began. "I would like to conduct an experiment here in this chamber and for it I will need six men. First, to dismiss Mr Napier's rather ugly Universe?" He brought forward the nobles who would take part in the Masque, some already wearing their costumes, disposed them with Earth at the centre, who happened to be the Maxwell, because he was wearing a lime green doublet and hose, the Moon and the Sun (or Lord Huntly) circling the Earth and then the other planets circling the Sun. He commanded them to begin and within minutes all the planets had bumped into each other and the Earth, to Maxwell's annoyance. Before a fight could begin between Maxwell and Mars, he stopped them, disposed them with Maxwell in the middle and Moon and Sun going around first, and the other planets in orderly pattern after. This began circling quite well and then Anricks spoiled it all by calling out "Mercury, go backwards" and "Venus, go backwards" which caused chaos. Again he stopped the experiment. "I am very sorry, Ptolemy," he shouted, "but your Universe will not answer." Everyone laughed, thoroughly enjoying the whole thing and especially that they weren't listening to a learned disquisition but watching drunken nobles falling over each other.

The King was watching with interest. Anricks, went to him, bent the knee and then spoke quietly to him which made him laugh.

Anricks brought the King into the centre. "Firstly, I should explain something. In this our play of the planets, for the real, the true Universe, we cannot use anyone other than the real, true King, even my Lord Huntly will not do. For the real Sun is much much bigger than the planets and it is a long way away. The fire of its heat is immense, it flames day and night, it IS day and night for when the Earth turns to it there is day and when the Earth turns away, there is night. The Sun is not really a planet, gentlemen, but it is most clearly a King."

He pointed at the King. "Here, gentlemen, we have the Sun, the King, whose light shines on all of us. We place him in the centre because the centre is the place from which all things flow. Now we put Mercury here, and Venus. The Earth comes next, with her partner, the Moon." He had Maxwell hold hands with the young man in silver tissue which made both of them uncomfortable since neither was a bugger. Then he placed Mars, then Jupiter and Saturn. "Pray begin my lords, begin your circles. Circle around the King, the Sun, as your lord and master and perceive the beauty and fitness of Copernicus his Universe!"

Despite all of them being drunk, the nobles did a very creditable job of circling the Sun; there were no collisions and even Maxwell and his Moon circled without incident.

"But Mr Anricks," said the King, his fists on his hips, enjoying himself immensely, "this would work just as well around the Earth, and does."

"Yes, Your Majesty, if we forget that the Sun is huge and at a great distance. It is, according to Arab calculation, millions and millions of miles away and millions of miles across. How can so great a celestial body circle something that is smaller and not made of flame? The Earth would be burned to a crisp. Here we have not only the solution to the problem of the retrogrades but also to the fact that the Sun is made of fire and enormous. I say that the Sun is naturally the King of the Planets and that naturally the planets dance attendance upon him."

He went on one knee to the King again. "My tale is done, Your Majesty."

Very prettily, because they were after all courtiers, the other nobles ceased circling and each knelt on one knee to the King in the centre who clapped his hands and laughed.

Anricks stood and backed, leaving the King to find for tradition and commonsense and say that the Earth was naturally the centre, as the Masque in the hall would shortly display.

Carey clapped him on the shoulder. "Mr Anricks, wonderfully done! If they had not set the whole Masque up to circle the Earth, you would be the victor."

Anricks was flushed with exhilaration and triumph. "I know," he said, "I think His Highness wishes he did not have to find perforce for tradition. But never mind. I have done right by dead Copernicus and that is all I ask."

Carey shook his head in wonder. "I have never seen a scholarly argument done in such a way before."

"This is what happens when you put all in the hands of the Almighty, I find," said Anricks, a little complacently. "I am afraid I can't take the credit."

Carey took his hat off and bowed to the philosopher. "Truly marvellous. Now all we need to do is find the assassin, arrest the Earl of Huntly for treason and our triumph will be complete."

Anricks looked concerned. "I suppose we need to leave that too in the hands of the Almighty," he said, "although that is always a risky thing to do. I could have stood mumbling like Napier, after all."

"You're right," said Carey.

In the bedlam of the hall at New Year's Eve, with everyone shouting once the drink had got to them and laying into the first remove of venison, boar, and a forest's offering of creatures harvested by the King's hunting, Carey concentrated on the wine rather than the food. He found himself surrounded by Danish girls who wanted to tell him something and couldn't say it in Scots, possibly because all of them were helplessly drunk.

He was just trying French on the youngest and juiciest of them when his sleeve was pulled from behind and he saw a wild-eyed Young Hutchin Graham, hatless and sweaty.

"Sir, sir," said Young Hutchin, and then Carey couldn't hear the rest because the girl next to him squealed loudly and started play-fighting the girl next to her until they both fell off the bench. He wasn't entirely clear how he had gotten himself surrounded by the girls. Their mistress the Queen was now sitting next to James and pretending not to notice as Lord Spynie sat himself down on His Highness of Scotland's royal knee."Ye've got to come wi' me," bellowed young Hutchin. "It's important, Sergeant Dodd says ye've got tae come."

Carey was suddenly no longer drunk. Sergeant Dodd had not made himself scarce, he wasn't needed to attend on Carey at a civic banket nor a Masque, but did this mean that Sergeant Dodd was about to earn his cash?

"Tell him to come here," he said, reaching out with his eating knife for the leg of a duck. "Why should I traipse off…?"

"Nay sir, it's important and Janet Armstrong wants ye too."

"Oh." Carey had great respect for Janet. "What's she doing here and not in Gilsland?"

"She came to tell ye stuff ye need tae know, will ye come?"

Carey looked across the roaring crowd. The King was lecturing both Anricks and Napier on something, there was the upraised finger.

"Oh, all right," he said, turned to bow to the juiciest Danish girl, kissed her hand and was rewarded by a clutch at him and alcohol-fuelled giggling. Disentangling himself from the other girl, he sidled across the floor between the benches full of people, bowed elaborately to the King who waved his finger and moved to the door where Red Sandy was waiting, an utterly alien presence in his plain jack and plainer helmet.

"What is it?" he demanded and found himself almost running across the courtyard and down the covered passage to the stables.

There in one of the small yards he found Sergeant Dodd, Janet, and an old woman waiting for him, next to a sturdy cart.

"I must get back…" he started.

"Sir Robert," said Janet firmly, her ginger eyebrows knotted and the freckles standing out on her nose, "one of the reasons I came all this way to Edinburgh was so you could hear Widow Ridley's story and decide what it means." Carey looked as patiently as he could at the old woman, who curtseyed to him, then turned to Janet.

"Where do I start?"

"With the cart you saw."

Over many minutes, Carey picked out Widow Ridley's story. "Foreigners?" he asked. "What kind?"

"The kind ye get in Keswick," Janet told him, "Deutschers. Though one of them spoke good English."

"Allemaynes? Go on."

In the cart were strange things. Widow Ridley enjoyed herself describing how witchy they were until Janet intervened, asking about the strange oil that burned her finger. She waved it.

"I think you are talking about an alchemist's labor-et-ora-torium," Carey said, who had seen the inside of one while he was down in London. "But it's not illegal unlike witchcraft…"

He saw Janet give her husband a look that should by rights have stuck four inches out of his back. Dodd ducked his head and glowered at his boots.

"The same man, Mr Hepburn, came back and talked to Sergeant Dodd."

"Oh?" said Carey. "Mr Hepburn?"

"Ay," said Widow Ridley, "And what did they talk about, that's the question."

Dodd folded his arms and kept glowering at his boots.

A heavy silence seemed to emanate like treacle from Janet while Widow Ridley watched with the interest of a lizard on a rock.

"Och, for God's sake," Dodd finally snarled, "he wis paying me to get oot of the way when Spynie was having another crack at killing ye."

"Oh, I know about that," said Carey. "I sorted that out with Spynie."

"Do ye know how much Spynie was paying my husband, Courtier?"

"Well no, Mrs Dodd, it's really his business. I object to the fact that he didn't tell me he was getting paid to steer clear of me at certain times, but I can hardly object to his getting the money…"

"I seen the tanks you saw, Missus Ridley," said Hutchin suddenly. "They're in one of the back stalls here, full of stuff…"

"One pound in my alehouse," said Widow Ridley.

"I know, it paid for his new helmet…"

"And ten pounds last night, according to what Young Hutchin Graham told me," said Janet, also folding her arms. "Sterling."

It was an awful lot for a simple bribe. Far too much really. "Well," Carey said, "I don't object to bribery. How can I? The entire governance of the country rests on it."

But his eyes had gone to an intense blue and never left Dodd's long angry face. There was a silence.

Carey spoke first. "Sergeant Henry Dodd," he said, back to the Berwick man, "if ye've been paid to kill me, now's yer chance, ye willna get another like it for I've come straight fra the King and he doesnae allow even daggers in his presence. As ye ken full well."

He drew his eating knife, useless though it would be against a man like Dodd. Carey stood waiting, trying to relax, trying to watch Dodd all over for his first move. Considering he was wearing a jack and helmet and had his sword, the fight probably wouldn't last very long, even if Carey could get in close and grapple, because Dodd was a far more skilled wrestler than him.

He wondered what his father would do when he got word his youngest son was dead. What would Lady Widdrington do or his mother—he didn't know, couldn't imagine. They were women and thus completely unpredictable. He swallowed.

At last Dodd lifted his brown eyes to Carey's. Carey saw black anger there that chilled him, struggling with something else. Dodd drew his sword slowly, as if for the first time in his life, he wasn't sure.

From the corner of his eye, Carey could see Young Hutchin had his dagger out and was backing. Then there was the sound of another sword being drawn and when he looked for the source of the sound, he saw it was Red Sandy Dodd. Well, that tore it, if he had ever had a chance, he didn't now.

Red Sandy moved fast towards Carey, who backed up quickly to get the wall behind him and prepared for the first blow...

And found himself looking at the back of Red Sandy's jack as the man turned and stood with his sword raised to cover himself and Carey.

"Brother," said Red Sandy thickly, "I let ye do something flat wrong before because I was nobbut a lad and couldn't stop ye. Ah'm bigger now so ye'll have to come through me to get at the Courtier, d'ye hear?"

"What?" Dodd's mouth twisted. "Ye?"

"Ay," said Red Sandy, his voice steadying. "Ah ken ye're much better than me wi' yer sword and yer fists but I reckon ye've gone woodwild so mebbe that'll give me a chance."

Another person moved suddenly and Carey at first couldn't think who it was. Hutchin? But he had climbed up to one of the high mangers and was sitting there with his dagger still out and his legs dangling.

It was Janet Dodd herself, standing on Red Sandy's left side where she wouldn't get in the way of his swordarm.

"Ay," she said, "I think Red Sandy has the right of it, ye're woodwild and dinna ken what ye're doing. How Wee Colin Elliot would laugh at ye, killing the man that beat them all wi'out a battle, ay, they'd raise their glasses to ye for that."

And she folded her arms again and tipped her hip and stared at her husband while Carey tried his best not to find her attractive.

Everything held in the balance for one second more and then just as Carey was trying to think how he could work with Red Sandy to disarm Dodd without getting killed or accidentally killing Janet, Dodd moved. He sheathed his sword impatiently and his face didn't move as he went to the next stall and started tacking up Whitesock, who nickered with interest.

"Ye're in charge of the men, Alexander Dodd," said his brother, "until himself sells the office anyway. I've business with Wee Colin Elliot."

He mounted up, bent right down over the horse's withers as he went out of the stable door and they heard Whitesock's shod hooves on the cobbles of the stableyard.

Carey let his breath out shakily. As always happened when he was ready for a fight but didn't fight, his hands were trembling. It took him four tries to sheath his eating knife and then he turned to Red Sandy and Janet who were looking stunned.

"Thank you, Mr Dodd, Mrs Dodd," he said formally, and saw with shock that there were tears in Red Sandy's eyes. Not in Janet's though.

"Ay," she said, "but be careful, he'll kill ye next time he sees ye, certain sure of it."

"Of course," said Carey, "if he's taken the money. Do ye really think he's wood?"

"Ay," she said, "he hasnae acted reasonable or hisself since Dick of Dryhope's tower. He's wood."

And then suddenly she crumpled and he had to catch her before she fell and she wept into the shoulder of his brand new damask doublet, risking watermarks, only for a second. Thank God she stopped before damage could be done, stepped back and used her apron to wipe her eyes and blow her nose. "I'm sorry, Deputy," she said, "it willna happen again."

Widow Ridley stood up from where she had taken shelter behind a feedbin and held Janet's hand. "Come on, Red Sandy," she ordered, "find us a place to stay in this palace. I'm going sightseeing tomorrow."

◇◇◇

Carey, thinking hard, went back to the hall which seemed to be rocking slightly with the noise. If Hepburn had given Dodd ten pounds to kill him, presumably half the final fee, it was clear he worked for Spynie and Sir Henry. If he was also an alchemist from the Allemaynes in Keswick, that was significant but still didn't mean he was looking to kill the King. Just because someone had written to a Deutscher in Deutsch, saying don't kill Solomon, it didn't necessarily mean Hepburn was also plotting to kill the King. Carey shook his head. He was sure the traitor was Huntly—but perhaps Hepburn was working for him. It might be an idea to find Hepburn and clap him in irons, though.

The ladies were giving a preview of their dance in the Masque, trotting about holding *papier mâché* globes painted with astrological signs and symbols and with a *papier mâché* god or goddess sitting on them. They were quite large but light because they were hollow. There went Mercury, Venus, Mars, Saturn, and Jupiter, very nicely painted. From the feathered wings adorning the pretty bare and powdered shoulders of the Queen's women, it was clear they were playing the angels who carried the globes on their shoulders and thus enabled them to move.

The girls handed the globes to the servants who carried them back to the hall ready for the Masque and everyone followed in a disorderly procession, talking at the tops of their voices and discreetly hurrying so they could be first in the queue for the banket of sweetmeats after the lords and ladies had served themselves.

In the hall the benches had been pushed to the side, a magnificent banket table laid along the other side so the central floor was clear for the dancing and it had even been swept clear of rushes. In the middle of the floor was a chair with arms and a kind of scaffolding over it, elaborately decorated with ribbons and garlands of holly.

There was Hepburn and two others, carefully carrying a magnificent *papier mâché* globe, painted with all the latest discoveries of the world. Cathay was there, decorated with curiously snaky dragons, and so was the great southern continent which clearly must exist to counterbalance the northern continent and which someone would discover any day now. The Americas were there, the bulge of New Spain and even some of the coastline of the northwestern part of North America, where only savages lived and also unicorns, griffins, and sphinxes.

It looked heavy and they were carrying it with particular care so Carey offered to help and they said they could manage. He watched while they set it on the high frame and sniffed.

"What's that funny smell, a sort of sourness?" he asked.

"The glue," said Hepburn, "unbelievable quantities of glue." He smiled.

Carey smiled back and asked, "The other globes were light enough for the women to carry. Why is the Earth so heavy?"

"It is made of lead to denote its firmness and immovability," said Hepburn. "Because it is at the centre of the Universe, the Earth must counterweigh all the other spheres so they can revolve around it."

For a second, Carey contemplated trying to arrest Hepburn immediately. Could he do it? He didn't think so. The man was organising the scenery for the Masque, the King would be very annoyed to have that disrupted. Carey would have to wait and take him after the Masque was finished.

Apollo the Sun went past, dazzling in golden armour, a little patched and let out, for the Earl of Huntly was wearing His Highness' refurbished costume from years before. With him was Artemis the Moon, a handsome young man wearing quantities of silver tissue, since women couldn't possibly act with the men.

Across the floor Carey saw Lord Spynie, now very prettily decked out as Aphrodite or Venus and he had a job not to roar with laughter since the breasts were strapped on upside down and Spynie was too drunk to notice. He was used to ridiculous costumes and stories for Masques but this was bidding fair to be something special. Maxwell wandered past, still in his bright green, talking intently to two of the Danish girls.

More Danish girls tottered past in a flock, carrying sugarplate bowls of sweetmeats and jelly and little spoons made of sugarplate too, while the gods, goddesses, and other gallant gentlemen went in hot pursuit of them, also carrying ridiculously dainty plates laden with sugar. It made Carey's teeth hurt to think about it.

Carey found himself some green cheese and nibbled that. Anricks was deep in conversation with his rival Napier again. Amazing how they could find so much to talk about concerning numbers.

Lord Spynie was now surrounded by his young henchmen— ah, somebody had spotted the breasts and was helping him to take them off and put them on the right way up. Sir Henry was there too, a cup of brandy in his hand and his face twisted with misery—what in God's name was troubling him now? Oh, his foot was swollen and wrapped in bandages, he had the gout. Automatically Carey scanned the room and found Lady Widdrington among the older women of the Queen's household, not unfortunately scandalously clad in bits of white silk and some straps. She was talking slowly and with many gestures to an old lady. For a moment Carey was lost in thought as he imagined what Elizabeth might look like if she was wearing some scraps of silk and straps instead of the doublet-style velvet Court bodice and a brocade kirtle in cramoisie that she was actually wearing. She looked well in it although as usual she had her modest married woman's cap over all her hair, so you couldn't tell what colour it might be except that it certainly wasn't blond unless she coloured her eyebrows, which of course she might...

Somebody was standing on his foot and there was a pungent smell of piss. Carey looked down and found Sir Henry had limped over and put his good foot on Carey's dancing slipper.

Carey looked down at Sir Henry, shifted his weight and then slowly and carefully put his other shoe on Sir Henry's bandaged foot, so they stood ridiculously caught, as if in the middle of some mummer's trick at the theatre.

"Really, Sir Henry," he said sweetly, "you should be more careful."

"Puppy!" gasped Sir Henry, beads of sweat appearing on his forehead, "Aaah, get off..."

"Certainly, sir," said Carey, increasing the pressure. "The minute you get off my foot."

Sir Henry moved his good foot and Carey slowly released his bad foot which clearly made the old man want to cry out. Spynie was looking their way and grinning under his fetching blond wig. Had it been his idea?

"Sir Robert," hissed Sir Henry, "I challenge you to a duel for looking lasciviously at my wife, sir. And for corrupting her."

Carey thought about this, breathing through his mouth so as not to smell the stink coming from the man. The bill was probably foul: Carey unusually had no idea what his face had been doing while he was staring at Elizabeth but judging by the content of his thoughts, it probably had been lascivious enough. To any other man he would have bowed and apologised profusely, but he didn't feel like it with Sir Henry.

"Certainly, sir," he replied. "Name your place and your weapons."

"Pistols," hissed Sir Henry. "We will have to find a place on the Border."

Carey stared at Sir Henry gravely, both eyebrows up. "Lord above, Sir Henry, aren't you going to choose a champion?"

"I will kill you myself," hissed Sir Henry, "you impudent cocksure bastard, so I can have the satisfaction of telling my bitch of a wife that you're dead."

Carey controlled his breathing as the best way of getting a hold on the fury building up in his belly. "Of course, it's more likely it will solve our problem and I will marry your grieving widow."

"Ye willna, because ye'll hang for my murder, so one way or another, I'll get you."

"Dear me," said Carey, "you have forgotten that I am a cousin to the Queen and have a right to ask for an axe. And I think this is a course of desperation, Sir Henry." He moved away in case Sir Henry tried to stick him with his eating knife and also to get away from the smell. "I suppose it's because the gout will kill you soon or perhaps your kidneys, since you stink of piss, Sir Henry, which I'm sure isn't healthy. Is it Spynie's idea for a duel? It's a better means of getting rid of me and you than his pathetic assassination attempt."

Sir Henry's face had such a number of emotions chasing across it that Carey felt like laughing, so he did. "Good God, man, can't you see it? He's bored of you and embarrassed by you. Well, never mind, I take your challenge, ye poor gouty old man, and may God ha' mercy on yer soul."

That was when he looked across the room and saw that Huntly was wearing a sword, against all King James' careful rules, he was armed.

There was dancing while the Masquers were getting ready and the ravaged remains of the banket cleared away, so he flung himself into it and found he was a great favourite with the incredibly drunk and funny Danish girls who weren't masquing, but used the figures of the dance to get across to the King as quickly as possible. The King was standing to one side and singing tunelessly along with the music. As soon as he was close enough, he went on one knee to him.

"Your Highness, the Earl of Huntly…"

"Ay, does he no' look fine in my old Apollo costume, even though he's a little too big for it…?"

"He has a sword…"

"Och, Sir Robert, it's made of painted wood, that sword, d'ye think I'm a fool?"

Carey suddenly felt very embarrassed. Of course it was, the King was emphatically not a fool. "Your Highness, I am the fool," he said. "I apologise for troubling you."

The King put his hand on his shoulder. "Up ye get, my dear," he said. "Ah ken ye mean well, but my dear Earl of Huntly wouldna hurt me."

"Well, Your Highness, he hurt the Earl of Moray…"

"Ay, true, but that was a deadly feud. Will ye no' join the dancing? I like to watch ye leap."

All of a sudden Carey had the feeling that he was driving a chariot, hopelessly out of control, heading for a cliff with a white and a black horse fighting each other in the traces in front of him, which he rather thought was an image from Plato.

Obediently he joined another row of dancers and jogged past the astronomical spheres on their stands and the leaden globe of the Earth on its scaffolding above the chair where the King would soon sit. There was something odd about that chair, it had a few little spots of black on it as if someone had shaken a dish of coals over it, but he didn't have time to wonder about that, he was holding hands with a Danish girl and spinning her round as they thundered past.

◇◇◇

Hughie could hardly believe his luck. He had only gone into the alehouse for a quart on the off chance and there was Henry Dodd himself, sitting by himself, stonily eating the ordinary which was haggis, of course, with bashed neeps and fried sippets of bread to soak up the fat, and drinking the ale while the alehouse racketed around him. He didn't look as if he was enjoying himself but then he never did and had got even gloomier after Dick of Dryhope's tower.

Hughie gave out that his name was Tyndale but it wasn't. He had had to be very careful coming back to Edinburgh and in fact until now he had not been into the town at all but had stayed in Holyrood House out of sight because it was less than a year since he had been banished from Edinburgh for a year and a day for the accidental killing of his uncle. Certainly the murder had looked like an accident, which Hughie had planned carefully to achieve. Since then his life had been transformed what with doing a few killings for the man who called himself Hepburn and a few for himself too.

There was only a month or two to go but he still didn't want the nuisance of being arrested again and certainly not of possibly being hanged. He had been all the way down to London to find and attach himself to Carey and had finally got himself a very cushy job with the man himself, if you didn't mind a fair bit of sewing, which he didn't. He was good at it, after all. In due course, Hughie would kill Carey and earn his thirty pounds sterling. Not yet. Hepburn had told him very clearly that Carey was off-limits until the day after New Year's Day, and then he could kill the Courtier any way he liked.

But in the meantime, here was Henry Dodd, sitting in a booth in an alehouse, grimly eating haggis and that was an opportunity not to be passed up because Hughie's right name was Elliot and he was a younger half-brother of Wee Colin himself.

So he elbowed his way through the crowd to the bar, using his size and height, got himself a quart, and came and sat down opposite Dodd. The face noted him and got longer and grimmer.

"What d'ye want?" said Dodd. "Did Carey send ye?"

"Nay," said Hughie genially. "Only I wis wondering why are ye here paying for food when ye can get it free at the King's Court?"

Dodd grunted. He was in his jack; his helmet—a nice new morion—on the table next to him where he could get at it easily. He hadn't taken his swordbelt off though. Hughie knew how to use a sword though he was better with a pike because of his size. However he had no plans whatsoever to fight Dodd with a sword, that wasn't his way at all.

No more words from Dodd. Hughie asked, "Where are ye going, Sergeant? Are ye taking a message."

"In a manner of speaking," said Dodd. "Wee Colin Elliot challenged me to a duel and I'm carrying my own message to say I accept."

"First blood or to the death?"

Dodd gave him a contemptuous look. "Death, o' course."

"Ay."

"Wee Colin's."

"Ay."

Dodd finished his ale.

"I hear ye took money to kill the Courtier," said Hughie carefully. "Is that true?

"Ay."

"So is he dead then?"

"What do ye care?"

I'm due a lot of money for killing him meself, Hughie nearly said but didn't. "He owes me wages," he said, because it was true.

"Well, last I saw of him, he wasnae dead," allowed Dodd.

Hughie smiled happily. "Och that's good news, is that. Nor wounded?"

"Nay."

"So where are ye going?"

"Ah told ye, Ah'm gaunae find Wee Colin Elliot, we'll fight and I'll kill him," said Dodd coldly. "And then I'll probably die meself."

"Och," said Hughie, "So ye'd rather kill Wee Colin than the Courtier?"

"Ay," said Dodd, "o' course."

Hughie sat back to think. Was it worth it? Yes, definitely. Could he do it? He thought so. Would Dodd believe him? Only one way to find out.

"I know why ye wantae kill Wee Colin," he said carefully. "And I'm really a Fenwick so I'd not be sorry to see him dead."

Dodd nodded once and waited. In the complex entanglements of the Border, the Fenwicks too had a long-running bloodfeud with the Elliots. It was quiet at the moment and there had been a couple of marriages to try and heal the breach, but nobody forgot a bloodfeud. How could you? A bloodfeud meant men dead.

"So," said Hughie authoritatively, "Ah ken where Wee Colin Elliot is the day. He's spending New Year wi' his sister and doing a spot of raiding in the East March. And I know his sister because her man's a Fenwick cousin of mine."

Dodd had sat back, his eyes slitted. "Ay?"

"Ay. I could take ye there in mebbe two days and then ye could do it and naebody to interfere. I cannae help ye get out again after ye do it and ye'll have to talk to the bastard Elliots, but I can take ye to where Colin Elliot is."

"Hmm. I just want the mither done with."

"Well, I won't help ye, I'm just a tailor, me, I'll leave the killing to ye."

"I don't need yer help."

"Good."

"What do ye want oot of it?"

"Your horse, the one ye call Whitesock," said Hughie, who had cast many covetous looks at the big sturdy beast. "I think ye willna be needing him again."

Dodd nodded. It was a fair price for the work as well. He looked into the distance as if he was talking to someone else and Hughie felt the hairs go up on his neck.

"Ay," said Dodd, with a short sigh. "Ay. It's a good idea. We'll need supplies and some horsefeed since the grass is under the snow, but ay. Is the tower near Jedburgh?"

"Nay," said Hughie. "Stobs." That was in fact where his poor sister lived, though he hadn't seen her for years. Never mind. They wouldn't get that far.

◇◇◇

At last the Masque had started although nearly everybody was too drunk to walk. His Highness was sitting under the leaden Earth, lolling sideways and laughing while the girls wafted about waving their arms and singing verses about Venus and Mercury and then formed an outer ring of angels, some of them semiconscious and distinctly fallen. The men pranced and kicked and jumped. Huntly was particularly good at this despite his size and large feet. Apollo the Sun had never been known to leap so high or disposedly when King James had been wearing the costume.

Napier and Anricks were deep in conversation like a couple of lovers and Carey looked around for the man organising the props in the Masque. He was nowhere to be seen and nor were his men. Carey poked his head out of the door and asked one of the guards where the four artificers had gone.

"Mr Hepburn went down to get some air, sir," said the man. "And his men with him."

Carey looked back at the Masque. Apollo was on one knee, speechifying in verse to the King and explaining that Apollo was the King's servant and sought only to do him good with his bow and arrows. He hurried over to Anricks, extricated him from his conversation with Napier and said,

"Something is wrong, Mr Anricks. Mr Hepburn, the masque artificer has gone and his men with him."

"An explosion?"

"Maybe. Will you search all the rooms nearby while I look in the cellars?"

He ran out of the door, down the stairs to the winecellars, searched through each of the arched vaults more by smell than sight since he only had a candle, found nothing apart from barrels of wine and more importantly, no lit fuse. He went to the stables, found Hutchin currycombing the horses, and learned from him where he had seen the tanks. They went to look and found the tanks open and empty, nothing else there and four of the better horses gone from the stables.

He sprinted back up to the hall, where the Maxwell and Huntly were advancing on the giggling King who kept slapping his arms as if he was being bitten by insects. Anricks was arguing with the musicians who were sawing away with a will as everybody circled around the King again. Apollo, the Sun, Mercury, Venus, the Moon, Mars, Jupiter, Saturn, all partnered with blond Danish girls with their costumes askew and their nipples popping out.

He used his fist on the open door and produced a loud thumping which made the nearer dancers slow and get bumped into by the next dancers. The whole stately sight tumbled into chaos.

"My lords, ladies, gentlemen, please leave the chamber at once!" He used his battle roar which produced a moment of silence.

King James stood up. "What are ye at?" demanded the monarch angrily. "*You* leave at once."

Carey looked up at the globe above the King, and suddenly got it. The round shape, the deadly liquid that Widow Ridley had dipped her finger in, everything.

He pointed at it. "Step away from the chair, Your Majesty…"
King James goggled at him. "Wha'?"

Carey saw it then, a crack from pole to pole in the leaden globe above the King splitting slowly, something oily leaking. "Ware the globe!" he shouted and started sprinting across the floor as the world went slow. Anricks saw it too and was nearer. He sprinted for the King before hunching his shoulders and making an excellent football tackle on the King which carried both of them sliding several yards away from the chair and the scaffolding, with the King underneath him.

The painted globe was opening like an egg broken by an expert cook, from the bottom to the top and from it came a quantity of oily liquid which poured onto the chair and the velvet robe the King had left there.

For a moment nothing happened and then smoke began to rise. Before their eyes the velvet robe and the upholstery and the very wood of the chair started to char and blacken as if it was burning in an invisible fire, and a horrible sour smell was growing while the invisible fire caught the rushes and floorboards and blackened them too.

Carey had never seen anything so terrifying as the slow ghostly fire, but he pulled down a tapestry to try to put it out.

"No," shouted Anricks, "this is oil of vitriol, stay back and find some lye quickly, or we'll have a fire."

The smoke was getting thicker. The King picked himself up off the floor, gasping and shaking. Suddenly he ran from the room, crying like a child. Anricks chased after him.

The Queen had already gathered up her ladies and swept them from the room, mostly frightened and not drunk anymore, although some were still giggling in bewilderment. Carey thundered down the stairs again, followed by a couple of bodyguards, across the courtyard, through the stables and into the yard behind where the laundry was and three lyedroppers standing in a row. They emptied them out carefully for the lye was caustic and put the lye into buckets which they carried upstairs into the hall full of smoke and tipped them onto the spreading fire. The first bucket produced a hissing and foaming which made one of the guards run, but the next produced less and the one after that, less again until there was a charred mess in the centre of the hall, bad-smelling smoke dissipating, and an expensive velvet robe and a chair turned to a charred mess.

◇◇◇

Anricks chased after the fleeing King of Scotland, up many flights of stairs and into the small rooms under the roof where the palace servants lived if they were important enough. At the end of the corridor the King ran into a room with just a bed in it, stood wailing for a minute and then crawled under the bed. After hesitating because of his new suit, Anricks crammed in under the bed as well.

"Your Highness, I must check your clothes for oil of vitriol…"

The King had his eyes tight shut and his thumb in his mouth and was making little whimpering noises.

"Please, Your Highness…" No response so Anricks found his tinderbox in his sleeve pocket and with shaking hands made fire and lit his candle stub. There were a few black-edged holes in the purple brocade but thank the Almighty, the oil of vitriol hadn't gone through the padding. There was a watch light on the windowsill and Anricks lit it and brought it under the bed where the King was rolled up tight, eyes still shut but tears pouring down his face.

"*Maman*," he was whispering. "*Ou est maman? Je veux maman, je vous en prie m'sieur, maman…*"

For a second Anricks didn't understand, but then he did. The King was begging for his mother who had been taken from him when he was eighteen months old.

What do I do, he wondered desperately and then he thought of his own children and what he would do for them. He crawled back under the bed and held the King tightly from behind, difficult with a fullgrown man.

"*Je m'excuse,*" Simon said, his voice shaking. "*Je suis désolé, votre majesté, mais votre mére n'est pas ici.*"

The King nodded, sucking his thumb. "*Je sais,*" he said, "*mais ou est-elle?*" Where is she?

"I don't know either," Simon said, still in French, "But you must be brave…"

James opened his eyes, turned over and blinked at Simon. "Brave?"

"Yes, Your Majesty, you must be brave. It's very important because you are the King."

"The King?"

"Yes, Your Majesty."

The whisper was almost too soft to hear and hard to understand with its lisping childish French. "But I am not brave," said the King, "I am a coward. I am always afraid."

"Well," said Simon, "so am I. I am not brave but I pretend to be brave, I do what a brave person would. I act, Your Majesty."

There was silence from the King. "*Ça marche?*" That works?

"*Oui.*"

"Oh."

"*Ça suffit,*" said Simon, suddenly hating the cold ambitious men who had taken the King from his mother all those years before. "*Vous étes brave, tres vaillant. Et soyez calme.*"

"*Oui,*" said the King, "*je suis calme.*" And the King smiled suddenly at Anricks and then shut his eyes and went instantly to sleep, lying there on the cold dusty floor, with Anricks holding him.

He lay for what seemed a long time and then heard light footsteps tiptoeing into the room.

Very carefully Anricks wriggled out and climbed stiffly to his feet and saw the Queen, still wearing her artful draperies but stone-cold sober.

"How eez he?"

Anricks crept to the door carrying the watch candle and beckoned her outside.

"He is sleeping, Your Highness."

"Sleeping? He never sleeps after somessing like zis, he cries and wails and says sings I not understand in French…"

Anricks gestured that the Queen should look for herself and held the candle so she could see.

"Good God," she said, "he is sleeping. How did you do it, sir?"

"I…ah…" Anricks hesitated, wondering if he should be tactful or honest. "I…spoke to him in French, which is a language I speak, and it seemed to calm him and so he slept."

The Queen suddenly smiled. "And you held him, no?" she said. "I see it from the marks in the dust. This is vot I should do. Yet he always say he speaks no French and vos late talking."

"I think perhaps when he is upset he remembers…"

"Vat?"

"His mother?"

"The mermaid Queen? Surely not. He vas alvays taught to hate her."

Anricks bowed because one does not contradict a Queen. She contradicted herself. "But yes, I have heard him say "*maman*" when he iz like zis. That is French for 'mutter', is not it?"

"Yes, Your Highness."

"Poor poor one." The Queen smiled at Anricks. "I vill hold him now and you may go downstairs and help Sir Robert find the vicked men who tried to kill him viz magic vater."

"Oil of vitriol,"

"Vatever it vos. I vill look after him. He vill vake up soon. I vill be here."

Anricks watched as the Queen slid herself under the bed. He bowed, left the watchcandle on the windowsill, went looking in the other bedrooms and finally found a shawl folded up on one of the beds. He brought it in and passed it under the bed to the Queen.

"Sank you," she said, "zo I not feel ze cold usually."

"Still," said Anricks. "When shall I tell your women where you are?"

"Vait at least two hours. In fact tell zem only I am viss the King."

Anricks went slowly down the stairs, feeling exhausted and longing for Rebecca, his own shelter and safe harbour, longing to put his head between her breasts and tell her what had happened.

◇◇◇

When they had put out the invisible flames with the lye, they gathered everything together using spears and pokers from the fire, and put it all into the Yule Log fire which smelled truly terrible but crackled and burned with ugly yellow flames. Carey was checking behind all the old dusty tapestries, in cupboards, nooks, window seats, because he couldn't believe there was no gunpowder. James' worthless father, Lord Darnley, had been blown up with gunpowder and because he had somehow escaped, then been strangled in his garden. Whenever Carey looked at the King of Scots now, mentally he heard the boom of a large explosion, which annoyed him almost as much as his repeated dreams of his own execution.

Huntly and Erroll had ridden into town, ostensibly to stop the Allemaynes getting away, which Carey didn't believe would do any good at all, seeing how they were both Catholics and Huntly was still his prime suspect for the originator of the plot. And so he went to the audience chamber where all the great and good of Scotland were discussing the doings at the tops of their voices, found Maitland of Thirlstane, got him to swear out a general warrant, and at midnight had the satisfaction of battering a door in and finding the Maxwell in bed with two of the Danish girls.

Ignoring a lot of angry shouting from the Maxwell after the girls had fled, Carey searched the room, found some ciphered papers and, joy of joys, hiding in a cupboard with a false back, a very dull-looking man who happened to be reading a Catholic breviary.

Scotland wasn't England but still Carey hauled him out of there by the scruff of his neck, and the Maxwell too in his shirt, hastily put on, and took them down to the cellars and locked them in separate rooms. It was immensely satisfying.

However, knowing the King of Scots' ridiculous softness, he reckoned he only had until morning.

Carey marched into the room where the priest was sitting in irons, looking pale and lost.

"I am Sir Robert Carey, Deputy Warden of the English West March, and acting for my Lord Maitland of Thirlstane." The man said nothing. "Your name?"

"William Crichton."

"Are you a Jesuit priest?"

"Yes. His Highness knows this, I have disputed with him theologically several times."

In England that would be enough to hang, draw, and quarter him, but this was Scotland where the King seemed intent on

convincing the Catholics that he was a Catholic and the Protestants that he was a Protestant.

Carey showed his teeth in an unpleasant smile. "Jonathan
Hepburn just made a hideous attempt against the sacred life of
His Majesty, in which he might have been burned to death by
oil of vitriol."

"Oh my God."

"What I want from you, William Crichton, is a full account
of the whole thing. From start to finish, including all main actors
and your part in it."

"In exchange for?"

"I will let you go. This isn't England."

"And if I don't?"

Carey leaned over Crichton and drew his finger across his
throat. "I'll do it myself," he said conversationally, "since it is no
sin for an Englishman to kill a Jesuit, as they account it no sin
to make attempts against the life of Her Majesty of England."

Crichton looked appalled. "I am a man of peace."

"Certainly you are, William," said Carey, still leaning, "and I
am not. I know the Maxwell may protest about his house priest
getting his throat cut, but probably not very much because of
all the things you know about him."

"My Lord Maxwell is a good Catholic…" began Crichton
and then stopped because Carey was laughing at him. "Well he
tries to be," he finished lamely. "How is His Highness?"

"I don't know."

"And you will let me go."

"Perhaps."

Crichton swallowed. "But…"

"Do you want me to give you to my Lord Spynie?"

Crichton went ashen. "But…"

"Speak up quickly then. I should think he's very upset at his
Masque being spoilt. He'll be here soon, I expect."

Crichton was silent a moment and his lips moved as if he
was praying. Then he tried to move his hand to the table but
rediscovered the chains on his wrist.

"Hepburn refused to tell us anything of his plans," he said, "he just guaranteed that King James would be dead or very ill...I thought poison..."

Carey said nothing.

"I was never happy about it," Crichton said. "If the King had been excommunicated it would be legitimate although still dubious, but he hasn't. Yet the paper came from the King of Spain saying, "*Fiat!*" And my Lords Maxwell and Huntly said it would be a great blow for Holy Mother Church. Besides he has no right to the throne, since his father was David Riccio..."

Carey looked nonplussed. "He inherits from his mother anyway."

"The Salic law..."

"Is in France, not Scotland."

"Well, anyway. Maxwell thinks that and it's hard to gainsay him. And Huntly."

Carey had his notebook out. "Anyone else?"

"Erroll of course, Angus, Auchinleck."

"Any more?"

"Fintry. I was never sure what he was going to do. Another of Hepburn's plans. And there was Sir James Chisholm of Cromlix, but that would be later when we needed to organise the supplies for the Spanish troops in Dumfries."

"Are there any there now?"

"No, the King of Spain refused to commit any troops until he heard that King James was dead or...or incapacitated."

Carey nodded.

"As soon as he hears that, the troops he has waiting in La Corunna will board fast ships, travel in three squadrons up the Irish Sea to Dumfries. By that time of course there would be civil war in Scotland and England and their landing would be substantially unopposed. Maxwell, Huntly, Erroll, and Angus would then march the troops south to Bristol, Oxford, and take London."

"And the first stage in all this was killing the King?" Crichton looked away. "When he had done nothing against you and indeed treated you with favour and gentleness."

"It was for Holy Mother Church."

"And a cardinal's hat for you." Carey was disgusted and spat deliberately into the corner. Crichton looked fixedly at his hands. "Anything else?"

"Sir George Kerr is waiting in the West near Paisley for the message that the King is dead. He'll take the papers to Spain…"

"What papers?"

Crichton hesitated.

Carey leaned towards him and said again, "What papers?"

"There are papers that…that the lords have signed…"

"What's on them?"

"Nothing. No, really, they are blank and the King of Spain can add to them whatever he likes."

Carey smiled. "Which lords apart from Huntly have signed these blank papers?"

"Maxwell, Erroll, Angus…"

"Has anyone sent a man?"

"I don't think so."

"The name of the ship?"

"*The Beauty of Lennox.*"

Carey showed his teeth again. "William," he said, "I think you have just helped me. If the papers get to Spain, that is the signal to send the troops? Yes?" Crichton nodded. "You were a traitor to your King and now you are a traitor to the Catholic Church, a much better thing to be. What does Kerr look like?"

"Like most Kerrs, he's red-headed, good-looking, one crumpled ear and corrie handed."

"Left-handed, you mean?"

Crichton nodded. "I never thought it was right to kill the King…"he began, but Carey had already left the room and locked the door, leaving him to sit in irons and contemplate his future.

Carey found Lord Spynie was waiting for him, and the ex-favourite immediately went with a troop of men-at-arms to Lennox. There was a good road to the little town of Glasgow and they rode out of the Court at three in the morning with a warrant for Kerr's arrest so there was every chance they would be at Lennox by noon. Carey considered riding with them but after some thought decided he needed to stay at Holyrood House and keep an eye on things there. Besides, he was due at the King's New Year's Day levée—Sir David Graham, one of the Grooms of the Bedchamber, had asked him personally if he would like to be there to give His Highness his cup of morning wine and wish him a Happy New Year, and of course he had agreed.

eδinburgh new year's δay 159[3]

Carey rose at dawn to get ready for the levée, after three hours sleep, proud in his new suit and Anricks tagged along because he said he had a petition to ask of the King. He was carrying two packages carefully wrapped in damask. They lined up outside the Kings Great Bedchamber, only to find he was in his privy bedchamber still and not to be disturbed. They waited while in the distance there came a characteristic hammering sound. Carey looked at Anricks and Anricks looked modestly at the ground.

"Is that the King and Queen…?" he asked.

"Maybe," said Anricks and looked prim.

The King eventually moved to the Great Bedchamber and they entered in a line, Carey and Anricks last, to find him sitting up in bed looking very perky although his shirt was revolting. The ceremony began with the Napkin with which the King sketchily wiped his face and hands. Then Sir David beckoned Carey to a table at the side of the room and gave him a goblet of wine after ceremonially tasting it. Carey took the goblet and a napkin for his shoulder, bowed, and walked slowly to the King in his bed, who was smiling at him, went on one knee to him as he would have done to the Queen of England. Just as he would have done at Whitehall, in the sight of the King he took a mouthful of the wine. And froze.

It was poisoned. He knew the taste, hidden by spices and sugar. Belladonna, just as it had been at Oxford, he knew it at once and his stomach twisted in reaction. He nearly spat it straight out, looked at the King, thought of dropping the goblet, thought of many many things, knew that the King had noticed, felt the poison furring the inside of his mouth, so he spat the mouthful carefully onto the napkin on his shoulder and mouthed to the King, "It's poisoned."

The King grinned and said, "Och it's nice to see ye, Sir Robert, gi's the booze then…"

He grabbed the goblet and to Carey's horror, tipped it up. But then he noticed the King's Adam's apple wasn't moving and so he didn't knock it out of the King's hand as his first impulse had been. Carey immediately stood and turned, looking all round the room, while his body hid whatever the King was doing with his goblet of poisoned wine.

Eight other petitioners were waiting patiently at the other end of the chamber, Mr Anricks was nearer the bed. The other Grooms of the Bedchamber were holding a clean shirt for the King, and his waistcoat, hose and doublet, his stockings and his shoes, but one man was walking slowly and ceremonially to the door with the jug of wine.

Carey went after him, through the small door and said, "Sir David, may I check that jug, please?"

Sir David put it on a table, turned and looked at him and the fear in his eyes told Carey all he needed to know. He grabbed the man's hand and found the little phial palmed in his left hand which was shaking.

Sir David brought up a small poinard he had hidden in his sleeve, against all James' careful rules and Carey grabbed his right hand with his left, got a little cut, grappled, trod on his toes, brought his knee up, missed the crotch but hit his thigh, then pulled his head back and butted Sir David on the nose so he went down. Moments later two of the guards came through the door and grabbed both of them. Carey was more concerned to keep the blood from his hand off his brand new duds and insisted on wrapping the napkin round it and holding it up so the bleeding would slow. They waited as the slow process of the levée continued, for all the petitioners had to have their say.

◇◇◇

Simon felt abandoned. He had counted on Carey to be there when he made his all important approach to the King—but Carey had suddenly chased out of the Great Bedchamber, in pursuit of the elderly nobleman carrying the jug of wine. The King had dribbled a lot of wine onto his already filthy shirt, had put the goblet on a small table by the bed.

Now other nobles, including Huntly, paced forwards to offer the King a clean shirt—which he refused—and then a magnificent Court suit of peach and pale tawny taffeta cannions and a doublet of equally splendid yellow and peach damask studded with diamonds and topazes. They helped him into it, with smooth practised movements, in itself a show of the King's magnificence.

He was feeling afraid, so much was riding on this. He had done his best with the Dispute, with the help of the Almighty, and now it was his job to find out…What?

What the King of Scots thought of Jews.

He waited whilst the other petitioners went forward to speak to the King…Two portly merchants, a Highlander looking uncomfortable in hose and doublet, a scrawny man with a lot of papers, a young blond Allemayne. All had presents for the King, of course, as it was New Year's Day. Thank the Almighty, he had remembered the necessity of gifts and taken the trouble to buy two suitable presents in Edinburgh in the week after Christmas, at a huge premium.

His hands were sweating. He held the damask-wrapped gifts with the tips of his fingers so the damask wouldn't be marked, waited modestly until the last. Carey had been invited, but Anricks had had to pay, rather a lot, in fact, to all the Grooms of the Bedchamber. Never mind. It was worth it.

"Ay, Mr Anricks," said the King affably, sitting in a carved chair and drinking more wine from a Venetian glass he had just been given by a merchant. "I enjoyed yer disputation last night."

"Thank you, Your Majesty."

"Get up off yer knees, mon, this isnae the Queen's Court. Now then. I've decided not tae clap ye in irons for knocking me over since ye had such a verra guid reason for it."

"Yes, Your Majesty."

"Ah dinna recall what happened after but my Queen says ye helped her and so Ah'm verra grateful," said the King with a smile which did not reach his eyes.

"Ah…My memory too is deficient, but I am glad Your Majesty's Queen is pleased with me."

"So. Whit have ye got me for my New Year's gift?"

Anricks presented his gift and the King unwrapped it to find a copy of Thomas Digges. He laughed. "Ye're determined to convert me to Copernicus, then?"

"Your Majesty needs only to read the Preface," said Anricks humbly. "I own the main part of the book is not new and in fact quite dull."

James laughed again at that.

"This is Sir Robert Carey's gift to you, Your Majesty," said Anricks. "It is a book on venerie, hunting, but I am afraid I cannot say how good it is for I have not…"

"Ah…wonderful! *La Vénerie de Twiti*! I've been after this for a long weary while, ye can tell the long-shanked Deputy Warden thank ye very much for it!" And King James opened the book and started reading immediately, but then remembered himself and put it down. "Mr Anricks, have ye a petition for me?"

"Yes, Your Majesty." Anricks took a deep breath. "I would like to petition you to look with favour on my people."

The King tilted his head, suddenly like a falcon. "Oh?"

"Perhaps you do not know, but I am a Jew, of the tribe and lineage of Abraham. I would like to pray you that you look with as much favour upon us as does Her Royal Majesty, your cousin of England."

There was a pause, but Anricks knew his cause was already lost.

"Ay well," said the King coldly. "I will, o' course."

"Thank you, Your Majesty, that is all I ask," said Anricks smoothly, backed three steps and then turned to follow Carey through the unremarkable door he had disappeared through. Inside he had a great yawning emptiness where before he had been afraid. For when Anricks had said he was a Jew, he had been watching King James' face carefully and across it he had seen travel, in the blink of an eye, a look of disgust.

The Ames, Anriques, Nuñez, and Lopez families would be buying land in Constantinople.

◇◇◇

Carey was checking the new napkin he had wrapped around his left hand where the cut in the web between finger and thumb was still producing blood when the King came through the door looking colder than he ever had in Carey's experience. He was carrying his goblet, still full of wine.

"Sir Robert, ye're wounded!"

"A cut from Sir David's dagger, Your Majesty. You didn't...?"

"Nay, I didna. I pretended. How did ye know..?"

"I was accidentally poisoned while I was serving the Queen on progress in the autumn. I knew the taste immediately."

"Ay? We'll hae this tested o'course but if Sir David had a knife..."

"And a phial to bring the poison in."

"I hate knives, I willna have them in my presence." He bent to Sir David and slapped his face, despite the blood and snot from the broken nose. Carey felt his forehead which felt distinctly sore. Not as sore as a broken nose though: mentally he thanked Bangtail, who had given him lessons in head-butting.

The slapping brought Sir David round more or less. "Sir David," said the King sadly, "ye've served me well all my life, I remember ye when I was a lad. Why? For God's sake why?"

"You...you debauched my wife, you...you..."

"I what? Debauched? Your wife?"

"My poor little Marguerite, you tupped her like..."

"Me? But Sir David, ye were serving me when the Duc D'Aubigny was here, ye know I'm no' a lover of women, or I wisnae until this morning. What made you think that?"

"The dresslength…She had a lover…Lovebites…"

"Ye're wood. I gave a dresslength to the Lady Schevengen as well, d'ye think I'm wapping her?"

Sir David rolled his eyes. "But someone was her lover, she had lovebites and I never give lovebites…"

"Fetch the Queen," the King said to one of the guards and the young man sprinted away.

Anricks had come through the door from the Great Bedchamber, found Carey holding up his hand with a bloody napkin round it and took him through to the antechamber where Anricks poured whishke bee on the cut until it stopped bleeding and then ripped up another napkin with his teeth to bandage Carey's hand properly. No more blood soaked through although hand wounds are often very bloody. Anricks didn't think it would need stanching or cauterising.

By the time they came back, the Queen had arrived and was holding the King tight while he smiled down at her. The Queen had tears in her eyes.

"What's happened now, Your Majesty?" Carey asked.

"Poor little Marguerite," the Queen said. "Poor poor girl. There vos no harm in her."

"It seems Sir David killed his wife last night, throttled her in his bed," said the King distastefully. "Dear God, man…"

"She had a lover, she betrayed me," muttered Sir David.

"Ay," said the King, "And you betrayed me. If it hadnae been for Sir Robert, an Englishman, I wad be suffering and dying by now. And ye thought I had swived yer wife. Dear God, when? I'm never alone."

He turned aside, his mouth wry. "Sir Robert, are ye well aside fra yer hand? Ye didna take hurt fra the poison?"

"No, Your Majesty, I spat it out." That wasn't entirely true since Carey was feeling quite sick and dizzy, but he put that down to reaction.

"A'right then, gentlemen, and my dearest Queen, nothing has happened. We'll review how the tasting is done, make it more English, I think. Sir David, ye'll confess the whole thing and…"

"But she betrayed me," whispered Sir David. "If it wasn't the King, who was it?"

"What d'ye think, my dear?" the King asked the Queen.

The Queen shrugged. "Sir David iss a fool," she said. "Ve all knew she vos haffing an affair with Jonathan Hepburn, it vos obvious."

For some reason Sir David started crying into his hands and would say no more.

◇◇◇

When Janet Dodd awoke, she found the Court like an animal that has had a fright: confused, uncertain, and taking refuge in the familiar. Then when the King and Queen showed themselves, walking through the snowy garden as if nothing at all had happened, it relaxed and went about its business.

Lady Widdrington came to find Janet and Widow Ridley, and found both of them in their best kirtles, and Janet with a wonderful green hat on her head, preparing to go to market to sell the linen and take a look round the town. She talked to them and heard the tale of the mysterious alchemist and brought them both to the audience chamber to tell the King and Queen.

King James had changed his doublet and hose, which was very unusual for him, and was magnificent in tawny and peach, although he still hadn't shifted his shirt.

He was affable and friendly and a little abstracted, wiggled his fingers at Janet for her promptness and Widow Ridley for her curiosity, gave the Widow a silver goblet with the King's crest that he had just got from a merchant. He promised Janet a pension.

The Queen came personally to see the linen sheets and aprons and ordered the elderly lady in charge of the Sweet Coffers to buy the lot of them at a very fair price, which Janet added to her moneybelt. She tasted the flowerwater and snapped that up too.

The money was enough for extra feed this year and even next year if they needed it, which God send they wouldn't.

Janet couldn't go home yet since Henry had disappeared and she didn't want to think about what he was probably doing. So she and Widow Ridley went into Edinburgh and exclaimed at everything, the house where John Knox hadn't lived but a silver merchant had, and the alehouses, and the Tron and the Tollbooth, and of course, the castle, partly wrecked and in piles from the gunpowder and cannon in the siege twenty years before, with scaffolding and masons getting on with rebuilding it.

◇◇◇

George Kerr was at Lennox, already aboard the ship that would take him to Spain through the dangerous winter seas, stowing his chest. He heard the sound of boots on the deck, looked through a hatch hoping to see his friend Sir David Graham and his men and instead saw the minister of Paisley, Andrew Knox, looking grim and behind him was Lord Spynie. He knew he was doomed. He took the two most important pieces of paper, the one from the Spanish King and the one setting out how and where the troops would land and be disposed in Scotland, and he gulped them down in strips with a lot of good wine.

He would have started on the blank sheets with the signatures of the Scottish Catholic lords, but by that time the cabin door was juddering to the kicking and the bolt broke and seconds later he was on his face on the deck, protesting that he was a merchant, until they found the papers and then he shut up. The minister of Paisley looked at him with contempt and then stood carefully on his hand.

"Traitor," he spat. "Traitor tae the Kirk and to the King and the realm."

"I am not a traitor to the true Church," he answered, rather well he thought, and got kicked hard in the ribs.

"Ye admit you are a traitor to the King and the realm," said Spynie, kicking him a couple of times in the crotch. "Good, that saves time."

They couldn't head back to Edinburgh without some rest, for the horses as well as the men, and Andrew Knox put them up in his manse in Paisley. They left Kerr in the town lock-up where the ministry of the town came to dispute with him and break his legs in the Boot. They slung him weeping across a horse three hours before the next sunrise, and headed back to Edinburgh.

On the 2nd of January 1592/3 they had acquired the full plan of the Catholic earls along with a complete account of the King of Spain's addendum requiring the murder of the King before he committed any troops, leaving both Scotland and England without an heir and safe for Spain to invade.

◇◇◇

James listened to Carey as he gave his report verbally—he started on both his knees but James soon had him on a stool with wine at his elbow. The two books that Mr Anricks had given him for New Year's presents lay on the table. One was Thomas Digges, on the revolutions of the planets, as yet unopened. The other book was the magnificent volume on hunting by Twiti which was lying open with a goblet keeping the place.

"D'ye think it could ha' worked?" asked James.

"Yes, Your Majesty," said Carey, "both realms are vulnerable until you have at least one son. With you gone and no issue, I hate to think what would have happened here or in England. It could have triggered the Bond of Association and started a general killing of Catholics, which would, as night follows day, have led to civil war. We have only to look at the state of France to know we want no such thing."

"The Bond of Association was originally against my martyred mother."

"It was, of course, because she would not stop plotting."

"Surely that was her duty, as a sovereign monarch detained illegally in another country."

Carey smiled. "It was, Your Majesty, and I conceived it as my duty if she succeeded to kill her and her fellow Papists."

"You signed it?"

"Of course. Most of the Court did, it swept the country."

James heaved a sigh. "What d'ye think to it now?"

"Perhaps I am less enthused," said Carey carefully, "for since then I have been in France and seen a land riven by civil and religious war."

James nodded. "All I ask, ye know, is that I may be a peace-maker. That's all."

"Her Majesty, too, wishes she could do away with war—though for her, her chief complaint is the expense of it."

"Ay," said James, "typical woman. So let's see these papers."

Carey handed over the blanks with their flamboyant semi-illiterate noble signatures across the bottom.

"No mair?"

"No, Your Majesty, he had disposed of any others. My Lord Spynie is not sure how as there was no fire nor ashes, but he may have eaten them since he looked green about the gills."

"Was he given the Boot?"

"Yes, Your Majesty," said Carey with a quick grimace of disgust. "The ministers insisted. It didn't take long."

"Ay," said the King, "the ministers are awfy keen on it, I find. We'll hang the poor fellow as soon as we can. We'll hang that fool Graham of Fintry as well."

"I think he is at least half mad."

"Ay and he has a verra nice inheritance which will have tae be confiscated for a while, I fear. I'm deporting Father Crichton back tae Spain."

Carey said nothing for a moment and then asked, "And the Catholic earls? Maxwell, Huntly? Angus?"

"Ay well, they've been verra naughty boys and will have tae be warded for a while, but then…"

"You will free them."

"Ay," James blinked at the window where it had started to rain an unpleasant mixture of snow and rain, a kind of flying readymade slush. "I know ye think Ah'm wood fer not clapping them all in irons and having their heads off. The ministers think the same—they are having a day of fasting in thanks for my deliverance, God save them."

"At least execute Lord Maxwell and the Earl of Huntly, Your Majesty. When I think of what they tried to do to you with the oil of vitriol..." said Carey, slipping off the stool onto his knees again.

"The engineer, Jonathan Hepburn?"

"I'm not clear how much he did nor who he was working for, but I know he brought the oil of vitriol from Keswick, whatever he was doing with Marguerite on the side. He rode from the Court as soon as it was set up and we don't know where he went."

"Might he have gone back to Keswick?"

"Yes, or he might have taken ship for the Netherlands at Leith."

"Find him," said the King. "Find him and kill him. He's an Englishman and now he's run, I dinna have jurisdiction and my cousin of England might be annoyed. So I leave it to ye, Sir Robert."

"Yes, Your Majesty," said Carey firmly, "I will be honoured to end his life. And Maxwell and Huntly..."

James leaned over and caught Carey's face between his two soft fleshy hands. "I know," he whispered, "if it werenae for the wee Jew philosopher that knocked me over and backwards, I'd likely be dead or burning to death in invisible flames. D'ye think I dinna ken that? D'ye think I dinna ken that they all think I'm soft as shite and silly and they call me Queen James, and worse, d'ye think I dinna ken? Ay, I ken, and still I'll forgive them and keep forgiving them and keep on forgiving them until they understand or someone else kills them. I will have peace, Sir Robert. I will have peace in my lands and with Spain and with France, too. I *will* have *peace*, by God."

He let go of Carey's face and drank so the Englishman wouldn't see the tears in his eyes, before he could snort them down, waiting for the cynical smile, the supercilious look.

Carey stayed where he was for a moment, his chestnut head bowed. When he spoke it was in an oddly strangled tone of voice.

"I think Your Majesty is the bravest Prince I have ever heard of."

"Ye do?"

"Yes. It's easy for a Prince to seek war, that's instinctive to men, it's expected of him. But for a Prince to seek peace—that takes true courage."

"Ay?" James thought about it. "Ay, perhaps it does."

"I will help you in any way I can, Your Majesty," said Carey. He sounded sincere. Maybe he was.

"Thank ye," said James. "Now be off wi' ye and take yer wee Maimonides south, too. There's nae more need for him to stay here and spy on me."

Carey rose gracefully to his feet, bowed, backed to the door.

"Ay, tell my cousin of England and her little hunchbacked Secretary, thank you for sending him."

"Yes, Your Majesty."

"And tell Lord Spynie to come in now."

Carey bowed again as he went out the door. James sighed. Such a pity the handsome Englishman was in thrall to the she-devil still, as Buchanan called all women, though his lady-love Lady Widdrington was a remarkable woman with almost a man's intelligence. In fact he had recently come to appreciate more the softer plusher charms of women and had enjoyed himself with his young Queen, more than he would ever have expected. Still...for companionship and sheer delight, there was nothing to match a young man, such as Spynie had been, or as his darling Esmé Stuart, Duc D'Aubigny had been before the lords had poisoned him. That he could not forgive, try as he might and the Gowrie family would pay for it one day. But Huntly and Angus and Erroll and all their silly conspiracies? They were just naughty boys, after all, Huntly especially whom he couldn't help sighing over.

James stood and looked out of the window. God had given him a mission and he had known what it was since the age of five when he had watched his foster father, the Earl of Mar, bleeding to death from a dozen stab wounds. He had promised himself through tears and gritted teeth that he would be a peaceful monarch and he would have peace. He had never forgotten it.

◇◇◇

Dodd kicked his tired pony up a small hill and down into the slushy valley. Half an hour before, it had started to sleet and they were still six miles from Stobs.

Dodd had said maybe four words the whole way and they had taken it in turns to sleep in a sheepfold. Hughie had thought he could kill the man then but found Dodd watching him every time he got up and so he pretended he had a flux and went out into the snow and wind each time.

Now they had been riding all day, slowed down by the slippery snow and the sleet. On the other hand, Dodd was tired. He was riding the pony because an unshod pony was much nimbler among the rocks and tussocks of the hills. Men guarding the herds in the infields had asked their business and Hughie had explained they were going to his sister at Stobs. Two men, one obviously not a good rider and not a reiver despite his size, were only a threat if they were scouting for a larger party. They were taking a message, they said.

Hughie was tired as well but the hope of seeing the pretty red blood on the snow and the anticipated joy of killing, actually killing Henry Dodd, kept him going. When he brought that head in to Wee Colin's hall, there would be fire and feasting for sure, he'd be the star, maybe Wee Colin would reward him. And then he could go back to Carey when the weather was better and tell him some lie about where he had been and then later on kill him too and get his thirty pounds from Hepburn.

He was trailing behind again but Dodd seemed tranced by the sleet and the difficulty of the ground. Maybe now? Very very quietly he took his favourite weapon out of the bag at his back. It wasn't a full-size crossbow but it had a very powerful bow that he was just able to cock. He stole another glance at Dodd who was negotiating a slippery spot. Quickly he fitted the crossbow stirrup to his toe and pulled upwards. It was hard but he was strong and he managed it with no more than a grunt. Lost in thought, Dodd didn't even look back.

Whitesock noticed and pulled at the leading rein Dodd was holding, tried to pull away, neighed. Dodd glowered at him and pulled the rein sharply. "Will ye get on!" he snarled.

Now was the time. Hughie kicked his pony up the little hillock, putting in the heavy bolt as he went up behind Dodd who was in an argument with his horse, up close to the jack, leaned across, close enough to touch him and his fingers were numb, but he levelled the crossbow and pulled the lever and the bolt went straight into Dodd's back, hopefully into a kidney.

"Aah…" he whispered, and that was good to hear, he was in agony. He clapped his hand to the bolt, found it—ay, it was a good way in—tried to draw his sword but couldn't do it, managed to draw his dagger with his other hand.

Hughie had backed off. Whitesock pulled free with the leading rein trailing and whinnied high and deafening, again and again. Slowly, like taffy falling off a stick, Dodd leaned over and over until he was lying alongside the pony's neck and then slower still he fell off into the snow where the sleet fell on him and the bolt sticking out of his back.

Hughie waited a minute and then dismounted from his own pony, drew his sword, went over to where Dodd was lying with his face in the snow, slowly writhing, his lips drawn back in a grimace of pain. Hughie set himself, trying to remember how did the executioner do it. He wanted Dodd's head off neatly, not with all meat and bone dangling, but through the neckbones and gullet where it was soft and easy.

"Ma name is Hughie Elliot," he said loudly, in case his blood enemy could still hear him, "And that's why ye're gaunae die."

He took aim with his sword and one eye half-closed against the sleet, lifted it and then screamed and dropped the sword.

The bastard had stabbed him in the calf. Dodd's dagger was sticking out of his leg.

For a minute, Hughie kicked Dodd as hard as he could, then he picked up the sword, set himself again…

And something bit his arm and pulled him over. He staggered on the ice, the blade in his calf hurting, dropped the sword again.

Then he saw Whitesock with his eyes white and rolling, his ears right back and his ugly tombstone teeth pulling and biting at him, rearing up, striking with his front hooves, shod they were… Hughie ducked once, and the second hoof caught him neatly on the head so he went down half-stunned. Then Whitesock turned his back, kicked out with both back feet, Hughie went down in the snow on his back.

The last thing he saw was the outraged horse rising up above him and he felt the front hooves come down again and again on his chest, trampling him with iron hooves until his chest was jelly and his heart had stopped.

He didn't hear Dodd making little pants and grunts because the pain was so bad and he didn't see the horse lie down on his belly in the snow beside him.

By that time Hughie Elliot's eyes had set and a crow had already spotted the unexpected meal and was dropping down through the falling snow with joyous caws.

Glossary

at the horn—outlawed

at the lure—flying a falcon at a piece of meat or a bunch of feathers on a string

attacks of the mother—original term for hysteria

hunting *par force de chiens*—hunting with dogs

infirmity in my bones—rickets

out on the trod—out in pursuit of reivers

take her chamber—a woman would stay in one room for the final weeks of pregnancy

Allemaynes, Deutsch—Germans

apothecary—like a modern chemist or druggist

bag pudding—steamed savoury pudding, often made with suet

banket—a buffet of sweets, creams, custards, and cheeses, after a feast

bedfellow—someone you slept with, not necessarily sexual

birthing stool—a stool designed to help a woman squat in the second stage of childbirth

blankmanger—medieval dish made of almonds, cream, and chicken bonds of manrent—hiring a man to be a soldier for a fixed time, Scottish

boozing ken—small bar or pub

Border reiver—a member of the riding surnames, persistent cattle thief, horse rustler, murderer

breeks—breeches, fighting breeches were made of leather

buttery—means buttlery, where the bottles were kept, later you could get food there too

Calvinist—variety of Protestant who follows the teachings of John Calvin

carlin—old woman

Carlisle trained bands—the men of the city would train together to fight, often as pikemen or arquebusiers

Candlemas—ancient Catholic festival on 2nd February; originally Imbolc

chalice—the cup that holds the wine in a Catholic Mass

chamberer—someone who would do slightly menial tasks like changing the Queen's bedlinen

codpiece—a flap of cloth tied at the top of the hose, to hide the privates; often stuffed to look larger

conniption fit—epilepsy or a stroke

cramoisie—very popular colour in Elizabethan times, dark purple red

dag—smallest kind of firearm, a large gun firing one shot at a time, with a heavy ball on the bottom of the grip to balance the barrel and hit people with when you missed

Demiurge/Aeon—Gnostic idea—an angel who had set himself up as the Ruler of the World, but wasn't God

dominie—Scottish word for a teacher

domus magnificenciae—the part of the Court that contributed to the King's magnificence, nobles, courtiers *domus providenciae*—the part of the Court that kept everybody alive, servants, cooks, men-at-arms, gardeners

dresslength—twelve yards (at least) of fabric, the minimum amount needed to make a kirtle

duds—London slang meaning clothes

dyspepsia—bellyache

fig—rude gesture formed by putting the thumb between forefinger and second finger, making a fist and waving it

first remove, second remove—a meal would be composed of a group of dishes, mainly meat and fish, and then the table would be cleared and a second group of dishes would be brought of poultry, cheese etc.

flowerwater—distilled spirits from summer fruits and flowers, eg elderflower water; not very watery

flux—diarrhoea

galleas—cross between a galleon and a galley, there were four of them in the Armada

gallowglass—Irish mercenary, allegedly from Gallway

gossips—a woman's best female friends, her god-siblings

Groom of the Bedchamber—gentlemen who attended the King in his bed

guarderobe—indoor toilet in a castle, a small room jutting out from the wall with a clear drop under the seat

haggis—Scottish delicacy consisting of a sheep's pluck (liver, lungs, etc.) minced up and mixed with onions and oatmeal, very tasty

hart—a mature male deer with at least twelve tines to his antlers, therefore six years old

heifer—cow before she has her first calf

hobby—small sturdy horse or pony, native to the Borders

Hobson's livery stables—a successful chain of livery stables, where you couldn't choose which horse you hired, hence "Hobson's choice"

infield—fields nearest the tower or farmhouse

insight—the contents of a house that were moveable, pots, pans, blankets, etc.

jack—two meanings: 1) a leather mug, 2) a padded leather coat with no sleeves and metal plates between the leather to ward off blows

jailfever—typhoid or typhus fever, not really distinguished

jakes—outside toilet

Justice Raid—the King of Scotland would run a raid on his subjects and burn down their towers to teach them better manners

kern—Irish mercenary

kine—old plural of cow

Knight of the Carpet—a knight who had never been to war

Labor-et-oratorium—literally, where you work and pray; shortened to "laboratory" which means very much the same

lamb's tails—little rolls of carded wool for spinning

lambswool—a drink made of hot cider and beaten egg

levée—the King's official getting out of bed in the morning

liege—a feudal lord

lungfever—pneumonia

lute—instrument like a guitar but with twelve strings and a round soundbox

Lutheran—variety of Protestant who follows the teachings of Martin Luther

lye—alkali formed by dripping water through woodash, used for cleaning and to make soap

manchet bread—best white bread, made of sieved flour

marker stones—notorious for going wandering, they marked boundaries

maslin bread—second best bread, with the wheatgerm and some bran left in; very nutritious

milliner—hatmaker

minion—male favourite of a King (or Queen)

minister—Protestant priest in Scotland

mithered—annoyed, cross

monopoly or patent—awarded to favoured courtiers by the Queen, they allowed the Courtiers to make money by being the only person allowed to sell a particular item—like sweet wines (Dudley, Essex) or playing cards (Sir Walter Raleigh)

morion—curved helmet of the period

muliercula—tiny woman, midget

nebbish—incomprehensible Northern insult

New Spain—the Americas

outfield—rough pasture, further away from the tower or farmhouse

palliasse—straw mattress for sleeping on the floor if necessary

paten—the plate to hold the Host during a Catholic Mass

pelican—alchemical device

petticoat forepart—the pretty triangular part of a petticoat that was deliberately displayed

pinniwinks—Scottish word for thumbscrews

poinard—long, thin dagger with a very sharp point

postern gate—small gate in a bigger one to let in one person at a time

pottage—thick soup made with beans, vegetables, and bacon; standard peasant food

Ptolomaic system—the Sun goes around the Earth, which is at the centre of the Universe

puissant—powerful

pursuivant—someone who pursues, heraldic term but also meant a secret agent

quince cheese—what the Spanish call membrillo

Rough Wooing of Henry VIII—the war he fought against the Scots in the 1540s to persuade them to marry the infant Mary Queen of Scots to the infant Prince Edward; failed.

serpentine powder—basic ordinary mixed gunpowder, quite weak

Spanish farthingale—the petticoats shaped and stiffened with hoops like a crinoline to hold the skirts out, first in a bell shape and then in a barrel-shape late in Elizabeth's reign

stays—boned and reinforced bodice or corset

swive—have sex with

terceiros, tercios—the troops of Philip II's 3rd legion, the best and most-feared troops in Europe

the Boot—instrument of torture which broke the legs from the ankles up

the Groyne or La Corunna—major port in Galicia

thrawn—stubborn

tup—have sex with, especially sheep, male sheep

Warden Raid—the Warden would raid a particular area and burn down towers to teach the reivers better manners

Warden's Day—a meeting between the officials of the Scottish and English march to sort out who had stolen what and try and arrange compensation; could be quite exciting

Warden's fee—what the Warden got for finding and returning your cattle

wet larder—where you salted meat and made pickles

whishke bee/uisge beatha—whisky
white lead—poisonous face paint
wood—woodwild, mad

Author's Note

This book is wrapped around the mysterious incident of the Spanish Blanks, in which certain Catholic Scottish nobles signed their names at the bottom of blank sheets of paper intended for the King of Spain. Why they did that had to do with a Spanish-backed plot the details of which are not at all clear but which the Protestant ministers took very seriously. As usual, I have speculated outrageously.

The more I wrote about James VI of Scotland, the more I came to like him. It's clear he was gay although like many gay men in those times, he was perfectly capable with his Queen when he needed to be. He was also remarkably patient with his subjects, his suicidally lunatic nobles and his dour and fanatical ministers of the Kirk. King from his babyhood, he was canny and cautious and determined and managed a balancing act between all of them until he finally succeeded peacefully to the throne of England in 1603. The fact that, unlike many of his ancestors, he lived long enough to do it is proof of his intelligence.

To receive a free catalog of Poisoned Pen Press titles, please provide your name, address, and e-mail address in one of the following ways:

Phone: 1-800-421-3976
Facsimile: 1-480-949-1707
Email: info@poisonedpenpress.com
Website: www.poisonedpenpress.com

Poisoned Pen Press
6962 E. First Ave. Ste 103
Scottsdale, AZ 85251